Tales From Rainwater Pond

TALES FROM RAINWATER POND

Billy Roche

Pillar Press

Copyright © 2006 Billy Roche

Tales from Rainwater Pond
First published 2006
Pillar Press
Ladywell
Thomastown
Co Kilkenny

www.pillarpress.ie

ISBN 0955082145

British Library Cataloguing in Publication Data.
A CIP catalogue record for this book is available
from the British Library.

Printed in Ireland by Betaprint

10 9 8 7 6 5 4 3 2

To Valerie, Andrea and Cathy – my three Graces

Maggie Angre first appeared in **Soho Square**, edited by Colm Tóibín. This rewritten version of *Maggie Angre* later appeared in **Irish Studies in Brazil**, edited by Munira H. Mutran and Laura P.Z. Izarra. *Northern Lights* first appeared in **Ascent** (vol. 28 Number 3. Spring 2004). *Haberdashery* was broadcast on BBC Radio 4. *Sussex Gardens* was originally commissioned for The Verb, BBC Radio 3.

CONTENTS

HABERDASHERY

I was standing below in the shop when she appeared on the stairs like a beautiful apparition, her lovely face slipping from shadow to sunlight as she stepped from step to step. She'd lost a fair bit of weight since I last set eyes on her and she looked paler than before, but still lovely nevertheless, and when I told her so she came towards me to touch my face with the back of her hand and she whispered my name like a prayer.

Andy was standing by the counter, a packed overnight bag at his feet. Peter was out front in the car, the engine revving and the wipers flapping. Andy said that he wasn't going to go up to the hospital with her today because he had no one to mind the shop – or his, 'feckin' aul' haberdashery,' as Evelyn always put it.

She sort of smiled then and took one last look around: at the shelves of shirts, the boxes of boots, the rows and rows of curtain material and the cluster of Wellingtons dangling down, and if I didn't know her better I'd swear her eyes betrayed some kind of affection for it all.

And then she looked at us, the so called men in her life: Peter peeping in from the car, prematurely grey in his denim jacket and big cowboy belt and his once tender eyes

1

now a deep angry blue; and Andy, a stocky middle aged man all of a sudden, his rugged good looks hidden beneath the life lines that mapped his ageing, handsome face; and finally at me, a four eyed baker still in my working clothes with flour in my hair and clutching a big bag of steaming doughnuts. Thirty years a growing … Thirty years!

Andy crossed the room and called down to the boutique in the basement, 'Sean your mother is going now,' and we could hear Sean stirring below. The rain tapped out her name on the flat roof. A cat purred at her feet.

It was the 5th of May, Evelyn's birthday. I had a wrapped up present tucked away in my pocket and a card that said *FROM LEO, ANITA AND THE BOYS*, (although, to be honest with you, Anita and the lads knew nothing about it). The present was, as far as I could tell, an exact replica of a heart shaped necklace we gave to Evelyn when she was seventeen. It had *EVELYN* inscribed on the front in what the silversmith called arabesque. *FROM ANDY, PETER AND LEO* was engraved on the back of it.

I was just the messenger boy here that time, riding my big bike up hill and down dale through the wind and rain for thirty shillings a week and a brand new rain hat every New Year's day. The bike had a huge basket on the front and *Carrington & Sons* was emblazoned under the crossbar.

Andy and Peter were the sons in question. Their father, old man Carrington, was a big burly sort of man who used to shamble through the shop like Attila the Hun, bawling out orders at no one in particular, a fairly dour sort of geezer with little or no sense of humour. If you told him a joke chances were he wouldn't get it and even if he did get it he certainly wouldn't be bothered laughing at it.

'The name above that door out there is *Carrington & Sons,*' he said to Andy one day. 'Not **Rebel Rebel, Johnny**

Rebel or any other kind of rebel either – with or without a cause.'

Andy wanted to set up a boutique in the basement, which he was going to call *Rebel Rebel*. And that's when I came through the door, wringing wet and wheeling the big bicycle.

'I believe all the lights went out in the Cinema Palace last night, Mister Carrington,' I said, and the old man furrowed his already wrinkled brow. 'Yeah,' I went on, 'the picture was startin' ... '

Oh, lonely are the brave, boy!

Andy was sulking behind the menswear counter as I told him about Mrs Hayes inviting me into the kitchen to open the parcel in front of me – a black negligée and a skimpy knickers. She held them up to her and asked me what I thought of them and then she laughed at my blushing face and tossed my hair affectionately. Andy said that he didn't believe me but this time it was true.

The shop was a fairly dismal place at the best of times in those days with Miss Corcoran working up in the elevated office and Jimmy Crane scratching his bulbous nose behind the hat stand. Old man Carrington might materialise out of nowhere then and move from counter to counter – or department to department, as he liked to call them – grunting and growling and giving out and generally making everyone's life a misery. The only one who could ever get any good of him was the birdlike Mrs Carrington. She'd stand on the landing and gaze down at him disdainfully until he began to behave himself again.

And then Evelyn would breeze in like Shalimar in her school uniform, one sock up and the other down, four or five freckles around her nose and her hair falling down into her eyes all the time. She was still going out with Peter that time although Andy had designs on her even then.

'Don't do it, Andy,' I said to him one time when I noticed he was trying to muscle in. 'Love her from afar,' I told him, even though I knew well enough he wouldn't listen to me.

Peter and Evelyn would sometimes do their homework on the shoe counter or else they'd slip into the Bed Department and sprawl themselves across one of the beds, their school books piled up all around them. One day they fell asleep in there, snuggled into one another as Miss Corcoran said, '*like two little babes in an old whistling wood.*' Peter woke up to find a laughing congregation around the bed. 'The square on the hypotenuse,' he said through a stiffled yawn. Peter was a dry little bastard even then.

Anyway the three of us sang Happy Birthday to her and gave her seventeen kisses between us and then we stood around and watched as she tore open the wrapping paper to admire the necklace, rolling it around in her hand and wrapping it around her nail bitten fingers. We'd all bunced in ten shillings each to pay for it and there was still another two and tanner owing on it. It was no lucky bag job in other words.

When Evelyn tried to put it around her neck, Peter, acting all sophisticated, moved in to help her fasten the clasp, but he couldn't really manage it all that well and Andy had to come to the rescue. And that was Peter's first mistake if you ask me. I could see she liked Andy's manly – what's the word? – … dexterity.

It was Thursday, half-day closing, and we all set out for Rainwater Pond. I was riding the big bicycle with Evelyn on the crossbar and Andy sitting up in the basket while poor Peter had to run alongside, trying to keep up with us. We went along the railway tracks. Andy was showing off all the time, standing up in the basket with outstretched hands, and jumping down at one stage to go and rob an orchard, coming back with plums for Evelyn, which she said she had never tasted before. We sang, *The Sun Ain't Gonna Shine Anymore*, and, needless to say, I was in heaven – Evelyn leaning into me and looking up at me, her husky voice singing and her strong little hands touching mine from time to time as we bumped from sleeper to sleeper.

'When you're in love,' she said, 'you die a little every day.'

Only a little? I couldn't help thinking as her face shone before me in the broken, mounted mirror.

We arrived at Rainwater Pond to find the place littered with stripped off messenger boys and hard cases of every description – big Shamey Shiggins the painter, Tommy Day the singer and Maggie Angre and all. All powerful swimmers. This was not a place for the faint hearted.

Peter and Evelyn went off hand in hand into the long grass as soon as we got there and, while Andy went over to bum a few drags from big Shamey Shiggins, I lay the bike gently down in the weeds with all the other old faithful steeds. When I turned around Evelyn was standing on a jutting out piece of rock with the necklace in her hand, threatening to drop it in and silently daring someone to dive in there after it for her. To tell you the truth I didn't think she'd do it, but she did. It slipped through her fingers like a silver eel and I watched it sinking like a falling star. *EVELYN EVELYN EVELYN.* Never to be seen again.

Andy was the first to go. He stripped off and dived in there like Johnny Weissmuller. We all watched as he dived down into the deep to disappear into the dark. He was gone for ages too and then he surfaced with a desperate gasp and he clung on to the edge of the pond and gazed up into Evelyn's disappointed face: he was empty handed.

I was the next to go, feet first. I was no Esther Williams. I tried to do it with as much finesse as I could muster, mind you. I didn't want Evelyn to know that it was the first time

I'd ever dived down there. And Jesus it was deep. And murky. But it had a strange sort of allure too though, you know. All the queer things trapped in the weeds – dead dogs and prams and rusty wheels and tyres and the buckled skeleton of an old bicycle and what-have-you. And that sort of what-do-you-call-it … under water sound. Sort of hypnotic or something. It took me my best to swim up out of it that day too I don't mind telling you, and boy was I glad to see that big blue sky again and Evelyn's sad eyes peering out at me from behind the reeds.

One by one the others had a go: big Shamey Shiggins, Tommy Day and a fellow they called Apache Bryne. But it was when Maggie Angre surfaced and shook her head that we all knew it would be useless to try again. That didn't stop me however. No, I went down there another three or four times after that. Made a bit of a show of myself I think.

Peter was the only one who didn't strip off and dive in there for her that time and I think he paid the price for it too. She sulked all the way home. I don't know if she was mad at Peter and black out with us for failing to retrieve the necklace. I often picture it lying down there at the bottom of Rainwater – glistening, rusting, dying.

We ran into a storm on the way back and we had to shelter under a big Devil's Tree. Evelyn stepped out into the open and invited the heavens down on her. Peter tried to coax her back into the shelter but she refused.

'No,' she said, 'I like the wind and rain. It's the calm that frightens me,' and she ran across the field away from us.

Andy rode after her on the bike and scooped her up onto the crossbar. We watched the pair of them riding around the saturated field, the thunder clapping and the rain pouring down.

And that was it. Peter had lost her.

∾

Peter ran away to sea shortly after that and he didn't come back for a few years. He didn't even come home for his father's funeral. Never came back for the wedding either. I was the best man. 'Ladies and Gentlemen,' I said. 'It gives me great pleasure,' and I sat back down again.

A year later Sean was born and Andy got his name over the door: *Andy Carrington & Son.* The following Spring Peter returned when he got word that his mother was poorly and he never went back to sea again. He hung around the town until all his money was gone and then Andy gave him a job running the *Rebel Rebel* boutique in the basement.

He went through the rest of his life drinking and gambling and carousing. He looked fairly cool at first, skipping from one back street bar to another, yesterday's paper jutting up out of his pocket. After a while though when the novelty wore off he just looked sort of silly. At least I thought so anyway.

Of course there were women. Well, girls mostly. They seemed to find him mysterious or something. Mind you, come to think of it, I suppose he did look and behave like some prodigal character from one of those dreary novels he was always talking about. He got a girl pregnant then and when he refused to acknowledge it her father and brothers came down after him and gave him an awful hiding. The beating left him with a bad gash over one of his eyes, which never truly healed, and he walked with a bit of a limp for a while too. And boy did he milk that one: The blind and the lame and the misunderstood all in the one God. He's knocking around out with a woman called Una Young at the moment. She seems to be mad about him, although he treats her like shit most of the time if you ask me.

Andy didn't fare out much better. As soon as he got his name over the door he lost his zing. Thinks about nothing only the shop now, talks about nothing else either. It takes me my best these days to visualise him diving into Rainwater Pond or standing up in the basket. I mean whatever happened to that little fellow anyway? – that brave young adventurer. Although, to be fair, it is fairly hard to be adventurous when you're up to your ears in buttons and bows, I suppose.

Evelyn was never cut out for this place though. Too dull. Vests and long johns and all the rest of it! I mean a woman like that needs mystery and intrigue and someone telling her he loves her all the time.

'What is you want?' Andy asked her once, trying to fathom her loneliness, but Evelyn could never find the words to describe her pain.

'She wants to be adored,' I felt like telling him.

She left him one time, went back home to her own place. But she didn't really get on well with her mother and a few weeks later she came back again. Andy didn't seem to care one way or another whether she came or went at that stage. Well, he never went looking for her anyway, let's put it that way. There was a rumour going around that she was having a long running affair with that prick who owns the Banjo Bar, but … I don't know if that was true or not.

And what about me? Huh? … Well, I took the first decent job that came along, married the first woman I met and I go home for my dinner every day. Adventurous? No. But I do know this though, every single thing I did in my life I did for her. For Evelyn. To impress her, like! Every handball match, every fancy phrase, everything. I learnt to play the drums and joined a local dance band because I thought it might intrigue her, etched out her name on my drumsticks and everything. Practised day and night – my flams and paradiddles – in the hope that she might come and see us sometime. But she never did. Not that I blame her or anything. The Toreadors – the only group in the history of modern music who started at the bottom and worked our way down.

I took French lessons and everything another time. 'Jaime L'amour, Evelyn,' I said to her one night, and I could see her eyes light up.

'What do that mean?' Andy wanted to know.

'I'm in love with love,' I told him and I kissed her hand like a Frenchman.

After that it was card tricks and jokes and stories galore, spilling out of me every time I was around her or near her. And believe me I conspired to be around her and near her as often as I could, coming into the shop every Thursday night for a regular poker game, dropping in most mornings too after work with a few cakes or a fresh loaf of bread. Any excuse to see her. Not to see her was death for me.

'Who do I remind you of, Leo?' she wondered one Thursday night as she tried on a new hat.

'Gina Lollobrigida,' I replied and she smiled, flattered. It was the right answer.

'Aah!' she cried then, pointing her finger at me

'Yeah?' I said, doing the same thing to her.

'Hah?' she said, moving towards me.

'Get out of it!' says I as we circled round each other, still pointing and prodding until our fingers finally met and our faces gently collided like a couple of steers locking antlers.

'Aha,' we both said then at the same time. 'There you are!'

Peter shook his head and sighed and turned away. Andy pretended he never noticed and left the room as he did every time Evelyn and I played this particular game. And I was delighted because it meant that I had entered a beautiful, private realm with her that neither of them could ever even hope to penetrate. It ended as usual with a soft Eskimo kiss and then she moved away from me, leaving behind the lingering scent of her breath in the air. And then, making a great show of it, I bawled across the shop to Peter who was still busy stacking shelves at eight 'o clock at night.'Are you playin' cards or workin' overtime now, Peter,' I said. 'Which?'

'He's conscientious,' Evelyn declared, putting the hat back on the stand. 'That right, Peter?'

'Mmn,' Peter moaned, his nose out of joint.

'Yeah well, Evelyn,' I said, 'I'm a conscientious objector. Now, come on.'

Through the corner of my eye I spied Evelyn trying on a different hat, cocking it to one side and consulting the mirror. Andy was coming down the stairs with a pot of coffee and a big plate of sandwiches.

'That's how drummers count seven beats in a bar, Evelyn, you know,' I told her. 'Gina Lollobrigida. One Two Three Four Five Six Seven Gina Lollobrigida. Cus Cus Cus Cus Cus Cus Cus Cus Cus Lollobrigida … … . I see your old flame up the town too, Peter. Young Una Young, hah! *You're too young says aul' Young when young Young was born.* You'd want to give this man a rise here, Andy, because he's after doin' the work of three or four men here today, boy – the Marx Brothers! Here, speaking of Gina Lollobrigida. What did the bra say to the hat? You go on ahead while I give these two a lift. Do you get it? You go on ahead while I give these two a … … … .'

Yeah, that was me that time! Yap yap yapping, a hundred miles a minute. Afraid to stop talking in case I'd say the wrong thing, afraid to listen in case I'd suddenly … understand.

'Pick a card there, Evelyn,' I said with a great fancy shuffle. 'And don't tell me what it is now.'

'But sure where's the point,' she said, 'when I just keep picking the same card all the time. There. I told you. The Queen Of Spades.'

'Don't tell me I said. '

'The same one all the time,' she said and she sort of hugged herself and shivered.

It was too. Five or six times in a row nearly now. The Queen Of Spades. The Dark Eyed Lady.

~

I arrived into the shop one evening to find Andy and Peter boxing inside the Bed Department. Evelyn was standing on the landing saying their names softly over and over again as the sound of crashing and banging and cursing came from within. Signs on it the fight had started in the shop. There was a standard lamp broken and all the hats from the hat stand were scattered and there was a smidgeon of blood on one of the display cases. I found out later on that Peter had stormed in on top of them, half drunk, and indignantly demanded his rights – his name over the door and that kind of thing. And the two brothers had argued about their father's will and their mother's wishes with Peter insisting that if he had not run away to sea that time his name would definitely be up over the door right now. Instead of that he was living in a dingy flat above the old carpet shop down the street there he said, a place they used to keep the waste paper in once upon a time. But of course it was all just *mar dhea* anyway. I mean every dog and devil on the street knew what this fight was really about. Evelyn knew it too.

'They're killing one another in there,' she said when she saw me, and her eyes were full of fire when she said it.

I needn't tell you what I was thinking as I rambled into the Bed Department to euphemistically bang their heads together.

~

11

Evelyn would sometimes ask Andy to take her to the pictures and now and again he would – reluctantly. She'd come back full of it all and she'd want to talk about it, the actors, the story, the music. Andy would sort of groan and go and bury his head into a mountain of skewered invoices and Evelyn would come over to tell me all about it. Sometimes I'd go to the film the next night just so I'd be able to discuss it with her and she'd be delighted. 'Cause she really loved the pictures, like you know.

Did I tell you the rain was tapping out her name on the flat roof? Did I say that? Well, it was. Tap, tap, tapping: *Evelyn.* And her hair changed colour too as she moved through a splash of sunlight – from auburn to chestnut to a beautiful golden brown.

Sean came up from the basement. He linked his mother and led her to the door. Sean kicks with the other foot I think. Andy picked up the overnight bag and followed them out onto the street. Under the dripping canopy I gave her the present. I think that was probably the best time to do it too. Even then I was still trying to impress her. Can you believe that?

She read the card. 'Leo,' she said, 'your own handwriting too.'

Or is that when she touched my face? I think it was. With the back of her hand. Like a blessing. Although, God forgive me, sometimes I nearly wish it meant something else. And then they helped her into the car and before I knew it she was gone.

'Are you sure you don't want to go up to the hospital with her,' Sean said to his father as the car pulled away.

'No, 'Andy said. 'Let Peter do it,' and they both went back inside.

I didn't. I stood there in the drizzling rain and watched the car disappear around the bend. I knew I'd never see her again.

I went home then and went up to the back bedroom. I got out my battered drum kit and put on an old Joe Loss record and sat down to play along with it. *In The Mood. Do Be Do BE Do BE Do BE Do BE Do Yeah. Do BE Do BE Do BE Do BE Do BE Do Ah. Do BE Do BE Do BE Do Be Do BE Do Cus. Do BE Do BE Do Be Do Be Do BE Do Do. Do BE Do BE Do BE Do BE Do BE Do Do And It's Gina Lollobrigida. And Do BE Do BE Do BE Do BE Do BE Do Do … …*

Anita called up the stairs to me that my tea was ready.

'It's all right' hon,' I said, 'I'm not wantin' any'

'What's that?' she said.

'I said it's all right, I'm not wantin' anything.'

'Yeah?' she said. 'Well now, there's a first.'

'Yeah well,' I said,' there's always a first for everything.'

'Come again?' says she.

'I said there's always a first time … for everything. Gina Lollobrigida … *Do BE Do BE Do BE Do BE Do BE Do Wham. Do Be Do BE Do BE Do BE Do BE Do Slam. Do BE Do BE Do BE Do Be Do BE Do Bam. Do Be Do BE Do BE Do BE Do BE Do Jam. Wham Slam Bam Bam Bam and it's Gina Lollobrigida. Cus … '*

NORTHERN LIGHTS

The back of the van was choc-a-bloc with stuff: honey and herbs and a batch of the lovely leather bracelets she made and a box of her tiny landscape paintings, which had proved to be a steady little earner, selling at €20 each in various outlets throughout the town. She had them down to a fine art now – fifteen to twenty minutes, frame and all. And then there were the potted plants: the busy lizzies and spider plants, geraniums and cactus, trailing ivy and hibiscus, all present and accounted for. Yes, between one thing and another she was doing all right. Well, keeping the wolf from the door anyway. In fact if things were different she might even be proud of the cottage industry she'd created, cottage being the operative word. The house behind her was tumbling down around her ears. She hadn't managed to do half the things she'd intended to do when they first arrived here. How long was it now? Years and years! The children were grown up and gone away and everything. Driven away.

The postman still referred to the place as The Apiary, which was nice. Whatever happened to that wooden sign? Blown down in a storm and blew away, probably ended up on someone's bonfire. She must give Mister Wright a call and ask him to take another look at the old grandfather clock on the landing. Still going slow. Or fast, depending on it's mood. Mind of its own, that clock. What a great name for a clockmaker – Mister Wright.

The battered old van was caked with mud and rusty around the wheels and one of the tyres was bald. The exhaust was tied up with twine and the front bumper was dented beyond repair. Beyond repair – the story of her life. She saw her own reflection in the side mirror, hair blown about, face chapped with the wind and her cardigan puffed up into a bulge so that from a certain angle you'd swear she had developed the makings of a hump on her back. She was nearly fifty years of age now and her face looked lined and jaded, ravaged by time. Well, she thought so anyway although people still told her she looked beautiful occasionally, and maybe she did. Sometimes she did.

He was there too, squashed into the mirror and standing in the doorway behind her, riddled with suspicion as usual. He looked older than his years, although he always dressed younger than he should, which was silly. I mean that haircut for Christ's sake. And those boots.

'Are you sure you don't want to come into town with me?' she called over her shoulder as she opened the back door of the van.

He shook his head and turned aside. He reached into the hallway and found his coat and walking stick, whistled the dog and went crunching up the gravelled yard like yesterday's hero and over the ditch without a word. He had the look of an alcoholic about him lately even though he rarely drank. Smoked like a trooper though, and the weight was falling off of him. He was definitely dying of something, she was sure of that. But what? And when?

She lobbed her homemade hand trolley onto the back seat of the van and then she returned to the house to bank up the fire. She rinsed her hands under the tap, dried them in an old tea towel that was lying around and she went up to the bevelling attic to fetch her winter coat. All around the room, displayed on easels and leaning against the wall and piled in a heap on the floor were what she called her real paintings: some finished, some half finished, some nearly finished, some abandoned, others in limbo. One day she would have an exhibition – in a gallery or the Desert Hall or The Menapia Hotel maybe. People standing around discussing her work in hushed tones, the significance of it and so on. Sipping wine and drinking cups of coffee and discreetly whispering her name whenever she'd sidled by. She hadn't told him all this of course, he'd only laugh.

Her latest painting was a winter scene of the house and the surrounding fields, the frozen tundra of her life. It was a heightened, Hopperesque sort of affair: a frozen water barrel in the yard, icicles dangling from the eaves, the gutters clogged with melting snow and pearls of condensation clinging to the clothes line as a mad swarm of bees flocked towards a beautiful and strange green tinted horizon.

'What is that?' he said the minute he saw it, squinting through those antarctic blue eyes.

'What?' she wondered, acting dumb.

'That?' he said, aiming his head in the general direction of the glowing, emerald sky, the first thing he said to her all day as it happens.

'The aurora borealis' she told him, and she knew well enough what he was going to say. He could be a right little encyclopaedia when he wanted to be.

'The Northern Lights?' he said, '-at this latitude?' and he shook his head, doubtfully.

'I know,' she retorted, 'that's the point.' And then there was silence and he sort of growled and creaked his way down the stairs and slipped out the back door.

She put on the drab winter coat (the third winter in a row now). She could see him through the window, traversing the drenched fields, the dog running along ahead of him. She wondered what he thought about as he strode past the dark pond where the hard cases dived in the summer and where young lovers laid down at night. Did he think about love? Did he think about death? Did he ever think about her at all? Did he ever even give her a second thought? Probably not. He was good with the dog though, and kind to the bees. But people! No. She couldn't keep a workman in the house with him. Her friends too all disappeared. And as for the kids? Well!

Like for instance the night he came back in a foul temper from one of his long walks with the dog, banging pots and pans and kettles in the kitchen and cursing the children for leaving their stuff lying around; and then about ten minutes later a gang of young men arrived to pound on the door, offering to fight him, threatening to drag him outside. They were out hunting apparently, had all the paraphernalia anyway: lamps, guns, dogs, sticks, sacks. And the noise, the cursing. She was petrified. So was he, although he made a bit of a show of it when they were gone, searching around for his shotgun and running after them as far as the end of the lane. What had he said to them on his travels? What had he done? She never found out. He never explained himself … Ever.

Some nights he wouldn't come back for hours. She'd be listening to the radio or watching the television or reading a book, and she'd glance up at the clock and wonder where he was and what was keeping him. She'd imagine him falling down a hole or slipping into Rainwater Pond or falling under one of the night trains that came and went behind the house. And then she'd hear the latch on the back door and the scrape of his mucky boots on the hard mat and, God forgive her, her heart would sort of sink.

They rarely made love anymore – if it could ever be called love. He stayed up half the night now, listening to the radio. Strange things. The Shipping News or something, anything. She'd go to bed and drop off and in the early hours he'd slip in beside her, turn his back and sleep. Sometimes she'd wake up in the morning and he wouldn't be there at all. She'd come down the stairs to find him curled up on the sofa with a blanket around him, a book on the floor, an empty cup nearby.

She had never painted him, even when he was handsome. She had forgotten that he was once good looking until she found a photograph of him recently in a jeans and a sloppy Joe – lean, tanned, tall, fair haired and handsome. That was that summer, full of hope then. Forlorn enough too as it turned out. Sick and tired of answering to someone else all the time he decided to set up a makeshift garage of his own at the back of the house, fixing cars and motorbikes and lawn mowers and that kind of thing. And everything would have been all right too only people insisted on asking him when they might have their property back, which caused great offence to Lord Muck of course. One woman got a tongue lashing for ringing up two days in a row, inquiring about her beloved Austin Martin, which she said she needed to get to work. Another man was practically frogmarched out of the yard one day just because he dared to question the price of something. In the end word got around about him and people stopped coming altogether and he was left tinkering around the yard all day everyday in a dirty overalls with nothing to do. No, she didn't think she ever would paint him now. He wouldn't sit still for her anyway. From memory maybe? No. How can you paint what you can't understand?

∽

In some people's eyes the three mile drive into town was probably idyllic: the river rushing towards the sea, the march reeds bowing and bending and dancing to some silent symphony, the sea gulls mewling like demented flutes and the quilted fields spreading on out and up towards the mountain. But you could get bogged down in that marshland and tangled up in those wild reeds, stuck and stranded in the muck and the mire. And it might be days before someone would come looking for you – weeks, months, years even. And when they'd eventually find you it could happen that you'd look so wretched that they'd think you weren't worth saving at all and they'd just turn around and leave you where they found you.

No, this area, this place, this spot ... And the people. Those boatmen with their lonely eyes. And the stories. A man found hanging in a barn. Another threw himself into the salty river. *GAVE HIMSELF BACK TO THE SEA!* And that old man in the white house who shot his sheepdog with a shotgun rather than pay a vet a couple of lousy quid to do it humanely (if that's the right word). The women with their hard faces and hard hands, stoic as they come, love and tenderness a thing of the past.

She was passing the white house now, the little white cottage. The old man at the gate waved to her but she refused to acknowledge him anymore. She watched him through the rear view mirror as he wondered what was up. And then she spied her own face there too and she deliberately softened her expression. Don't want a hard face now do we? I mean hard hands are one thing but a hard face. I mean ... Jesus!

Anyway, love and tenderness were not a thing of the past. Although for a while there she thought they were. Three years and she hadn't shed a single tear, over anything. Until the night Nicky Spain kissed her beneath the stars, took her in his sculptor's arms and kissed her.

'We can't do this Nicky,' she said, falling into him. 'I'm married, you're married.'

'You're the most beautiful woman I've ever seen,' he said as if that made everything all right and then he kissed her again, all over the face, licked her face and everything.

'I'm forty seven now,' she told him in a feeble attempt to staunch his passion.

'You'll always be beautiful,' he said, 'and I'll always love you.'

It slipped out of him so naturally that she was inclined to believe him. And later back at her car she wept, lay into his sturdy body and wept, tear after big fat tear spilling out of her eyes and rolling down her face with the same perpetual motion. And he wrapped his arms around her to comfort her and he told her it was all right, everything was all right, and he seemed to understand her grief. And then she got into the car, rolled down the window and looked up into his worried face.

'You've the tenderest eyes I've ever seen,' she said, and she went home.

❧

In the town she found a handy place to park between the row of chestnut trees. Ideal really. She could do all her business in one fell swoop now. Big fat Anthony Mahoney was standing outside The Cherry Orchard Supermarket having a smoke, striped apron and silly looking butcher's hat. He daubed his cigarette, prodigally planted it behind his ear and came towards her. He opened up the back door of the van and automatically proceeded to lug the boxes of honey into the shop for her.

'Thanks Anthony,' she chirped, getting out.

'Are you wanting cash for these?' he wanted to know with a great air of authority.

'Yeah, if you can,' she called after him. 'The invoice is in there.'

He grunted and waddled his way towards The Cherry Orchard, truly smitten by the looks of it. She smiled to herself as she loaded up her trolley with most of the potted plants and then she rolled them over to The Garden Shed Nursery opposite.

Twenty potted plants at €4 each – €80 – and she was owed another €50 from the last day. A hundred and thirty all in all. Great. Mrs Heinz was here today. Cheque signed, crossed, dated and everything. And when she returned to the van Anthony was waiting for her with an impressive wad of money. Brilliant. He helped her to load up the trolley again: first the honey and herbs, then the bracelets, then the small landscape paintings. Pick And Choose, Lamberts and your man in The Bull Ring. In that order. Oh, and The Angel Boutique – three potted plants and a landscape painting. Anthony took the keys from her, locked up the back of the van and then gently returned them as if it was all in a day's work. She winked at him and smiled at the bald headed Mister Byrne, the manager of the Cherry Orchard, who was giving her the thumbs up from inside the shop, a signal that her honey was still going great guns. Under her spell too, no doubt. Ah well … Some of us have it as they say.

◦

Nicky Spain's studio was beside The Cherry Orchard. A cobbled yard led into the dark cavern where he worked. She could see sparks flying and spitting and a blow torch glowing in the dark and she knew that Nicky was in there somewhere, although she couldn't make him out, sleeves rolled up, holes in his jeans, holes in his jumper, dirt on his face. She wondered if he could see her. No, probably not. If he did he'd come out to her, for sure. What was he making in there anyway? A magic horse to take them both away? She was sorely tempted to go towards the light.

'Light,' he said, the first time she ever laid eyes on him. 'People go on about light all the time as if it was the be all and end all of everything. It's not. It's just one aspect of painting.' He was giving an art class in the Desert Hall to a handful of wide-eyed students. 'Light to me,' he went on, 'is like a beautiful melody. It should be surrounded by discord and hidden in what-do-you-call-it … cacophony so that it sneaks up to ambush you when you least expect it. Boom.'

Later they all went down to the Thomas Moore Tavern for a few drinks and she ended up sitting beside him and that's how she got to know him better. He sang a song that night. *As I Roved Out.* So did she, something silly. And afterwards he walked her back to her car.

It would be nearly nine years though before he'd kiss her beneath the stars, after some do or other. Another two months before they began their brief and beautiful affair. Three months it lasted all in all. Three beautiful, petrified months of whispered phone calls, scribbled notes and love letters, hands held in coffee shops and bars and discreet meetings in the city. And then it was all over, finished by her, afraid to go on. She had seen Nicky's wife Phil coming out of the bank a few days before and noticed that she was very pale looking and had lost a lot of weight. It was just a glimpse really, but enough to make her curious, and when she asked around she was told that Phil was unwell. The big C, someone told her. And then, two or three days later, Nicky's young daughter Carmen had followed her about, skulking along silently behind her in her school uniform. Along the main street, the girl's eyes burning into the small of her back. Up a side street and there she was again, keeping at a safe distance, giving her the evil eye. In the end she was forced to take refuge in a nearby waterfront café. And still Carmen didn't call it a day. No, she hung around on the corner for a long time, her collar turned up like a private detective. Carmen was soon joined by her young brother Aidan who shuffled to keep warm and blew into his hands and seemed kind of confused about it all to say the least. A truck pulled up then in front of the window, blocking the view. She was tempted to make her escape there and then, but she didn't in the end. She waited, her heart pounding. The lorry driver eventually returned to his vehicle and drove off and she looked out the window to find that the two children were – thankfully from her perspective, mysteriously she suspected from theirs – no longer there. The damage, however, had already been done by then.

That last phone call. God.

'Don't go,' he pleaded when she gave him the bad news.' I don't want you to go,' he said. 'Not yet.'

'I have to,' she told him, 'for all our sakes.' She hadn't, of course, elaborated.

'What was she afraid of?' he wanted to know then. 'Happiness?'

Six months later she slipped in to see Nicky's exhibition in a local gallery when she knew he wasn't around. A Romanian girl was manning the door, prematurely grey and beautiful. A devotee? A lover? All her jealousy was dispelled however when she moved around the room and saw herself everywhere. Carved in wood and chiselled in stone and sculpted in bronze, her lithe, svelte body everywhere. Standing up and sitting down and walking away. Naked and adorned. And faceless. (Was he trying to forget her or could he not recall? Or protecting her perhaps? Yes, all of these.) Lovers too, in love and making love. And that divine piece etched in ebony, depicting two lovers tangled up and entwined like dancers in a dance. That night at Rainwater Pond, her legs wrapped around him, his face close to hers. 'Look at this,' he said. 'A work of art!' And it was too. A work of art! And later they both hid their faces from a passing night train and after it was gone he scratched her name in the dust.

Meanwhile back at the studio the sparks continued their dainty dance and the glow from the blowtorch illuminated Nicky's masked and shadowy outline for the briefest of moments. And then he was gone again, disappeared in a puff of smoke like some ghostly conquistador, and she turned on her heels and wheeled her clattering trolley down the leafy avenue and onto the narrow, bustling Main Street.

'The herbs and honey for Lamberts, the bracelets for your man in the Bull Ring, the landscape paintings for Pick And Choose. Wait there now. The Angel Boutique first. Should have put that honey on top. Don't matter. Hang on now. Lovely suit. Classy blouse. Nice price too, I'd say. Still. Must get my hair done. Tch, the state of it! Now. Three potted plants and a landscape. Well, seascape. *Wexford Harbour In The Gloaming.* Nice title, even though I do say so myself. Ding … Love that sound. Money from the till. Great. Snobby little bitch. One of these days I'll come in here and buy the shop. You'll see.'

∾

Lunchtime. She popped her head into The Centenary Stores. All the girls were there, Margaret and Annette and young Rosemary, in their bank uniforms. She joined them, ordered a toasted special and a cup of coffee.

'Yum yum pig's bum,' Margaret said when the food arrived. The barman looked at her askance and the girls giggled when he was gone. And then they were down to business. What's what and who's with who in the bank. And when Annette and Rosemary went back to work Margaret took an hour that was owed to her and they each had another cup of coffee.

'So?' Margaret said. 'What's going on?'

And so she told Margaret about her life with him again and the story sounded so gloomy that they both had to laugh about it.

'Well, what did you expect?' Margaret said. 'I mean it is marriage after all,' and she laughed again in spite of everything as Margaret reached across and swept a strand of hair away from her lovely face and murmured,' Let the cat see the rabbit,' under her breath.

Later Margaret slipped out to the Ladies and she was left alone at the counter.

She looked around at all the young people heading back to work, paying their bills and kissing their lovers goodbye and making plans to meet later on. She wondered what it would be like to go to the pictures or something, hold hands in the dark. Or maybe a nice meal in an Italian Restaurant, a nice bottle of wine. Or a concert somewhere, in the quaint Protestant Church perhaps. Slip down to the pub afterwards for a few drinks and that. She called for the bill and thought about leaving him for once and for all. Move into town with her stuff, take a cheap flat somewhere, over The Banjo Bar maybe. Leave him the bees and the honey. Live on her painting. It could be done. Keep making the bracelets though. Margaret returned to find her singing softly to herself. *When I Turn Around/ To Embrace My Darling/ Instead Of Gold / Sure Tis Brass I Find.*

'You know, I was just thinking there,' she said to Margaret as she waited for her change. 'What would stop me from moving into town, find a cheap flat for myself.'

'Nothing,' Margaret said. 'Absolutely nothing.'

∽

She put the trolley into the back of the van, locked it up and rambled towards Nicky Spain's studio, down the cobbled path and inside. She found him leaning over a strange looking contraption, a sculpted piece, which was probably ingenious, although its significance eluded her.

'How are you, Nicky,' she wondered when she saw him and he rose up and came towards her, took her hand in his and said her name softly to himself over and over again like an incantation.

He looked tired she thought as she touched his face. 'How's Phil?' she asked.

'Not too good,' he said. 'She's in and out of the hospital all the time now, up and down to Dublin every second day nearly. We're all exhausted. The lads are in bits over it … .. No hope, I'm afraid. A matter of time.' She had already heard that on the grapevine. He shrugged, tears in his eyes. Cé Sera.

They went into the back room and he made a pot of coffee. She sat down on the car seat that served as a sofa and he sat beside her and put his arm around her. She lay her head on his shoulder and she wept again. That man. What is it about him?

'Are you working?' he inquired when things had calmed down, kissing her forehead.

'Yeah,' she said through her tears. 'I am. I have about twenty done now. I'm thinking of showing them soon somewhere. I have a bit more work to do on them still, mind you,' she said, searching his eyes for some sign of approval or something. Or scorn even. 'It's hard to work out there though, you know,' she went on. 'A bit cramped and that, with no real light worth talking about.'

'There's a room upstairs there you can use if you want,' he told her. 'Anytime.'

'Yeah? There's not a bed in it by any chance is there?'

'There is actually,' he said. 'Why, do you want to fool around or something?'

She slapped him playfully. 'I wouldn't mind to tell you the truth,' she said, 'but … better not, eh? '

'I wouldn't have the energy anyway,' he confessed, and when she laughed he drew her closer to him and whispered, 'That's better,' in her ear; and then he wiped her left over tears away and he kissed her slowly and lovingly and he told her in a roundabout way that she looked beautiful and that he had always loved her and would always love her, no matter what.

Later she took a look at the room. Sparsely furnished: a bed, a locker, a built in wardrobe, high ceiling, plenty of light, a deadly looking chair. She could move in here straight away if she wanted to. Go to work. Be here to help Nicky through the hard times ahead. Of course people would talk but … Let them. There was a bathroom across the landing. Needs a woman's touch, this place. A few curtains, a bit of finesse.

She could hear Nicky working below and the sound of a radio playing some beautiful love song and she knew then in her heart and soul that she still loved him even though she had never told him so. Afraid he'd get carried away, she kept that secret to herself. It wasn't for her own sake she had ended the affair but for his. After all he was the one with the sick wife and a young family who doted on him. Her own lads had already skedaddled at that stage, Sinead in London and Darren still in college. Although she often recollected feeling fearful of the outcome at the time.

'You'd better not tell anyone about this,' she warned Nicky one night, gripped with panic. 'He'll go mad if he finds out … Kill me … '

Was that the first time? Yes, it was, the very first time. The pair of them tucked up in bed together. And before that, earlier on that same day, as she stood at the sink. The

Angelus was on the telly. The phone rang and when she answered it Nicky was on the other end.

'Are you on your own there?' he wondered.

'Yeah,' she whispered, 'sort of. He's going hunting with big Lar Larkin for a few days.'

She could see the two men through the window, packing all the stuff into the back of the van: guns, traps, tents, ropes, knives and fishing nets. God only knows what they were hoping to catch. The dog was going with them too, evidently, bundled into the back anyway.

'As soon as he's gone I'm coming out to see you,' Nicky said and the sense of urgency in his voice set a secret part of her on fire. 'Right?' he said.

'Right,' she heard herself say, and then Nicky hung up and never gave her a chance to change her mind.

This thing between them had been building up for weeks now. Will we or won't we? We might, we can't, we will, we must, we have to, where and when and what does it all mean if we do? That kiss beneath the stars that night was one thing, its aftermath was another. She had gone on home and tried to forget all about it and, apart from the odd lapse now and again when she longed to hear his voice or to smell him close by, she thought she was doing all right. Until Nicky rang her up one morning out of the blue to see how she was getting on and before she knew it they were sitting in a coffee shop somewhere together and holding hands under the table. And here she was now on the cusp of God knows what.

Lar Larkin was locking up the back of the van now as the other fellow came into the house to say goodbye to her.

'Back Monday or Tuesday,' he said, grinning. Over the moon he was, kissed her and everything.

Was he going hunting at all? she wondered. He never brought anything home with him from these trips. Did they eat all that they caught? The thought crossed her mind that he might be going to a whorehouse in Dublin or something. Or some other woman maybe. She had often fantasised about him coming in and telling her that he had found someone else. She would act indignant of course and kick him out and then jump for joy when he was gone. Or would she?

Fifteen minutes later Nicky arrived. He must have passed the other car along the way, the cheeky devil, because there was only the one road out of here. He abandoned the car in the middle of the driveway, driver's door still open and everything, the radio playing. He ran into her arms and swept her into the kitchen, devouring her with kisses, clothes coming off and flying everywhere: cardigan, blouse, skirt, pants, jumper, stockings, shirt, the lot. Cushions dropped to the floor too and then they slid to the ground and melted into each other like a hand in a glove. She don't know how it happened but they ended up in bed. Did he carry her there? He must have. Yes, he did. He carried her up the stairs, her naked body wrapped around him, past angels and saints and empty holy water fonts.

Later as the evening shadows crowded around the room she snuggled into him and worried about it all – his wife, her husband, their children. Nicky told her not to worry about it.

'There's a whole lot of different ways of loving,' he whispered. 'The fact that we only have the one word for it is our hard luck.'

He was forever saying that until she got fed up hearing it and reared up on him one night as she lay in his arms beside the moonlit lagoon. 'You're always saying that,' she said, 'and it gets on my nerves. The truth of the matter is there's only one kind of love and this is it.' It was the nearest she had ever come to telling him that she loved him and he had only laughed, kissed her and slid her gently into the water. She swam away from him earnestly, as if for good, disappearing into the bulrushes – *A Nymph Among The Reeds* – and as she climbed out she caught a glimpse of herself and for once she saw what he saw when he looked at her and she just knew that she was beautiful.

Yes, this room would do nicely if only she had the courage to take it. On second thoughts better not though, eh? All the trouble it'd cause. Her family, her mother and sisters and all. And his family, passing them in the street and that. And the children. And facing him when he'd come into town looking for her, a face of vengeance on him. No, stay the way we are. Ride it out. The devil you know and all of that.

Downstairs she found Nicky polishing a sculpted piece – a cold cast bronze statue of an emaciated woman with cropped hair and terror in her eyes, a majestic angel at her shoulder showing her the way. In the corner she spied a bronze bust of Phil in happier and healthier times. And elsewhere Phil in blue jeans wheeling a bicycle, Phil in childbirth, Phil at prayer. She instinctively put her arms around him and cuddled into him from behind. He reached back and touched her face and it occurred to her that she would soon try and paint this very hunched over image: the pair of them fused together like that, wracked with pain and lost in loneliness.

'I never did get over you,' he said as darkness fell. 'I don't suppose I ever will now.'

∞

The lights were on in the white cottage as she drove past and smoke came curling from the chimney. Two devoted swans alighted on the river. A black diver dived. A fox roved through the fields. A train rumbled by. Fog surrounded the mountain and the wind in the wild reeds piped out a faint and lonely note. Life's beautiful melody you might say.

When she arrived at the house she found the dog's dish overturned. She upturned it, filled it with water from the water barrel and peeped in to the kitchen through the tiny window. He was sitting over the fire, toasting bread skewered on a fork. Startled, he looked towards her and when he saw her his eyes were filled not with suspicion or jealousy as she had expected, but with a terrible sinking disappointment that she had come back at all.

'Oh,' she said to herself. Now she understood.

Tonight after tea she would go up to the attic and paint a portrait of him: a loner alone sitting in front of a window against a sliver of night sky. She would do it honestly and without malice and tomorrow after he was gone for his long walk with the dog she would pack all her things into the back of the van, say goodbye to the bees and leave.

MAGGIE ANGRE

Maggie Angre, a rolled up towel under her arm, stood on the edge of Rainwater Pond and gazed out at the very spot where her brother Steven had perished. This old abandoned quarry, which had been filled up to the brim with a mixture of seawater and rain: black and bottomless, tanged with salt, home of the otter and the eel, where the drowning Steven had called out her name, called out to her even though he must have known in his heart and soul that there was no way could she swim out that far. And even still his voice echoed here, echoed through the trees, was blown on out to sea only to return year in and year out to this desolate and magnetic place.

On the far side the march reeds bowed like pageboys, and in the distance, beyond the railway tracks, the mountains lay heaped against the sky as Maggie began to undress, kicking off her muddy shoes, taking off her pants and jumper and flinging them up into the bushes. She had her bathing costume on underneath her clothes, which was straining now to bear the brunt of her bulging physique. She knelt down and dipped her hand in the water. She blessed herself and she looked up at the cloud rolling sky and she remembered once again what it was like on the day he drowned. Their bedraggled gang huddled together on the bank: Steven and Albino Murphy and big fat Anthony Mahony from Selskar, herself and one or two others; and how they all got a bit of a fright when two white swans materialised out of the reeds opposite and began to drown the tiny ducks, holding them under water with their wings. Albino tiptoeing along the top of the old submerged quarry wall, which made him look like he was walking on the water and he waving out to the wide-eyed passengers on a passing train.

It was a fine afternoon. There was a blue sky. Or was it raining? No, it was … It was all kinds of weather on the day he drowned and it was no particular time of day, it was all day and every day and all day long there were sun showers. They sheltered under the dripping bushes. They ate beans and crab apples and they sang a jaunty calypso song that Albino had taught them. *Rich Man Underneath The Apple Tree/ Rich Man Singing/ You Can't Catch Me/ I Own The Apple/ I Own The Pear/ Rich Man Say/ That He Don't Care.*

Steven was a good-looking boy. Handsome. Not like Maggie at all. You'd never think for a minute that they were brother and sister. And he was brave too. He was the one who swam all the way across to the other side of the pond while the rest of them were afraid of their living lives to venture more than a few feet from the shore. Steven was fearless that way. And he was very good with people. You can ask anyone about him. He was well liked. Very well thought of, Steven was! Very well respected! When he went to work in Delaney's Grocery Store that time, doing the messages after school, they were all dying about him there. Mister Delaney said he was one of the best young fellows he'd ever taken on. Always in good form, he said, always laughing and joking and that. Tossing coins with all the boys in the laneway at the back of the shop and all. And riding the big bike with no hands, coming down the hill. He was a devil at that. But dependable. Absolutely dependable. You could always rely on Steven. Give him a message to do and he'd always do it. Worth his weight in gold, Mister Delaney said he was … Yes, gold.

Actually Steven not only rode the bike with no hands but (unknownst to Mister Delaney) he could also ride it standing upright on the saddle like a cowboy in the rodeo, which he often did to amuse the other lads on the street. He could snap twine too and there wasn't a street or alleyway or shortcut in the town that he didn't know. And what about the time they all went on the annual shop outing to Dublin? – in a bus. Steven was only working there nine months at that stage and although you were supposed to be over a year in the place before you were considered eligible nevertheless Steven was allowed to go. That's how much they thought of him there. Steven came back with great stories to tell that time, recounting them to Maggie across the dark expanse of the freezing cold bedroom they shared in the pokey house in Keyser's Lane. And she pictured them all sitting in the swanky dining room of The Metropolitan Hotel in Dublin as the waiters danced attendance all around them. Steven was sitting beside old Denny Dempsey who didn't know what to do so that Steven had to tell him which knife and fork to use and all that kind of stuff. First the soup arrived, Steven said, piping hot. Cream of vegetable, his favourite. 'And did you know which spoon to use for that, Steven,' Maggie asked, even though she knew well enough that he did. 'Oh yeah,' Steven replied. 'The roundy one for the soup and then you just work your way inwards.' Some of the men – in fact most of the men – broke their bread rolls up and let them float around in their soup, but Steven didn't do that because someone once told him that that was a terrible ignorant thing to do, and Maggie felt so proud of Steven then because he always knew the right thing to do. You could always depend on that. Then, as Steven called out the rest of the menu to her, under the cover of darkness, she reached beneath her pillow and treated herself to another suck of the sweet stick of Dublin rock that he had brought home to her.

Maggie stood on the jutting out piece of bank where Steven had stood. Awkward and ugly she felt in the daylight as the folds of flesh fell down around her and the fatness of her chilblained legs reflected in the water. And then she dived, leaving behind her footprints in the mucky bank, dirty bits of clay clinging to the soles of her feet as the river rose like a shroud to hide the monstrosity that she called her body. And when she dived her arched body resembled a bird in flight and when she rose up it was with an amphibian grace that she ploughed through the water, eating up distance with every stride, cutting down space with every stroke, her head rising and falling, her arms shooting out tiny white spurts of water as she swam. Maggie Angre was a powerful swimmer. When she swam people stopped to look at her. She could swim out to Useless Island and back again and then without a feather off of her she could just turn around and swim the entire length of the Woodenworks. She loved the water. Yes, Maggie was in her alley when she swam.

A seagull screeched and swooped and landed like the Holy Ghost on top of the old submerged quarry wall. The afternoon train ploughed past too, the driver blowing his lonesome whistle at Maggie to spur her across the pond. A few drops of rain fell with a gentle pit pat on the surface of the water and the early September breeze made the nearby furze and bramble bushes rustle and sway. All these sounds and motions were there too on that fateful day, all these and more. A swarm of bees droned somewhere, a butterfly gently fluttered and the trees were alive with birdsong. The sound of a transistor radio played softly from the long grass, some courting couple probably. And Slattery's peacock let out its unmerciful shriek that day too so that each and every one of them stiffened like statues. Steven made fun of them all and sort of imitated their terrified faces, but Maggie couldn't help thinking afterwards that this must surely have been some sort of omen. And then a young girl appeared out of nowhere – a beautiful apparition in the clearing of a cluster of crab apple trees. She was accompanied by a crippled boy who lurked in the long grass like he was her guardian angel. The girl secretly smiled at Steven as he stepped up to the edge of the bank to take his dive.

'Hold my towel Maggie,' Steven said. 'And when I come back you're to hand it to me like a cloak … cause then I'll be the King Of The Kyber Rifles,' and then he blessed himself and with the words, 'In Saecula Saeculorum,' on his lips he was gone, into the water and away, one of the last things she'd ever hear him say as it turned out.

She would have handed him his cloak that day too. She would have forged a crown for him if he had asked her for it, whatever he wanted. If he was here today he would have definitely elevated her to another level, she was sure of that, instead of the freak that she had become, which, let's face it, is what she was. Working in that old slaughter house yard three days a week, which wasn't right, no matter what way you looked at it, it wasn't right, and although she always washed herself from top to toe every evening in the basin after work she knew well enough that she still reeked of the place whenever she went out at night. Of course everyone just assumed she was inured to it all but she wasn't. Far from it in fact! Only the other day she nearly keeled over when she caught a glimpse of her own simian-like self in a shop window: a rough looking woman in a man's suit, the blustery wind reddening her chiselled, pock – marked face and betraying her scarcity of hair, ballooning up her coat so that she looked twice the size she already was, as if she wasn't bad enough.

And there's no doubt about it but if Steven was here today she wouldn't be still living in that damp old house in Keyser's Lane now either. He would have moved her out of there long and ever ago. They'd be living on a boat by now. That old forlorn coaster called the Santa Maria that was neaped in the Crescent Quay for as long as she could recall. Steven was always going on about that. How great it would be to buy it and do it up and live on it like a couple of bohemians. A pot bellied stove installed in the galley with wooden benches running all around for people to sit on whenever they'd come to call, and a special private cabin for Maggie to sleep in with a pipe from the stove running through the wall to make it nice and cosy. Or maybe they wouldn't live on a boat at all, perhaps he'd build a nice new bungalow on the edge of town somewhere and she could keep house for him and when he got married and had a family she'd get on really well with his wife and she'd be called upon from time to time to mind the children for them whenever they went away for weekends to Dublin or London or wherever.

And Steven would stand up for her if he ever heard tell of anyone saying anything against her or anything. He'd put on his coat and go down after them. Just like that time in the snooker hall all those years ago as she waited for him to finish his game of billiards and some teddy boy said something unkind to her, something she'd rather not repeat now if you don't mind, not realising she was Steven's younger sister. Steven threw him a murderous look and the fellow nearly died. He apologised and everything, said he never knew. But Steven just kept glaring at him until the fellow skulked off to the far end of the room with his tail between his legs. And later on the same lad, to make amends, slipped out to the shop and he came back with a choc-ice for Maggie.

She could have done with Steven by her side the other day too when she stopped to browse through the array of frayed hardbacks and torn paperbacks that were on display on a stand outside that second hand book shop in the Mall. She found a book that she had been searching for this long time. She picked it up and leafed through it, her stumpy fingers gently turning the pages from which vaulted the lovely, musty fragrance of some other little untold tale. She read the first page and then the last page and she closed it and hugged it lovingly to her bosom. A young, svelte student girl was frantically thumbing her way through the collection of books on the same rack, obviously searching for something specific. A funeral procession was inching its way towards them. The owner of the book shop, a small pernickety man who always pretended he never saw you before no matter how many times you went in there, came out onto the stoop and invited Maggie and the girl to step inside and when they did he closed over the door so that the funeral could pass in peace.

And so Maggie found herself locked within the dusty bookshop with the young student girl and a middle-aged man who looked like a professor (tweed coat, horn-rimmed glasses and a corduroy pants), and another married couple who were so in love that they were reading the same book. The owner of the shop was at the till, engrossed in some serious calculation, and a soft stream of rain-soaked sunlight flooded the window. All we need now are cathedral bells everywhere, Maggie was thinking, stepping up to the counter to pay for the book. For some reason or other she felt at home here as the shop window darkened for a moment or two with the shifting shadows of the shuffling mourners outside. Perhaps she had found her niche at long last. Perhaps she should pack in her job at the abattoir, move away to the city, close to a college. Take classes maybe. Live in an attic, a vase of flowers in the window, a high Nelly bike in the hall below. Read and write and go to plays. Dabble in poetry maybe. Lose herself in the midst of her own kindred kind. She was smiling sweetly to herself when the owner of the shop opened the door again and, as the tail end of the funeral breezed by, Maggie's heart dipped when she overheard the man on his way out muttering to his wife, 'Was that a man or a woman in there?'

She was reaching the far bank now, touching it, kicking away from it, travelling under water for maybe ten or fifteen strides. And then she surfaced, her drenched hair behind her like a wet mane, plunging onwards gracefully until she came to the very place where Steven had perished. 'Aw,' she cried, a lonely, atavistic sound. Here's where he splashed, here's where he kicked, here's where he called out her name. She could still hear those pitiful sounds now and that last inarticulate yelp before he was swallowed up by the dark, treacherous place known as Rainwater Pond.

'What did you call out to me like that for, Steven?' Maggie began. 'You must have known that I wouldn't be able to swim out here and save you. You must have known! I mean why me? Why not Albino Murphy or one of the other bigger boys? Or were you just calling out to your only kin in sight Steven, was that it? That was it, wasn't it? You were saying goodbye to the little sister that you loved. You did love me, Steven, didn't you? Ah, of course you did. Sure wasn't I your little sister and weren't you always minding me and holding my hand and didn't you always take me with you whenever you went on any of your daring adventures, robbing orchards and knocking doors and calling out to the Dummy Doyle and all the rest of it. That lovely summer's day, Steven, one of those dog days, coming up John Street, do you remember? There was a gang of us in it, like The Bowery Boys we were. We all clamoured onto the running board at the back of the big railway cart, the driver up front oblivious to it all as he steered the big dray horse around the bend, his railway hat tilted to one side like a Yankee soldier in the pictures. And we all laughed at each other as the wind whipped in around us and lifted our hair into all kinds of comical shapes. Albino looked like a madman that day, swinging there upside down with his hair on end and his feet wrapped around the sides of the cart. A proper madman. Your shadow on the road, Steven, with your hair all tossed, and you so particular. Big fat Anthony Mahony falling off and calling his mammy. *Oh Mammy,* says he. And when you all jumped off at the bottom of Hill Street I was carried away because my jumper got caught up in a nail and I had to call out to you. *STEVEN ... STEVEN* so that you had to run your best to catch up with me and you climbed on board again and set me free and you told me to hang on a while longer until the dray horse slowed down from a gallop to a trot. The sound of the clopping, Steven. And the rancid smell of the street that day. And the old street sweeper's song, his arms outstretched, like he was giving a concert to an invisible audience. *Like A Golden Dream/In My Heart Ever Smiling.* Old Mrs Healy standing there on the corner, disgusted, shaking her head and silently vowing to tell our da on us as soon as she got back to the street.'

'*Hang on Maggie*, you said to me. *Hang on*. And I used to love it when you said my name like that. And when you'd put your arm around me in a crowded place. I used to love that. *Now Maggie*, you said. *Now. Let go ... Let go Maggie*, and I did and the driver glanced over his shoulder and frowned at us and you waved at him and that seemed to solve everything, that seemed to cancel all the wrong we did, one pleasant wave from you. My legs all scraped. And your red face, Steven, from all the running. The rest of the lads coming down the road towards us, grinning. Anthony Mahony limping and laughing at his own misfortune. *Oh Mammy*! And that was that day, Steven, that was that morning, and in the afternoon we rambled the roads together and in the evening you made me pancakes for tea – with butter. And jam. That glorious day.'

'The night of course is a different story. Because I read somewhere Steven – and I do believe this is true – that the night is supposed to be older than the day; it tries to teach us all the things we have no real need to know. It was night time when you brought me into the parlour to see my poor Mammy laid out. And you told me she looked like an angel, but I didn't look, Steven, I couldn't look. Just a glimpse is all I got of her and she looked so pale, so white, practically transparent she was, lying there in the coffin, like that marble statue of the martyred saint in the chapel. My poor Mammy. And then you led me out of the room and you put your arm around me and I watched my da trembling with grief in the hall. And later I saw him crying like a baby in my uncle Jimmy's arms. And you kept your arm tight around me, minding me all the time. All the time, minding me like I was some precious, sweet, fragile thing.'

'It was night time too when they fished you out of the water, Steven, the surrounding area twinkling with flash-lights and the black pond spangled with moonlight as the beery breath and fugitive sounds of the worn out searchers pierced my poor little broken heart. And when they brought you home to the house in a bag and laid you out in the parlour I made sure to look this time, Steven. I looked long and hard. Because I knew then that someone like me would probably never get the chance to see the likes of you again. The house was packed that night, the hall was crowded too, pouring out onto the street and everything they were. Old Mrs Healy had to practically beat her way into the parlour. That beautiful girl from the clearing was there as well, mingling red-eyed in the midst of the curious crowd, the cripple praying hell for leather at her shoulder. Johnson's dog, Sally, howled on cue. Everyone said it was the banshee, but it wasn't. It was Johnson's dog, Sally. And then, just like that, they all went home and left us to our fate (had someone given a silent signal or what?).

'My poor Da was dying alive about you though, Steven, you know. He was never the same at all after you were gone. He just couldn't get over it. I mean he never put much pass on me one way or another but after you were gone I sort of disappeared too. In a way, I suppose you could say, Steven, I perished too.'

In Saecula Saeculorum, Maggie heard herself say as she dived down deep, down among the eels and the tiny fishes and all the other old rusty things that dwelt down there. And, while she was down there, Maggie confided in herself again, and the things she told herself were not for human ears: sins and other odd ephemeral things that cannot be caught or put into words. And when she had juggled them all backwards and forwards and up and down from the mortal to the venal to the pathetically immaterial, she saw herself standing once again on the edge of Rainwater Pond, gazing out at her drowning brother Steven as he kicked and splashed and squealed his way into eternity. She heard too Steven's last few frightened yelps, which always reminded her, God forgive her for even thinking it, which always reminded her of the sound The Dummy Doyle made that day when the policeman came up to the street to shoot his dog for biting a child. But before all this, before the splashing and kicking and the muted cries, Steven had clearly and distinctly called out her name; and his voice had echoed through the trees and resounded across the railway tracks and winged its way homewards past the factories and bars and pigeon lofts and rooftops and monuments of the town, and then all that young girl called Maggie could do was to stand on the bank and watch as her big brother sank like a saturated log into the misty belly of the pond. And after that there was nothing, nothing but the ghost of the echo of her name somewhere, nothing but the grey sky and the grey water and the greyness of the two dirty swans below.

And so Maggie Angre surfaced and wept once again for her dead brother Steven, wept once again for her lonely self, and as the salt tears she shed dropped into the water she remembered the first time that she had been brave enough to swim out this far and how the taste of her own teardrops had led her to believe that it was Steven's last few tears that had turned this stretch of water to brine.

On the way back she swam with all her might, every inch of water purging its own portion of blame, every foot of ground washing away another sin from the face of the earth. She was swimming for Steven now. She was swimming for herself. She was swimming for Albino Murphy who was killed in the Congo.

When she got back to the other side her eyes were still red from crying and so she sat shivering on the bank with a towel around her until her grief had subsided. She rolled her wringing wet costume up inside the towel and then she climbed up to the top of the ferny bank to sink in the sun. She lit up a cigarette and she examined her nicotine stained fingers and then she gazed down into the tranquil waters where two white swans swam.

A LUCKY ESCAPE

Tommy Day? Yeah, I know Tommy Day. Tommy Day the singer, you mean? Yeah! He used to sing with a dance band called The Toreadors once upon a time. Well, he sang with other bands too, but that's what most people remember about him. A nifty sort of fellow. You 'd often see him coming out of a side street or nipping up a back street or slipping in and out of betting shops and all the rest of it. That's more or less how he lived his life really. Plenty of talent. No ambition. No plan. Some people are like that. Until they wake up one morning and realise it's all over.

He'd be over fifty now, Tommy! He was never much to look at, but there was always something about him, especially when he sang – deadly hand movements and that kind of thing. I mean he had something, you know, heart or soul or something. I don't know … It's hard to explain. I mean you knew that he meant what he said when he sang, let's put it that way. And I'll tell you something else for nothing but no one could ever sing a love song like Tommy Day. And I know most people say they were just words to him, that there was never really anything to him, but … . no. He knew about love all right. He'd been to the garden.

He never married, lived with his mother all his life. His father died young so I suppose Tommy was a source of comfort for her, singing to her and that. Not financially of course. No, Tommy was no breadwinner. Although to be fair to him she always knew exactly where to find him if ever she was looking for him: hanging over a jukebox or down in the snooker hall or up to his ears in a back room card game. He'd bet on two flies going up the wall, the same fellow.

Tommy joined The Toreadors when he was seventeen, singing at the Saturday night dances in the local Desert Hall. So by the time his eighteenth birthday rolled around he was a fairly seasoned singer. Johnny, the old bandleader, came through the double doors at the back of the room with a cake and he carried it across the powdered dance floor towards the bandstand. Tommy was mortified. He was on stage, surrounded by an eight piece band, trumpets and trombones and saxophones and what-not, and big Leo Whats-his-name – I can't think of his surname now – ... he was a baker ... on the drums. The musicians were wearing these red sparkly coats and white frilly shirts. Next week the coats would be turned inside out and they'd be blue. Ingenious? Yeah, well, maybe. It wouldn't do to look too close though. All that glittered wasn't gold back then.

The band played Happy Birthday and the dancers sang along and then Tommy blew out the candles with three half-hearted puffs.

'Take your pick,' Johnny said to him, picking up his old battered saxophone and Tommy looked at him with wide eyes and wonder.

'What do you want to sing?' Johnny explained and a stillness fell over the hall.

Now this was 1967, don't forget ('*Flowers In The Rain,*' and '*Strawberry Fields Forever,*' and all). But Tommy was basically an old fashioned singer at heart and everybody knew that he wouldn't pick something straightforward from the charts. In fact the band had made bets on it and everything. It was bound to be Sam Cooke, Bobby Darin or Conway Twitty – Tommy's idols. For that very reason he was rarely allowed to pick a number.

'Somethin' from this century, Tommy,' Leo called from the back of the band.

'Yeah and preferably before the century is over,' Johnny chirped and the band launched into an old Laurel and Hardy riff to highlight the joke.

'Cupid?' Tommy eventually suggested and Leo Whats-his-name gave a triumphant roll on his snare drum.

'Fair enough,' Johnny said and counted them in. 'A one, two, a one two three and ...'

Cullen ... . Leo Cullen! That's it.

'*Cupid*,' Tommy crooned, stepping into the spotlight. '*Draw Back Your Bow/ And Let Your Arrow Go/ Straight To My Lover's Heart For Me / Nobody But Me ...* '

She was standing down at the back of the hall, flicking her hair behind her ears all the time as young girls do and singing along to the song and smiling at Tommy's hand movements and lovely – what only could be termed -Frank Sinatra gestures: the wry smile, the slight tilt of the head, the expressive shrug of the shoulders and so on. She blushed when someone asked her to dance, but she got up anyway and before the song was over she was dancing close to the bandstand, laughing at the winking musicians and thrilled by Tommy's beautiful stage antics.

Tommy couldn't take his eyes off of her. He watched her all night long as she moved about the dance floor – sitting down and standing up and dancing and trying to hold the hard cases at bay. Her name was Clare Kearney and from the moment he saw her and heard her name spoken out loud I'm afraid it was all over for him. And I'm sorry to have to report that from that day on Tommy's life was just another sad, sad song that he'd never get to sing.

That night Tommy didn't sleep a wink. He tossed and turned and thought about her all the time. He wanted to hold her hand. He wanted to say her name out loud. He wanted to marry her. '*When My Little Girl Is Smiling,*' kept cropping into his head. The next few days he spent in a trance, mooning and moping about. His mother was worried about him because he wasn't eating his dinner. 'You don't owe anybody any money or anything, Tommy, do you?' she asked him one time after tea. She knew well enough, like his father before him, that he was a bit of a gambler.

The following Saturday night Clare was back at the dance again and every other Saturday night after that. It was about the third or fourth Saturday though before Tommy got a chance to talk to her. She came up to the bandstand to put in a request for her friend's birthday.

'What would you like me to sing?' Tommy asked her, going down on one knee.

'Far away,' Leo cried from behind his drums.

'*Bus Stop,*' she said. 'She loves *Bus Stop.*'

'Alright,' Tommy promised. '*Bus Stop* it is,' and he took the slip of paper from her and stuffed it into his top pocket and watched as she kind of tiptoed her way back to her place by the wall.

'A bit recent for you, Thomas, ain't it?' Johnny said to him when Tommy whispered the request in his ear. 'What's her name again?

'Breda Lacy,' Tommy told him.

'Alright,' Johnny said. 'Fair enough … . Ladies and Gentlemen, a special request for Freda Lacy who's seventeen today. And it's the one and only Tommy Day to sing *Bus Stop.*'

'I wish the bus would stop,' Leo said, 'Til we all get off.'

That same night (or perhaps it was some other night, I don't know) after he had helped to put all the gear into the

47

back of Johnny's old battered van, Tommy fastened up his coat and rambled home alone. She was standing at the foot of John's Gate Street hill, looking a little apprehensive to say the least. A drunken man was out in the middle of the street singing, '*Don't Laugh At Me Cause I'm A Fool*,' at the top of his voice and she was afraid to pass him by. Tommy went over to her and told her not to worry and volunteered to walk her home.

'*I'm Not Good Looking*,' the old man sang as they passed.

'That's for sure,' Tommy said under his breath and Clare laughed with relief: a fairly husky sort of sound.

And so the young couple walked through the deserted streets of the sleeping town – Tommy on air. They must have passed other people along the way, someone putting out a bin or a man and his dog or some courting couple arguing or something, but if they did Tommy never noticed, he never noticed a thing. And I know it wasn't a date or anything. I mean he wouldn't get to hold her hand or kiss her goodnight at the door, but it was still lovely nevertheless. It was still something worth remembering. 'Cause there was stars in the sky and everything.

She told him she was working in Rafferty's Department Store now, which he already knew: in the office. Mister Rafferty she said was all right to work for, a bit cross at times, but generally speaking he was all right. Mrs Rafferty on the other hand was a right bitch. You wouldn't want to put your hand in her mouth. Clare told Tommy then, confidentially, that she'd much sooner be working down in the shop with Thelma Mahoney and all the other girls; but Clare had Commercial Commerce you see and so her mother had insisted that they put her in the office, which could be a dull old place at the best of times if the truth be told. When she spoke Clare had a slight catch in her voice, and although she talked all the time you always got the feeling that there was something about herself that she would never tell you, that there was something about her you'd never know, something she'd never reveal. Tommy wasn't so sure he liked that about her.

Her friend, Breda Lacy, was going out with Apache Byrne now and that's why she was walking home alone. She asked Tommy about Apache Bryne, what kind of a person he was and all that, and Tommy told her that he was all right, that he wasn't half as wild as he pretended to be. On the other hand, he said, he wasn't called Apache for nothing.

Her mother was waiting for her at the door when they got there, wondering what kept her. So she told her mother about the drunken man singing, '*Don't Laugh At Me 'Cause I'm A Fool,* 'at the top of his voice and about Tommy coming to her rescue.

'Who was it, Tommy?' her mother wanted to know and when Tommy told her she just folded her arms and threw her eyes to heaven.

'What happened to Breda?' was the next question.

'She had to go home early 'cause she felt sick,' Clare replied.

'What was wrong with her?'

'I don't know,' Clare said. 'She was sick, that's all. '

'Mmn ... ... How's your Mammy, Tommy?'

'Grand.'

'She misses your Daddy terrible though I think, don't she?'

'Ah yeah,' Tommy agreed.

'She looks lost sometimes – without him ... God help her ... Yeah. Sick, hah! You must think I came down in the last shower or somethin', Miss, do you? Huh? Go ahead in there. Night Tommy.'

'Night Mrs Kearney.'

'Thanks Tommy, 'Clare called softly from the hallway.

'Yeah, right, Clare. See yeh, eh?' Tommy said and the door was gently shut in his face.

The drunken man was singing his way up the street towards him as Tommy turned for home. A milk float came silently round the bend. *On The Street Where You Live* sprang to mind. Vic Damone, eh!

❧

The following week Marty Maher came home from England with two French letters in his wallet and all hell broke loose. Tommy took a break from the bandstand and went into the Gents to find big Shamey Shiggins with a bursted lip and spouting blood all over the shop. There was blood everywhere: in the sink, on the floor and caked on the wooden frame of the cubicle. Marty Maher had dropped him with a head butt. Everyone just stood around in awe. No one had ever dropped big Shamey before. Shamey looked dazed. Or pale and wan as they say.

To make matters worse when Tommy went back outside Marty Maher was dancing with Clare. Luckily enough it was a fast set. The next set was a slow one though and he danced that one with her too. It nearly killed Tommy to watch her snuggling into him. *'The Twelfth Of Never,' 'Unchained Melody,'* and ... I can't remember what the third number was now.

She danced with him all night after that. At one stage she was sort of sitting on his lap. Tommy was dying up there. He was hoping that she'd shake him off as the evening wore on, but she never did. At the end of the night, as the band played, *'The National Anthem,'* Tommy watched them like a hawk. He could read their lips from afar as Marty asked her if he could walk her home. 'O.K,' Clare replied. 'Hang on 'til I get my coat,' and as she tripped gaily out to the cloakroom Tommy's heart sank like a roller coaster and to his own astonishment he heard himself gasping her name under his breath. 'Clare,' he said, and he was suddenly consumed with a terrible, old aching disappointment.

∽

Sunday afternoon at Rainwater Pond. Blackberry pickers moved from bush to bush as Shamey Shiggins nursed his swollen lip and Apache Bryne boasted about his exploits with Breda Lacy (or Freda Lacy as she became to be known from then on). Tommy Day lay on his belly, plucking moss from the big rock and dropping it down into the dark water below. An abandoned boat lay stranded in the long grass and beyond the waving meadow the sea shimmered like a fragmented mirror in the sun. A train trundled by and a passenger looked out and wondered about the gang of wayward boys who basked beside this strange looking lagoon. The stranger seemed to wonder too about Tommy's lonely frown and he appeared to understand. Perhaps that's the answer, Tommy thought as the man's face evaporated. Get on a train and go away.

A bunch of spancelled old timers arrived then with walking sticks and blackthorn sticks and dogs, talking all the time about everything under the sun – this, that and the other. The dogs dived in and swam about and came out glistening with brine. One old man, Jakey Brown, called out to the lads, 'Morrow boys.' Jakey was an expert on birds. He could imitate the plaintive cry of the curlew and the back to front wolf whistle of the grey plover. The sparrow has twenty different melodies he'd tell you too and if you gave him half a chance he'd whistle them all for you. 'Never trust a peacock,' was another one, 'because it was the one that showed the Devil the way to Paradise.' And then he'd throw back his head and cry like one.

'I wouldn't have a blackthorn stick next or near me,' Jakey was telling one of the other old men. 'The blackthorn is a terrible unlucky tree, you know.' Tommy had heard that before somewhere: The Crown of Thorns or something. Is this what's in store for them? Tommy wondered as the old timers yapped their way out of sight – himself and big Shamey and Apache Byrne rambling the roads in forty years time with blackthorn sticks and dogs, whistling like curlews and crying like peacocks. Men without women!

And then Marty Maher and Clare showed up, hand in hand or arm in arm – I don't recall. Of all the places to come! Or was that that day at all? Maybe not. So long ago now!

'He must be runnin' out of French letters by now, lads,' Apache Bryne declared as the two lovers climbed over a gate and disappeared across the meadow. 'Unless of course he's havin' them dry cleaned or something,' and big Shamey, in spite of everything, spluttered out a painful laugh.

Tommy watched her going towards the ocean to vanish into the waving corn and he told himself that he must learn to despise her otherwise the pain will be too hard to endure. He must relinquish all hope. The nape of her neck though!

∽

A month later Clare announced to her mother that she was pregnant and Marty Maher bailed out for London and left her in the lurch. Needless to say she was the talk of the town. She lost her job in Rafferty's and everything over it, for fear she'd lower the tone of the place. And she was the butt of everyone's jokes for the next few months – on the street corners, in the bars, at the Saturday night dances, her name bandied about like Salome. And I wish I could say that Tommy Day became her Lancelot, but no, he didn't. He scoffed with the rest of them or pretended to at least and in his heart he told himself that he didn't care, that it didn't matter. She was never anything to shout about anyway.

The Toreadors got the sack from The Desert Hall around that time. Father Howlin took Johnny to one side and told him that he wanted to try something different. He said from now on he was going to hire a small group known as *The Bandits.*

The following Saturday night Johnny turned up with his gear as usual and Father Howlin came to him, red faced and fuming.

'Johnny,' he said, 'I told you last week that I was hiring a group called *The Bandits* from now on.'

'Yeah I know you did, Father, 'Johnny said. 'We are *The Bandits.*'

Tommy Day was the lead singer with *The Bandits* and people swear there was a hurt in his voice that hadn't been there before and maybe there was. He seemed a bit rougher certainly. A little angrier maybe as he belted his way through Johnny Kidd and The Pirates' *'I'll Never Get Over You.'*

∽

Ash Wednesday, the beginning of Lent, and Tommy was out of work again. No more dances for the next seven weeks, no more weddings or reunions either. Tommy rambled around the place, skint. Now and then his mother would take pity on him and throw him a couple of quid, but Tommy would only squander it on a horse or try his luck in a poker game and before he knew it he'd end up back where he started.

He got a job as a night porter in The Menapia Hotel for a few weeks, which turned out to be a fairly handy number until the manager paid a surprise visit in the middle of the night one night only to discover big Shamey Shiggins and

Apache Byrne and all the boys drinking on the house in the resident's lounge at four o'clock in the morning. Everybody out!

One night as he was going home with a bag of chips Tommy happened on Clare who was sitting on the wooden seat at the end of Saint John's Road. She called out to him and he said goodnight to her, matter-of-factly. He had intended to just go on by about his business, but he didn't in the end. He crossed the street and sat down beside her and before he knew it she was dipping into his bag of chips and telling him all her news. He was surprised how chirpy she was, considering, like! She only had about six weeks to go now, she told him, all being well. She was hoping for a girl, but it didn't really matter, she said, as long as everything turned out all right. That was the main thing. She got a letter from Marty a while back, she said. He didn't really want anything or anything, just wondering how she was getting on and that.

'That was nice of him,' Tommy mumbled, sarcastically, and her eyes sort of darted in his direction as if she didn't quite get the drift.

She had really tiny ears and a perfect mouth and her eyes were of the faintest blue, kind of drained of colour, almost soul-less in fact. Another reason not to love her?

Tommy walked her home that night and shortly afterwards when the child was born, a few days prematurely, he went up to the hospital to see her with a squashed bunch of flowers under his coat. It was a baby girl -Deirdre – and the first time she wheeled the pram down the town Tommy went with her. He took her into Nolan's Cafe for a sundae and a coke and they listened to the jukebox. He knew that people were talking about him, laughing at him more than likely. He wished that people thought the baby was his, but he knew well enough that they didn't, that everybody knew the whole story. His mother was looking at him sorrowfully. Mrs Kearney on the other hand was all over him. Cups of tea and plates of biscuits to beat the band, his feet under the table as they say. *Alright!*

And when it came time to christen the child Tommy was invited to the party. The party (well it wasn't exactly a party, just a few cakes and sandwiches and tea and soft drinks) was held in the spacious living room. Apache Byrne was there with Breda Lacy. And later on Tommy nipped out and got Sean Corcoran who played the guitar with The Toreadors and Eddie Shaw who played the trumpet and they had a right session. Eddie Shaw had to put the mute on his trumpet to dampen the sound. Mrs Kearney came into the room at one stage as Eddie was playing, '*Oh My Papa.*'

'I can't believe that child is sleeping through that racket,' she said. 'Rip Van Winkle has nothing on her!' and everybody laughed.

At the end of the evening Clare gave Tommy a huge hug in the hall on his way out. He was tempted to kiss her there and then but something stopped him and he didn't in the end. He knew in his heart and soul that he would regret not kissing her later, but, apart from everything else, Eddie and Sean and Apache Byrne were waiting for him outside the front door. (Breda had gone ahead home in a bit of a sulk because the boys kept calling her Freda all the time.) And then, as if to stem the tide, Clare gave Tommy a harmless peck on the cheek and she raced to the door to say thanks and goodnight to the others.

The next morning Tommy woke up in a state of confusion. Things were going all right, he assured himself. Clare had invited him to the party. She had sat beside him most of the time and she had given him that big hug in the hall on his way out. Her face glowed when he sang to her and she laughed at the funny things he said sometimes. And the other day they had gone out to Rainwater Pond together, sat in the sun and returned home along the railways tracks, the two of them talking and laughing and singing and the first two buttons of her blue blouse open and she kept asking him questions all the time.

'What do you feel when you sing a sad song now?' she wondered. 'I mean do you feel anything? Or do you just sing it, like?'

'Oh no,' Tommy told her. 'I feel it. I feel everything.'

'Yeah?' Clare said and she made a bit of a face as if she didn't quite approve or understand what he was getting at.

'I can't imagine it,' she said. 'I mean how you do it, like!'

And that's the way it went all the way home. It was as if she was trying to fathom it all. And just before they reached the edge of town she said something strange to him.

'Did you ever think of livin' somewhere else, Tommy?' she began.

'Yeah,' Tommy lied, 'sometimes.'

'Yeah, me too,' she confessed. 'I often think about going away and living somewhere else, somewhere foreign maybe. Then I could really be myself for a change instead of going around pretending all the time.'

Tommy was disappointed to hear her say this and he looked towards her to witness her gazing moodily out to sea as if the place she dreamt of going to was just somewhere over the horizon. A dark shadow shaded her face and her eyes were vague and distant and Tommy felt a meanness welling up inside of him. Did she intend to go to this other place without him or what? And if she was not who she pretended to be all the time then who was she? I mean who was this girl that he thought he had got to know lately? Or had she only gulled him again? On the other hand he was well aware that she had just confided in him, let him in on a secret that, in all likelihood, nobody else had ever heard before and he was glad about that. No, at the end of the day and taking everything into consideration, he was convinced she felt something for him all right! He was sure of it in fact. Absolutely! He'd put money on it!

So why did he feel so inconsequential then? Huh? The friendly kiss on the cheek? The distance between them when they walked? Those vacant, soul-less blue eyes looking through him all the time? What? … Who knows? He just did.

As it turned out he was right to feel that way. Tommy went down to Kearney's one night before tea only to find Clare doing herself up for a date with Marty Maher who had just come back for the summer. He was taking her to the pictures. Wasn't it great? Yeah. Great.

Tommy got into a row down in the snooker hall that night and had to be put out of the club. Over tea earlier on he had snapped at his poor mother and made her cry. And in the pub when someone asked him to sing a song he sang something so vulgar that everyone wondered what was up with him. Around midnight he went up and hung around outside Clare's house and waited for them to come home. He intended to tell them exactly what he thought of the pair of them and maybe fight Marty Maher too if that's what he wanted. But it turned fairly cold and started to rain and in the end he just skulked on home via the back streets with tears in eyes.

Tommy bumped into the two of them on and off over the next few weeks and whenever he did he averted his eyes or crossed the street or pretended he never saw them in the first place. Clare seemed to be going out of her way to let everybody see that she was going out with Marty now, holding his hand in public and linking him and sitting on his lap at the back of the dance hall and all that carry-on. She never once came to Tommy to explain it all to him. In fact it was Marty Maher who eventually came and put him out of his misery.

Tommy was sitting at the counter in the Banjo Bar and Marty sidled up and sat beside him.

'Listen Tommy,' Marty said. 'I know you were fairly fond of Clare and all the rest of it and you're probably wonderin' what's goin' on and all that but … Well, the truth of the matter is Clare is goin' out with me now.'

'So I see,' Tommy said and he looked directly into Marty Maher's lousy eyes.

'Yeah well …' Marty said and grimaced as if he understood what Tommy was going through. 'Clare and I have to do the best for the child's sake, Tommy, like you know. I mean … whatever, you know.'

'I know,' Tommy said. And he meant it when he said it.

'I'll be straight about it,' Marty told him then. 'She's always talkin' about you. Gets on my nerves sometimes to tell you the truth, but sure what can I do? … Anyway, I just thought you should know all of that and not be avoidin' us all the time. Alright?

'Yeah.'

'Wish us luck?'

'Of course'

'Shake on it.'

'Yeah,' Tommy said and held out his hand. 'Good luck.'

Clare married Marty Maher before the year was out. She had two more children for him – a boy and another girl – and Marty sort of settled down after that. Of course there was the odd scrape, the odd fight in a bar, the odd day in court, the odd affair with another woman. But generally speaking he settled down all right, generally speaking he did all right by her. Generally speaking!

Clare turned more matronly with each passing year. She put on a fair bit of weight and her legs grew sort of dumpy and her clothes looked on the staid side and her conversation was inclined to be old-womanish. In fact if you saw her now you'd probably wonder what Tommy ever saw in her in the first place, but there you go.

Tommy moved from one band to another after that. After The Bandits he sang with The Ray Flynn Quartet and one or two other groups he'd rather not mention. He entered a few national talent competitions, which were sponsored by **The Golden Brown Boot Company**, and although he sang on the radio a couple of times he came nowhere and eventually he lost heart and just gave up the ghost and stopped trying altogether.

He sings in the Banjo Bar every weekend now with the hunch backed Ray Flynn on the piano. Real moody sort of stuff: Frank Sinatra and Paul Anka and that – *Blame It On My Youth* and *Diana* and *The September Song*. And an upbeat version of *Mona Lisa* – Conway Twitty's version.

Did he ever fall in love again? No, I don't think so. Although he did take up with this girl called Eithne Reilly somewhere along the line and she was absolutely mad about him and would do anything for him until she got fed up of him turning up late and turning up drunk and turning up broke and sometimes not turning up at all. She eventually opted for a more sensible chap who she married. She continues to see Tommy on the sly though when her husband is working the night shift.

'Tell me you love me, Tommy,' she says.

'I love you,' he tells her as he buttons up his pants.

Most weekdays he rambles the roads now with Shamey Shiggins and Apache Bryne: walking sticks, dogs, the lot, talking about everything under the sun – this, that and the other. They marvel at all the people dying all around them.

Marty Maher for instance who died of heart failure at forty-eight years of age. Apache Bryne said it served him right when he heard the news and laughed and glanced in Shamey's direction and big Shamey flashed a forgiving smile and muttered, 'Poor Marty,' under his breath.

Every Friday night Tommy slips the two boys into the Banjo Bar for free. They sit down in their favourite corner to watch the show. Once in a while a drink on the house arrives for them.

'Fair play to you, Tommy boy!' Apache Bryne says as he takes another gulp and he sits back to enjoy Tommy singing, *It's All Only Make Believe*. 'I like this one,' he says to Shamey over the introduction.

'So do I,' Shamey agrees. 'So do I.'

'*It's All Only Make Believe.*'

Tommy saw Clare the other day, clattering down the street with a couple of – what must have been – Deirdre's children hanging out of her (a grandmother now if you don't mind). She called out to him from the other side of the road. She seemed genuinely pleased to see him too. He was tempted to go on over and talk to her, but he didn't in the end, he just walked on by. Better not start all of that up again, eh? A lucky escape really when you think of it.

'Yes It's All Only Make Believe.'

ONE IS NOT A NUMBER

Who would have thought it was all going to end up here, eh? – our life long love affair – right back more or less where it all started in the first place, at Rainwater Pond. And as I meandered in and out of the maze of people that had gathered here to pay their respects I managed to take a peek now and then through a gap in the wall of donkey jackets and duffle coats and burly bodies as she lay there on the grass verge, covered from top to toe with an old grey, faded army blanket. And, hand on my heart, I can honestly say that I felt little or nothing for her, less than nothing in fact. Well, nothing akin to grief anyway: a little numbness maybe; a little excitement too, at the drama of it all, which is only natural, I suppose, under the circumstances. But other than that, nothing. No remorse. No sense of loss. No ... nothing. Nothing at all. Why? I don't know why. Too much water under the bridge, I suppose. All my feelings and emotions had all been winnowed away or something – by time.

All around me her name sort of leaked from reluctant lips: the last time they saw her and the first time they met her and all the things she said and done and didn't do. Imelda said this and Imelda said that and then Imelda said the other thing. And all I knew (not that anyone was asking me now or anything, but) all I knew was that she was always there, right from the word go, always there and wherever she was I was never too far behind. That's all I knew. That's all I could say about her, if any of them ever even lowered themselves to ask me, that is. A montage of memories bombarded me then, a clatter of black and white images: the way she walked (well a kind of a glide really), her strong hands (nails bitten to the quick), her sweet secretive smile, her husky laugh, her mirthless beauty as someone once remarked, and that slightly cruel, defiant stare of hers.

Above us the seagulls were hoarsely hurling her name over their shoulders at one another, breaking it up into three distinct syllables – Eee-Mel-Da. Sharp needles of rain pricked the surface of the water. A train rolled by too, making the soft earth rumble.

It was not deliberate or anything, but I found myself standing alongside Ely who looked like a worn out old man all of a sudden. He gazed directly into my eyes, but of course as usual he refused to acknowledge me, my very existence. Even then, at this terrible time, it was still beneath him. Can you credit that? Blessed are the meek for they shall inherit my bollicks. Ha!

He looks older than time now, I was thinking. And sadder than sin. And you know what, it served him right. He tried to hold on to her too long. He held on when he should have let her go. A shadow fell across his face. He sort of winced, like he had a touch of heartburn or what-do-you-call-it … indigestion or something (on the other hand you might have just read my mind of course.). I couldn't help but wonder who owned the old faded army blanket? I mean where had it come from in the first place? The back seat of someone's car? The F.C.A?

'Who owns the blanket?' I asked him over the din.

'What,' he wondered, twitching like a startled bird as he turned his drained face away from me again. One of the Bradley brothers had come over to shake his hand. Don't ask me which one – Tom, John or Josie. I'm hard set to tell them apart these days. Well, it can't be Tom anyway. Ely was riding Tom's missus for a while there so it's hardly him. And Josie has a moustache, so it must have been John.

'Sorry for your troubles, Ely,' John was saying. Whether he meant it or not now of course is another story. Only the other day the three brothers had ambushed Ely at the back of the Shelter wall and here was one of them now suddenly shaking his hand and sympathising with him. I took myself elsewhere. Fuck that! Among them be it, I say!

I limped my way over to the body and bent down to take a look at her, drawing back the blanket. To my surprise she was naked under there, and milky white.

'What's the cripple playin' at, eh?' someone in the crowd wanted to know, one of the Bradley brothers again, with the moustache this time – Josie – and of course this prompted Harpo Hayes to get on his buckin' bronco over it.

'Hey, hey, hey,' he cried out just to let me know that I was out of order.

I held the palm of my hand up to him, like a policeman on the beat trying to quell a potential riot, and, for the time being at least, he fell silent. Not that I gave a monkey's about any of them, mind you. This was the least I deserved if you ask me, for my life long devotion to her. One last glimpse: that dark tuft of hair; two mounds of flesh; her shoulders bared; her body smeared with a kind of scummy green; nostrils flaring; eyes wide open and her hair all tangled. Not like herself at all in my opinion, a sort of underwater rendition of her. I was sorely tempted to kiss her on the lips to tell you the truth, but thought better of it in the end and respectfully … *refrained.* The Bradley brothers would just love that now, an excuse to string me up from the nearest crab apple tree. So I blessed myself instead and pretended to pray, moving my lips fervently. I read somewhere that prayers don't count unless you move your lips, you know. So I moved my lips and made a soft sibilant sound like an old woman saying the Stations Of The Cross in the chapel. I bowed my head too at the very mention of His name, reverently. Not that I give a shit about all that of course. If I had my way there'd be a picture of Judas hanging on my wall. Yes, Cain is the boy I'd adore.

'Hey, hey, hey,' Harpo Hayes continued (so called by the way not because he resembles the famous comic or anything, but because he is a man of few words). He has a hoarse, high falsetto voice at the best of times with practically no resonance to it, but today for some reason it cut through the din like a Mac's Smile blade so that everyone within earshot shut up and turned to look at me.

I returned their gaze, looking from one pathetic face to another. There they all were, red faced and raging – arms folded, arms akimbo, hands clenched, eyes narrowed, varicose veins throbbing as their big, loitering lips muttered secret and silent curses in my direction. And judging me too if you don't mind! Yes! Every last one of them, judging me. Me! – the one who loved her most of all, the one who came whenever she called, no matter how faint or feeble the cry. Oh yeah. The barist hint, the merest gesture, the … wispiest whisper and I'd be there at her command. I tell you here and now for nothing but I had a good mind to curse them all into a knot. Dig a great big hole and fired the lot of them into it be fucked. Shit all over their heads. Drop my pants and say, 'Here, does that remind you of anyone?' I wanted to ask them all, '*Who owns this fucking blanket?*'

But of course I didn't. I blessed myself again and covered her up and rose to hobble my way out of there, nodding to this one and that one as I went so that anyone watching me who didn't know any better would swear I was David Niven or someone. And as I walked away I turned around and glanced back over my shoulder at the body and muttered, 'Poor Imelda,' to myself, enunciating the name so that they all could see how upset I really was over it. In actual fact, to be honest with you, privately I was sort of relieved it had all finally come to an end to tell you the truth. Maybe now, at long last, I might get a bit of peace for myself. Start anew – if I can! *Me Fa Me Re Do So Me Fa Do. Tra La La La La La La La La.*

⟋

We were born a few doors down from each other, Imelda and me, in that squat row of houses called Salty Way. Step out the front door and you could smell it – the briny stench of the sea. Take a few steps down the grassy bank and across the railway tracks and you're at the water's edge. Look left and there's the Shelter where the fishermen still moor their sturdy flat-bottomed boats all the time. Turn right and you're on your way to Rainwater Pond.

Old Mosey Clark and Tenacious Doyle and Jakey Brown ruled the roost around here in those days of course. Ely and Harpo and The Bradley Brothers and my big brother Ian and all the boys were only young lads that time, hanging around the boats and listening to the old fellows nattering – hardy miniature versions of what they would soon become. And I'd come sliding down the bank, a delicate gangly fellow with a snotty nose and a club foot and a wheezy chest and I'd try once again in vain to wheedle my way into the gang. But of course, try as I might, the answer was always the same. *'No. Nay. Never!'*

'Why not?' I pleaded. I honestly couldn't fathom it in those far off days, my excommunication. What had I done to deserve this anyway? I mean the name of my crime was … what … exactly?

'A fellow is only as good as the company he keeps,' Ely informed me one day as he played with my lapels, and then with a gentle slap on the back of the neck he banished me once and for all from the fold.

At first I was crestfallen. To try and live without their acceptance was beyond me. I refused to believe it and tagged along behind them whenever they went anywhere. I'd follow them all over the place: down the town to the snooker hall or into Nolan's Café to spy on them from the doorway as they played on the well worn old football table. Or up the railway tracks towards Rainwater Pond to watch them plunder nests and rob orchards and ride jennets and donkeys and the tinker's piebald ponies through the fields, keeping at a safe distance of course, skulking along behind them like a whipped whippet. This only infuriated them all the more and once in a while they'd hatch a plan to try to teach me a lesson. They hid behind the bushes and jumped out on me one day and ducked my face in the water and held me down until I kicked and squealed and begged for mercy. Another time they opened my laces and urinated en masse into my big boot. My leg stank for weeks after that. The final straw came when they tied me to a post and lined up to tickle me with nettles.

In the end I more or less gave up the ghost altogether and turned my attention to the girls – Loretta Lane and big Diana Dempsey mainly. And of course young Imelda who was just a freckled faced tom-boy that time. The girls weren't that keen on me either, mind you, but at least they didn't hit me or try to hurt me all the time I did tricks for them all to impress them: handstands that went awry and made them laugh; card tricks too that sometimes astounded them; and number games, which they couldn't resist playing, despite their obvious aversion towards me. 'Think of a number,' I'd say to them, and nine times out of ten they would.

I brought them tiny presents from time to time as well – an apple from a nearby orchard, a cake I'd swipe from the back of a bread man's van, an ornament from some scrap heap maybe. 'Yuck,' they'd say, making a face and dropping whatever it was I brought to them as if it was infectious or scaldy.

Imelda always took my gifts though. She'd wrap them up carefully in a dainty laced handkerchief and bury them in her secret hiding place in the overgrown graveyard – the trinket, the brooch, the bracelet, the plastic toy from a lucky bag, whatever. I used to follow behind and watch as she pulled back the briars to reveal her stoney tabernacle where she stored all the treasure I had foraged for her. It was of course just a childish game she was playing with me, Imelda casting herself as the high priestess and yours truly here as the twisted, adoring acolyte. I had a good mind to sprout a hump for her too while I was at it, just to pacify her – my Esmerelda in blue jeans. Ha!

She very seldom spoke to me in those days. Just a mysterious look that seemed to convey all she wanted to tell me and everything I needed to know. In fact in all the years I'd known her I do believe she only spoke directly to me three or four times, five or six at the most. That time when a child on the street got knocked down by a bicycle and Imelda, who couldn't have been more than eleven or twelve herself at the time, cradled the boy in her arms and told me to go into her house and fetch a blanket from the cupboard beneath the stairs. 'Hurry Matty,' she said as I hobbled along, delighted to be recognised by her at long last, thrilled to hear my Christian name tripping out of her like that. When I returned with the blanket she wrapped it around the young lad and cuddled into him and stroked his hair and muttered, 'Good boy,' to him and all that kind of stuff until the ambulance arrived. For weeks afterwards, I might as well be honest with you, I longed for some minor calamity to happen to me. I was tempted to stage a bit of a pratfall or something. Or throw myself off a wall or what-not. But alas, as luck would have it, something wicked this way just wouldn't come.

Five or six years later Imelda was moving around the neighbourhood in a muslin dress, a fairly see though affair so that you could kind of make out the outline of her underclothes. Lace sometimes. And black, the elastic of her panties showing. The top of her leg revealed whenever she sat down – where the ocean meets the shore, if you follow my drift. Ha! … She was a real outsider then too, having divorced herself from Loretta and Diana, finding their company tedious with their endless talk of boys and clothes and new born babies. Yeah, she sort of isolated herself and took to rambling alone, lost in a secret world of her own. I could see that the others were just as glad to be shot of her. Her sullenness annoyed and alienated them. What they didn't know then though was that in the fullness of time she would also use it as a sexual weapon to wipe both their eyes.

The only one she couldn't shake off was yours truly. I used to follow her down to the deserted railway station where she'd climb up into the elevated signal box and look out to sea, out towards Useless Island and beyond, dreaming of God knows what. Meanwhile I'd wait in the shadows below, whittling a piece of stick with a knife like a browned off gunslinger in the pictures. Or else she'd go in the opposite direction, up the line towards Rainwater Pond, kicking off her shoes to walk along the gravelled beach, paddling in the water as she roved. And wherever she walked I was convinced pretty flowers would spring up in her wake – lovely little sea pansies and wild wine-coloured sand roses and strange looking hybrid things that were yet to be named. I'd envy the puddle her toes had touched and the berries she plucked from the bushes. I envied the bushes and the banks she was forced to scale and the niched, holy well she'd stoop to drink from. I longed to be the sandpiper that was allowed to land on her trailing shadow, and the pond itself, which would soon mirror her sullen, untamed image.

Once I saw her swim there – naked. It was a late summer's evening, the end of another sweltering, sultry day. There was a tacky looking carnival on the green and all the usual suspects were hanging around there. Ely had taken up with big Diana Dempsey and he spent most evenings now kissing her at the back of the Merry-Go – Round with his hand up her jumper. Imelda was in one of her sulky moods and rambled off alone. I followed her along the railway line to Rainwater Pond and hid myself in the long grass, holding on for dear life to my contrary mongrel Tailor who was anxious to be off. And as I inhaled the rank stink that seeped from the damp ditch where I was hiding she shed her muslin dress and the rest of her things and soon I saw her sliding naked into the water, the sound of the carnival churning out *The Merry Widow* in the distance.

I broke out in a sweat as she took those three or four vital steps to the water's edge. A sort of silky mist shrouded her so that all I could make out was a veiled silhouette of her beautiful, broad back, her bare backside and a glimpse of her pert, young breasts. She swam out to the middle of the pond – an awkward breaststroke of sorts – rolled over onto her back and floated like a dolphin at play.

Darkness crept stealthily over the land and soon she was just a blurred image to me, and as she splashed around out there and hummed some familiar love song I cocked my head to one side and sighed and basked in the very notion of it all. From time to time I worried about her too though, whenever she stopped humming or if the sound of her splashing diminished. Rainwater Pond was a dark and treacherous place, bottomless they say. You could throw a stone or a coin in there and watch it fall, go home and have your tea and go to the pictures and come home and go to bed and sleep and dream and wake up and go to work or to school or whatever and it would still be falling when you came home for your dinner.

I used often go to the edge and sit and look into the water and wonder about its endlessness. I'd take off my boot and let my poor old withered leg dangle in the water awhile and dare to believe that this particular place had magic properties that could somehow heal me. I'd remove my foot from the water only to discover that it was whole again. And then I'd submerge my face and the same thing would happen. I'd look into the pond and there I'd be – straight and strong and handsome -and the fellow I'd become would be tall and fair and broad of shoulders and clean and good and kind with blond hair and a few freckles here and there to ensure that he always looked youthful no matter how old he'd become. And he was the other me, the real me, the one marooned inside me, the invisible one who stood beside me or behind me in times of trouble, the one Imelda (or anyone else around here either for that matter) didn't even know yet. My other self so to speak!

The dog whined and struggled to be free. A bird or a rat or an otter or some such thing had rustled the nearby ferns. I held on to him and hushed him up. He barked. 'Shut up, Tailor,' I whispered as he growled and wriggled in my arms.

'Who's that?' Imelda called from behind the mist. 'Who's there, I said.'

I held my breath and stroked Tailor to be still. Imelda laughed and began to sing again, words this time, her grandda's favourite song. *Fairwell Fairwell/Beloved Land Farewell* ... And with that she was gone, underwater. I let the dog off and rose myself up to catch a glimpse of her black form disappearing out of sight. I crept closer to the pond and peeped into it. I picked up some of her clothes that were lying around, caressed them and kissed them and then hung them gently on a stumpy tree trunk and I lingered at the water's edge – her lusty sad-eyed centaur.

My heart was in my mouth as I waited for her to surface again. I began to imagine what it would be like if she ran into trouble out there. I would run to her rescue of course even though, to my shame, I couldn't swim a stroke. I had come out to the pond on a few occasions hoping that the boys would relent and let me tag along and teach me to swim and dive and all the other things that young boys are suppose to do together, but Ely had only mocked me and drove me away.

'If he takes off that boot, lads,' Ely said, 'we'll all get sick. And if he leaves it on he'll sink like a stone. And I don't know about any of you fellows, but I've no intention of goin' in there after him.'

'Neither have I.' my brother Ian said, who could be worse than any of them, and with that they sent me home, drove me away with flying stones and abusive language. (The things they called me!)

The fact that I couldn't swim a stroke wouldn't have stopped me from going in there after her that day though, if she had run into trouble I mean. Or any other day either for that matter. No, I would have plunged myself in there whole-heartedly and strapped myself around her with my big-buckled belt, and as my bloated boot filled up with dirty water we would have danced a merry dance together, her hair floating upwards and the hair between her legs all frizzled and her breasts bobbing about and the bubbles escaping from my mouth as I mumbled, 'Imelda, I love you,' in her ear. And with that we'd sink towards the bottom in slow motion, lost in each other's arms as if we were free falling through time and space forever and ever and ever and ever and ever more ... .

I was lost in this reverie and never even noticed her clambering out. I had to slip slyly into a marshy ditch and make a pillow of my closed fists, missed the whole sideshow in the process. She dressed hastily on the bank and then rambled homewards, her hair still wet, her damp clothes clinging to her. She stopped to pat Tailor who had rambled up to her and then she looked sideways up into the dyke where I was lurking and called out to me. 'I know you're up there Matty Larkin,' and that was the second time I ever remember her saying anything directly to me. Or indirectly either for that matter, depending on which way you looked at it. Ha!

I hadn't a minute's luck for a long time after that that night though, you know – for looking at her I mean. On the way back I slipped and sprained my good ankle and struggled all the way home, on my hands and knees most of the way. Tailor turned turk on me too and snapped at my hand when I reached down to put the collar on him. I got a thorn in my other hand then (which turned septic on me over the next few days so that I had to endure a rake of hot poultices to make it better), and it started to lash rain and everything. And when I went home, wringing wet, and mentioned that Tailor had snapped at me my mother sighed irritably and my father lost his rag and rose up and dragged the poor old dog outside to shoot it. 'No son of mine,' he said, 'is goin' to have a dog that does the likes of that …' I begged him not to, but he just swept me aside and tied poor Tailor up and went to get his shotgun. I was as white as a sheet as I gazed from the whining dog in the yard to my mother who was sprawled slovenly across the couch. 'Don't look at me,' she said. 'As far as I'm concerned it serves him right. And it serves you right too because you ruined that dog if you ask me. Pattin' and kissin' him and all the rest of it!'

The gun backfired in the yard when my father tried to shoot the poor thing and nearly took the hand and all off of him, and just for that he took off his belt and gave me an awful thrashing, made my legs bleed and everything. 'You ruined that dog,' he said as he swung the belt. 'Ruined it you did, you crooked little bastard!' And then he went and got a basin of water and drowned poor Tailor, holding its head underwater with a sweeping brush.

I cried myself to sleep that night, rocked myself back and forth and forward and played with myself and cursed myself for ever mentioning Tailor going to bite me in the first place; and I tried to think of her naked in the water, but all I could see was her looking up sideways at me in the dyke and saying my name over and over again and I knew I deserved all that I got, lecherous little animal that I was at that time. And although I was thoroughly ashamed of myself, nevertheless I vowed there and then to rise up in the world and make her proud of me someday. I'd go back to school, do the Leaving Cert and get a good job for myself somewhere, in an office. That's it. A clerk in a solicitor's office or something. Up in court, handing your man the papers and all that. Some murder case maybe. Imelda sitting down the back, amazed. I'd be wearing a suit and tie and your man would depend on me. I'd be his right hand man. 'He's my right hand man,' he'd say and Imelda would overhear this and smile.

But unfortunately my da wouldn't let me go back to school. 'Back to school,' he said, 'to live the life of Reilly! I will in me hole,' and he pretended to give me a backhander. Not that I was surprised or anything. After all he was the one who took me out of school in the first place – at fourteen years of age. He took me out and sent me down the town selling newspapers. And after that he got me a job selling apples and oranges in The Bullring and that's where I learned to sing my little coster song: *Apples a penny each/Ten for a tanner.*

I wouldn't mind but I was fairly handy in school. You know, reading and writing and all. And sums. And algebra. Isosceles triangles and all that. The teacher pleaded with my da to leave me where I was, but he wouldn't. Mister Morrissey. A great teacher he was. In that school for wayward boys and girls beside the police station there. 'One is not a number,' he'd say. 'The first real number is two and with it mathematics and multiplicity begins.' I never forgot that: one is not a number.

But of course my Da thought it was all a load of balls anyway. 'Get out into the world and earn your keep,' he always said. He'd be stationed in the hall every Saturday night to take my earnings from me as soon as I came through the door so he could go off to the Shark Public House or somewhere. My mother would be parked on the top of the stairs too, waiting for her share so she could slip out to the Bingo bus. In the end I used to have to hide a thrupenny piece in the lining of my old coat, otherwise I'd have nothing left for myself.

On Saturday nights the boys would all get dressed up to go to the dance in The Desert Hall: Ely in his black snazzy suit and Harpo in a collarless coat, which was all the rage then, and my brother Ian and the Bradley brothers, all going off to see Tommy Day and The Bandits. I came down one night to join them, picking my way carefully down the bank. I had just bought a new suit on the never never and my shoes were shining and my hair was slicked back neatly into place and for some reason I thought this would make me eligible this time.

'Where do you think you're goin'?' Ely said to me when I tried to mingle unobtrusively with the rest of the gang.

'Nowhere,' I said.

'Good,' Ely said. 'Because that's exactly where you're goin' with us tonight – nowhere.' And then he ridiculed my outfit, tossing the lapels and spinning me around and generally belittling me in front of all the other lads.

Amid howls of laughter I skulked away, glancing back over my shoulder to see the girls arriving, dressed to the nines and chewing chewing gum and smelling of Eau de Cologne. Ely was telling them what he had just said to me, and the girls were all tittering and pointing in my direction, as I became an inconsequential speck in the distance.

That night at the dance I hung around at the end of the hall, sometimes sitting, sometimes standing, now and then sort of bopping to the beat of the band, shiny beads of sweat on my brow as the place filled up to capacity. Tommy Day was on stage, singing into one of those big fat microphones. Ely was dancing with Diana and when the band played a slow number I caught a glimpse of him smooching with her, nibbling her ear and his hand on her arse.

My brother Ian and Harpo and the Bradley brothers hung around the door, smoking cigarettes and guzzling from flagons of cider and Baby Powers of whiskey and mingling with all the other stony faced hard cases who were all too cool (or too shitty) to ask anyone up for a dance. I sidled up beside them all at one stage and prayed that for once I might just blend in (because I was lost standing over there on my own), and for a short while at least they tolerated me. One or two of them let me have a slug of cider and my brother Ian left me his last few drops of whiskey. I gulped it down and shivered and they all laughed at me, and then I laughed at them and I turned around and included anyone else who was standing nearby so that in the end everyone around was laughing and I shivered all the more.

I wasn't used to drinking and it went right to my head and I moved around the hall then asking girls up to dance right, left and centre, scattering them all like flamingos wherever I went. In the end I winded up dancing on my own in the middle of the dance floor, a silly convoluted dance that had everyone around me in stitches. And the more they laughed I more I did it – jumping up and down and turning around full circle and hopping on one leg and then the other, arms flailing, head bobbing, arse wriggling like a busy bumble bee. *Oh I'm The Boy To Tease Her/And I'm The Boy To Please Her/And I'm The Boy To Squeeze Her/And I'll Tell You What I'll Do.* Girls passing by put their hands to their mouths and tried to hold in the laughing. The roving bouncer saw me too, shook his head and threw his eyes to heaven when I blew him a kiss. *I'll Court Her Like An Irishman/ Da Da Da Da Da Da Da Da.* Tommy Day pointed at me from the stage and everything, prompting half the hall to look my way. Tommy was not singing this time. The bass player was doing the honours. Too corny for Tommy I'd say. *Da Da Da Da Da Da Da Da/The Bould O'Donohue.*

'Do you not know this one, Tommy?' I called out at the top of my voice.

'What?' Tommy said, holding his hand to his ear.

'Do you not know this number I said,' I bellowed back to him.

He waved me away and laughed and away I went again, off around the hall, bumping into the other dancers and nearly knocking people over and everything. *I'm The Boy To Squeeze Her/ And I'll Tell You What I'll Do ...* And then I spied a couple of posh fellows grinning and pointing at me and, feeling all important in myself now, I went over to them and asked the two of them what they thought they were gawking at.

'What?' the first fellow wondered over the band.

'I said what are you two gawkin' at? Are you deaf?'

'What did he say?' the first fellow said to the second lad.

'He wants to know what we're gawkin' at?' the second lad told him.

'Not much,' the first one said with a gentle push and when the two of them turned to walk away I let a great big hocker fly, which missed its mark and landed on a girl's dress who was coming towards me. She let out a wild shriek and when she told her boyfriend that I had just spat on her he gave me a box on the ear and with that I began to throw up all over the dance floor. *Like The Bould O'Donohue.*

To my surprise, and relief, all the boys came to my rescue – Ian first, then Ely and Harpo and eventually the Bradley brothers, downing the boyfriend of the girl, hammering the two posh lads too before they proceeded to punch and kick and head butt anyone else who got in the way. A right, royal rumble. The fight escalated, involving fellows who had nothing at all to do with it in the first place. Nearly wrecked the place, the boys did. Fellows were floored. Girls screamed. Chairs went flying. The band stopped playing and everything. And Ely was the master of them all, I'll have to give him that, taking on two fellows at the same time and standing up to the bouncer when he eventually showed up.

'Come on,' Ely said to him, egging him on. 'Let's see what you got?'

I was on the floor by then, delirious with drink. I spied Diana in the midst of the crowd, biting her lower lip anxiously and secretly proud of Ely's bravado. Loretta had an exhilarated look in her eye too as she watched one of the Bradley brothers – Tom I think it was – banging someone's head off the wall. I caught a glimpse of Imelda between the dense, disembodied forest of shoes and feet and legs that scuffled and shuffled above me. She was retrieving her coat from the cloakroom, heading on home early without me. She took one last, unimpressed peek in at the fight and bailed out.

'Imelda,' I cried, dribble on my face. 'Hang on … . hang on … .' Needless to say I would have gladly followed her but the place was spinning around me at that precise moment in time.

It was on one of these dance nights that Imelda asked me to take her out to Useless Island, and although I was no use in a boat nevertheless I agreed to take her there. I wanted to borrow my brother Ian's sailing cot, but Imelda insisted we go in Ely's, which she said was much better. Much prettier anyway, she said. Painted blue and with the words *The King Fisher* inscribed on it. My heart was in my mouth as I pushed her out to sea. Imelda was standing up regally in the boat and I was wading in the water. We could hear the noisy gang of boys and girls approaching, coming home from the dance, singing one of the love songs they had heard Tommy Day singing earlier on. *No Man Is A Island* or something. Ely would probably take big Diana up into the elevated signal box, I figured. And Tom Bradley would, more than likely, be trying to get Loretta to slip into the shadows of the deserted railway station. Meanwhile I continued to push the boat away from the shore, shuddering as the cold water inched up around me. I prayed to God that I would be able to scramble up beside her when the time was right.

'Hurry,' she commanded, sensing the others were drawing near.

As luck would have it the Gods were good to me that night and I managed to struggle my way up into the boat all right. I rowed us there in silence beneath a crescent moon and as we rounded The Black Man a solitary seal raised its head and wondered about us and the North Star winked at me as I tried to think of something intelligent to say to her. Not that she was that pushed one way or another whether I said anything or not, but … nevertheless. If it was now I could have told her about the stars, pointed out some constellation to her. Orion The Hunter, traipsing across the night sky maybe, his club against his shoulder, his sword dangling from his starry belt. And Sirius the Dog Star, scurrying faithfully along behind him, one of the brightest stars of all. I might have found a constellation that looked like her. And another that resembled me and we could have laughed about it. 'There's you,' I could have said to her. 'Proud and beautiful in the sky. And there's me, gazing up at you adoringly.' But I didn't know all that stuff that time. I didn't know nothing then. All I knew was that she wasn't like the other girls around here. She was different and didn't belong here. That's all I knew. And I knew that that wasn't exactly an original thought or anything, but if I could have found the right words I think it might have been an effective thing to say to her. I know now what I should have said of course. I do. Too late now I know, but … 'You don't belong here, 'I should have said to her. 'You're a palm tree, growing in the wrong country.' That's what I should have said.

Imelda sprang from the boat once we landed and she ran around the island like a girl in a musical. This side and that side and then up onto a mound of earth to let the wind tangle up her hair. She lit a fire and she scraped her name with a sharp stone on the broken down wall as if she was staking her claim on the place, and she hummed the same old love song that the others were singing earlier on. She seemed to be under the impression that she was the first girl ever to come out here, but I knew for a fact that she wasn't. Last week after the fight in the dance hall Ely had brought Diana Dempsey out here and they didn't get back till all hours.

I kept my distance from her, sitting by the boat for a while and eventually moving closer to the fire to warm myself as she went off around the deserted island, exploring, a dried up old furze bush burning like a torch in her hand. I was tempted to let the boat adrift so that we might be stranded out there together for the night. Imagine, the two of us lying there beside the fire. Apart at first. But then as the night grew colder and the strange eerie sounds of the island increased she'd grow fearful and slide across beside me and snuggle into me like a baby, her head on my shoulder. And with every kiss I'd slowly change, metamorphose. And in the morning when we woke I'd be transformed – straight and strong and handsome. 'You're a palm tree,' I'd softly say to her. 'growing in the wrong country.'

Imelda returned suddenly, in a bit of a huff over something. 'Come on,' she said. 'Get me out of here,' and she kicked out the fire, her eyes ablaze.

'What's wrong?' I wondered, but of course she didn't even deign to answer me. 'Hardly worth our while coming out here in the first place,' I complained as we climbed back into the boat again, and she snatched the oars from me and sat down sulkily to row the boat ashore herself while I was confined to the back seat like a chastised schoolboy. And then I saw it. Diana's name scrawled everywhere – on the trunk of the tree, on the edge of the boat, on the wooden plank in front of me, on one of the oars even. *Diana loves Ely.* Oh dear!

Ely was standing on the shore waiting for us when we got back to the Shelter. His head was cocked to one side and he was sort of smirking dangerously to himself. He shook his head and his lips moved as he uttered some dark, secret threat over and over again that I tried in vain to decipher. I thought sure he was going to kill me for taking his boat, but he didn't. He hardly noticed me in fact. He caught the rope which Imelda brazenly threw to him, and then he held out his hand and helped her disembark, and she stepped lightly ashore as if it was her divine right.

'Tie her up,' he said to me, tossing me the end of the rope and the pair of them disappeared into the darkness together. And that was the end of big Diana Dempsey.

It was around that time too that most of the boys and girls in the area dropped out of school. The Bradley brothers all went to work in The Bacon Factory where their uncle Ernie worked. Harpo had a job in the nearby car plant. Ely got a start in a local garage. My brother Ian was gainfully employed with Powers Coal Merchants – delivering the coal to be specific. Imelda, along with most of the other girls from around here, went to work in the laundry.

In the mornings I'd see her toddling down the bank and along the railway tracks, taking the short cut to work, dressed in white overalls and a bandanna for her head. At one o'clock she'd come back home for her dinner and then I'd follow her back to work at two. At five she'd finish for the day and there I'd be again waiting outside the laundry gates to follow her home. She'd meet Ely every evening after tea and the pair of them would go off to the pictures together or down to Nolan's Café, or else out to Useless Island in the boat. I'd go down to the deserted railway station and climb up into the signal box and watch them through the old rugged pair of binoculars I'd just bought for half nothing in Ned Stand's Pawn Shop. Not that I saw very much or anything. They had a habit of concealing themselves down behind the broken down old wall out there so that most times all I could make out was the back of their heads from time to time and the distant glow of the camp fire.

One day she never showed up for work. I saw her going down the bank as usual that morning, but apparently she never made it past the clock-in desk. At one o'clock there was still no sign of her. In the afternoon I searched frantically up and down the place: the old deserted station, the overgrown graveyard, Nolan's Café, up into the elevated signal box with the binoculars and anywhere else I could think of. No sign of her anywhere. At six o'clock people became alarmed. By eight o'clock the penny was beginning to drop. Ely was missing too. Some of the girls were sent for. They knew nothing. Imelda never told them anything lately. My brother Ian was summoned, but he knew nothing either. And Harpo was given a bit of a grilling by Imelda's granny. Anyway, to make a long story short, it emerged that the pair of them had run away together to get married. They were in Swansea, someone said. Imelda's grandda was duly dispatched to bring them back.

When they returned there was a great stave organised in The Shark Public House to celebrate their wedding, guitars and accordions going great guns. Tommy Day showed up and sang *From The Candy Store On The Corner*, especially for the bride. I hung around outside the pub, listening to the ribald songs that roared out of there. *Whiskey In A Jar* and The *Wayward Wind* and *I Don't Work For A Living*. My father was in right form and brought me out a glass of lemonade and a packet of Marietta biscuits. Ely came out to get a bit of fresh air too as I was munching the biscuits and hopping off the lemonade.

'Congratulations Ely,' I said and – transferring the biscuits from one hand to another and wiping the crumbs from my mouth – I held out my hand to him, graciously in my book.

'Go away from me will you,' he hissed, took one of the biscuits, which he fed to a passing dog, and then he laughed as Harpo Hayes fell out of the pub with his shirt hanging out, fluthered. Diana Dempsey came bursting out soon after, crying, and although Ely tried to comfort her she broke away from him and hurried home.

'What's ails her?' Harpo wanted to know, his eyes all glazed and his hair unruly.

'She's still mad about me,' Ely said proudly, and I could tell by the face of him that he was tempted to go after her.

Imelda was two months pregnant by then and seven months later their first baby boy was born. To mark the occasion Ely packed in his job at the garage and went fishing full time in his faithful boat, *The King Fisher*. He signed on the dole at the same time to supplement his meagre income. He also took to wearing a peaked leather fisherman's hat on his head all the time, cocked to one side in an impudent fashion or else placed back on his skull drunkenly. He was full sure that this made him look more interesting.

If you want my opinion Imelda sold herself short when she married that lad and from that day onwards everyday she spent was a bit harder than the one that went before it. And I won't deny it either but I retreated into myself around that time. I felt betrayed to tell you the truth. So I hibernated for a while, locking myself away in the cramped back bedroom, inventing things – traps and snares and electrical appliances that gave you a shock when you accidentally touched them. And I read avidly. Paperbacks usually at first: Ray Bradbury and Denis Wheatley and Louis L'amour mostly. Big books too, eventually. The bigger the better. Encyclopaedias and National Geographic and science books and that kind of thing. I read everything I could get my hands on to tell you the truth in the hope that I might find some equilibrium for myself. Or a centre of gravity maybe. Because everything was out of kilter with no rhyme nor reason to anything anymore – without her in my dreams.

That's more or less when my reign of revenge began really, around that time. At night mainly. I paid them all back for every misdemeanour that was ever perpetrated against me over the years: Ely and Harpo and Ian and The Bradley brothers and anybody else who had sided with them. Oh yeah. I got them all back. I shit in their boats, I pissed in their flasks, I hocked into their cups-of-soup and I came in their coffee; I hung their cats and poisoned their dogs and killed their ferrets and either raided or set fire to their fluttering clothes lines; and whenever any of them came up to the house after me and accused me of anything I threatened to send them a solicitor's letter in the post, and every single one of them backed away because they were all afraid of their lives of the law and anything written down on paper.

My mother, God be good to her, was well and truly gone by then of course, ferried off to the big Bingo Hall in the sky. Ha! ... Yeah, she collapsed in the yard on the way out to the lav in the middle of the night one night and it seems no one ever even heard her pitiful, feeble cries – if there were any. My brother Ian found her in the morning, frozen solid and clutching the frosty middle pole of the washing line, locked into rigor mortis and delicate thin layers of melting ice all around her. I've been plagued ever since with this strange image of her immured inside a block of ice, curled up like a potential butterfly. The last I saw of her the morticians were humping her bent up body down the narrow hall and out the front door to the waiting hearse. I heard afterwards that they had to break her legs and arms to get her into the coffin. Ah well, at least we could watch whatever we wanted on the telly from then on.

I used to sleep on the old disembowelled couch downstairs most nights. There was too many fellows upstairs in the bed that time and anyway I'd be tossing and turning all night with the pain in my foot. So I used to camp out on the couch in the kitchen, an old-fashioned curlicued chaise – longue with the guts hanging out of it, propped up with old pillows and blankets and old coats from the cupboard. It was grand except for the nights when my father would come in drunk and make himself a feed of chips or something, banging around in the pantry and spouting bullshit out of him. Sometimes he'd be as good as gold. He'd sing me a song and toss my hair and tell me I was unfortunate and then he might take a great figeary and make me a few pancakes. Other times he'd just turn on me and give me a whipping with his belt or a backhander in the face because of something I said or for looking at him a certain way or something, and he'd insist I call him the boss. 'Who's the boss?' he'd say, twisting my arm behind my back, viciously. 'You are,' I'd say, in agony. 'You are.' And he was too now that my mother was gone. Until that Christmas Eve he took a bad turn in the kitchen and sank to his knees, frothing at the mouth and gasping for breath. I had read somewhere that a dolphin is supposed to turn all the sad colours of the rainbow before it dies and that's exactly what it reminded me of. Only my father turned forty shades of blue – first light blue, then dark blue, then black, then grey and finally ashen. He couldn't speak and was pleading with his terrified eyes for me to do something for him, get a doctor or phone the ambulance or something sensible like that. I was tempted to go out to the shed and get the hatchet and hit him in the forehead, but I didn't in the end.

I just sat there and watched him die. My sister Betty was there too, in a state of shock. Ian came running down the stairs when she eventually called him and he couldn't believe his eyes. My father was dead on the kitchen floor and I was just sitting there, calmly singing. *I Swear By The Cross On The Back Of My Hide/ I Was There On That First Christmas Morning.* I should have hit him with the fuckin' hatchet. Tra la la la la la la la la.

∽

It was a cold, clear, blue skied late September day when Ishmael came to town. I was up in the front bedroom cutting letters from various magazines and pasting them together to form a ransom note to send to Mrs Hayes – Harpo's mother. Her favourite cat had just trespassed once too often into my back yard. If she were to leave a twenty pound note in a jam jar in a certain place then I would assure her that her pussy cat would return home safe and sound tonight, otherwise she could look forward to never seeing poor old Tissy alive and kicking again. The cat was of course already dead and buried by that time. I would also send a note to a certain other individual (a young local tearaway who had given me dog's abuse on the street for the past few months), telling him that there was treasure hidden in the jam jar in the lane behind his house in Oyster Avenue. Signed, *'a girl who loves you.'* Harpo and his brother -and maybe Ely too into the bargain -would be watching that jar like hawks and as soon as Killer Dino dipped his hand into it the boys would pounce and rearranged his features with a couple of good clatters and from that day onwards the two families would feud like fuck. Ha!

Anyway I was busy at my work, glancing out the window at the harbour now and then where a little armada of short masted sailing boats tacked their way around Useless Island, their sails flapping and furling with the breeze as Harpo Hayes and the Bradley brothers – well Tom and Josie anyway – and my brother Ian practised for the forthcoming regatta. Dirty-faced guttersnipes were playing on the street, skipping and arguing and complaining. And, down near the Shelter, Ely was caulking his newly built boat, the tarry whiff of burning pitch wafting on the wind as the muffled sound of his hammering came and went like far away music.

And that's when I saw Ishmael for the very first time as he bent his back and knelt to examine a forsaken puddle the retreating tide had left behind. I instinctively picked up my binoculars and honed in on him. He was wearing a leather jacket, a soft one with fur on the collar like someone in the American air force. He had surveying equipment close by and a big old-fashioned box camera on a tripod, which he lugged behind him wherever he went. Some of the old timers were watching him suspiciously. The women would wonder about his seed, breed and generation. The men would want to know what his game was. The children mauled at him and followed him around all over the place like he was the Pied Piper, which he didn't seem to mind.

'I wonder what his name is?' I heard myself say as I sat down on the edge of the bed to put on my shoes and stockings.

By the time I got down the stairs and out the door and down the bank he was gone. I followed his trail along the railway tracks towards Rainwater Pond. A few children said he had stopped to take a photograph of them huddled together inside the niche of the holy well. Jakey Brown told me he had just passed him too and called after me not to be bothering the man. 'The other way around, Jakey,' I yelled over my shoulder as I sped. 'Yes, the other way round, boy,' and I could feel Jakey's honest old eyes boring into the small of my back as I left him there.

There were four or five houses clustered in and around the pond. One was a family home. Another was deserted, covered in cobwebs and riddled with rats and the windows all smashed and the stink of you – know-what out of it. The third one was rented to a painter or an artist or some such. The two end houses closest to the sea were joined together at the hip like Siamese twins. The man I was looking for – whose real name was Richard Drew by the way – had taken these two houses. One he used as a storeroom, the other to live in. The two houses had half doors and as I stepped up to the first one he appeared in the doorway above me – the bottom half of the door closed, the top swung open – so that I found myself gazing directly into his aqua-blue eyes. And what I saw nearly knocked me for six. There he was, my doppelganger (for want of a better word), – straight, strong and handsome, sandy rather than blond and no freckles to speak of, but you could see that as a boy he might have sported a few here and there. He had a fairly youthful complexion and he smoked a pipe, a nice affectation I thought, and he had a grand speaking voice, which he very seldom overused. Our meeting like this reminded me of a book I once read where the main character rose up out of the bed in the middle of the night, not knowing who he was or where he came from and then he went warily to the mirror and looked at himself as if for the very first time. *The Strange Case Of Henry Williams,* I think it was called, a sort of a murder story.

Anyway I introduced myself to him and welcomed him to the area and told him all about my club foot and the hardship I was accustomed to, and about my mother falling and dying in the yard, and about my father beating me and taking me out of school, and about all the other boys up around here ignoring me and whatever. He just nodded and sighed and smiled and hummed and hawed now and again. I learnt little or nothing about him that first day. In fact all I know about him even to this day is what I either guessed or garnered over the next six weeks or so. For instance, I don't know if he was married or not, but I suspect that he was – divorced I'd say or separated at least. I don't know if he had a family but I'd take a chance and say that he had not, not the fatherly type I'd be inclined to think. I don't know where he came from, but – judging by his accent – I'd say he was probably born in England, educated in Ireland and lived in various parts of the world all his life. Or maybe it was the other way around, born here and educated there, I'm not sure. He was more or less my own age, one or two years older perhaps. And there was a sort of subterranean loneliness about him that you just knew in your heart and soul nothing, neither love nor money, would ever shift. It struck me later (much later in fact) that perhaps I was his alter ego too, sitting on his shoulder on the other side of the world, whispering, '*I wouldn't do that,*' in his ear.

I offered to do any messages he wanted done and to light the fire for him and anything else that needed doing and he agreed that would be helpful to him. After a little shilly-shallying ('What seems fair?' 'I'll leave it to yourself.' 'No, no, please …' 'You tell me.' 'Shall we say …') we decided on a price and shook hands on it, and he gave me some small change to use as a kitty so I could buy a few provisions for him and he told me he'd leave a key under the mat for me and that was that.

'My name is Richard by the way,' he called after me as I hobbled away. 'Richard Drew.'

Nice of him to volunteer that information, I thought as I rounded the corner, after all I told him. My name is Richard! Richard Drew! 'Well Richard Drew,' I swore as I went. 'I'm goin' to smelt you down and pour you out, boy!'

The next afternoon I toddled up to the house with some milk and bread and butter and sugar and a little cheese and let myself in. I put the provisions on the kitchen table and had a good look around. A small living room, covered with books and documents, a tiny kitchen just big enough for a fridge and a stove and a few shelves. There was a small toilet at the back and a bedroom, aglow with daylight, which overlooked the sea. I snooped around, picking things up and putting them down again: a panoramic photograph of the harbour, a conk-like seashell on a shelf, a few drawings of birds – a heron, a corncrake, a curlew, a cormorant, a snipe, an exotic looking king fisher. And calculations all over the place: the prevailing winds, the tides, the depths of the mudflats, the precarious nature of the silted harbour and the shallowness of the channel that led in and out of it and so on.

I touched the slender old-fashioned spyglass that lay like an ornament on the sideboard, picked it up and to my surprise discovered that it was actually functional (much sharper than my old binoculars). I went to the window in the bedroom and looked out to sea and marvelled at the birds landing on the slob lands a few miles away – gannets and guillemots and puffins and terns – and at the expanse of ocean that, as far as I was concerned anyway, led to the very edge of the world. I put the spyglass back in its proper place and browsed some more, opening up a ledger where he had doodled a few symbols and shapes and asterisks and scribbled some notes – *fertile enough mudflats.*** Troublesome harbour.*** Healthy birdlife* and that sort of thing. And there was a pencilled sketch of a woman scrawled somewhere, which I suppose, although I wouldn't swear to it, could have passed for Imelda.

There was an impressive collection of books lying around too, one on top of the other – *Billy Budd* and *A Tale*

Of Two Cities and *Moby Dick*. I picked up *Moby Dick* and read the first sentence. *Call me Ishmael.* 'Fair enough,' I mumbled. 'Ishmael it is,' and I closed the book and continued my quest. I was searching for something personal belonging to him, some clue as to who he really was, behind the pipe so to speak. I felt like a spy spying on myself to tell you the truth. I heard a gentle footfall approaching then and I hurried to the fireplace, knelt down and proceeded to clean out the grate.

Imelda soon appeared over the top of the half door and looked in at me, suspiciously.

'What are you doin' here?' she wanted to know.

'Your man asked me to light the fire for him and that,' I explained as she reached in and unclasped the lock on the bottom end of the door and entered.

'Huh!' she growled as she moved around the room, putting groceries into the fridge and the vegetables into their various compartments in the kitchen. He must have asked her to come too, I reckoned, as she swished on by.

Imelda had five children by this time – from fourteen down to five years of age, steps of stairs would be a fair description. She still looked pretty good though. I mean she was still fairly slim and nimble. Her face appeared drawn from time to time all right and she always looked a bit worried about something or other, but the pain I saw there and the deep-seated sadness only enhanced her beauty and gave her more depth from my point of view.

'Where are you wantin' these, Imelda?' Ely cried from the doorway, peeping in over the top of the half door. He was carrying a big bag of wooden fire blocks on his shoulder.

'Fire them into that other old house there,' she said and he did, returning to the doorway with the empty sack.' Is that all you got?' she called out to him from the kitchen.

'What?' Ely said, wondering what I was doing there. 'No.'

'But sure they'll be gone in no time,' she scolded as she came back into the living room again.

'Harpo is on his way with another bag now,' Ely barked back. 'I mean I haven't a hundred hands or anything. What's he doin' hangin' around here?' he said then, referring to me.

'Don't ask me,' Imelda said, shaking her head at the length of time I was taking to set the fire.

'I was invited here,' I called out to him, but he was already gone at that stage, giving Harpo his orders to toss the second bag of blocks into the other house. And as the pair of them arrived like a double act in the doorway I put a match to the fire, which was now set, and I stepped back to admire my handiwork.

'That should do the trick now,' I said softly to no one in particular. I had a special way of setting a fire, sculpting sticks and carefully placing peat briquettes here and there and judiciously planting bits of coal about the place until I'd built a beautiful edifice that would suddenly erupt into flames as soon as I put a match to it.

'Throw us in a few of them old logs there, Ely,' Imelda said, and when he did she planted them roughly into the fire grate, disregarding the symmetry of my work. And then, taking control, she slipped on her apron, turned on the radio and hunted us all away from there – Ely, Harpo and me. The Three Wise Men! Ha!

I decided to give the two of them a wide berth on the way home and hung back awhile. Harpo's voice got on my nerves lately and Ely was just as pass remarkable as ever.

'I hope she'll get us the money for them,' Harpo was saying as they vanished. Mean as shit that fellow is.

I found a skinny secluded crab apple tree opposite the house and sat myself up into the fork of it. The radio was playing inside now, some Country and Western song. I could hear her humming along as she came out to shake the dust from a mat, which she hung on the half door to air, and for a moment or two I basked in her primitive beauty once again as I had a thousand times before. And I knew that just before I die – or the minute I die or whenever it is that your whole life is supposed to flash before you – that that's what I'll see. Imelda in some guise or other: coming home from school in her school uniform, satchel on her shoulder and her blazer askew; or traipsing back from the corner shop in the whirling snow; or gazing with neurotic eyes out the window as the rain pelted against her kitchen windowpane. Her hair bleached with the sun in the summer. Her face pale and wan with the worry in the winter. One image piled on top of another as season followed season and one year became the next. Maiden, mother and moon.

I went back to the house that evening to find a tired looking Richard Drew sitting at the table, mulling over his notes and writing in his ledger and sipping a mug of coffee. He had a few candles lighting around the place, as was his wont, preferring, as he later confessed, candlelight to bulb any day of the week. Dishes were piled up in the sink and there was a smell of fresh bread in the room. I peered in over the half door at him.

'How's it goin', Ishmael?' I called into him.

'Huh?' he said, looked around at me and lit up his pipe, puffing it like an English army officer in the pictures.

'How's the fire?' I asked him.

'The fire?' he said, confused.

'Not so hot by the looks of it,' I said. 'Hang on, I'll get you a few more what-do-you-call-its from the eh …' and I slipped into the other old house next door and picked up a few logs and this gave me a licence to step aboard. Once inside, I banked up the fire and turned to face him, my boney arse to the flames.

'Snug enough?' I asked him.

'Yeah,' he replied. 'Not too bad. A bit drafty at times, but ...' He shrugged.

'That's good,' I said, and I looked around the room to give the impression I never had the pleasure before.

It seemed to be dawning on him now where we had first met and he began to remember our little business deal and with a soft sigh of recognition and remembrance he reached apologetically into his coat pocket for the money he had promised me. I protested of course, but he insisted and in the end I relented and took it. No, he wouldn't be needing me after all, he said. He had hired a local woman to look after things around here. She would light the fire every afternoon and tidy up and make him his dinner every evening and whatever else needed doing.

'Imelda?' I said.

'Yes, indeed,' he said. 'Imelda,' and I smiled at the sound of her name floating back and forth between us like that around the room.

'She's some woman, ain't she?' I ventured.

'You think so?' he said with a big, broad smile.

'Oh yeah,' I said. 'Don't tell me you never noticed now.'

'Well, I can't say I've given it much thought to tell you the truth,' he said, and I do believe he reddened around the gills.

'Well you should,' I said to him. 'Because she's one fine lookin' mare, boy. Not that she's up for grabs or anything now because she's not. So you can get that out of your head straight away.'

He was about to protest at this suggestion, but I stopped him dead in his tracks with an upturned palm.

'She's a one man woman as they say,' I told him. And then sort of sotto voce if you get my meaning, I said,' I can't say the same for Ely, mind you.'

'No?' he said.

'No,' I said, moving closer to the table. 'Ely's knockin' around with Tom Bradley's missus this long time – Loretta,' I whispered. 'He takes her out to Useless Island every chance he gets. And he's not playing tiddlywinks out there with her either if you know what I mean. Nor snakes and ladders neither for that matter.' And I winked at him to indicate that we were both men of the world.

'No?' he said again, taking another puff.

'No sir, he is not … .' I said and I laughed. 'Ha!'

'Oh!' he said then. 'That's a shame. She's seems like a nice person.'

'Who's that?' I said, 'Imelda? She is, a very nice person. She's a very special person. In a mysterious sort of way now I mean.'

'Mysterious?' he said, crinkling up his nose at me. It wouldn't have surprised me to hear him say. 'Matty, what a funny chap you are!' Like one of those silly bowler hatted fellows in the plays on the telly.

'Oh, very mysterious!' I continued. 'I mean you never know what she's thinking. You watch her sometime. Try and figure her out. You won't be able. And she changes all the time too, you know. She wears a jeans and she's one thing. Put her in a dress and she's another. You know?'

'If you say so,' he said with a smile that seemed to imply he had me well taped.

But I knew I had him, I knew well enough he was hooked. So I changed the subject. 'So how's the work goin'?' I said and off we went with me asking all the questions and him avoiding all the answers.

Every morning he'd go off about his business, surveying the place, examining and measuring. He'd catch an eel, measure it and weigh it and sling it back. He'd find a fish, open it up and scrutinise its innards. He'd scrape the cankered boats and inspect the contents under a micro-scope. He dissected crabs. He tested cockles and wild mussels and periwinkles and lobsters. He took samples of the water from various sides of the harbour. He sipped the water from the holy well. The seabirds seemed to interest him too – what they'd eat and where they'd land and where they'd lay and how long they'd stay and that. Using the big box camera he'd take photographs of the region: the bay, the harbour, the island, the Shelter, Rainwater Pond, the local graveyard, the men and women of the area, the boys and girls. (Although I suspect some of this was only diversion.) He'd sketch birds and plants and flowers and he'd make maps of the coastline. He persuaded a couple of salmon poachers (who shall remain nameless for obvious reasons) to take him up the river one moonless night, and they were chased by the bailiffs and everything, nearly caught them too he was telling me the next day. Real heart in the mouth stuff. He talked to the old timers for hours on end – Jakey Brown, Mosey Clark and Tenacious Doyle-, plying them with ridiculous questions and jotting down their answers.

'It's terrible unlucky to kill a robin, you know, 'Jakey Brown was telling him one day as I was passing. 'Even a cat won't kill a robin.'

Meanwhile Imelda continued to work about the house most days. He'd come back from his long day's trekking to find his bed made, a fire in the grate, the place spic and span and his dinner in the oven. Imelda would usually be on the verge of leaving as he arrived, her coat and hat in her hand, and they'd have a short conversation as she served him his meal and made him a pot of tea and put the biscuits on the table. He'd hang up his sketches and his photographs and pile his notes all around the room, and soon the place was alive with all his material, soon it was a real home away from home for him.

One day I went up to the house when I knew that Imelda was there on her own (because your man wasn't making any headway with her at all as far as I could see). I glanced in over the top of the half door to see her scurrying around the place, polishing and cleaning and humming along as usual to a song on the radio. She didn't notice me there at first so that I had a chance to watch her as she paused momentarily on the threshold of the bedroom where a lovely dappled pool of sunlight fell. She gave a bit of a start when she turned and saw me standing there, her hand on her heart.

'Is your man wantin' any messages done?' I wondered.

'No,' she said crossly and turned away again.

'No?' I said, but of course I received no answer. That was one of the things I loved best about her to tell you the truth. She never ever repeated herself unnecessarily. You could always depend on that.

I talked on anyway as she breezed into the bedroom and out of sight. Sometimes I think she was trying to convince herself that I didn't really exist at all, that I was some kind of figment of her imagination or something, that if she just ignored me I might somehow magically disappear. On the other hand I was fairly sure that part of her really needed me too though, you know, had always needed me. What I had to give her I mean – my adoration, my religious devotion, my unswerving loyalty, my … obsession, whatever you want to call it.

'He's a fairly nice fellow, ain't he?' I called into her.

'Who's that?' she wondered from the other room, acting the old gom.

'Ishmael,' I said, and although I couldn't see her face I'd bet money on it that she flinched. She didn't like that. Me, calling him Ishmael! But that's what everyone up around here called him now.

'A queer interesting fellow,' I continued as she materialised in the bedroom doorway again with a rag in her hand.

'Yeah?' she said, going about her business.' In what way, like?'

'I don't know. His life. His … way of life. I mean I can't disclose all he told me 'cause it's confidential, but … you can take it from me he's had one fairly interesting life so far. And as he said himself, it's not over yet either. Not by a long shot, says he,'

'I hope it keeps fine for him,' Imelda muttered on her way to the dustbin and I had to laugh at her sarcastic tone of voice.

'Ha!' I said and I continued to sing Ishmael's praises to her, awarding him mystery and fabricating adventures for him and so on. And so the seed was sown.

On the day of the regatta Ishmael, fair play to him, like everyone else around here, took the day off. He rambled from one event to another, displaying a childish exuberance for all that he found. Flags and bunting and pennants were festooned from house to house. A marching Fife and Drum Band paraded. A priest in full garb blessed the boats. Music poured from The Shark Public House, which was packed to the rafters all day long. The children were treated to a puppet show on the green and every child was given a hat and a badge and a bag of sweets. Stalls and stands and a makeshift marquee tent were erected where at the end of the day all the results of all the various races and events were posted. Ely won the boat race. Harpo came first on the greasy pole. Old Mosey Clark won the arm wrestling competition in The Shark again and Maggie Angre was the winner of 'The Big Swim,' from Useless Island to The Shelter.

Imelda came in first in the mother's race and received a medal for it. Ishmael clapped and cheered and whistled loudly as she stepped up onto the podium to accept her award. She did a dainty, delicate curtsy in his direction and he gave her the thumbs up. Ely witnessed all of this and came across and plonked his shiny fisherman's hat on Ishmael's head and told him he could keep it. 'I saw you admirin' that on me the other day there,' Ely shouted to him over all the noise.

When Ishmael got back to the house that night – slightly inebriated – he was surprised to find Imelda standing on the inside looking out at him over the half door. She had her medal around her neck and as he drew nearer she held it up to him, proudly.

'Did you see me?' she asked, beaming.

'I did,' he told her. Ely's old hat was perched on the side of his head. 'And I was proud of you,' he said as he took the medal in his hand and caressed it.

She was delighted. 'What are you like?' she said then, snatching the hat and tossing his hair and plonking it back to front on her own head.

I was nicely nestled in the fork of the crab apple tree by the way and although I can't relate to you every word they said verbatim, nevertheless I can give you a fairly accurate account of what went on in there.

'I brought you some brown bread and scones,' she declared as she opened the door for him and he went inside, retrieving the hat on the way, and from what I could gather she lit the candle on the table and made him a pot of tea and sat opposite him and talked to him for a good while.

What did they talk about? About the regatta and about the day and about something one of her children had said or done. And then she told him about the race and she tried to find the words to explain to him how she felt when she won it, the first thing in her life she ever won, she said.

'Loretta Bradley was raging,' Imelda rejoiced and Ishmael, who hadn't uttered a word for ages, threw his head back and laughed. I could see his magnified shadow on the wall: head back, front legs of the chair off the ground, hat balanced waywardly on the side of his head again and his pipe in his mouth.

'Do you know something,' he said to her then, slurring slightly. 'You should get out of here altogether. Sprout a pair of wings and beat it. Cause there's no way you belong in this place ... No way,' and he sort of chortled and shook his head vehemently to emphasis his point.

'I don't?' she said, awaiting the bullshit.

'No,' he said. 'You don't. And I've looked at it everyway – up and down and over and back and I've come to the conclusion that you must have fallen from the sky or something, or rose up out of the water one morning, cause you're not from around here and that's for sure and certain.'

'Now we're getting' somewhere,' I heard myself say and I stood up in the tree and practically rode one of the scrawny branches.

'You're a palm tree,' he told her then, taking her hand in his – according to their shadows on the wall anyway. And Jesus I felt the tingle. Oh, Lort! ... 'You're a palm tree,' he said, 'growing in the wrong country,' and then there was silence and shortly after that, with a beautiful '*goodnight*,' from the doorway, she went home – on gossamer wings as they say.

The following afternoon Imelda took him out to Useless Island. She wanted to show him her secret place she said where she assured him the mussels blossomed in abundance. They came back late that evening, laden down with stuff – buckets of cockles and mussels and periwinkles and a few bottles of white wine and a loaf of fresh brown bread and a big lobster he purchased from a fisherman on the pier. And then, filled with a strange enthusiasm for the day, she told him she was going to cook a big pot of mussels for them and she slipped off her coat and put on her apron and began tying her hair back until he stopped her and insisted on showing her a new way of doing it (in white wine and with a hint of garlic); and while he rooted out the saucepans and pots and opened up the wine, she washed the mussels in the sink and rinsed the glasses under the tap and set the table and cut the bread and lit the candle and out of the corner of her eye she slyly watched as he went whistling about his work. And in no time at all they were sitting down to a steaming feast together – lobster and mussels and creamy cockles cooked in milk – crunching shells and clinking glasses and classical music on the old second-hand gramophone he bought yesterday for half nothing from a stall on the green (delivered, incidentally, by The Wellington brothers in a horse and cart and we had an awful job trying to get it into the house, but that's another story).

And from my usual perch I watched and I listened – to their oohs and aws and their hahs and their whats and their yeahs and their whys and their maybes, and as the light waned their shadows danced around the walls until in the end one of them stood up and stepped over to close the upper half of the door. And not too long after that the candle went out and I just silently sat there with my beating heart thumping inside my shirt, sporting a Chinaman's smile and a beautiful bugle and wishing to God I'd learnt to play the piccolo. Me Fa Me Re Do So Me Fa Do. Tra La La La La La La La La.

∽

And so the affair began in earnest with good old yours truly here, the instigator of it all, left on the outside looking in – through a crack in the shutter or an aperture of light. Or maybe listening at the keyhole night after night and just when I'd be about to hear something worth talking about a train would trundle by or a flock of gulls might swoop down, screeching and wailing like fallen angels. Or else he'd put an old crackling record on the gramophone – *Madame Butterfly* or *Some Enchanted Evening* or some other ancient aria. And sometimes it seemed as if Mother Nature herself was looking after the pair of them (the wind, the rain, the drifting moon or whatever), masking their every move and camouflaging their secret love for each other, enfolding them, you could say, in her ever-loving arms.

From time to time I did get lucky of course. Once I caught a glimpse of her without a screed on, slipping from the bedroom to the toilet and giggling back over her shoulder at something he said from the other room. Another time I saw him – corpulent enough in the alto-gether – stepping up to the tap for a glass of water, drinking it down and filling it again so he could take one back to her in the bedroom. And the two of them sitting at the kitchen table another night, her wearing his unbuttoned blue shirt.

And that's more or less the way it went really: day after day he'd wait for her to come to him and night after night she'd return. They'd bolt the door and pull down the shutters and draw the curtains and speak so low that half the time you'd be hard set to hear what they were saying to one another – lovely little murmurings that had the where-withal to make me shiver. They grew bolder with each passing day of course as lovers do and the bolder they got the more careless they became: a curtain not fully drawn, a shutter only half way down, a light left lighting in another room. And as they grew bolder I got braver. I'd circle the house and hide in a bush beneath the bedroom window and glimpse them curled up together in that big dishevelled double bed, her dress draped across a chair, her shoes kicked off in the doorway somewhere as the rain dripped down the window pane to conceal the sin. Or I'd peep through the gap in the front door as they lay half naked together in each other's arms on the mat in front of the blazing fire.

'I hate goin' back here now,' she was telling him one night. 'Doors and windows flung open and Harpo Hayes sittin' over the fire, drinkin' tea and spittin' into the flames and all the rest of it. Makes me sick sometimes.'

'You deserve better,' Ishmael told her.

'I wasn't lookin' for sympathy,' she sort of snapped.

'Oh!' he said, fearing he had overstepped the mark. 'Sorry.'

'You're so mannerly sometimes, do you know that,' she grumbled, getting up to put her clothes on.

'Am I?' he replied, turning to look at her, propping himself up on his elbow with his head cupped in the palm of his hand. 'Is that good or bad?' he wondered, drinking in the sight of her.

She didn't of course answer him and he was left wondering whether mannerly was a good or bad thing to be in her book. She was good at that – making you question your manliness.

That was the night Ely and Harpo came by the house. They were out hunting – lamping rabbits – and were returning home with the dogs and their big boots and their shotguns and a necklace of dead rabbits around their necks. I had to duck down out of sight or they would have seen me.

'Your man is still up anyway,' Ely was saying as they passed the house. He had another hat on his head, the very exact same as the last one (where did he get these from, I sometimes wondered). 'Must be readin' a book or some- thing,' Ely continued, nodding his head in the general direc- tion of the back bedroom, and with that the pair of them were engulfed by the darkness, belatedly whistling the dogs who were still sniffing around the outside of the house.

Little did the other two inside realise how close they came that night because a few minutes later Imelda emerged, completely unaware, and scuttled on homewards. Ishmael, an old blanket around him, watched her from the window, bewitched and uncertain – propelling himself off into the future, I'd hazard, where no doubt his limitations lay in wait.

To say that all of this impinged on his work would be putting it mildly. He didn't get out of bed most days now until about eleven or twelve o'clock. He'd appear in the doorway every morning with sleep still in his eyes, drinking coffee and staring blearily into space. And she wasn't much better, going around with a distracted look and miles away whenever anyone asked her a question. No, they lived only to see each other now and whenever they did she'd run into his arms like a lovesick schoolgirl and before you'd know it they'd be at it again – door locked, shutters down, curtains drawn. And while they played or slept or fooled around I stood guard, watching and listening and looking out for the two of them – a faithful little sentry in a rained on duffle coat.

Eventually of course they had a lover's tiff over something and fell out. Don't ask me what it was. All I heard was their raised voices one night as I crept closer to the house – something about him talking to Loretta Bradley on the green I thought she said – and before I knew it she came storming out the door and away she went. He came to the door and called out angrily after her, all sense of decorum gone. God, how I envied him that night.

For three days and nights she never came next or near him. He moped about the house most of the first day and night, waiting for her to show up, listening to Neapolitan love songs on the gramophone into the early hours of the next morning. The second day he took a walk around the area, I suspect in the hope that he might happen on her. That night he ended up drinking in The Shark and rumour had it that he bought a round for the house – 'showing off' as she later described it. He was seen chatting and laughing with Loretta Bradley who was working behind the bar now while her husband Tom played darts in the rarely-opened upstairs lounge. The next day Ely was back in the Shark again and he stayed there all day this time, drinking and singing to Loretta and arm wrestling unsuccessfully with the Bradley brothers all afternoon. He practically fell out of the place that night, drunk as an owl. I had to help him home.

'*Farewell Farewell/ Beloved Land Farewell ...*' he sang as we stumbled along the railway tracks. He was wearing denim jeans and a jacket and the jaunty fisherman's hat on his head along with a three-day stubble: gone native if you don't mind.

'Jaysus,' I said to him, 'you'll be rollin' your own next.'

'I'm in love Matty,' he informed me that night as I put him into the bed. 'Lovely, lovely, love,' he said drunkenly, and as soon as he fell asleep I covered him up and turned out the light and, after I rifled his biscuit tin, I went to the half door with the spyglass to gaze into the distance: past the pond and the cluster of crab apple trees and into the moonlit cemetery, scanning along the rusty railway tracks past the holy well to the Shelter where the sailing boats bobbed and rolled. A brilliant instrument – in every sense of the word. The Black Man, Useless Island, the breakwater and bridge and beyond all that, the river Slaney gushing darkly towards the sea. And then back again to see her sitting in the fork of my favourite skinny crab apple tree, Imelda, looking at the house, looking at me. She knew that I saw her too. And do you know what? She didn't care. She couldn't have cared less in fact! Maybe, in her book, I didn't really exist after all. Ha!

They made up in the end of course, the very next day. I went out to the house and the place was all boarded up like a fortress.

'They're at it again,' I chirped, and sure enough about a half hour later she came out the door and hurried home to get the tea ready.

'Are you off Imelda?' I said to her as she brushed on by me.

'Yeah,' she mumbled, putting no hiding on it anymore. And that worried Ishmael I think, the thought that she might be actually prepared to just leave it all behind and go with him.

Meanwhile Ely was still seeing Loretta on the sly, unaware that the shoe was also on the other foot of course. Yeah, I'd bump into the two of them from time to time too – Ely and Loretta that is – coming out of Slattery's Field together, him fairly nonchalant, her all flustered. Or else I'd see her rushing stealthily down to The Shelter to meet him in the middle of the night, a scarf pulled up over her head – as if that made any difference.

'Someone should write an opera or somethin' about this place sometime,' I mentioned to old Jakey Brown one afternoon.

'Yeh reckon?' he said.

'I do,' I said to him. 'With all the goings on anyway. '

'Oh now,' he said as if he knew exactly what I was talking about.

Oh and listen, by the way, before anyone goes pointing the finger at me I want it put on record here and now for nothing that the ending of this tale has absolutely nothing whatsoever to do with me, right? I mean to say I only set the wheel in motion. Where it stops is anyone's guess. So … Don't blame me as the song goes.

One night I went out to the house to find Harpo standing on the threshold, giving Ishmael a good talking to.

Had he found out about the affair? I wasn't sure. And I never did find out for certain either, although I have my suspicions.

'Go and get it,' Harpo was saying, ordering him almost, and what's more Ishmael obeyed him. While he was gone Harpo slipped into the other old house and returned with a hatchet, which he stowed away inside his coat. Ishmael came out with Ely's old hat in his hand and presented it to Harpo. 'You get out of here now, boy,' Harpo warned him, stuffing the rolled up hat into his pocket. 'Do you hear me?' he said earnestly over his shoulder as he scarpered.

Maybe I should have stayed with Ishmael, but my instincts told me to follow Harpo and so I did. He led me to the edge of Slattery's Field where Ely was waiting for him. Shorn of his hat, Ely looked gaunt and grey and more than a little unsure of himself all of a sudden. When Harpo produced the hat Ely snatched it from him thirstily and put it on his head, fixing it and straightening it and adjusting it (anyone'd think he was entering a competition or something). Harpo showed him the hatchet inside his coat and the pair of them took off apprehensively down the bank together towards The Shelter where The Bradley brothers were waiting to greet them, plainly poised for trouble.

'The OK Coral be Jaysus!' I was thinking as I watched them from afar. And I wasn't too far off the mark either as it turned out.

As soon as they all came face to face, Tom Bradley stepped forward and flung a crumpled fisherman's hat at Ely and accused him of something or other. Ely protested and pushed him away. The others joined in and a bit of pushing and shoving and jostling ensued. Harpo calmed them all down, one hand on the hatchet inside his coat.

'Whoo lads,' Harpo was saying.' Take it easy now.' His was the only voice I could hear clearly, borne on the wind for some reason.

'Hat?' Ely seemed to be saying. 'What hat? I have my hat.'

'My missus came home last night and bla bla bla bla bla …' Tom Bradley said, spluttering all over everyone as usual. (I found out later that Loretta had gone home the night before wearing Ely's hat. The silly bitch hung it in the closet and when Tom – her husband – found it, the inquisition began.)

Ely threw his hands in the air and looked at Harpo imploringly. He was a good actor, I'll give him that. Josie put in his tuppence worth then, stabbing the air with his finger and pointing his thumb towards the houses to indicate some point or other. 'Humty dumty do,' he said.

'I'm goin' to tell you one thing.' John said and the guttural sound that emanated from him indicated that he was not a happy man either.

'True enough,' Tom agreed. Or words to that effect.

Ely said something to placate them, his outstretched hands beseeching them all to have a heart.

'But sure that looks like your man's hat,' Harpo declared. Clear as a bell.

Josie's raspy voice again, asking another question.

'Whats-his-name!' Harpo told him. 'Ishmael!'

Well you dirty little splapeen, I was thinking, and then I ducked down because Ely was looking directly at me, over the heads of the others.

Josie turned his head away in disbelief. John shuffled. Tom almost buckled at the knees. Ely and Harpo waited. I strained to hear what was coming next.

'Mickla-fuckin' – tishla (or something),' someone said. Tom I think it was.

'Not necessarily,' said someone else. Josie more than likely.

And then, just like that, they were off, lumbering up the railway tracks towards Rainwater Pond and Harpo took his hand off the hatchet.

'Take it easy Tom,' Ely called after them and, with a sly glance in my direction and with the tiniest of gestures – an infinitesimal nod of his head – he appeared to tell me to go and warn Ishmael that they were coming to get him.

'All heart that lad is,' I said as I bolted. With his, '*take it easy.*'

I was half hoping I might get there before them, but I didn't in the end, hampered as I was with ditches and bushes and dykes. They were inside the house when I arrived on the scene. I could hear the ransacking sounds from within as I crouched in the long grass. Was he still in there? I wondered. I hoped not. My fears were answered though when Tom came out and yodelled through a pair of big cupped hands.

'Ishmael!' he roared, his voice catching with furious tears. 'Ishmael! ... I know you're out there. I have your whoremaster's hat here. Why don't you come and get it? ... Hah? Come on ... Come and get it ... .' and, as his sobbing voice – which reminded me by the way of one of Ishmael's operatic tenors, weeping and sobbing into their soup – echoed back to taunt him, his big fist nearly punched the top of the half door off its hinges.

I thought I heard the faint sound of breathing nearby and I looked to see Ishmael lying in the dirty ditch beside me. His frightened eyes were pleading with me to tell him what to do. Stricken with fear, I knew, given the slightest encouragement, he would gladly flee and I was a little disappointed in him if I was to be absolutely truthful about it. What did I expect? I don't know. Fisticuffs at the back of the house. A duel in the sun. Pistols at dawn. Something noble like that. But no, guilty of one thing and blamed for another, as soon as I gave him my blessing – a silent, dimissive hand signal – he took off like Quick Joey Small, scaling the ivied wall to drop into Slattery's Field and out of sight. Did he say anything before he fled? Yes, he did actually. He said one thing. 'Tell Imelda,' he whispered,' his eyes darting around in holy terror. 'Tell her I meant everything I said,' he said and away he went.

I was fairly sorry to see him go I have to admit. (Yes, I knew there and then that I'd never see him again.) 'Cause there was so much more I wanted to tell him, so much more he needed to know. It was never going to work between him and Imelda anyway. Never in a million years. Different planets. Different worlds. She was too salty for him. He was too naive. I mean for one thing, a cat will kill a robin. I saw one kill a robin one day in my back yard and he didn't have no qualms about it either. None whatsoever! And that's just one thing. You know?

I could see him now racing up the steep grassy incline, scattering a herd of Friesians, his white shirt black with dirt, his frightened eyes practically glowing in the dark. He tripped and fell, rose up and ran again – my frowning, fleeing doppelganger – and to think that I once envied him, that I once yearned to be him.

I was tempted to shout something after him, a few words of advice or something to send him on his way, but it wasn't a good time for that, so I just ducked back down to watch, and enjoy I have to say, the wrecking of the house. And, as the old gramophone came crashing through the window and the big box camera came flying through the door, I have to admit that my heart sort of went out to them all – to Ishmael and Tom Bradley and Ely and Loretta and anyone else who was tangled up in this affair. And above all to poor Imelda of course who'd come up here tomorrow morning and find him gone – no note nor nothing. I felt sorry for her, you know. For all of them. No, I did though. Straight up. Well, I mean, it's only natural, ain't it? I mean … you're bound to feel something. Sure you wouldn't be human otherwise.

◇

Of course that was all a long time ago now – fifteen odd years ago nearly now – and things have changed around here since then. Slattery's Seafood Company stands where the old Bacon Factory used to be. They catch and process and sell and export all kinds of things: crabs and eels and lobsters and mussels and punnets of cockles and periwinkles and the like. Most of the boys from around here work in the plant now – Harpo and Ian and two of the Bradley boys – John and Josie. Ely is about the only one who still goes out fishing these days. Impudent as ever, he goes about his work with the hat tilted on his head and a mischievous twinkle in his eye. He built himself another boat recently and called it *IMELDA'S CHILD (Imelda had a sixth and final child, a little girl who was christened Vivian but was always known as Imelda's Child for some reason),* which was all very fine and dandy until Loretta Bradley saw the name of the boat and, incensed, she went straight home to confess her long forgotten sin to her husband Tom who didn't particularly want to hear about it in the first place. The case was settled out of court so to speak – at the back of The Shelter wall.

I don't know if Imelda knew about all that or not. I'm not so sure she cared one way or another to tell you the truth. As the years slipped by she disappeared inside herself, reared her children and buried her granny and granda and then tended her own grandchildren; and regardless of what life threw her way (and life was cruel to her at times: her oldest lad was in and out of jail by the new time and her second grandchild was born with a serious physical defect), Imelda somehow dealt with it all with the same sweet secretive smile, with that same old cruel, defiant stare of hers.

I still shadowed her of course, kept my vigil, skulking along behind her, clutching the little spyglass (yes, I managed to salvage it from the wreckage – a little flotsam and jetsam). Now and then I'd see her swimming in Rainwater Pond or nestling in the fork of my favourite crab apple tree, gazing over at the empty house, Ishmael on her mind. Once in a while I'd catch her sitting inside the grotto of the holy well or watch her standing statuesque in the boat as her oldest lad rowed her out to Useless Island for the afternoon.

' We'll be reading about that one in the paper one of these days,' old Tenacious Doyle said to me early one morning as Imelda passed us by without even saying hello to the two of us. And as it turned out he was right.

She's buried in the local cemetery. Her ghost still haunts this stretch of shoreline every chance she gets. You can hear her voice in the wind as it whistles through the dancing backyard washing lines; you can see her footprints in the trail of wild flowers that lead from the graveyard to the Shelter and from there all the way to Rainwater Pond. And there's no doubt about it but she's the one. She's the one who makes you walk the Via Dolorossa, she's the one who sends you to the water's edge to look at yourself as if for the very first time. And some people call her this and some people call her that and others call her something else. I happen to call her Imelda, and sometimes I call her Love. Lovely, lovely love. Ha! … *Me Fa Me Ra Do So Me Fa Do/ Tra La La La La La La La La.*

ON A BLACKTHORN LIMB

Mother May I Go Out To Swim
Yes My Darling Daughter
Hang Your Clothes On A Blackthorn Limb
But Don't Go Near The Water.

What exactly it was she saw in him we'll probably never really know now. She came into his cluttered shop to have her bicycle mended and he treated her with the same contempt he seemed to show for everyone who came through his door. She wanted new brakes, a new basket, a new saddle, the broken spokes mended, the chain oiled and righted. He looked it over and frowned and with an ignorant jerk of his head he indicated to her to leave it by the wall, and as she consigned it to the so called designated spot she felt foolish and a little mean, like she ought to buy a new bike or something instead of having this old dilapidated thing repaired. She was a trifle confused, mind you, when she looked around the room and saw no new bicycles for sale anywhere in the place.

'The cheek of him,' she thought as she watched him write it all down in a well-thumbed notebook. The place by the way was a hovel, and a chaotic one at that.

'The day after tomorrow or thereabouts,' he told her, whipping out a comb from his back pocket and running it through his slick, coal-black hair as he swung to admire himself in the mirror. Really loved himself, obviously. Although secretly, she had to admit, his vanity made her tingle.

He had a swarthy complexion, which probably made his teeth look whiter than they actually were. Nice teeth though. Even. And white. But his eyes were cruel, his eyes were cruel and his hands were dirty and his mouth curved down into a sort of a snarl when he smiled. His image in the mirror was handsome, however. How was that? He was not handsome. He wasn't even good looking. She looked from reality to reflection and back again and then she noticed that he was glaring directly at her through the looking glass and sort of grinning at her, leeringly. She decided there and then that she detested him. She left in a flurry, sorry she had ever gone there in the first place and vowing never to go there again as soon as she got her bike back. Imagine, grinning at her like that. Lort! He must be forty-eight years of age if he's a day, more than twice her age. Old enough to be her ... something-or-other. Oh Lort!

Two days later she popped her head in again to see if her bike was ready. It wasn't. It still lay in the corner, untouched. He was behind the counter, reading a newspaper. Match him better to be mending her bicycle. His eyes were black with silent scorn. And deep, like a lagoon. Sink or swim they seemed to say, it's all the same to me.

'Give me your number,' he said, irritably. 'I'll call you when it's ready.' Clearly he didn't want her dropping in there every five minutes. A pity about him!

'I'd rather not, 'she said. 'I don't like giving my number to strange men.'

'What's strange about me?' he wanted to know and she gave him a remonstrating glance and he sort of grinned at her again. Who did he remind her of? Somebody.

'Oh, I want a bell too,' she told him before she left. 'One of those old fashioned, roundy ones.'

'A bit old fashioned, ain't it?' he said

'Well, what if it is?' she snapped back at him.

He just shrugged and sort of scoffed and threw his eyes to heaven as if he was asking God a question. Jesus, he was arrogant.

They said he had a wife one time – and a child. She left him or something, or died. She couldn't remember how the story went now. She didn't know what had happened to the child. She asked her mother about it and was told the same thing – wife ran away or died or something.

'And the child?'

'Was there a child?' her mother wondered and gave it some thought.

Paddy Taylor called up to the house that night and took her to the pictures. They got chips on the way home, but he wouldn't come in, even when her mother tried to coax him from the doorway. No, he had to work early in the morning, he told her. Thanks all the same. So had she, in the office of Jones' Foundry. Miss Farrell, invoice this and then bring me that and then do the other thing when you get the time, mauled every time she came in or went out of the office by Mister Morris who was under the impression that he was God's gift. Lort!

'I'm going to hit the hay now, Mam,' she said and went up the stairs, her room full of dolls and cuddly toys and puffed up pillows and posters all over the wall.

'O.K,' her mother cried. Her mother was still at the door watching Paddy going down the street towards his own house. What did she think was going to happen to him? Hijacked and held to ransom and fucked up the arse or something. Paddy was whistling as he walked. Some march or other. He played the cornet with The Confraternity Brass And Reed Band. Lips like sandpaper.

'Good night love,' her mother cried as she banged and bolted the door. 'Sleep well.'

'Yeah, I know,' she mumbled as she undressed, 'and don't go near the water, right?' She did, in her dreams. Deep, deep lagoon, falling in and sinking down and under. Those dark eyes. And that grinning, leering face. And an underwater voice – her own voice – declaring over and over, *'he's not even good looking.'*

A few days later (she deliberately gave him about two days grace) she called in and found her bike all ready and rearing to go: all shined up, new basket, new spokes, new chain and everything. She tried the brakes. Deadly. Over the handlebars if she's not careful. And the bell. She rang it a couple of times, a fairly high-pitched jangle, and he frowned at the din. She felt childish. She rang it again though for spite as soon as he turned his back. He shook his head in disapproval, handed her a pump and bent his head to write something else into his dog-eared notebook. She took the pump from him, even though she had not ordered one. The sound of opera music was coming from the back room. And she thought she heard a woman's voice in there too, humming or something and moving about, talking to a child. Or a dog maybe. She cocked her head to listen more intently. And them she noticed that he was staring at her and smirking. 'Jealous was she?' his look seemed to say. Yeah, in your dreams pal. She paid him and left, struggling to open the door in front of her, encumbered as she was with the pump and the basket and the bike.

'Would you?' she wondered and she indicated to him that she was in trouble with the door. Should go without saying really.

He sighed and came out from behind the counter and held the door ajar for her.

'I thought you people were supposed to be emancipated by now,' he said, lifting the flap and coming out from behind the counter.

You people. Unbelievable! She struggled past and mounted the bicycle and rode away. She could feel him standing in the shop doorway, watching her from behind. She rang the bell and waved without looking round. Just before she rounded the corner though she glanced back: he was not there.

She went for a long ride into the country, stopping at the old Norman castle that overlooked the river. She climbed up to the precipice and stood on a bed of wild flowers, which from the road she knew made her look like she was standing on a multi-coloured cloud. Like Isis. Or the Virgin Mary. Make a great picture if she had a camera. And someone to take it of course. Later she went down to the fisherman's shelter and sat on the wooden seat. The lovely smell of burning wood, the dying embers. Charred kettle. Dirty mug. Empty, rusty biscuit tin Beached driftwood. The rugged hut redolent with summer rain. The aroma of rope and the scent of the sea. And the beautiful smell of some other … indefinable thing – hope or something. Or maybe it was just the seaweed.

It was turning dark when she turned for home. A lamp, she forgot to get a lamp. She knew that Paddy Taylor would be waiting for her in the house now. They had arranged to meet. He'd be wearing his sports coat probably and polo shirt. Always clean, spotless clean. And his nails shining. Dandruff sometimes though, on his shoulder. Tiny specks. Hardly noticeable really, but there nevertheless. She would be well and truly late at this stage – for their rendezvous. He wouldn't mind, just laugh or something. Did everything right, Paddy. No real go in him though, no real jizz. Well, not sexually anyway. She had made all the first moves. That night in the pictures to his surprise she opened his zip in the dark and put her hand inside his pants and he just lay back and, judging by the faint sounds that emanated from him anyway, he seemed to enjoy it. But he didn't return the compliment, for want of a better word – then or since. And later in the week she did it again in the living room after her mother had gone to bed, put her hand inside his pants and taught him the meaning of the word ecstasy. He left the house in a state of shock.

'Disgraced,' she said, saturated, and she had to laugh as she locked and bolted the front door.

The lamp, she must have a lamp. She pulled up in front of the bicycle shop, parked and rapped on the door. When he answered he was not surprised to see her there, he seemed to be half expecting her in fact.

'I need a lamp,' she said and he glanced at his watch: it was half eight at night.

He beckoned to her to come in and she doubled back for her bicycle, which she parked in the hall, and then she banged the front door shut behind her. He was not in the shop when she got there. She followed the music into the living quarters at the back. He was in the drab so-called parlour, standing in front of a three bar electric fire. Opera music was playing: *M'appari*.

'Do you want a drink? he asked. He was drinking whiskey and his lips were juicy.

She shook her head and looked around. Dark, footy, miserable place. The only thing worth talking about in the room, dominating the room in fact, was a large, framed photograph of a beautiful woman above the mantelpiece. The woman, who was wearing a light summer dress and a dainty knitted cardigan, was standing beside a bicycle in front of what looked like a lake with a train rumbling by in the background and a glimpse of the sea in the distance. She had a pale, youthful face and her smile was sad and lonely so that you couldn't help but wonder about it and worry a bit for her peace of mind. *Forever Young* was scribbled across the picture.

She was just about to ask him about the woman when he lowered his whiskey, plonked the glass on the mantelpiece and came towards her to take her in his arms. He kissed her roughly on the lips and before she knew it she was sinking into him, running her hands through his tangled hair, roughly tugging at it, running her hands down his body to find his zip, opening it and plunging her hand inside. He stripped her at the same time, expertly popping buttons and slipping off garments until she stood there half naked before him. He slid to his knees then and covered her with kisses, those kind of urgent and desperate kisses that she had only read about up to now. Meanwhile she practically ripped off his shirt (literally), and she sank to the floor and then, just like that, he was inside of her, his body rising and falling above her until she felt the explosion.

'Yes, she said. 'Yes.'

At long last!

It was early morning when she woke. The birds were singing in the rafters. A feeble shaft of sunlight fell across the end of the bed. He was gently snoring, his back turned to her. She wondered and sort of worried about her bike in the hall. Silly really. The room was truly masculine, devoid of any frills. The curtains didn't quite fit the window and they didn't go with anything else in the room either. The blankets were a hopeless mishmash of colour and of unequal length and breadth. There was an old fashioned bolster underneath the pillows and the pillowcases were like chalk and cheese. On top of the wardrobe sat a child's red Wellington boot. A damp odour suffused the room. Nice though. It reminded her of something she had never known. She would soon have to change everything of course.

Just then the door creaked open and a black dog peered in at her. The dog – a cross between a greyhound and something else, a sort of whippet if you like – sniffed its way around the room to his side of the bed. A few minutes later she heard a woman's voice outside and before she had time to react a strange looking creature was gazing in at them: neurotic eyes and a pointed chin and dyed black hair, the colour of ink.

'Bitch,' she said. Come on. Out of it. Bitch .... Come on.'

The dog trotted its way obediently towards the old crone and they both left. She could hear the front door slamming. The sound woke him up. He sighed and turned towards her, surprised to find her still there. He kissed her roughly and mounted her again and when he was finished he rose up and she listened to him unashamedly relieving himself in the bathroom. She had a vague memory of him coming back into the room before she drifted off to sleep again.

She woke at mid-day, got out of bed and dressed. She toddled out to the living quarters. Voices were coming from the shop. She made herself some tea and toast, but there was no butter in the fridge and so she went without the toast. After breakfast she went snooping about, opening cupboards and drawers and reading the scribbled notes that she found on the back of old envelopes that were left littered around. There was just the small kitchen, the living room (or the parlour as he liked to call it), and the bathroom and one bedroom and a box room that was locked for some reason. She tried the door in vain a couple of times and she wondered about it and then she thought she heard him coming and she hurried back to the parlour to sit on the sofa, nursing a cold cup of coffee.

She sat there for a while alone, silently surveying her dreary surroundings and then instinctively she rose and began to tidy up. She found some cushion covers in the hot press and she removed the dirty ones and replaced them. She hoovered the carpet and scrubbed the dirty kitchen. She took away the electric fire, which was covering up the fireplace, and she lit a proper fire in the grate. She changed the sheets on the bed and the curtains on the window and she washed up all the dirty cups and saucers and spoons that were dotted about the place.

When he came in for his lunch there was a clean table-cloth on the table and some soup made for him with brown bread on a side plate. (She had nipped out earlier on to get some butter and a few other things that were needed, slyly slipping across the street to the Cherry Orchard Super-market, hiding her guilty eyes behind a pair of sun glasses, her hair tied up in a sort of bandanna. As it turned out, however, as we will soon discover, her little expedition to the outside world had not gone unnoticed.) He had his soup and brown bread and a scalding mug of tea and he listened to the news on the radio and then he went back to work and barely uttered two civil words to her throughout it all.

'Don't say thanks whatever you do,' she called after him, although in the depths of her innermost secret self she felt strangely contented.

He shut the shop early and arrived with a Chinese take-away. She was sitting by the roaring fire, reading a book. (Even in the middle of the summer it was a freezing, cold place.) She rose up when she saw him coming and got the plates and cutlery and a few glasses of water and they both sat down to devour the food. Later he disappeared out of sight and she heard the sound of the shower and she went in to the bathroom, undressed and got in with him, cuddling into his broad back, the soap running down the pair of them like a foaming river. He turned her around and entered her from the rear. And later he carried her drenched body into the bedroom and lay her down gently on the bed, his glowering silhouette above her, the whites of his eyes glistening in the half-light and the sound of children playing in the narrow laneway at the back of the shop. A man like that, she thought, could cut your throat if you crossed him. Bury your body out the back somewhere and say it was all in the name of love when they eventually caught him.

'Move over in the bed,' he growled and she did and he lay down beside her and he kissed her wet body and he whispered strange things to her and he told her to roll over and when she did he tickled her back until she fell asleep.

The nine o clock night news was on the telly when she woke up. He was not there. Darkness was falling, stealing stealthily across the room. Angry voices were coming from the shop. She got up and put on one of his shirts and she slipped barefooted out to the parlour. It was her mother's voice.

'What do you mean you don't know where she is?' her mother was saying. 'She was here with you today? All day? But you don't know where she is now? Was she here with you last night 'cause she never came home last night. I was worried sick about her. I very nearly called the Guards and everything. I couldn't believe it when someone told me today that she was here with you. Making a holy show of herself like that. I mean what's she doin' here with you anyway? I've a good mind to call the Guards on you.'

'Look,' he said to her, 'I don't know what she's doin' here. You'll have to ask her that. All I know is she came here of her own free will and if she comes again the same thing will happen again. And don't give me that 'she's too young shit' either. She's big and ugly enough now to decide for herself … Now if you don't mind … .'

'Oh but I do mind.' her mother said, indignantly. 'Yes, I do mind, Mister Indigo ... .' It was a nickname on the street for him because of the blueness of his stubble. Paulo was another one, due to his Mediterranean complexion.

She peeped out through the curtain. The shit would surely hit the fan now. He was holding the door ajar and her mother was resisting.

'Alright,' he said,' let me put it this way,' and he leaned into her and whispered something in her ear.

Her mother looked silly in a gaudy coloured dress and short knee length stockings and for the first time in her life she had to admit to herself that she was ashamed of her. All those years, coming out of school to find this strange airy looking creature waiting for her at the gate, the other children laughing at her. And later after the Saturday night discos she'd be standing outside the nightclub so that the boys were all afraid to ask to walk her home. And then the questions, the endless questions. Who were you with and what did he say and where did you go and what did you do and all that kind of stuff. And the rumours going round about the mother of this fatherless child. And the time she got it into her head that a certain individual was her father and she followed him around the town all over the place and sort of stalked him until he got tired of it and confronted her and asked her what she wanted. She was about ten or eleven then.

'Are you my Daddy?' she asked him outright.

'What?' he said, astounded. 'No.'

He was dressed immaculately and of noble mien. She so wanted him to be her Daddy. But he just got into his car and drove away.

'Bitch.'

The black dog scurried past and out to the shop. When she turned around she found the creature with the neurotic eyes standing in the middle of the room. An icy chill accompanied her. Where had she come from? How did she get in here? And what did she want? She was just about to summon up the courage to ask these questions when she heard the front door slam and she looked out to the shop to find that her mother was gone and he was bolting the door. What had he whispered in her ear? Some dark secret, maybe? Or the devastating truth, perhaps! He came into the parlour with a big serious face on him and she felt sure he was going to ask her to leave now, but he didn't. He took her in his arms and kissed her again, popping the buttons of the shirt open and plunging his hand inside, oblivious to the old woman close by.

'It'll all end in tears,' the old one said, cackled and left furtively through the back door, the dog scuttling along behind her.

'Hatty,' he said when she was gone as if that explained everything.

The next day Paddy Taylor came down to the shop and reared up on the two of them.

'Calm down boy,' he said to Paddy who was ranting like a maniac.

'Calm down?' Paddy said, and he made a fist and suddenly struck Indigo, or whatever you want to call him, in the face and although he made his nose bleed it was a fairly ineffectual blow. Well, it didn't even shift Indigo, let's put it that way. When Paddy threw a second punch Indigo or Paulo or whatever his name is grabbed his arms and wrestled him to his knees and told him to be a good boy.

'Whoremaster,' Paddy bellowed as he rose up and moved backwards towards the door. 'A whoremaster and his whore … . Like your ma. The very same as her.'

'Yeah, right,' Indigo said (let's call him that and be done with it), and he contemptuously tossed the young man a half eaten apple. 'Here,' he said, 'before you jaw lock yourself there.'

Paddy caught it, took a big bite out of it, spat it out and backed his way onto the street where he flung the heart of the apple viciously against the window before running off down the road with his shirt hanging out.

'The things we do for love,' Indigo said and wiped the blood from his nose as he sauntered back into the living quarters like nothing had happened. She went to the window, exhilarated.

A few days later she went back to work and Mister Morris had the cheek to call her into his office and, with his hand gently on her arse, he asked her where she had been for the past few days.

'On the nest,' she said and she reached out and grabbed him by the testicles and softly squeezed.

He never bothered her again after that.

Each evening after work she came back to the shop where he'd be working and she'd go into the back to make the dinner. He'd shut up about six and come in to warm himself in front of the fire before going into the shower. He'd arrive at the dinner table spic and span and usually the pair of them would end up in bed before eight, the washing up piled up in the sink.

'Let Hatty do it,' he'd say, and although she never actually saw Hatty doing anything, nevertheless, sooner or later, it always got done.

Her mother rang her practically every day at work and begged her to come back home again. Sometimes she took the call, sometimes she didn't. Once or twice Paddy Taylor was waiting outside the factory for her in the evening. She managed to avoid him by dodging out the side gate and soon he got the message and stopped coming altogether.

'You don't know anything about this lad,' her mother

warned her on the phone one day. 'I mean he could be anyone, done anything, you don't know.'

'I know enough,' she snapped, angrily.

'Try and leave him then and see what happens,' her mother said. 'Kill you more than likely. Or worse even.' and she held the phone away from her ear as her mother rattled off a litany of all the various possibilities.

Sometimes in the middle of the night on her way back from the bathroom she'd stop in the hall and try the door to the locked room or she'd bend down and try to look through the keyhole. Other times she'd stall in the parlour to wonder about the picture above the mantelpiece, strangely luminous and mysterious all of a sudden, thanks to the red glowing Sacred Heart votive lamp in the corner. On closer examination she could see that behind the woman in the photograph a torn, elaborate scarf was lodged in the branches of a gnarled old blackthorn tree. And far away the shadowy shape of the mountain peeped out from behind a misty bank of low-lying cloud. Two swans decorated the lake and smoke billowed from the chimney of a nearby cottage.

Who was this woman anyway – with her Mona Lisa smile? Wife? Lover? Phantom something or other? Or the true ruler of this dark little realm perhaps? And can she be usurped, that's the question? She had an urge to draw a moustache on her or something, and a pair of round glasses. And once when no one was looking she actually took the picture from the wall altogether just so she might see what the room would look like without her in it. Another time while he was sleeping she reached up to the top of the wardrobe and took down the dainty red boot. She measured it and studied it and rolled it around in her hand and tried to see a shoe size or something and she got a bit of a fright when he woke up and asked her what she was doing.

'Nothing,' she said, putting the tiny boot back in its place, and then she tiptoed out to the bathroom again even though she had just come back from there.

One evening she discovered Hatty sitting at the kitchen table, reading the tarot cards. She looked over the old woman's shoulder to see the picture of a heart with three swords sticking in it. The Hanged Man was another one. And The Lovers – two naked figures in what looked like Paradise.

'What does it all mean, Hatty?' she said. It was the first time she had ever spoken directly to the old woman.

'It means.' said Hatty, 'that something's gonna give,' and she laughed that cackling laugh again.

She was tempted to ask Hatty about the child's red boot on top of the wardrobe and about the woman in the photograph and about the room behind the locked door, but she was half afraid of the answers she'd receive. She had her own version of events already sorted out in her head anyway. The red boot belonged to his three year old daughter who she'd often picture in her mind's eye climbing on board a train, holding her mother's hand. The child would be crying and calling out to her Daddy who was standing on the rain drenched platform with his collar turned up and tears in his eyes. Other times she'd imagine Indigo finding the boot lodged in the mud flat of a swollen, gushing river, pulling the boot out of the swamp with a hopeless sucking sound; and then she'd picture him tearing his hair out and calling out the young one's name. 'Jennifer! Jennifer!' or 'Molly! Molly!' She'd imagine too how it would be when she'd find the key to the locked room in the back of the old clock on the mantelpiece or under the washed jam jar that held all the screws and nails and old fuses and other bits and pieces. She'd open the door only to find a shrine to the missing child –a rocking horse and cradle and a rag doll and a sad, sacred beam of sunlight slanting in gently through the recessed sash-window. Or else the room would be dedicated to the woman in the picture: a big double brass bed with puffed up pillows and a four-poster canopy. Mirrors all over the place and a photograph beside the bed of the family. And yes, there were times too when she dared to imagine the unimaginable. Blood stained hatchets and the like.

'That door is not locked, you know,' Hatty said to her out of the blue as if she had just read her mind. 'Well it is, but the key is above the doorjamb there.'

Was she looking towards the door or something? She must have been!

'So?' she said.

'You mean to tell me you don't want to go in there?' Hatty enquired, narrowing her eyes.

'No,' she lied. 'Not particularly.'

'You're right too,' Hatty said. 'Although according to this you will go in there sooner or later,' and she planted another card on the table and cackled again.

∾

'I'm going home for a few days, Bronson,' she announced one day out of the blue.

Bronson, that's who he reminded her of – Charles Bronson. Although in reality he looked nothing like him.

'Fair enough,' he said calmly and she had to admit that she felt a tad disappointed. She had expected a bit of a fight over it at least.

Her mother sulked most of the time she was there, thawing out gradually. Paddy Taylor was broken hearted, her mother told her over dinner one night. Well, barked at her. One of the few things she did say to her that first night. Paddy had come up to the house on several occasions with tears in his eyes, her mother was saying as she strode into the kitchen with the dirty dinner plates.

'You should have given him a good seeing to, Mother,' she called out to her from the other room.

'What?' her mother asked, incredulously, as she came back in with the dessert.

'Nothing,' she said. She must stop doing that.

'*Seeing to*?' her mother said. 'What do you mean '*seeing to*?' I did see him. He was here, the poor chap, with tears in his eyes.'

They went to a recital the following night. Some visiting Welsh tenor was the top of the bill. The Confraternity Brass And Reed Band opened the first half of the show.

'Mother,' she sighed under her breath when she realised.

'What?' her mother wondered, the very essence of innocence.

Mister Morris was sitting opposite with his wife and family. She winked at him brazenly and he turned fairly crimson. Paddy Taylor turned red too when he saw her there in the audience. He played a few duff notes in his solo.

'He's off form tonight,' someone whispered in the row behind her.

She felt all-powerful. She put her tongue out at a woman who was staring at her. Her mother was raging with her.

'Well, what can you expect from an illegitimate?' she said to her mother on the way home.

'I'll have you know, miss,' her mother said,' that your father was a very respectable man.'

'So why didn't he stick by us then?' she asked.

'He was married,' her mother snarled.

'To who?'

'His wife. And don't ask me again who he is. I'm not at liberty to say.'

'It's all right,' she said. 'I don't need to know now.'

'What do you mean you don't need to know now?'

'I don't need to know any more, 'she said. 'In fact I don't want to know. I know who I am now.'

'Oh, get out the violin and play us a rhapsody there why don't you,' her mother said, sarcastically. 'You know who you are!' And then for some reason she hummed the theme to Coronation Street.

A warring peace reigned throughout the house for the next few days until she declared that it was time for her to go back to him again and then her mother relented and grew contrite and sorrowful in herself and tender towards her, packing things for her to take back with her and so on. She promised her mother that she would come back and stay with her every so often and everything seemed to be going hunky-dory until it was nearly time for her to go and then her mother suddenly lost the run of herself again and threw a tantrum, cursing the bicycle mender and all belonging to him into a knot for taking her away in the first place.

'Bad cess to him anyway,' her mother wailed. 'I hope he withers away to nothing and dies roaring in the bed. And you needn't come running to me either Miss when he lets you down, 'cause I won't want to know.'

'I'll see you, Mam,' she said, kissed her mother and hurried off down the street.

'Mother of God and all the saints in heaven,' her mother was saying as she went. 'What did I ever do to deserve this at all?'

He was serving a contrary-faced customer as she came through the front door of the shop with her things. She was so glad to be back that she dropped everything in the middle of the floor and threw her arms around him and kissed him, much to the alarm of everyone concerned.

'Did you come back? 'Hatty said to her when she went into the kitchen.

Hatty was at the sink, up to her ears in dirty delph.

'Yeah Hatty, I did,' she replied. 'With a vengeance.'

She had bought a rake of new stuff for the place: duvets and tea towels, new mugs and a few table mats, matching pillowcases, a china tea pot, some decent wine glasses and a few rolls of wallpaper and a tin of paint.

'What do you think, Hatty?' she wondered, holding up the wallpaper. 'I'm going to paper the top of the wall and paint the bottom with a fancy border in the middle.'

'I'm a dab hand at the papering,' Hatty said, abandoning the washing up. 'Even if I do say so myself.'

When he shut up the shop and came into the parlour that evening he found the two women up to their ears in paper and paint, Hatty papering while she took care of the painting. He sighed at the state of the place and went and had his shower. When he returned they inveigled him into putting up the border and then he had to paint the skirting board and the kitchen doorframe. And later they sent him out for some fish and chips.

'Do you see that picture there,' she said to Hatty when he was gone and she pointed towards the photo of the beautiful woman above the mantlepiece.

'What about it?' Hatty said abruptly.

'Where was that taken?'

'What do you want to know that for?'

'I want to have my picture taken there too,' she said.

'What for?'

'I don't know,' she said, 'I just do. I'm going to hang it on the wall opposite. Where was it taken? Do you know?'

'It was taken behind my place,' Hatty told her. 'One summer's day.'

'Will you take me there?'

'Maybe,' Hatty replied, rubbing out a few wrinkles. '…
We'll see …'

'We won't see at all, Hatty,' she said. ''Cause I'm going
there anyway – with or without you. I'm going to ape that
photo to a tee and then we'll see who rules the roost around
here.'

'Oh Jerciful Maysus,' Hatty said under her breath.

'Mine 'll be twice as big, mind you,' she said. 'Twice the
price too. The frame.'

'Bitch!' said Hatty and looked away.

'Huh? 'she said.

'Hah?'cried Hatty.

She looked around. The dog was nowhere to be seen
and she threw Hatty a suspicious, sideways glance, but the
old woman was too engrossed in her work to notice. Hang
on. Was that a cackle?

∽

What do you need Hatty for exactly?' she asked him one
night when they were snuggled up in bed together.

'Ah, you know,' he said, vaguely.

'No, I don't know,' she said. 'Tell me.'

'You always need an old one about the place,' he said.

'Why?'

'To nurse you when you're young and to lay you out
when you die and all that malarkey,' he said.

'Mmn.' she said, unconvinced. 'Where does she live
anyway?'

'Newton's Cross,' he told her, 'where the three roads meet!'

'That's what I thought,' she said.

'Yeah?'

'Yeah,' she sighed. 'And another thing,' she said, digging
him in the ribs. 'What do you mean I'm big and ugly
enough?'

'What's that?' he wondered, innocently.

'Oh yeah,' she said. 'As if.'

'As if?' he said. 'As if what?'

'As if … . nothing,' she said and she puckered his cheeks playfully, his face radiant with joy as she turned her back to him in the bed. He threw his weary arm around her and drew her closer to him and he whispered her own name in her ear as if it was a magic spell or something. (This would become a common occurrence.) They did not make love at all that night, which in itself was beautiful. And in the morning she saw him kiss the dented pillow where her head had lain.

The following morning she found the key on top of the doorjamb and she opened up the dusty box room. It was full of junk, bursting at the seams nearly. One cursory glance and she realised that there was nothing worth worrying about in there. She turned around and got a bit of a start when she saw him standing in the hallway behind her.

'Look at this place,' she said to him, brazenly.' It's full of dirt.'

'Yeah, I know,' he said.' That's why I put it in there.'

'It's a waste of a room though', she said and he tacitly agreed with her. 'I'm going to hire a skip in the morning,' she told him. 'Get rid of this lot … Gain ourselves a room,' and he mumbled something or other and disappeared back into the shop again.

A few days later she called to Hatty's white washed cottage and the old woman led her up the lane to the very spot where the picture was taken – pond and mountain and railway tracks, blackthorn and sea. The very place. It nearly took her breath away.

Hatty sort of stage-managed her into position beside the bicycle and then she produced a quaint old fashioned box camera of her own, declining to take the brand new one that was on offer.

'No,' Hatty said, 'I'll use my own, thank you very much,' and then the old woman placed a torn scarf in the branches of the blackthorn tree and sat back to wait for the mid-day train.

'I think I'll pack in my job, Hatty,' she was saying as two white swans glided diagonally across the water behind her. 'Take over the shop. Put him in that back box room, let him do all the repairs out of sight. What do you think? 'Cause he has no manner with people anyway. There should be new bicycles for sale in that place. And old ones too – done up. There's going to be a college here soon and then bikes 'll be all the rage, all the students and all. He'll make a fortune. I mean just think what you could do with that place though Hatty: a new shop front, new shelves, new everything … '

Hatty was not even listening to her. Instead she looked into the box camera and considered the composition and then she got a big stick and hunted the swans to the far side of the pond where they were supposed to be.

'Is this the same as the other picture, Hatty?' she wondered.

'No,' Hatty answered. 'It's not.'

'Why, what's different about it?'

'She was much better looking than you,' Hatty recalled.

'She was in her shite, Hatty,' she said. 'With the aul' veiled eyes on her.' The old woman cackled and gazed towards the railway tracks.

'Whist,' Hatty declared. 'Here she blows.'

A train soon sliced through the land and she felt the icy shiver of de ja vu.

'Smile, 'Hatty cried as she aimed.

'I am smiling, Hatty,' she said, nervously. 'I am smiling … '

'Bitch,' Hatty said and she took the shot.

THE DAY OFF

For some unknown reason – inexplicable you might say – Daly woke up one morning and decided on a whim to take the day off work. Twenty five years working as a clerk in Lawson and Sons Firm of Solicitors and this was the first time he'd ever been so bold, although God knows he'd often threatened as much.

'Yeah, right,' Crosbie would say sarcastically, fingering his frothy Cappuccino in the Coffee Pot Café. 'In your dreams, pal!'

'I will. I'll do it,' Daly would swear.

'When?'

'I don't know. One day ... Someday.'

'I'll tell you when,' Crosbie might hiss. 'Never!'

Well, today was the day. His wife – a no nonsense merchant – stirred in the bed beside him and squinted at him sideways through those sly, hooded eyelids as if reading his wayward thoughts, she even muttered something to imply that she had him well taped. He held his breath and stayed perfectly still until she fell back to sleep again, and then, being a creature of habit, he rose up as usual on the dot of seven thirty, shaved and showered and tiptoed down the stairs to the kitchen in his stocking feet. He had his breakfast and made his sandwiches – well, cream crackers actually and cheese and mayonnaise with a few grapes on the side, wrapped in tin-foil and imprisoned in a see-through Tupperware container – along with his usual flask of vegetable soup. He even raided the small change jar for money for his eleven o'clock cup of coffee in The Coffee Pot Café, which of course he wouldn't get to have today.

Upstairs he could detect his wife moving around and he hastily slipped on his slip-ons, gathered all his things together, – sandwiches, flask, brief case, jumper and jacket – fumbled his way through the front door where he bundled the lot onto the back seat and climbed into the car with a weary sigh of relief. She'd be coming down the stairs any minute now to face the world. 'What's that smell?' she would have said to him had he been there, referring to his aftershave which she saw as an affectation and an invitation to debauchery. It was a standard joke nowadays between himself and Crosbie behind her back: that and 'Where were you, ye liar?'

Daly revved the engine, let it warm up for a minute or two as was his style, steam rising like mist around the bonnet and sides (which for a while there – well in the beginning anyway – unbeknownst to him, made him the laughing stock of the street), and then he noisily took off out of the quiet cul-de-sac, a slightly comical, diminutive, finicky figure behind the steering wheel. He drove past the corner shop and away, through the streets of the bustling little town, booting down the hill past the side windows of Lawson and Sons Firm of Solicitors where he worked, or in this case – today at any rate – he didn't work.

He was sure people would notice him driving by: Linda from the Coffee Pot Café for one who was busy putting out the outside sign. Green eyes like a cat. 'Meeow', he felt like saying sometimes. What if he did, go in there someday and starting purring at her like that as she poured out his coffee?

Crosbie thinks, given half the chance, she'd scratch the back off you. God, imagine the inquisition.

'Where did you get those?'

'What?'

'Those marks on your back? '

'Penance for my sins.'

'What sins? What have you been up to? Where were you, ye liar?'

There's Bernard, the faithful messenger from the bank, wrenching up the heavy steel shutters. Bowing, bending, he's in. Oh my God, the dickie-bowed Mister Brown the manager is tied to a chair inside, bound and gagged, beaten and buggered. 'Quick Bernard, get out the Sudocream. In my office, Bernard. In the cupboard above the … Hurry Bernard, hurry. That's it … Gently Bernard, gently. … Oh, Bernard!' … And there's the roving traffic warden, hat tilted rakishly, slyly pretending not to notice a few potential lawbreakers. '*Go on park there, I dare you … . Park there you … red headed bastard.*'

Daly drives by, unseen. What's one to do? Bamp the horn? Spit into the wind? Drop the pants and moon? But no, nobody flagged him down, no one waved him in to the side of the road and demanded his passport and licence and the gory details of his final destination.

The town would soon be in his rear view mirror he couldn't help thinking as he headed for the brindled countryside: The Swan monument, the Faythe Primary School, the Celtic Laundry, Our Lady's Grotto, The Rocks, the sea and the road to Mandalay … .He switched on the radio. Yes, Brendan O'Dowda singing, '*La Golondrina.* Lovely. 'To *Far Off Lands/ The Swallow Now Is Speeding/To Warmer Climes … .*' Oh dear, there's young Mister Lawson, like the ghost of Christmas past, on his way to work. Did he see? No, too busy at other things. Stop picking, we're not playing today. That was a close shave. About twelve o'clock it'll dawn on him, the dopey dope! *'Were my eyes deceiving me or did I see Daly this morning, driving out of town to the tune of **La Golondrina?'***

There's that field, full of golden sunlight. And a pheasant, doing his little dance.

∾

The seaside! A walk along the beach. Crunch, crunch, crunch, crunch … Hate that sound. And the feel. Aah … . The seagulls circling and whinging and the tarry whiff of the ocean, marred by the reeking stink of the dry-docked fishing boats. A couple of schoolboys nipping down a sandy avenue, playing truant more than likely. Here's your brother! *'Cut out that smoking, it'll stunt your growth – little midgets going around with brown stained fingers, bad teeth and a smell off your breath.'*

The Guillemot Lightship, tied up in the harbour – a maritime museum this weather! How much to go in? A fiver? Go on then. Up the gangplank. *Ah me 'earties, them that dies be the lucky ones.* A tourist – in one's own backyard would you believe? There's no accounting. Crow's Nest first. No head for heights. Don't look down. Look out and up. Windmills on the horizon. And what's that in the distance? Is it? No, can't make it out at all. Well, God knows you were warned. Oh, for twenty twenty vision. Down into the galley afterwards to peep into the tiny cabins. Miniature existence when you think of it. They lived like monks according to this – the Lightship men. Rosary and everything during Lent, so they say anyway. Crosbie did a stint out here once. Well not here, out on the sea when the Lightship was … operational. Off the coast of … Arklow or somewhere. Boring he said it was. Up to the light to do your watch, down to the galley when it was your turn to cook, into the cabin to read your Louis L'Amour. One fellow who never said a word, another who never shut up and a third lad who was constantly sick over the side. *Oh Mammy. Mammy Mammy Mammy ... .Mammy Mc-feckin' – Grath ... .*Never again, Crosbie vowed. But then again it could be said that Crosbie was inclined to be a bit backward about coming forward on the work front. The job in the Banjo Bar didn't suit him he said – the hours were all wrong. The Civil Service was for arse lickers. And before that again, just out of school, he'd been offered an apprenticeship in a men's drapery store down town which had lasted all of three weeks. The manager was a sergeant-major for starters, he explained, and measuring men's inside legs was not exactly Crosbie's forte either. *I Joined the Navy/ To See The World/ And What Did I See/ I Saw The Sea ... .*

A few miles up the road Daly went into a pub and ordered a half of ale and a bag of peanuts. The place was in an awful state from the night before – screwed up racing dockets and bits of old newspapers and a mark that looked like someone had dragged a dead body from A to B and back again. Jesus, what went on here? The barman served him, handed him yesterday's soggy Evening Herald and told him to go sit in the corner out of harm's way with the added addendum, 'We're not even supposed to be open yet.'

The barman – who must also have been the owner – was going hither and thither, filling the shelves and calling into what sounded like his wife in the living area at the back of the shop. Daly could hear her distant replies,' Ask my arse,' being one of them.

'I'd rather not,' the barman muttered to no one in particular.

And then a red faced mariner came in. 'Did I leave a big rope here last night?' he wondered accusingly from the windy doorway.

'Ask herself inside there,' came the answer. '… if she's done with it!'

The red faced mariner disappeared into the living quarters and returned a few minutes later with his rope intact, mumbled a fond farewell and left, leaving the door ajar after him which Daly took it upon himself to close.

'Did you recognise that fella?' the crouched barman wished to know, his head appearing like a puppet over the tip of the counter.

'No,' Daly piped.

'Martin Hall. Tug-of-War. No? … He's a whore for ropes, that lad is. Goes through them by the new time I believe.'

Apart from that incident there was no real atmosphere in the place and so Daly drank up and left, bringing the unopened peanuts with him. They'd be missing him at the office round about now. Young Mister Lawson would be inquiring after him. Karen would agree that it was odd: no phone call, no doctor's note, nothing. Twenty five years and never missed a day. Well, granted, he did go home early once or twice – an earache one day, and a sudden bout of vertigo another. And of course from time to time he'd feel a bit under the weather – colds and flus and the like. But a few Beecham's powders and a hot toddy at lunch time (old Mister Lawson's remedy) usually put paid to that.

He pictured them all, well Karen and Crawford anyway, rummaging round for stuff: a file they couldn't locate, a notice that needed an urgent response of some sort. They'd probably ring his home to see where he was. His wife would take the call. Naturally enough she'd jump to all manner of conclusions. Crosbie, the seasoned gambler, would get the blame – try the race track, or the betting shop, or that new snooker hall in the Mall. Or an accident maybe, a frantic search through drawers and dressers for that insurance policy which she'd threatened not to renew. No, Marian Bowles though. Daly had been engaged to Marian Bowles once upon a time and her name was never too far below the surface, dredged up to whip him with in times of trouble. Marian Bowles did this and Marian Bowles did the other thing. 'Go back to Marian Bowles, why don't you,' was the constant refrain.

Crosbie might be hauled in for questioning. And even from the dock he'd play her like a violin. 'What was he wearing when he left the house? You don't know? Did he shave? Shower? Shampoo? Aftershave? Ah, yes, I see said the blind man.' In the end, like an overwound cuckoo clock, she'd put on her coat and go down to Healy and Doyle's Department Store to make sure that Marian Bowles hadn't taken the day off too.

On the way back into town Daly pulled over to the side to study his favourite field again – golden and glorious as it swept down to the sea. He often fantasised about running through this field with his shoes off. Or walking through it with some woman maybe – hand in hand. Not his wife, no. Marian Bowles perhaps. Yeah, Crosbie spying on them from the long grass as the pheasant hecked and hopped and hobbled nearby. Marian Bowles had hinted once or twice when she was going out with him that he wasn't nearly half as adventurous as she'd like him to be. What on earth did she expect him to do to her he couldn't help wondering sometimes. When it was all over between them, with Daly's reluctant blessing, Crosbie decided to tackle her himself, only to get short shrift.

'You're vain, ignorant, self centred, mean, thick, over-weight and ugly,' were some of the reasons she rattled off when Crosbie asked her why she wouldn't agree to go out with him.

'No need for it,' Crosbie complained. 'I mean a straight-forward "*I'd rather not,*" would have done me.'

⁓

The Pond. Some people called it The Otter Pond, others referred to it as Rainwater, but himself and Crosbie knew it merely as ***The Pond***, as if it was the only one. Daly pulled into the patch of waste ground and with the radio on he drank his soup. The cream crackers and cheese he'd save for later. What's the time? Eleven thirty three. By right at this moment in time he should be in – no, coming out of though – the Coffee Pot Café. Linda might ask someone about him, one of the young solicitors or the junior clerk, or Karen if she happened to slip across for a croissant.

'He's gone walkabouts apparently,' Karen would tell her.

'Is he now?' Linda was sure to say. 'Mmn … he's a dark horse.'

Daly had been coming out to ***The Pond*** for more years than he cared to remember. It was not officially his neck of the woods of course. In fact Crosbie was the one who had introduced him to it first, when they were both in short pants practically. And although the place was usually frequented by hard cases, (who by the way were fairly tribal about their territory) nobody ever bothered them. Chances are they had Daly pegged as a harmless birdwatcher, which somewhere in the depths of his secret recesses he sadly lamented. Or maybe it was Crosbie who could be described as an unknown entity to say the least: a policeman's son who was big, confident, brash and reasonably wise to the ways of the world. No, while other interlopers were frowned upon and at times punished – tied to posts, dumped headfirst into the water, shoes taken, chased off with stones, shirts ripped and torn, faces washed and fed with horseshit and God-only-knows-what other form of torture – for some strange reason or other Daly and Crosbie were generally left alone, ignored almost. And so while the locals – Tommy Day and Apache Bryne and the Bradley brothers and the boys – went (like fugitives from some cowboy film) about their business, Daly and Crosbie would sit hunched on the rock in the sun, taking it all in.

The day Maureen'Custard' Healy challenged them all to some sort of a contest, for instance! Maureen 'Custard' Healy was a wild, ferocious creature with broken teeth and dirty fingernails. The first time Daly laid eyes on her she was involved in a fist fight with a little cockney guy who had dared to laugh at her accent. She beat him senseless, knocked him down a grassy bank and into a bed of nettles where he gladly lay lifeless until she was out of sight. And here she was on this bright May day leading the rowdy gang into the roofless house-cum-handball alley, spurring Daly and Crosbie to sit up and wonder. Daly didn't dare follow, fearing he'd be roped into something inappropriate, but Crosbie did, with the haughty air of a paid observer whose duty it was to report back to Party Headquarters. Riddled with misgivings, Daly sat there, timidly waiting, until Crosbie, arms swinging, came strolling back with the news. Maureen 'Custard' Healy had challenged them all to an up-the-wall pissing competition, he announced. She went first, Daly was told, squatting down and widdling an inch or two up the wall to much derision and laughter. Apache Bryne was the next to go. He opened his pants and whipped out his weapon (Seamus O Hoolahan Flynn in Crosbie's terminology) and proudly pointed it towards the ceiling, grinning like a chimpanzee until Maureen 'Custard' Healy stepped forward and insisted on a '*No Hands*' rule.

'And that' declared Crosbie, 'was that!'

Another afternoon – later that same summer – the gang decided to settle for once and for all who was the biggest and best. Maureen 'Custard' Healy, in spite of the fact that she was no Venus in blue jeans, was called in once again to act as judge and jury. Yet again Daly watched aghast from afar as Crosbie, in the thick of it, witnessed one after the other of them whipping out – as he put it – Seamus O Hoolahan Flynn to be considered and felt and measured and weighed in the noon day sun. In the end the award surprisingly went to a little wizened character with a pigeon chest and a club foot who had appeared unbidden out of nowhere. Maureen 'Custard' Healy took one look and swore he was in a league of his own.

'Yes, out on his own she said he was,' Crosbie maintained.

'Yeah?' Daly cried, incredulously.

'Yeah, 'Crosbie assured him. 'Well, let me put it this way,' he said then just to drive his point home. 'You wouldn't want it over your eye for a wart.'

The fact that Daly grew up to become a solicitor's clerk proved to be a godsend for many of these people who were, by nature, delinquent. They'd seek him out at the back of the courtroom to ask him what the judge meant by '*consecutive*,' and '*concurrent*', and '*sub judice*'. And even today they still looked for him as their children and grandchildren came before the courts – drunk and disorderly, drunk and incapable, drunk and abusive, drunk and in charge of a bicycle. Not one of them ever admitted to being sober at the time of their arrest which led Daly to presume that they were using it as some sort of a defence against something – a charge of snobbery most like.

In fact it was a son of Maureen 'Custard' Healy's (Murphy was her married name) who was to turn the unwitting Daly into a sort of a working class hero. The young man showed up one morning for trial in total disarray – unshaved and shabby with an unironed shirt and a rumpled old jacket and his hair tangled and unkempt. Mister Moran, his solicitor, shook his head and groaned at the sight of him as Daly ushered the culprit into a nearby lavatory where he produced a comb and an electric razor and proceeded to brush down the dusty jacket before loaning the lad his green spotted tie. The solicitor was delighted with the transformation and when the accused got off with a warning it was mostly put down to the tie. The following week some other ne'er-do-well asked Daly for the use of it and the same bloke – who should have received six months by right – got off with a light fine and a stern warning. The green spotted tie became something of a good luck charm henceforth with criminals of every shade and hue lining up to wear it.

'What is this green tie business?' a visiting judge was overheard to say to old Mister Lawson one day at the top of the winding staircase. 'Some sort of a secret sect or something?'

Daly, hands in pockets, was standing beside the dark pond, watching a curlew and a sandpiper dart and darn. He rambled down onto the pebbled strand to catch sight of a heron wading across the mudflats on its spindly stilts. A hint of rain sent him into the planked makeshift hut where he studied the graffiti: *What Are You Looking At?* the cracked mirror wanted to know in smeared lipstick. *Prick … . Shit … . MINGE …* and *SHARON'S MOTHER IS A WHORE …* Very nice!

Daly's wife would have called in the sisters at this stage – all three of them. They'd be planning and scheming and ringing around, despatching their hen-pecked husbands off in different directions to look for him. Crosbie's influence would be brought up and no doubt other episodes recalled.

The time Crosbie had to carry him home from the Forester's Reunion might be revisited. Talk about drunk and incapable.

'You were like our Lord on the cross,' Crosbie would remind him later when he disputed the story.

'I wasn't that bad now, Crosbie,' Daly protested, a little ashamed that three pints of Guinness and a half an ale shandy could have got him into such a state.

'I had to carry you up to bed,' Crosbie pointed out. 'Over my shoulder like a sack of spuds.'

'Oh yeah,' Daly conceded.

'Yeah.'

The midday train went rattling by and he had a good mind to do something mad, rise up and put his tongue out at someone or give someone the finger or something; or pull his hat to one side maybe and slouch along like a dribbling imbecile beside it. '*Chu chu train … Chu chu … train …*'

It began to rain for real as he hurried back to the car where he ate his cream crackers and drank the rest of the soup and listened to the radio for a while before falling asleep in the back seat. When he woke up the rain had stopped and it was sunny. He got out and scrambled up onto the mossy rock where he sat hunched in the sun in a fashion reminiscent of the past.

'Any sign of him?' one of the sisters would be screeching into her mobile phone at this point in time. In fact all the sisters would be talking simultaneously, anxious and loud and cacophonous, embracing the tragedy for all it was worth. His wife would remain silent however, earnestly preparing for widowhood and secretly hatching her plan to call the children – Damien in London and Doris in an adjacent estate; they'd need to be told before she reluctantly agreed to drag the streams, rivers and local reservoirs.

Daly, prising open the bag of peanuts, began to hatch a plan of his own. He'd need an excuse, a good excuse. For Young Mister Lawson tomorrow, who it must be said was full of his own importance these days, conveniently forgetting that he was once a bit of a rake himself. That was when old Mister Lawson ruled the roost in the office. An old established man – with his '*Daly*' and his '*Crawford*' and his, '*send the lassie into me this instant.*' Young Mister Lawson was constantly in trouble back then: a fight in a dance hall, an illicit affair with a married woman, a drunken escapade or two, rugby songs sung and chanted in crowded taverns and bars. Daly and Karen and Crawford would often line up outside the main office, listening to Old Mister Lawson giving the young man inside a good dressing down. Recently though young Mister Lawson had taken to wearing three piece suits in place of casual slacks and jacket, and he proudly sported striped braces of late instead of a buckled belt. He'd gone pale and grey practically overnight. And, as if on cue, he was going bald as well. He ate mints and dined out at lunchtime. He'd even joined the Rotary Club for God's sake.

'Something came up,' Daly would tell him tomorrow from the mat. 'Something important … .. Personal.'

'What?' he'd want to know.

'I'd rather not say.'

Young Mister Lawson wouldn't like that of course. He'd make that nasal sound and pinch his lower lip and he'd knock the desk with the first two knuckles of his right hand and murmur, 'Fair enough, ask Karen to come into me,' as if he was going to run the matter by her before meting out the necessary penalty.

Daly wouldn't mind but young Mister Lawson was only a wet day in charge. In fact it was Daly who first happened on the dead Old Mister Lawson, sitting upright like

Buddha on the toilet bowl with his glasses askew, a magazine on his lap, and his pants down around his ankles. Daly couldn't believe it at first. He called out to him, reached in and tipped him and everything, which was odd because the dead man's eyes were wide open. And then, weighing up the situation and realising that the first one on the scene would be the one who'd come in for most of the hassle – ringing the ambulance and the doctor and the police and explaining it all to everyone and all the rest of it, maybe even becoming involved in cleaning up the old man, pulling up his trousers and all that that entailed – Daly, his heart pounding, decided on a different course of action. He'd pretend he never knew. With that thought in mind he closed over the toilet door and a few moments later he was peeping into the outer office to inform Karen that he was taking an early lunch, and he grabbed his coat and slipped down the stairs and across the road to The Menapia Hotel, where they'd never think of looking for him. When he got back it was all over. Karen was crying into a rolled up handkerchief on the landing and Crawford was on the phone to young Mister Lawson, and the police and the ambulance and the doctor had been and gone. Daly acted shocked and horrified, hugging Karen and comforting Crawford, and when young Mister Lawson arrived he shook his hand and sympathised with him, and when the young man had left he took it upon himself to shut up shop early and give everyone the rest of the day off.

Crosbie made him tell the story several times, interrupting him on and off and plying him with questions. What magazine was the old man reading at the time, and what page was open, and what kind of an expression was he wearing? Daly answered as best he could, feigning distaste now and again while secretly enjoying it all, particularly when Crosbie made him retell how he had closed over the toilet door, grabbed his coat and left them all to their fate. Crosbie said it put him in mind of the night porter from the Menapia Hotel years ago who could sleep with his eyes wide open, hence inadvertently scuppering the wily plans of small time con men and randy commercial travellers. What was his name? Benson! Or Fenton? Something like that.

Daly stood up and stretched, looked around and embraced the rain-drenched wilderness. He must do this more often, he silently pledged. He should have done it before in fact. Pity Crosbie hadn't tagged along really, for old time's sake.

'I'd keep out of his way for the rest of the week if I was you,' Karen might advice Daly as she'd pass him in the corridor the following morning. 'He's not that happy with you at all, you know … .Where did you go anyway?'

'Ask my arse,' Daly would feel like saying to her, but of course he wouldn't.

MYSTIC

Some people called him a mystic, others labelled him a bum while Butler's da was of the opinion that he was a bit of a hippy with long, greasy red hair down to his shoulders and the makings of a ginger beard and a rake of tattoos: one on each arm and one on his forehead and another on his backside depicting the devil shovelling coal up his rear end; although how Butler's da knew all of this was another matter. They also said that Mystic (which is what the boys decided to call him), slept in a hammock and he wore a big, gold earring in his left ear all the time. He could charm the birds out of the sky too they said, to alight on his outstretched arms and land on his shoulders and even the top of his head sometimes, eating bread and crumbs and scraps of food from his tantalising fingertips. But more important than all of that, Mystic kept a real live pet snake and if he liked the look of you he just might let you see it.

Derek was the first to arrive at the meeting place, down on the quay where the skateboarders rendezvoused and already, at ten to twelve on this cold September Saturday morning, the place was heaving. He spied one of the boys from his class out there, popping tricks and flipping and rolling and grinding, his arms extended like a skier and his breath steaming from his mouth like cigar smoke. Derek had never tried skateboarding – although he knew most of the terms – and looking at it up close like this he didn't think he ever would try it now. For a start you would have to hurt yourself first before you got the hang of it; you'd fall or slip, graze your knee or bang your shinbone or scrape your elbows off the ground. You might even break your leg. A boy he knew (well a fairly big lad actually) fell off his board last year and broke his leg in three places. He spent most of the summer in the hospital where the food was supposed to be awful – the dinners anyway!

Derek wished it were possible to learn to do something without any pain, without any anguish. Sometimes it seemed that absolutely everything, even safe pursuits – joining the library or a computer class or the boy scouts or even the altar boys – held their fair share of grief for a novice; if not physical pain then there was bound to be embarrassment of some sort; not knowing where to sit or what to do when the break came, whether to bring sand-wiches or not or should you just bring the money to buy something from the shop: if there was a shop.

Derek gestured gently to the boy from his class, Wedger Ruttledge, who, to Derek's surprise, gladly waved back to him and gave him a high five and called his name out loud. 'Derek,' he cried, joyfully. Wedger took a tumble, but he got straight back up and went at it again, nose grinding his way over to the sloping sea wall, showing off, Derek thought, now that he knew that someone was watching him. Mallon approached, wearing a hooded jacket and a nifty bag on his back, well equipped for the expedition by anyone's standards. He looked up and down the road several times before he crossed the busy street.

Derek had got out of bed early enough that morning, careful not to disturb his younger brother Anthony who was still snuggled up and sleeping in the bed beside him. Derek covered him up and tiptoed out onto the landing where he put on his pants and shirt and rustling jumper. He went down the stairs to find his father lying on the couch with a few blankets pulled up around him. His father got up and put on his trousers and said, 'She was in her act again last night,' and he tidied the blankets away, bundling them carelessly into the hot press. 'I'll tell you,' he said, going into the bathroom. 'I've just about had it with her now.'

Derek didn't really know what '*in her act*' meant. His mother had headaches from time to time and she was inclined to take to her bed for days on end. Was that an act? And what did he mean by '*had it*'? He switched on the radio and made his breakfast: cornflakes and toast, a big glass of orange juice and a pot of tea. His father came out of the bathroom, mumbled one or two incoherent sentences, swallowed a quick cup of coffee, affectionately tousled Derek's head of hair (which in hindsight would hold some hidden significance), and then he went down the hall without a word and the boy heard the front door slam. 'In her act,' Derek mumbled, just to see how it sounded coming from his own mouth.

Derek had his breakfast, checked on his pigeons, fed and watered them and swept out the loft and then he returned to the house and went back upstairs again to peep into his mother's bedroom. The place was in complete darkness, the curtains drawn tight around the windows. Clothes were strewn wildly around the room, arrayed on the end of the bed and dangling from the back of a chair and piled in a multi-coloured heap in the corner, like some mad woman's lair. There was that usual stale smell in there too. Vic or ointment mingled with the smell of something else, porter or whisky or something. Her pills were spilt out onto the dressing table, the cotton wool spewing like innards from the overturned container. An upended coffee cup sat on the floor beside the bed, dripping its coagulated contents onto the already well-stained carpet. Two miniature empty bottles of whisky posed like a still life on the bedside locker. Anthony used to love to save those bottles. He'd tear off the labels and wash the bottles clean and play shop with them. He had a fairly plentiful supply of them too until his father, in a fit of temper one day, swept the lot of them up into his arms and dumped them all into the dustbin in the yard, oblivious to Anthony's tears.

His mother must have had another pain last night. She must have had one of her headaches, or *one of her spells* as she sometimes called them. Derek stepped inside the threshold. 'Are you all right Mam?' he asked, tentatively.

'Mmn,' she mumbled without even turning around, barely stirring in fact.

'I'm goin' now,' he said and waited. 'Mam!'

'Huh?' his mother murmured, her voice small and faint.

'I said I'm goin' now,' he told her, but she did not reply. He was hoping she'd give him some money to spend. Just before he left the room she slowly turned and gazed at him through a pair of sorrowful, lifeless eyes, a look he was learning to detest.

Mallon arrived at his side, taking off his glasses and wiping them in his jumper.

'Any sign of the others?' he wondered.

'No,' Derek told him. 'No sign yet anyway.'

'There's Wedger,' Mallon cried excitedly and called out to the boy from their class in the distance who signalled back at him and appeared to be telling some of the other skaters – much to Mallon's delight – that the two of them were from his class.

Derek hoped that Wedger would not want to tag along with them to see the snake when he found out where they were going. Mystic didn't like too many people showing up (or so they said anyway). Not that Derek begrudged Wedger a chance to see the snake or anything but Mystic might get annoyed and chase them away.

'I hope this fellow won't expect us to hold this snake now or anything,' Mallon was saying. 'No way would I touch a snake. Would you Derek?'

'I wouldn't mind,' Derek said, although in his heart of hearts he was hoping that he would not be called upon to do so.

'Well, you're on your own then,' Mallon confessed.

Mallon was afraid of everything and not ashamed to admit it either, whereas Butler was afraid of nothing and would have a go at anything, regardless of the danger or the inevitable consequences. Derek was somewhere between the two, afraid of everything but willing to risk anything to save face in front of the others. Derek sometimes wondered if maybe it might be better to be one thing or another – an out and out coward or a foolhardy fool. If Mystic asked him to handle the snake then he would, but he wouldn't lose any sleep over it if he didn't get to hold it.

'Where are you goin', Derek?' his kid brother Anthony had asked that morning as Derek tried to creep quietly down the stairs. Anthony was standing on the landing in his ruffled pyjamas and his hair on end.

'I've to go out for a while,' Derek told him.

'Will you turn on the telly for me before you go?' Anthony wondered in a sleepy voice.

'Are you not wantin' to get back into the bed for a while?' Derek suggested. The house was cold.

'No,' Anthony replied. 'I'm wantin' to watch the telly.'

'Alright,' Derek said. 'Get a blanket then and I'll turn it on for you.'

Derek left young Anthony on the couch watching the television, a blanket wrapped around him and a tray on his lap with cornflakes and hot milk and luke-warm tea in his Manchester United cup.

'I hope Butler won't ask this lad Mystic to show us this snake now,' Mallon was saying. 'I mean you know Butler when he gets goin'.'

'He won't,' Derek assured him.

You weren't supposed to ask Mystic to show you the snake by the way. You weren't supposed to expect anything from him that he was not prepared to give you of his own accord. Butler's da said that he heard that Mystic gave a couple of lads the bum's rush one day last week for jumping the gun, chased them off down the beach brandishing a big blackthorn stick, and all because they asked to see the snake when they should have waited for an invitation.

The mid-day train was thundering towards them, humping and bumping and clattering over the sleepers, the driver hooting the horn to warn everybody that he was coming. The skaters stopped skating and turned to wave and the two boys stopped talking and Derek gazed up at the mute and miming passengers who resembled characters trapped inside a moving tableau and he felt both equally at home and at sea with them, all at the same time: a sad eyed lady drinking tea from a polystyrene cup; a man with a quiff smoking, plumes of smoke curling up all around him; a uniformed conductor moving from seat to seat, chastising the man for smoking in a public place; the man with the quiff protesting that there was no sign up and the conductor issuing an ultimatum. There was a child there too, a young girl, kneeling up and looking out the window, singing softly for her own amusement. Derek wondered what she was singing, some nursery rhyme more than likely. And he wondered too who was supposed to be minding her: no one as far as he could make out. When the coast was clear again Egan was miraculously standing on the other side of the tracks.

'Where's Butler?' Mallon called out to him.

Egan aimed his head towards the skaters where Butler could be seen in full flight, balanced precariously on Wedger's board, his arms outstretched and his face twisted up in an aspect of delighted agony. Derek frowned and looked to Egan for solace but of course, as usual, Egan's face betrayed no impression one way or another. Derek sometimes harboured the notion that Egan would one day join the French Foreign Legion and die on some foreign battlefield in some far away land and no one would ever really be any the wiser about him.

Mallon called out to Butler to come on and Derek joined him in the refrain but between the two of them the sound they made hardly constituted a noise at all. Butler came in his own good time. He had a baseball hat turned back to front and baggy pants and a big woolly jumper that went right down to his knees.

'Any of you bring any sandwiches?' he wondered and then without waiting for a reply he said, 'I'm after eatin' all of mine already,' and Egan silently testified that this was true.

And off they went, ambling along the railway tracks, bidding farewell to Wedger Ruttledge who was clearly wondering where they were bound. Around the first bend they stopped to gaze in at the old defunct gas works yard, which always put Derek in mind of something from a science fiction story – gigantic vats and pipes and rusty gantries and steel vertical ladders going nowhere.

'One match now lads and … boom,' Butler declared, his heavy face pressed against the bars of the big wrought iron gate. 'The whole town, boy. Well, half of it anyway.'

Mallon's eyes grew large at the very idea of half the town going up in smoke. Egan remained stoic as ever. Derek made a faint ambiguous sound that, as far as he was concerned anyway, neither confirmed nor contradicted what Butler had just said; but Butler sensed the mutinous intention and glared sidelong at him and snarled and belched directly into his face so that Derek blushed and wished he could be like Egan who was able to conceal his thoughts so well. And then, just like that, Butler decided to race them all as far as the deserted railway station and he took off, pushing the nimble Mallon back and cursing Egan for passing him out.

Derek did not like racing and so he walked, shuffling from sleeper to sleeper one minute, tiptoeing on the track like a ropewalker the next, and finally stepping gingerly along the narrow sea wall for comfort. The wall was covered in seaweed, which squelched and popped beneath him, and the bittersweet bouquet of the sea was everywhere. A green wreck of a boat was careened on its side on a rugged patch of beach, weeds and wild flowers sprouting through the cracks. A seagull landed on it and fluttered. Derek took a pot shot at it with a make believe catapult as the train moaned in the distance and wriggled off to the far side of the sandy peninsula.

The other boys had reached the station by now and were calling to Derek to hurry up, their voices faint and distant. 'Yeah, right,' Derek said softly, so low he was hard set to hear it himself. Anthony would be getting bored round about now, flipping from channel to channel, maybe getting up from the couch to get himself a biscuit, running back to his warm blanket again to watch another cartoon. He'd hear his mother's footsteps on the landing, slipping across to the bathroom and then he'd hear her stumbling back to bed again. Someone might rustle the letterbox and

Anthony would grow nervouse and he'd turn up the volume on the telly to drown out the sound.

When Derek arrived at the deserted railway station the others were hiding on him in one of the waiting rooms. He went in through the door and they nipped noiselessly out the window and when he heard them tittering outside it made him feel foolish, like that time at the party when he was the first one caught out in the game of musical chairs. He looked out the window to see the three boys stealing towards the lofty signal box, Mallon stalling on the wooden weathered staircase to marvel at it all: the ghostly station with the nettles and thistles and dandelions growing up through the paving slabs and the navy blue bench rotten to the core now and the dilapidated sign saying *The South Side* dangling down, hanging by a tread, and the windows all smashed and the roof gone and the wind whipping the dirty cans and old newspapers up into tumbleweeds.

Derek had actually come across an old photograph of this station recently – down in the snooker hall or behind the counter in the Banjo Bar or somewhere. He couldn't really recall where he had seen it now – somewhere: the platform was swept clean and a packed train was standing at the station, puffing and impatient to be off; and the station master was there in his uniform and glistening whistle as a young woman ran for the train beneath a clear summer sky, holding on to her hat; and beyond all of that there was a vague, distant lustre of sea. Where was it he had seen that now? – somewhere!

As Derek made his way up into the signal box he could see Butler standing in the doorway imitating a well known local tour guide, mimicking his clipped accent to a tee and exaggerating his hand movements as he called out all the things worth seeing from up there.

'On my left we have the harbour,' Butler was saying, 'both ancient and modern all at the same time. Ancient from the point of view that it's old ... very old. And modern because it's not. Ha Ha Ha ... On the other hand I have four fingers and a thumb ... '

Mallon was laughing uproariously – overdoing it in Derek's estimation – and even Egan was not immune to it all. When Derek entered the room Butler put his finger to his lips to indicate that an interloper had just infiltrated the ranks, and when Derek was safely inside Butler ushered the others out and banged the door in Derek's face, shutting him in. And they laughed and pointed and jeered him through the glass partition and then they tramped noisily back down the wooden staircase again without him.

Derek turned to survey the shimmering harbour: the Black Man, Useless Island, the bridge spanned across the river where the cars and lorries looked like dinky toys. He could see the trawlers and dredgers and mussel boats and the yachts competing out beyond the bar. And off in the other direction the town with its grey slanted rooftops. He must bring Anthony up here someday soon and show him all of this, he vowed as he turned to leave.

He came down onto the platform again to find the others crossing the tracks towards an old, abandoned carriage that had been left stranded on the far side of a disused section of the railway line.

'Were any of you two ever in here before?' Butler was asking them.

Mallon shook his head. Egan shrugged.

'What?' Butler wondered and Egan repeated the performance. 'Was that a yes or a no?' Butler asked him, niggled now. Sometimes Egan could get on your nerves, the way he went on, making out that he knew everything when he didn't. 'Huh?' Butler said again, putting his ear to Egan's mouth, but Egan just made a face and pretended he didn't know what Butler was on about. 'Well we were, weren't we Derek?' Butler called over his shoulder, his voice reverberating across the deep ravine of tracks that contained him.

'What?' Derek called after them.

'In here before!' Butler bellowed as he led the others up into the carriage.

Derek stayed on the opposite platform, looking up and down. He knew what was in there. Some local lads had turned the place into a sort of a clubhouse – candles and kettle and cups and posters and all that kind of stuff. The last time (the first time they discovered it) Butler and Derek got caught red-handed in there. A few young lads came in and told them to beat it. Butler told them to get lost, that this didn't belong to them, that it was public property and that their days were numbered, and the young fellows ran off to get their big brothers and Derek and Butler were chased off down the railway tracks by a posse of bigger boys who soon arrived on the scene, stones flying and curses hurled after them. When they were halfway home Butler produced the rusted silver cup he had stolen – a sort of a trophy – and Derek didn't see why he had to go and do a thing like that, but of course you couldn't say anything like that to Butler or he'd just turn around and do the same thing again, or worse even!

'Derek,' Mallon cried from the doorway and he beckoned for Derek to come on over and see it.

Derek turned aside and silently cursed Butler. Why couldn't they just get to where they were supposed to be going instead of this lark. This was the other side of the town as far as he was concerned. Salty Way and Oyster Avenue and Mermaid Lane and Harbour View. The boys and girls from around here were salty people. They had weather beaten faces and hooded eyes. Their fathers were fishermen and their mothers usually worked in the laundry. And they wouldn't take too kindly to them marauding their clubhouse; they hadn't the last time and they certainly wouldn't this time either.

Derek stepped off the platform and crossed the tracks towards the railway carriage. He hoped Anthony would be all right. He hadn't lit a fire because he knew there wouldn't be enough coal to last the day and anyway he was afraid that Anthony might set fire to himself with the big blanket wrapped around him. His father usually worked a few hours overtime on Saturday mornings and would spend the afternoon in the Banjo Bar, nipping in and out of the betting shop before the start of every race. His mother would probably not get out of bed until early afternoon. She'd come down the stairs bleary-eyed and mope about listlessly for the rest of the day and would probably go back to bed in the evening. He hoped Anthony would be all right. Maybe he shouldn't have come here today. Maybe he should have stayed at home to mind him.

He entered the carriage and found Butler and Egan and Mallon sprawled all over the seats, making themselves at home in there.

'Come in,' Butler said to him. 'Sit down there out of that and take the weight off your feet.' And then he laughed – a menacing sound – and Derek knew that the visit would be prolonged even longer than was necessary because Butler was well aware that Derek was on edge over it. And when it was eventually time for them to leave Butler encouraged the others to fill their pockets with stuff: a hurling ball and sweets and a set of darts he pulled from the dart board and a pack of playing cards and a picture of Robbie Keane in action and anything else that took their fancy. And although Derek did his best to hide his annoyance, nevertheless, his face was full of it so that Butler grabbed hold of him around the neck and held him in a playful head lock in an attempt to make light of it all.

The next stop was the Shelter where the fishermen moored their flat bottomed boats: blue ones and green ones and red ones with names scrawled and painted on their sides – *Shenandoah* and *Inishfree* and *The Wild Rover and Laramie.* A handful of men were gathered there, sitting on an upturned boat and conversing loudly, their angry dogs close by. The boys passed beneath their suspicious, feral gaze, like weary pilgrims. Well, they would have passed had Butler not decided to go over to them at the last minute and addle them all with childish questions. What's this and what's that and what do you use this for and all the rest of it?

'That's a noodle na,' one of them declared, a contrary looking man. 'For catchin' winkles,' he said with a conspiratorial wink to the other men who smirked and smiled crookedly at one another.

'Ha ha ha,' Butler said over his shoulder as he walked away. 'Very funny. Tell us when to laugh.' And then Butler shouted something rude at them and took off at a lick and the others followed suit, little Mallon laughing nervously as he ran. And Derek had to run too this time because one of the men cursed loudly and picked up a buoy which he half heartedly flung after them, and Derek was glad that Anthony was not there to see him running away like that.

∽

'Make a wish,' Butler said as they drank from the Holy Well and Mallon closed his eyes and his lips moved.

Egan caught some water in his cupped hands and slurped it up and then dowsed his face with whatever was left. Butler plunged his whole head under the spout and then he filled his baseball hat with water and put it on his head so that little rivulets sluiced down his back and face comically. The Holy Well was encased inside a roofed niche and the words *Aqua Pura 1948* were embossed on a plaque overhead.

'What do that mean?' Butler wondered as he stepped back to let Derek into the alcove.

'Aqua Pura,' Derek read. '1948 … Well Aqua means water and I suppose Pura means pure so …' and Derek sort of shrugged to indicate that the answer was fairly obvious.

'Huh?' Butler said, sitting up on the ivied roof of the well now.

'Pure water,' Egan announced as if he had just solved the conundrum.

'I know that you dumbo,' Butler snarled back. 'The 1948 part I mean? Was it built in 1948? Did they first find it in '48? Did they put this sign up that time? Or was that the year your dumb da bawled his big red headed way into the world? What?'

'Whose dumb da?' Egan asked him earnestly.

'Your dumb da,' Butler challenged, climbing down to plod Egan's chest with the tip of his index finger. 'Why, what about it?'

'Nothing,' Egan replied and then under his breath he muttered wryly, 'It's just that my Da was born in '52.'

'Yeah,' Butler said then. '1852, judgin' by the wrinkles … Dumbo!'

Derek suppressed a smile – someone else's turn for a change. He took a few sips of water and declared softly that it tasted sweet.

'Did you make a wish, Derek?' Butler wanted to know.

'No,' Derek told him.

'Why not? … Not into it?'

'No,' Derek said, which was true; he had wished and hoped and prayed for things in the past and it never seemed to do any good.

'How about you Butler?' Mallon inquired.

'What,' Butler snapped.

'What did you wish for?'

'World peace!' Butler announced and he stuck his tongue out and made a face at a few children who were playing on the nearby grassy bank.

'I wonder what kind of a snake is it?' Mallon mused as they tramped along the railway line.

'I heard it was a python,' Butler said. 'A beautiful looking thing I believe. Although someone else said it was a viper.'

'Let's hope not,' Mallon said. 'They're poisonous.'

'A boa constrictor'd be worst,' Butler informed him. 'Crush you to death. Slowly.'

'It won't be crushin' me to death anyway,' Mallon assured him. 'Because I won't be next or near it in the first place.'

They were at the back of the laundry now. A weary collection of women were taking a break, standing on top of the bank, smoking cigarettes and eating Tayto crisps and drinking from tins of coke, which they passed back and forth from one to the other.

'How are you Bernie,' Butler called up to one of them.

'How's it goin' young fella?' she shouted back down to him. 'Where are you goin'?'

'Rainwater Pond to see the snake,' Butler told her.

'Oh, right,' she said.' How's your da?'

'Grand.'

'Did he get his new teeth yet?'

'Yeah. Last week.'

'Lovely,' she said.

Derek spied a friend of his father's up there too. A dark haired woman with a pretty face and what could only be described as a petite nose. Derek first saw her sitting up at the counter with his father in the Banjo Bar. It was the day

Anthony got his hand caught in the door and his mother was having one of her spells, and Derek had to go down and ask his father to come home. And another time as he was passing the bar he had looked in through the window and there they were again, sitting at a table – this woman and his father. And one more time on the street he saw them together. Derek wondered now if she recognised him, but he got no hint of it from her if she did.

'Do you smell that lads?' Butler was saying as they moved along, stopping in his tracks all of a sudden.

'No,' Mallon said, anxiously. 'What?'

'Plums,' Butler said and his eyes lit up as he looked from one boy to the next.

'Butler,' Derek pleaded, reasonably. 'The plums are that way and we're goin' this way.'

'Not necessarily,' Butler said and he branched off up the bank with the others at his heels.

Derek stood stock-still: he didn't need another detour.

'What's the matter, Derek?' Butler called down to him from the top of the hill and then drifting into a deep southern drawl he said, 'Cat got your tongue?'

Mallon laughed, recognising the film the line came from, and he gave Derek an exaggerated signal to follow.

Derek caught up with them in the wild overgrown graveyard. They walked in succession and in silence; even Butler was somewhat subdued as they trampled through the tangle of briars and brambles and nettles and ferns, stepping on and over hidden gravestones and graves. Butler, from time to time, would glance over his shoulder at the others and grimace at some crooked wooden cross or some shadowy shape or some airy graveyard sound. The foliage was so thick that Mallon practically disappeared from view at one point.

'Where's Mallon gone?' someone said.

'I'm over here,' Mallon shrieked like a friendly ghost.

A big proud looking oak tree demarcated the boundary between the graveyard and Slattery's Field and this is where Butler hatched the plan, mapping it out on the ground with a piece of stick, behaving like an army general in *The Thin Red Line*.

'Right you guys,' Butler said in a fake American voice, taking off his hat and hanging it on a branch of the tree. 'Here's where we are. And there's that ditch there and just over it on the other side of that field of green yonder lies *The Orchard Of Plums*. All we're required to do now is to go in and get them.'

'Hang on Butler,' Mallon interrupted. 'Is that a wall I see?'

'A wall?' Butler said. 'Why of course. You don't expect them to grow the plums on the outside where every Jack the Shilling can just walk up and take them of their own free will now do you? There's a six foot wall there and we have to scale it.'

'How do we get back out?' Egan asked him, sensibly.

'Tell him Derek,' Butler said.

'There's a side gate that we can open from the inside.' Derek answered.

'Yeah and when I give the word we're all out of there,' Butler barked. 'No matter how many plums you have in your pockets or your mouths or your hands! Right? I've never left a man behind me yet and I've no intention of startin' with you lot. Now, any questions?

'Yeah,' Mallon piped up.' What happens if we're caught.'

'Tell them your name is Wedger Ruttledge and run,' was Butler's advice.

They clambered over the ditch and into the field that sloped down to Slattery's Mansion. A crucified scarecrow with a tattered old hat marked the centre of the field and this is where they squatted to hear Butler's final instructions so that anyone watching them from afar would swear that the scarecrow was part of the platoon too.

'There it is lads,' Butler said. 'Slattery's Mansion. Fourteen windows they say, fifteen rooms. One of the windows is blacked out. Why? Because they have a maniac son who's boarded up in there, that's why! And they say he hates intruders. If he catches you he'll bite into the side of your neck with the only two teeth he has left in his head – his fangs! So don't get caught … Getting caught is not an option. Mallon, we'll lift you up first. Peep down into the yard and … '

'I don't even like plums, Butler,' Mallon said in protest.

'This is not about plums, Mallon,' Butler informed him.

'It's not?' Mallon said, sarcastically.

Butler sighed and shook his head and continued. '… We'll lift you up first. Crawl along the top of the shed and peep down into the yard and make sure there's no one down there, give us the bend then and it's up and over and every man for himself. It's twelve forty five now. By one o' five this operation will be complete. Let's move it.'

And that's what happened. They helped Mallon – who was now wearing the scarecrow's confiscated old hat – up onto the wall and he crept carefully on all fours across the roof of the shed (a little too carefully for Butler's liking), peeped down into the yard and called to the others that the coast was clear. Derek was the next to be hoisted aloft and then Egan and then they had to reach down and pull Butler aboard – a mission that had to be aborted several times first before it was brought to a successful conclusion: once because Butler couldn't stop slipping, once because he couldn't stop laughing and once because Derek lost his grip. Finally Derek had to climb back down again and shove him up from behind with both Egan and Mallon furiously hauling from the other end. When Butler was safely perched on high the others reached down to lift Derek home. And then – after a short interval in which Butler treated them all to some very unwelcome last minute advice – they dropped down into enemy territory one by one: first Butler, then Egan and then Derek who waited to catch Mallon as he lowered himself down.

They moved across the yard, crouching like marines, and then in full view of the mansion they crawled on their bellies in the long grass until they reached the outskirts of the orchard. And there were the plum trees in one corner, flanked on all sides by apple trees and pear trees and rows and rows of gooseberry bushes.

In primitive silence the boys set about their task and each boy had a different technique of plundering: Butler fashioned a sort of a sack from his jumper, tying the arms together and moving from tree to tree, stuffing his makeshift knapsack with fruit and shrewdly edging his way closer to the side gate all the time, retrieving his snagged baseball hat from a thorny bush with a silent curse; Egan on the other hand went at it literally hand over fist, climbing up into a tree, eating and stuffing his pockets all at the same time, the slender branches complaining beneath him; and Mallon, who had not been lying when he said he did not like plums, was helping himself to the apples and pears, turning the battered old hat into a bucket.

Derek ate a plum first before he began filling his pockets, the juice squirting out onto his chin before dribbling uncomfortably down the inside of his jumper. If he had known that they were going to come pillaging plums today he would have worn a different jacket with more pockets. He was determined to bring a few home with him this time – for his mother and Anthony. The last time they had raided this place he had panicked and only taken a handful and had eaten them all in no time and tramped home empty-handed. This time he would take his time, fill his pockets and have plenty to go around at the end of the day. As he worked he kept an eye on the others and all of them, without exception, were conscious of the big house, which looked like a huge watchful animal with its gleaming windows for eyes and its majestic doorway of a mouth. A dog barked somewhere but Butler silently informed them all that it was nothing to worry about – the dog was either tied up or belonged to a different household.

Once when Derek looked up at the mansion he thought he saw a figure at one of the upstairs windows, looking down at them and shyly waving. His heart skipped a beat as he gazed up into the far away lonely eyes of a hunched up dwarf-like anaemic creature who, to all intents and purposes, was smiling at him now. Derek was so wrapped up in it all that he stopped picking altogether and never even noticed the others slipping out the side gate without him. Butler had to return and whistle to him loudly to hurry him up and, with a light skip in his step, Derek sped towards him, glimpsing the window one more time as he went so that Butler couldn't help but wonder about it.

Out in the lane the boys sat in the dyke and treated themselves to the plums, eating ravenously – pips sucked to the marrow and the remnants booted away with relish. Fingers were licked and wiped, stories swopped and the adventure bisected and trisected and analysed until in the end there was nothing left to talk about.

'Destroy the evidence, lads,' Butler advised them, his hat turned sideways and his lips dyed purple. He was kicking the pips of the plums and the hearts of the apples and pears into a small hole and covering them up with dirt.

Derek moved a few plums from his pants pocket into his jacket in case they'd be squashed and he tried to picture

Anthony's face when he'd produce them. On the way out that morning he had banged the door and then shouted back in through the letterbox at Anthony that he was not to answer the door to anyone. 'I won't Derek,' Anthony promised him. 'Don't worry.' And as Derek walked away he looked back at the house and, apart from everything else, the absence of smoke billowing from the chimney on this cold September Saturday morning suffused his heart with shame.

'Right you crowd,' Butler was saying, kicking the soles of their feet like a sergeant in a war picture. 'Let's get to where we're supposed to be going.'

They rose up amid a stream of innocuous protests and as they were plodding down the rutted laneway they met a farmer coming the other way, herding a few cattle in front of him. The boys saluted him and he absentmindedly waved back to them and when he was gone Butler turned and called after him. 'Thanks for the plums,' and he took off again and, even though they all knew that the orchard did not belong to this particular man, the others fled too. All except Derek that is who was reliving the moment his father tousled his hair that morning, his stumpy fingers lingering there longer than usual as if he was bequeathing something to his son or seeking absolution from him for some sin that was yet to be committed. Derek watched the boys disappear around the bend and by the time he caught up with them again his mind was full of stuff and he was polishing off his last remaining plum.

They passed a man and his son digging bait, wielding sprongs and knee-deep in mud; and further down the line they met two women wearing identical head-scarves, the very image of each other in every detail, sisters, without a doubt. They were picking blackberries, bending and plucking in unison as they dropped fistfuls of berries into the same shiny tin can.

'The Beverly sisters,' Butler whispered under his breath as the boys cruised on by them and Butler wrapped his jumper around his head like a scarf and he fluttered his eyelids and did a bit of a dance and sang a song about sisters in a woman's high pitched voice, causing the others to snigger so that the two women straightened up and looked sternly in their direction as if they had overheard everything.

At a five-barred gate the boys encountered a donkey poking its sad eyed face through the opening. They patted its hard, nuzzling head and fed grass into its gaping mouth, and Butler told them to hold it steady while he climbed up onto the gate like a rodeo rider and lowered himself onto its back. The donkey was a fairly docile creature until Butler touched down and then it became restless and started to shift and splutter and finally move wildly away from the gate.

'Yahoo,' Butler yodelled as the donkey took off, gambolling and bucking and kicking and humping and braying, sending Butler up into suspended animation like something from a comic strip so that when he came back down again he was not sitting astride the donkey any more but side saddle like Lady Godiva; and with that he slid off and was running alongside the donkey, holding on to its neck. He managed to control the beast and corral it into the lee of a nearby ditch where he ordered one of the others to climb aboard. Egan was the chosen one. Derek made a stirrup of his hands and as soon as Egan had mounted Butler hit the donkey a hard slap on the rump and let out a wild shriek and away it went again, Egan writhing and wincing with pain and rising and yelping until he was deposited unceremoniously into a thorny gripe.

'Hold on to him,' Butler screamed as the donkey bolted across the field. 'Hold on to him, I said.'

Butler pursued the donkey into a copse of trees, and Derek was half hoping that he wouldn't catch up with it because he knew that he was next in line. He pictured himself on the donkey, clutching on with one hand and shrieking unashamedly. Egan picked himself up and brushed himself down and then chuckled with relief.

'What's it like?' Derek asked him.

'Sore,' Egan replied.

And then Derek's prayers were answered when a ferret of a man appeared out of nowhere and hurried towards them, shaking his fist and cursing. The man was a sooty looking fellow whose face and clothes and hands were so besmirched that he could only have been a chimneysweep by profession. Needless to say Derek didn't wait to confirm this suspicion. He darted towards the gate, preceded by Mallon who, to Derek's surprise, vaulted over it with amazing agility. Derek was climbing over the gate when Egan bounded by too, up and over like a cross-country runner. Derek scrambled to the other side and followed the others, slipping and sliding and tumbling pell-mell down the bank to hide behind a mound of earth on a piece of waste ground, catching their breath and giggling nervously and getting ready for the off again if necessary.

No sign of Butler though. No sign and no sound! They waited and wondered. Had he been captured? Mallon ventured. Egan said there was a caravan in the corner of the field, that that's where the man had come from. Perhaps Butler was tied up in there, Mallon suggested, that they would have to pay ransom for him. Or else they'd have to sneak around at night and set him free. They all laughed about it but as time drifted by the joke wore off and they began to worry. Should they go back and tell the man they passed? Mallon said. The one digging bait! Or the two women perhaps? Where would be the point in that? Egan sanpped and Derek agreed with him. No point! They shouldn't have been riding the donkey in the first place.

They waited for ages until by general consensus they decided to make their way to Rainwater Pond and wait for him there in the hope that he would soon be released.

They travelled in silence, feeling a trifle guilty, leaving Butler to his fate like that. After all Butler wasn't the worst of them. He could make you laugh sometimes. And once when Derek got into a fight in the schoolyard with two hard looking jokers from a different class Butler charged across the yard and trounced the pair of them. And another time Butler came to his rescue when Derek fell into a bog hole. Butler hauled him out and then fished out his left behind boot with his fishing rod. Although on the other hand in his heart Derek was thinking that Butler deserved all that he got. Why couldn't he just leave things alone? Leave them be and get to where they were supposed to be going in the first place instead of always … Ah, what was the point?

But of course they need not have worried. When they arrived at the pond Butler was sitting on the wall, waiting for them.

'About time,' he said with a big broad grin and Mallon ran towards him and jumped up onto his back and gently cursed him for getting them all worked up about him in the first place.

∽

Mystic was living in a disused cottage on the edge of Rainwater Pond. It had no front door so that a sheet of sacking hung down like the entrance to a tent. Butler called out, but no one answered. The boys nervously regarded each another as Butler called again. 'Hello.'

'Maybe he's gone,' Derek said. 'Moved on.' It was wishful thinking.

'He's not gone Derek,' Butler said. 'He's here alright.' And with that he called out again and drew back the sacking and peeped inside. It was dark in there. The windows were covered with sacking too and black refuse bags. When his eyes had grown accustomed to the darkness, Derek discerned the outline of a hammock dangling down, and a sleeping bag tossed carelessly across it. A tea chest was laid like a table with a tea towel for a tablecloth and a bag of sugar and a box of teabags and a stained mug and a rusty spoon and an unlit night watchman's lantern for light. Mallon's eyes lit up with wonder. Butler grimaced at the state of the place and held his nose at the smell. There was a covered up box in the corner of the room and it was fairly obvious that all four boys were collectively wondering if that was where the snake was kept.

'Let's check round the back,' Butler said and he led the way around the side of the house and down a grassy slope to a shale-peppered strand.

Mystic was sitting on a sandy bank at the water's edge, whistling softly and smiling obliquely as the boys drew near. And Derek had to admit that he was all the things they expected him to be with broken teeth and long greasy red hair down to his shoulders and the makings of a ginger beard and a big silver earring in his left ear and tattoos everywhere.

'Morrow Mystic,' Butler cried when Mystic turned to stare at them through a pair of ocean blue eyes; and then Mystic turned away and sort of shook his head and in a little reedy voice he made a soft, cymbal-like sound that seemed to suggest that he had been half expecting them all along. And, as the boys moved closer, Derek knew that he would indeed soon get to see the snake, and he thought about his mother and father and Anthony again and something told him – deep down – that all was not well in the world.

TABLE MANNERS

Birdsong In The Early Morn
The Ringing Of A Bell
The Stillness Of A Frosty Dawn
Sea Sounds In A Shell
The Rain, The Wind, The River's Purl
The Droning Of A Bee
All Bow Down And Pander To
Sweet Mystery ... .

Michael was forced to abandon the car at the end of the lane and walk the remaining hundred yards or so to the cottage: a truck, a van, a battered old jalopy and a big blue jeep were parked haphazardly along the route. A couple of carpenters were walking across the roof of one of the nearby houses, banging here and there and measuring and frowning like mathematicians. Next house but one he noticed a young labourer working a cement mixer. The young man bent and shovelled and spilt the contents out onto a small wooden sheet and then he carried the muck in a bucket into the house where, going on the sounds that came from within, a group of plasterers were at work. The youth called out to Michael and saluted him. 'Mister Farr,' he cried. 'You're a long way from home,' (or something of that sort). Michael couldn't make him out against the glare of the autumnal noon-day sunlight, one of his past pupils, odds on it. Dropped out and was now making his living the hard way. Brawn over brain.

The five or six tiny houses that were dotted here and there around Rainwater Pond had been purchased by the local entrepreneur Harry Hall who was still busy buying up half the town. These buildings used to be terrible dilapidated until Harry got his hands on them, and to his credit he had set about putting them right. Now it was fairly obvious to everyone concerned that he would soon have a cluster of up-market holiday homes on his hands just three miles from the town centre, a real steal when you considered that they had the lovely vista of the pond in the front and the sea to the rear.

The cottage Michael sought was the last one in the block and it was the only one that was completely renovated and refurbished. It was actually two cottages knocked into one. The old fashioned half door was still in place on the end house while the other half door had been turned into a big bay window so that when Michael looked in over the open top of the door he was surprised to see the place flooded with sunlight, spilling in from all sides. There was a horseshoe above the door and the proverbial Bridget's cross over the mantelpiece. (Trust Harry Hall to think of everything.)The kitchen-cum living room was decorated in the fashion of an old style farmhouse with a stacked ornamental sideboard and an ornate wooden pew and a sturdy table and chairs. Maria Callas was singing an aria on the C.D. player in the corner – from *Norma*, Michael thought – so that Michael had to knock loudly and call out several times before the lady he was looking for emerged from the bedroom with a look of alarm painted across her freckled face.

'I'm here to take you into town,' Michael announced when he saw her – a vision and a half in the doorway with those languid blue eyes and her hair russet in the sun while the rest of her body was latticed in shadow.

'Oh right,' she replied as if he were far too early, which he was not. 'Hang on,' she said and she disappeared into the bedroom again. 'Are you early or am I running late?' Michael heard her say from the other room. ''Cause I wasn't expecting you yet. Well, not for another … three minutes at least.'

'That's half my problem,' Michael replied.' I'm too prompt.'

'I hate that in a man,' she chirped. 'You're not Jim Belton by any chance are you?'

'No, I'm Michael Farr,' Michael replied.

'I might have known. You're too good looking to be Jim Belton.'

'To tell you the truth I'm too looking to be Michael Farr too but what can I do about it – nothing.'

She laughed and Michael thought he heard her talking to someone in there. Or perhaps she was on the telephone.

Michael hoped that she didn't think he was a taxi driver or a hackney man, or any other sort of hired hand for that matter, and if he were to be absolutely truthful about it he'd have to admit that he felt a trifle miffed, being outside the door like this. He took a good look around while he was waiting: first at the workers working, the carpenters on the roof and the young labourer conferring with one of the tradesmen on top of a pile of rubble; and then the pond, where a silent trio of ruffled swans gently sailed; and finally returning his gaze to the cottage again to find that everything was where it was supposed to be except for her few personal belongings which were slung and flung willy-nilly about the place, books and notes and manuscripts and grooming utensils.

He wondered what her own place would be like, this beautiful, wild-looking poet. Ramshackle probably. Where did she live anyway? Galway or somewhere. Well, the west certainly, judging by her accent. A white washed cottage of her own by the sea in some wild place, woods and lanes and wildlife all around her. Baroque furniture. Or rococo maybe. Well, strange definitely. A big four-poster bed, creaky and inviting. A window filled with daylight – and moonlight. He wondered too what she made of this place, Harry Hall's manufactured cottage, and he couldn't resist putting words in her mouth. 'Devoid of soul,' she'd say. 'Devoid of … aesthetic.' They were in no position to complain of course. Harry Hall had donated this particular house to them for free. Well, free would be a bit strong wherever Harry was involved. In return for the house he would receive complimentary tickets for all the events in the festival along with a large add in the programme. Not that Harry would avail of the readings and poetry recitals or anything. No, he'd pass his tickets on to some potential clients who would turn up red faced at the door, hoping they were genuine.

'I'll tell you what,' she said, peeping out around the doorframe again. 'I'll meet you at the car in a minute. I just need to …' and she indicated that she needed to do something or other. The word '*chiaroscuro*' sprang to mind and when she was gone she left a sort of luminous afterglow in her wake.

'Fair enough,' Michael called after her. 'No hurry,' he muttered and before he walked away he thought he saw a second shadow, a man's shadow, in the bedroom doorway behind her and for some unknown reason he felt betrayed somehow.

As he trudged back to the car he was sure that she was under the impression that he had been hired to drive her to and fro. He hoped not but that's what it looked like. Her expression and the way she sort of dismissed him that time. He recognised the young labourer now and he waved up at him. Not the brightest apple in the barrel. Found his true calling after all from what Michael could remember of him.

Back at the car he snapped a bar of Aero and reclined his seat and thought about the poet. He had heard her once or twice on the radio recently, promoting her new volume of poetry, and he had seen her a few times on the telly too. She was one of those celebrity poets who very soon would become a household name if she didn't watch out. A bohemian beauty. Just the sight of her that time in the doorway had caught him unawares: those pouting lips and that flaming hair and her voice, clear and distinct and full of resonance; and those strange, myopic eyes exuding ... mystery.

Mystery! That was it! That's what was missing from his life. Mystery! Mystery and danger. And intrigue. That was the name of that adolescent poem he had written back in those heady days of his youth. *Mystery.* His search for his Desdemona, his quest to solve the riddle of his own ... incompleteness. Oh, God! The angst! How did it go again? Something about this fellow whistling up a street or something. Or walking down an avenue. No, most of it gone now ... No, hang on though. ... *You're Putting On A Thin Disguise* (or something) / *Hoping Nobody Can See.* That's it! The middle section of the first what-do-you-call-it ... stanza. *You're Putting On A Thin Disguise/ Hoping Nobody Can See/ But There's No Need To Apologise/ For Mystery ...* Yeah.

The young labourer was drumming on the roof of the car. 'Are you buyin' one of these?' he wondered as Michael wound down the window.

'Why, are you selling?' Michael responded and the young lad laughed loudly.

'Do you remember me?' the boy wanted to know then, bringing his big, red-chaffed, slightly idiotic face even nearer.

'How could I forget you?' Michael said to him, although for the life of him he could not recall the young man's name, and again came the loud laughter. Yes, that laugh was familiar. Hayes or Hynes or something. Or Harris. Yeah. Tommy Harris or something like that. Well, Harris anyway. Definitely.

Someone whistled out, a signal of some sort, and with a dirty tipsy wink young Harris made his way in his mucky boots back to the spluttering cement mixer. Just as well. She was coming down the lane, looking around anxiously, wondering where the car was parked and stepping gingerly across the planked roadway. Should he bamp the horn? Or flick the headlights maybe? Might seem a bit forward. No, she saw him, frowned and hurried towards him. 'If she gets in the back it means she thinks I'm hired to drive her about,' Michael was thinking as he watched her approach. Kitty Shaw was her name and her hair was still damp. And yes, she got in the back and placed all her stuff on the seat beside her. Michael turned the car around and drove away, beeping and waving to young Tommy Harris who was practically incandescent with the sheer excitement of it all, a real red letter day for him, no doubt.

'The Menapia Hotel,' she said in a tone of voice that implied there would be a hefty tip in it for him at the end of the journey.

You're Walking Down The Avenue/ You're Whistling Up The Street … Oh yes. Gone but not forgotten. *Mystery.*

'Is the house comfortable enough for you?' Michael asked her when they had gone a mile or so down the road, watching her through the driving mirror.

'What?' she said with a minute arch of her eyebrows. 'Yes. ... It is ... Very nice.'

'Well if you need anything just give us a shout,' he said. 'I'll give you my number and ... you know ... if you need anything.'

'Thanks,' she said coldly and she began looking over her notes and he resigned to leave her in peace. He knew how she felt. Well, kind of knew how she felt. He had done a few readings himself in his time – in The Desert Hall and in The Menapia Hotel in the early days of the festival; it was mainly local artists and writers and poets in those days. Malachy Dillon was the head honcho back then, the founding father of the festival when all was said and done. Good old Malachy with his cravat and blazer and dramatic comb over, holding court in the back bar of the Menapia Hotel every Monday night, surrounded by his loving disciples who hung slack-jawed on his every utterance. Earnest young men for the most part and every last one of them as odd as the next; and afterwards they'd all traipse back to Malachy's terraced house with a few six packs and the occasional bottle of wine, and Malachy's eldest daughter Sheila would produce the tea and biscuits and hover coquettishly in the shadows, giving Michael and the others the inaudible come on. The fact that it was Harry Hall, who had inveigled his way into the camp under false pretences, who eventually deflowered her in the back seat of his car behind the reservoir says more about this unusual band of brothers than anything else. Malachy was oblivious to it all of course, too busy being judge and jury and acidic executioner. Although to give him his due he was rather taken with Michael's poem *Mystery* when it was first recited. 'You're on to something there,' he told Michael, confidentially. 'There's something pagan about it, which I like,' he confessed and then promptly proceeded never to mention it again. *You Never Get To Hear Her Voice/You Never*

Get To Speak! You Never Get To … (Something Something) … / You Never Get To Meet … Oh yeah, she'd need a bit of space now all right, a bit of silence. The tummy rumbling, the hands shaking, the voice growing faint. Oh yes, I remember it well. … *Kiss Her Lips!* That's it. *You Never Get To Kiss Her Lips …* . Yeah. … *Mystery.*

He pulled up outside the Menapia Hotel and he got out and opened the door for her. She climbed out and hurried into the hotel without him. He locked the car and followed her into the lobby. She was standing at the front desk talking to Jim Belton who was explaining the procedure to her. The lunchtime reading would take place in The Alcove – a small, secluded room just off the main bar. No, it wasn't as small as it sounded, eighty or so people. She asked to see the room and the set-up and Jim Belton led her there. Michael followed the pair of them sheepishly across the lobby and he stood at the doorway of The Alcove and watched as she stepped up onto the podium and tested the lectern and tried the microphone, adjusting the height of it and wriggling it about and so on and so forth, and then she gazed down at the area where the audience would soon be sitting, imagining what it would be like, envisaging it all.

'Alright?' Jim Belton droned, anxious to be off and making no bones about it.

'Yes,' she said, earnestly. 'I think so.' But she did not budge from the stage. Instead she dawdled and contemplated, ignoring Jim Belton's nervous fidgeting and key jangling. Michael liked that, her self-possession.

'Well, if there's anything else you need just let us know, 'Jim Belton was saying as he guided her back out to the lobby again.

'Is there some place I could go to eh …' she said and she indicated that she would like to look over her notes and poems before the reading.

'Yes, of course,' Jim Belton assured her, although Michael knew well enough that there would no such place available in the hotel right now.

Jim Belton accompanied her to the bar and returned shaking his head.

'She wants a dressing room,' he said under his breath. 'I mean it's a lunchtime reading for Christ's sake, not *H.M.S. Pinafore*. The nook in the bar will have to do her. Listen, Michael, Jenny Sewell hasn't turned up –again, – so you'll have to do the honours I'm afraid.'

'What else is new?' Michael reminded him. Jenny Sewell did this every year: joined the committee at the last minute (usually when all the fund raising was done and all the decisions taken), volunteered her services and then half the time never showed up to do the door or to usher people to their seats when she was supposed to. She never failed to turn up for all the wine receptions though and the book launches. And she never forgot to collect all her free tickets to all the events either, which pissed everyone off no end as you can imagine. (Although, to be fair, secretly Michael had a soft spot for her – and her for him too if the truth be known.)

'Where's the cash box?' Michael cried.

'There it is there in front of you,' Jim Belton told him. 'Oh and listen she wants her books on display too she said, so you might set up one of those tables to the side there with the books laid out and all the rest of it ...' he was rushing away as he was saying all of this and added just before he went that she had left a box of books behind the reception desk.

Michael went about his work, setting up the cash box and the stumpy book of tickets and the handwritten sign to advertise the reading; and then he dragged across another small table to set all her books upon, laying some of them down flat and others upright like a display in a regular bookshop. The books had been parcelled up in what looked like a publisher's package. There was a poster in there too, which contained an opaque photograph of her standing beside a lake: the farther you stood back from it the clearer you made her out, apparently. This he tacked up on the wall behind the table. Very impressive. She had three volumes of poetry for sale: *Redye The Roses*, *The Furze But Ill Behaves* and *Table Manners* – five copies of each, which he spaced apart symmetrically. He was halfway through this task when his wife Eleanor and her sister Nuala and their mother (his mother-in-law) came through the door.

'What are you doing there?' Eleanor grumbled when she saw him.

'It's a long story,' he told her.

'I thought whats-her-face was supposed to be here today?' she said, coming closer.

'Yeah, well ...' he said and he made a wry face that told her the whole sorry saga.

Eleanor shook her head and blurted some harmless curse. 'But sure we might as well get our tickets now while we're here,' she called to the others then, 'save us queuing later on,' and the three women reached into their bags for their purses and argued about who was going to pay for them.

'*Table Manners*,' Nuala remarked, rummaging.

'What's that?' Eleanor asked.

'*Table Manners*,' Nuala replied, pointing out the book on the table. 'That's her latest one.'

'Oh yeah,' Eleanor said then, picking it up and flippantly leafing through it. 'Kitty Shaw. She was on the radio the other day talking about that. I wasn't all that gone on it to tell you the truth, what I heard of it anyway. Now ...'

Michael had to admit that he felt kind of funny, selling tickets to his own wife, but he did it anyway and then the three women took themselves off into the bar for some soup and sandwiches.

⌒

The Alcove was practically filled to the brim and the cash box was overflowing with money when Jim Belton led Kitty Shaw out of the bar and across the silent lobby to the door of The Alcove. He would introduce her, he told her, in a hushed whisper, and she gently indicated that she understood. 'Is there anything particular you want me to say?' Jim Belton broached before he went, giving her new book on the table the once over.

'What?' she said, nervously, as if this kind of thing was beneath her (which made Michael feel very ill at ease). 'No,' she said then. 'Nothing,' and she turned away disdainfully.

'Right so,' Jim Belton said and with that he was gone, unaware of the terrible hubris he'd just committed.

The door of the Alcove swung open, affording them a brief glimpse of the audience and a brief sound of their hubbub and then all went quiet as the door slid shut again. She paced nervously about as Michael carried on, counting the money and sorting the ticket stubs. She smelt of expensive soap and her face radiated and she had tiny, dainty feet that padded about the place in what looked like hand made moccasins. She apprehensively eyed the books on the table. He was sorry he hadn't managed to sell any yet, although people had shown an interest in them. People had been looking at them, picking them up and slyly putting them back down again. He wanted to say something to reassure her, but he couldn't bring himself to say anything. After the reading he might sell a few of them. He hoped so anyway, for her sake. He intended to buy six of them himself actually, three for his own use and three more for the school library. From inside the Alcove came the sound of laughter, which Michael couldn't help but notice had an unsettling effect on her. God only knows what Jim Belton was saying in there. He could be uncouth enough when he set his mind to it.

'Are you all right?' Michael inquired in the hope that it might wring from her a glimmer of recognition: it didn't.

'Mmn,' she mumbled, distractedly.

And then Eleanor and her entourage breezed out of the bar and came tramping towards The Alcove. Michael was mortified. He had forgotten all about them and never realised that they hadn't taken their seats yet.

'Has it started?' Eleanor wondered, handing him her ticket. If she recognised the poet then she never let on.

Michael threw her a dirty look as he herded them inside. 'You'll have to sit down the back somewhere,' he whispered as he opened the door.

'It's all right,' Eleanor said. 'There's three seats there'll do us,' and she pointed out three seats to the side of the stage.

'But sure you'll see nothing worth talking about from there,' Michael warned her.

'What's there to see?' Eleanor said to him, leading the way.' I mean she's not going to sing and dance or anything, is she?' and Nuala gave a smoky laugh behind him as she ushered her mother ahead.

Jim Belton had actually stopped his announcement until the three ladies were in their seats and he was just about to begin again when Father Corish entered, reeking of chicken soup and garlic bread and a few breadcrumbs on his chin. He thrust some money into Michael's hand and hastened to the place that Nancy Byrne was holding for him. The two chairs that had been reserved for Malachy Dillon and Sheila were still vacant and Michael couldn't help thinking that it was a bit of a waste to have two empty seats up front like that when people were crowded uncomfortably together down the back. He was sorely tempted to beckon a couple of people forward, but then what would happen if Malachy and Sheila turned up at the last minute? Ructions!

'All right?' Jim Belton beamed, unctuously, and when everyone was settled he continued.

Michael went back outside to find Kitty Shaw fiddling with the books on the table, rearranging them.

'... mainly from Table Manners, which of course is her latest volume of poetry,' Jim Belton was saying inside as the door closed on its own steam, blotting out the sound of nearly everything. Kitty Shaw got worried then because she could not hear what Jim Belton was saying and she went to the door and put her ear to it so that she might know when the time was right for her to enter, and Michael felt his stomach churning with worry for her. And then the sound of clapping told her that the introduction was over and done with and, suddenly electrified, she opened the door and stepped over the threshold to tumultuous applause.

Michael had everything in order by the time Jim Belton came back out to him.

'Why do we do this, eh?' Jim Belton complained.

'What's that?' Michael asked, absentmindedly.

'Put ourselves through this every year. I don't know ... Here's Nicholas now ... You hang on here will you? I've to go over to the eh ...' and with that he was gone out the door to oversee some other event.

The big, blue jeep had pulled up outside and Nicholas Holden, the distinguished and well-known novelist, got out of it. Michael could see him through the hotel window, buttonholed by Jim Belton who very soon hurried away. Nicholas Holden stepped into the lobby, filling up the doorway with his broad frame and his greying, handsome features. He dithered on the threshold awhile as he scratched his forehead and considered the door of the bar and the door The Alcove with equal measure. It was a moment that defined him somehow or other in Michael's estimation; although if Michael had been asked to elaborate or to write it all down then he didn't think he'd know what to say.

∽

Michael sold nine books all in all after the reading – the six he bought himself and three others – two copies of *Redye The Roses* and one copy of *Table Manners.* The remaining books he returned to the cardboard box, along with the money he had collected for the nine he had sold. The crowd were still milling around the lobby when Jim Belton arrived back and inquired how Michael had fared out.

'Grand,' Michael told him. 'No bother.'

'Good,' Jim Belton said. 'Guess who I bumped into up the town there?

Michael had no idea.

'Jenny Sewell!' was the answer. 'Looking hale and hearty … 'and with a violent shake of his head Jim Belton disappeared into the bar where Kitty Shaw could be found in the nook, drinking coffee with Nicholas Holden.

Michael deposited the cardboard box behind the front desk. He was still in a state of awe. He had only caught the tail end of the reading, slipping in and standing at the back of the room, the cashbox cleaved sensibly to his chest as if he feared some thief might at any minute suddenly burst in and try and wrest it from him. Kitty Shaw, adorned with a stylish pair of spectacles, which Michael suspected she didn't really need, was reading from her latest volume *Table Manners,* swaying gently back and forth as she recited:

> The Hand That Rocks The Cradle
> Is The Hand That Holds The Gun
> Sator Arepo Tenet Opera Rotas

And I'm Weeping In The Moonlight
Instead Of Grinning Neath The Sun
Sator Arepo Tenet Opera Rotas

You Led Me To The Garden
Where I Weaved My Wicked Spell
Sator Arepo Tenet Opera Rotas

Now I'm No Maiden Marian
And You're No William Tell
Sator Arepo Tenet Opera Rotas

Veni Vedi Veci
I Thought I Heard You Say
Sator Arepo Tenet Opera Rotas

And Then You Had The Nerve
To Try And Teach Me How To Pray
Sator Arepo Tenet Opera Rotas.

Michael stood spellbound at the back of the room as one poem followed another – poems about sinners and love-lorn creatures for the most part, poor things who were guilty of all sorts of unforgivable things: murder and abortion and betrayal and unkindness of every kind. Curses and spells – palindromic and otherwise – and broken promises and heart rending disappointments permeated the poems; lovers left and came back in due course only to repeat the performance all over again. *The Killing Fields* and *Fat Chance* (from the *Table Manners* collection) and the pleading *Redye The Roses* were just three of the poems he heard that day and they were all delivered in quick succession with Kitty Shaw reeling them all off, all these wicked things, in a voice that was calm and dulcet in essence, contradicting herself some might say. And to cap it all a mote-filled beam of sunlight stole in accidentally through the round window behind her, giving her, at times, an angelic aspect that was totally at odds with some of the beautiful and terrible things she was saying.

Michael was not the only one that was affected. He looked around at the audience to find many of them captivated: some showed signs of embarrassment while others were clearly entranced. One woman was silently weeping. Michael couldn't help wondering what Malachy would have made of it all.

'I'm speechless,' Father Corish said to him on the way out. 'I mean … I'm … 'and he threw his plump hands in the air to indicate that words failed him and Nancy Bryne just nodded in mute agreement by his side.

Michael silently agreed. Although his own paltry poem kept running itself round and round in his head all the time. *You Never Get To See Her Cry/ And You've Got Company/ There's Not A Man That Wouldn't Die/ For …*

'Powerful,' someone else was saying. 'Yes, powerful stuff.'

Yes, people were impressed. People were moved. Eleanor, on the other hand, appeared to be impervious to it all. She led the others into the bar where she bought them a drink and then she went home without saying goodbye to him and she never even mentioned the poet or her poems.

Mystery!

∽

It was nearly dark when Michael dropped Kitty Shaw back to the cottage that evening. He'd gone back to school in the afternoon in a daze where he sleepwalked his way through a class from three o'clock to four. He supervised after school study from four fifteen to five thirty, picked up his fourteen year old daughter Sara from violin lessons at quarter to six, went home and had his dinner by seven and he was just about to crash down into the armchair in front of the telly for the evening when the phone rang. His heart skipped a beat when he heard her voice on the other end. He tried to remain calm and collected, but he was sure that the whole family could hear his heart pounding and the slight tremble in his voice as he vowed to come and fetch her.

'Who's that?' Eleanor asked him when he hung up, although Michael suspected she knew well enough who it was all the time. 'Huh,' she growled when he told her, 'that one must think you've nothing else to do only tote her about the place or something.'

She was waiting under the canopy of The Menapia Hotel when he drew up on the far side of the street. He rolled down the window and timidly called out to her. It was the first time he had called her by name and it felt strange. 'Kitty,' he cried. 'Kitty …' She looked at him vacantly, only vaguely recognising him at first, and then when the penny finally dropped she extinguished a cigarette on the ground with her heel, picked up a canvas bag that lay at her feet and stepped off the footpath. She clambered into the back seat and immediately lit up another cigarette. She opened the window and exhaled. Her breath smelt of white wine and something else that Michael could not detect. She seemed a little tipsy. Michael felt compelled to tell her how much he had enjoyed the reading and she mumbled some inane reply, and then he reminded her yet again that he had left the box of books and the money he had collected behind the hotel desk for her (€75.30); it spilt out of his mouth like a babbling schoolboy.

'I know,' she said, offhand. 'You told me already.'

'Did I?'

'Yeah … Well, somebody did.'

'And did you get it?'

'What?'

'The money? The seventy-five thirty?'

'Yeah, I got it,' she sighed. 'Got it and spent it,' she said.

'Yeah?' he grinned. 'On what?'

'Wine gums,' she told him. '… and sherry trifle,' and with that she sniggered and when Michael caught her scornful eye in the driving mirror he knew that he had said the wrong thing and he could have kicked himself for saying anything in the first place. He decided to say nothing for the remainder of the journey. She said little or nothing either – an odd weary sigh now and again – until they reached the pond. 'Look at it,' she murmured when she saw the stillness of the water. 'Like glass!' she said, and Michael couldn't help thinking that if he had said something like that it would have sounded silly.

The workers were gone and the place had an eerie feel to it. A heron was perched stock-still on a nearby fence, like a wise old owl. Michael went past it without comment, although he secretly wanted to shout about it as a harbinger of some sort. He drove her right up to the door. She got out, bade him goodnight and went inside, a couple of bottles of wine clinking together in her canvas bag. He waited until she was safely inside and watched her as she tinkered with the alarm switch and then, when she looked around at him suspiciously from the dinky hallway, he beeped the horn and drove away again.

He sat in his armchair that night and read from *Table Manners*, flicking from page to page and from poem to poem, sighing and cooing at some of the things he found there.

'What?' Eleanor demanded at one stage. She was standing by the window, ironing a tower of clothes and when Michael read the particular phrase out to her she just shrugged it off. It was something about the two sides of a woman or something. 'It'd be a poor woman that only had two sides to her,' Eleanor declared, disappearing up the stairs to the hot press.

And later in bed as Eleanor slept he tossed and turned and thought about it all, all these wicked things that happened within the confines of the poems. Had they happened to her in reality? All these lovers! And that one particular, enigmatic man she kept mentioning all the time? Who was he, this Heathcliff type creation of hers?

'Where's Nicholas Holden staying exactly?' Michael had asked Jim Belton out of the blue over a bowl of soup in the hotel bar after the reading.

'Here,' Jim Belton replied. 'In the hotel. We got a good deal though,' he said. 'Three nights for ...' and like an old washerwoman he mimed the price of the room with exaggerated lip movement.

'Was he booked in here last night?' Michael pried.

'Last night?' Yeah. Why?'

'No reason. Just wondering,' Michael said and he turned away from Jim Belton's inquisitive stare.

The next morning Michael picked Kitty Shaw up again and brought her to his school where she was due to read and talk to some of his students. He walked her down the impressive, cloistered corridor of the college, their footsteps echoing mockingly before them and behind them.

'Do you teach here?' she suddenly asked.

'Yes,' he answered, startled. (She hadn't uttered a word all the way in: the back seat again by the way.) 'In fact this is my class you'll be meeting.' he told her.

'Oh!' she said and she gave a small secretive smile that seemed to imply, *'so you're not a mere go-for after all.'*

To say she bewitched the class would be an understatement. The hushed silence that accompanied her recital was unprecedented and even when the bell rang -which was normally a clarion for pandemonium – in the middle of one of her poems nobody stirred. In fact Michael had to dismiss the class several times, clapping his hands together loudly and calling out to them, before many of the boys left the room.

Michael introduced her to the headmaster afterwards who held onto her hand longer than was necessary. And later on they had a brief conversation with a couple of awed English teachers in the vestibule; the pair of them watched with obvious envy as Michael led her along the corridor and out the main door to the car again. She sat in the front with him this time. They had lunch together down town in a local lounge bar.

'We're being watched,' she said, excitedly, as he returned to the table with their soup and brown bread.

'Are we?' he said, looking around him, and sure enough a couple of women he knew by sight were keeping an eye on things from an adjacent table.

'Or to be precise,' Kitty Shaw whispered, 'you are.'

'More than likely,' Michael said, dismissively, and he shrugged it off. He was, however, needless to say, fairly impressed by it all.

'Are you married or something?' she teased in a mock reproachful voice when he was safely seated opposite her again, and he reeled off the usual hackneyed response – wife, family, house and home, number of years in the job and all that palaver. She listened intently, chuckling and smiling airily at the sweet and tender fatherly things he'd say about his daughter or his eleven year old son as if she had never witnessed this kind of affection in a man before; and whenever a lull arrived she'd ask him another question and, rather chuffed, he'd gladly oblige, talking, talking, talking all the time.

'What about you?' Michael eventually said to her when he finally ran out of things to say.

'What about me, what?' she challenged, cocking her head to one side as if the question was a loaded one.

'Are you married yourself or anything?' he asked, shyly.

'No,' she emphatically told him. 'At the moment I'm sort of … . Well … No, is the answer to that question.'

And that was that. She was a mystery. Over coffee, in a moment of weakness, Michael confessed to her that he was a bit of a poet too. He was sorry the minute he said it but what could he do? It just slipped out of him.

'Give me one of your lines,' she implored, teasingly. 'Go on … Your best line now.'

'My best line,' Michael said. 'Oh, I don't know … *Looking Like You're In Control/ Feeling Incomplete..*' he said with a shrug and she gave it some thought and winked her approval and then she tore off a corner from a table mat and pretended to write it down, covering up her writing with her free arm and pouting like a petulant schoolgirl.

Later he fixed up the bill while she slipped out to the Ladies and when she came back he led her out the side door past the spying women, his hand resting gently on the small of her back.

Afterwards he borrowed the key to Saint Selskar Abbey from the curator and he showed her the ruins. He watched her move from gravestone to gravestone and from place to place, her long flowing headscarf streeling in the dirt behind her. He gathered it up and wrapped it around her neck when the chance arose and as he tried to tuck it in around her lapels she grinned mischievously up at him, so near now that he could smell her sweet smelling breath and hear her faintly breathing; and it made him tingle to think that he could have almost counted the number of freckles and tiny blemishes that blossomed here and there about her fascinating face. And then she broke away again and kicked a path through a mound of leaves and disappeared out of sight inside the walls of the old Abbey.

He sat on an ancient parapet and watched her shadow dance and vanish and reappear again as she moved from portal to portal. And while he was waiting he came to the conclusion that the edifice he called his life had been constructed not on terra firma as he had always suspected, but was resting instead on sand that was now shifting restlessly beneath him. There was a yawning chasm growing between where he presently stood and where he once used to be. On the other hand the gulf that existed between him and Kitty Shaw had narrowed considerably in his estimation; it was not by any means out of the question that he would soon be holding her hand or kissing her lips and he had to admit that the safe life he used to inhabit in the not too distant past was, all of a sudden, a risky enough place to be.

He caught sight of her now, standing at an old gravestone, her gaze fastened on some scribbled inscription. She had all the poise of a fallen angel: slightly sinful, her skin translucent, her hair aflame and her body full and feline. And yes, he wanted to throw his arms around her and lose himself in the mystery, to change everything, to cast off the shackles of respectability and run amok, to take one last daring, quixotic leap into chance and uncertainty.

'All the names,' she said, coming towards him.

'What about them?' he called out to her.

'They're strange, that's all,' she said. 'Very strange. And this place … 'and with a wild, theatrical flourish she indicated its mystical nature.

The sun went in and she frowned at its disappearance. And then it started to rain, a sudden torrential downpour, so that they had to run and shelter under the ivied wooden battlement. They crouched down and huddled together as he gallantly tried to shield her body with his own, and when they had sort of settled themselves she leaned her head on his shoulder and hummed a rainy lullaby as she studied the menacing sky. Michael wasn't sure whether it would be right and fitting for him to put his arm around her now or not. He wanted to of course but thought better of it and, fearing rejection, he didn't in the end.

Footsteps thundered overhead – school children on the rampage. They both cast their eyes upwards and smirked. Raindrops glistened on the beams above them and fell one by one in what seemed like a choreographed tumble. A robin drank from a puddle close by. A big brindled tree shook free another fall of leaves. A paperboy yodelled his whereabouts, two or three streets away. And still she was silent. Michael drifted away dreamily into the future and was flattered to think that she might one day write a poem about this very event: the dripping drops, the robin, the tree, the falling leaves, the far away paperboy, their mystical surroundings. '*Rainy Monday,*' she'd call it – even though it was in fact Tuesday; and then just as suddenly as it had arrived the rain went away again.

'It's stopped,' she said, stepping out into the open and testing the air with her fingertips.

'So it is,' he said and tut-tutted to express his disappointment.

'What can you do?' she said with a shrug and a sweep of her hand and this gesture gave him the courage to put his hand gently on her shoulder.

'Seen enough?' he wondered

She indicated that she had seen enough and she slipped her arm gently around his waist as the pair of them sauntered out the gate together like two young lovers in love. He even summoned up the nerve to kiss her lightly on the crown of her head on the way out. Some small talk followed with the curator at the door, Michael's heart thumping inside his shirt and the curator's voice droning on and on and Kitty Shaw (who clearly had no time for small talk) rambling off without him so that Michael had to break away abruptly and hurry to catch up with her again. And later while he went back to work she decided to go gadding about the town, the scarf wrapped around her and a merry twinkle in her eye.

'Are you sure?' Michael pressed when she refused his offer of a lift out to the cottage.

'Certain,' she said, touching his hand. 'You go back to school. I'm going to ramble about the place. Take a look around. '

'Fair enough,' Michael said with a boyish grin.

And as she tripped lightly away from him up the street he boldly stood with his hands in his pockets and watched her go, putting no hiding on it anymore.

In class he asked the boys what they thought of her. He felt connected to her all of a sudden and was anxious to hear that she was well received. Some said she was all right, others thought she was fairly good; someone down the back piped up that 'she was a nice bit of stuff,' and the whole place erupted.

'Yes, all right,' Michael scolded, desperately trying to hide his glee. 'That'll do.'

Out in the staff room, when her name came up, one of the teachers said he'd gladly run away with her any time – day or night. 'That's nice of you,' Michael heard himself say as he made a cup of tea. 'Hard to hold on to though,' someone else insisted and the general consensus was that it would be nigh on impossible to hold on to a creature like that, and Michael (who – we must remember – was sailing in uncharted waters right now,) felt a sort of forlorn hopelessness gnawing inside of him.

After school Michael went looking for her again. He parked his car and went nosing about, combing the meandering side streets and alleyways, peeping into the cluttered antique shops and boutiques and quaint, empty pubs and coffee bars. At times he thought he sensed her near, smelt her fragrance or thought he heard the strains of her velvet voice somewhere. He'd barge into a snug or coffee shop and maybe say her name under his breath only to find that he had been mistaken and he'd have to retreat out the door again. And off he'd go once more, following her invisible trail around the town, and although he'd have to admit that a great part of him was all-at-sea nevertheless life was crisp again, there was an edge to it.

It bemused him to behold his own almost comical twin mirrored in a clouded puddle of rain as he waited to cross the busy street – in his suit and tie and gleaming white shirt and apologetic smile, his gold fáinne pinned to his chalky lapel and his top pocket sprouting a rake of 4B pencils. No, wayward was the thing to be now he told himself and to hell with pensions and security and a job for life and living for tomorrow. To hell with all of that. He would live for the moment from here on out, for the here and now, and you can stick your well-planned future. With a woman like that there was no future anyway. You lived for today and that was all you dared hope for, that was all you were entitled to. One kiss, one glance, one moment was worth everything. Walking hand in hand with her maybe by the banks of a river, hands clasped and fingers entwined. Or hearing her whisper your name when no one else was around. Or dancing with her – holding her close – to a song on a jukebox in some bohemian bar somewhere else in the world, anywhere. And yes, she would take you apart and put you back together again in her own image and to her own liking. He knew that. Or maybe she'd empty you out and fill you up again with emptiness and loneliness. Well, what of it? At least you'd be alive, alive and kicking instead of living this safe and moribund life he was living right now. And true, in time she'd leave you too of course – sooner or later – when it suited her. 'Nothing lasts forever,' you'd hear her say and when you turned around you'd find her gone. He knew all of that and he accepted it, welcomed it actually, if the truth be told. Welcomed it because then at least he'd have something to write about at long last, then at least and at last he might have something worth while to say.

He finally caught up with her in the smoker's corner of the Menapia Hotel. She and Nicholas Holden were regaling each other over a blazing log fire, the pair of them hidden behind a mantle of cigar smoke and sipping a couple of hot toddies. He heard her voice first and Nicholas Holden's hoarse laughter. Michael walked towards the sound, past the dishevelled bellboy, past the troubled manageress, past the Alcove and the Roundroom Grill and then he turned the carpeted corner and there they both were. They stopped talking when he arrived on the scene and looked up at him inquiringly. Neither of them asked him to pull up a chair and join them and so he stood before them like an attendant. He asked her if she would need a lift back out to the cottage at any stage and she thanked him and told him *no, that she would be all right*. He should have kept his mouth shut then but he didn't, he just kept talking, thinking that he would rescue her or something – from Nicholas Holden's unwelcome clutches. Michael reminded her that she was due to do another reading that night in The Desert Hall (it took him his best not to wink at her). He wondered if she would like him to come out to the cottage and collect her and take her back into town for it. She seemed somewhat taken aback by this. She thought about it and with a furtive look in Nicholas Holden's direction, seeking his permission almost and silently receiving it, she eventually, reluctantly, agreed. And still it didn't sink in. Michael, full of vigour now, said that he would pick her up at about seven thirty or thereabouts (still thinking he was doing the right thing, that this was what she would have wanted him to do) and she said, in a half hearted sort of way, that that would be great and then with a curt, irritable sigh she turned back to Nicholas Holden again and without missing a beat , as if Michael was no longer there in fact, they immediately took up where they had left off in their previously interrupted conversation.

Michael felt his face redden as he realised that he had been unceremoniously dismissed and, feeling more confused than shunned at that stage, he very quietly and quickly turned tail and fled. It was only later when he thought about it all that he began to resent what she'd done to him, it was only later when he considered it through and through that he realised that he had been well and truly spurned.

Michael was in a foul humour as he drove out to the cottage that evening. And to make matters worse he passed Nicholas Holden's jeep going into town on the way out. The workers were still there when he arrived at the pond. Young Bobby Harris – Bobby, that was his name, not Tommy, Bobby. – hailed him but Michael was in no mood for him and didn't even bother to respond. Instead he swung the car up to the front door and sounded the horn aggressively. She came out and climbed gaily into the front seat beside him. She said hello to him, mentioning his name for a change. Michael grunted a greeting and took off at a lick. Again Bobby Harris waved him on his way, which Michael once again chose to ignore. She very soon realised that things were not right and she watched him out of the corner of her eye as he drove, his eyes glumly ahead.

'Look at the crane,' she said, more for something to say than anything else.

Michael drove on in silence. It was a heron not a crane he wanted to tell her, but what was the point?

When they got into town, instead of dropping her at the door of The Desert Hall, he pulled up around the corner from it.

'I'll let you out here,' he said. 'I need to find a place to park,' and when she got out he pulled away abruptly and hardly gave her time to collect her things. She was standing in the middle of the road when he drove off. He could see her in his rear view mirror, watching him through a pair of piercing blue eyes that, to his delight, were full of fury.

The place was filling up when he arrived on the stairs of The Desert Hall. He had to fight his way through the queue that had formed all the way down to the front door. Jenny Sewell was posted at the door of the auditorium, collecting the tickets and pointing people to their seats. Another parcel of Kitty's books had been opened up and lay on a table on the landing at the top of the stairs, a poster overhead.

'Help!' Jenny Sewell exclaimed when she saw Michael standing there and she grimaced in horror as he walked away from her again.

Yes, she'd be reliving that never to be forgotten kiss right now – in the broom cupboard on the first landing of The Menapia Hotel. The festival before last was it? No, the one before that again though. God! 'You'll get me shot,' she protested, pressing her body eagerly against him. And he, all fingers and thumbs, fumbled about, getting nowhere, teeth and tongues clashing as her cupped hands engulfed his face. And the sounds the two of them made that day – the rustle of her clothes and the little sweet nothings they both murmured and the metalic clang of the empty bucket at their feet; and she felt so clean and crisp and she smelt so sweet and he would have told so too only they thought they heard someone coming and were forced to disengage. 'Call me,' she pleaded, straightening her attire as he left with a brush and mop that he never really needed in the first place. And although he promised her that he would call her, he never did.

Michael looked into the small side room where Jim Belton was nattering with Nicholas Holden and Kitty and a young classical guitarist who was also on the bill. They were deciding on the order. First the musician would play a number, then Kitty, followed by another musical number and then Nicholas Holden would finish off the evening, reading from his latest novel, *All the Way Home*. Jim Belton would once again do the honours and he wrote a few things down on a scrap of paper and plunged it into his top pocket and then he went out into the noisy auditorium to see how things were progressing out there. Kitty retired to one corner of the room and Nicholas Holden to another and the young musician took his guitar out of its case and began tuning up. Michael was still standing in the doorway watching all of this, although he might just as well have been invisible for all the pass that was put on him there.

Out on the landing he was short with Jim Belton when he was asked to fetch three glasses of water for the artists, and even though he softened somewhat when Jim Belton asked him what was up, nevertheless he still didn't go and get the water. Jenny Sewell had to oblige.

The young guitarist began with O'Carolan's *Sí Beag Sí Mór*. Michael stood earnestly at the door with his arms folded and watched as Kitty Shaw stepped up to the microphone and even though he did his best to brace himself against it all, still and all he died a death with every word she uttered and with every single move she made.

She actually did a very clever thing. She read the three title poems right off the bat: *The Furze But Ill Behaves,*

Redye The Roses and then her latest one *Table Manners,* hence advertising the three books she had on sale outside on the landing all in one fell swoop. As a result of this ingenious strategy her books sold like hot cakes during the interval. This was bad news for Michael of course who was hoping to waylay her in the wings and straighten things out. Instead he had to get behind one of the tables and give Jenny Sewell a hand. Kitty Shaw stood to one side and autographed the books as people lined up in droves all around her. Now and then Michael's eyes would drift in her direction or his sleeve might brush against her shoulder or he'd have to reach across her to take someone's money, but she was so totally engrossed in what she was doing that she didn't appear to notice him there at all.

The young musician opened the second half of the evening with a beautiful arrangement of *My Lagan Love,* and then Nicholas Holden appeared in the spotlight, dressed in a black open necked shirt and a white pants and red framed spectacles. Kitty Shaw was nowhere to be found. She was not in the audience. Michael scanned the crowd and could not see her anywhere. Father Corish and Nancy Bryne were sitting in two seats at the very back of the hall (holding hands?); and Malachy Dillon and Sheila were situated in the front row of the tiny balcony. Malachy, a rheumy-eyed old man now all of a sudden with a dickie bow and fancy scarf and a walking stick straddled across his lap. ('It's unlucky to mock a poet, to love a poet or to be a poet,' he'd often rhapsodise to Sheila in the shadows from his sagging armchair.)

Michael took the image with him when he went back-stage. Kitty was not there either. Some of the card-playing backstage crew wondered about him as he hunted high and low about the place for her. By the time he came back out onto the landing again Jenny Sewell had restocked all the books on the table – mainly Nicholas Holden's novel this time.

'Eleanor is inside there, you know,' she mentioned softly, as if she knew what was going on.

'Is she?' he said and his voice was sad.

'Yeah, in the third row, ogling Nicholas Holden with the rest of them.'

'It wouldn't surprise me,' Michael said, lamely.

'Ah well,' she said, coming closer, and she covered his hand with hers and gently squeezed it; and then she touched his face, murmured some little tender thing – '*poor Michael*,' it sounded like – and she moved away from him again.

'I'll take a gike at him myself I think,' she said as she tiptoed to the door of the auditorium. 'He is fairly dishy all right though, ain't he?' she whispered, peeping in from the back of the hall and then, just like that, she was gone.

～

Michael was on the look-out on the footpath outside The Desert Hall as the crowds came piling out to flock all around him. Kitty was still nowhere to be seen. He huddled there with his collar turned up and gazed about him frantically. People greeted him and waved to him and spoke to him and jostled him, but he did not reply. Lost in a world of his own, he just stared right through them all. Even the dewy-eyed Malachy Dillon was given the short shrift when he tried to communicate with him helplessly from across the divide. The last Michael saw of him (and this can be taken literally) Malachy was toddling feebly down the road, holding on to Sheila's arm to keep an even keel.

No, Michael was running out of time now, he was very nearly out of time. Tomorrow she would be gone and God only knows when, if ever, he might get to see her again. It was all a misunderstanding anyway. If he could just see her, meet with her and talk to her face to face then he was sure it would be all right, he was sure it could all be ironed out.

Jenny Sewell said goodnight to him and disappeared into the night on the arm of her dull dentist husband. Part of Michael wanted to call after her, say something nice to her, but he couldn't really think of anything worth saying and so he just let her go in the end. Father Corish and Nancy Bryne were there too, disappointed with the evening's performance as it transpired. Michael shrugged like a delinquent when Nancy Bryne listed off her misgivings. And then Eleanor and Nuala and their mother swept out and mingled with the bustling throng and the whole lot of them gradually gravitated down towards The Thomas Moore Tavern. And that's when Michael glimpsed Kitty coming out the side door of the Coffee Pot Café across the street and his eyes lit up and his heart began to pound, until he spied Nicholas Holden pulling up alongside in his big blue jeep and she got into the front seat beside him and they drove off together.

'They're going for a meal,' Jim Belton informed him as he sidled up behind him.

'Where?' Michael earnestly wondered.

'I don't know,' Jim Belton said. 'He wouldn't say – for some reason. I fixed him up and all the rest of it. Financially, I mean ... We made money on him actually. '

༄

Michael parked the car in the shadows beside the pond. The cottage was lost in a shroud of darkness: clearly they were not here yet. Earlier on he had driven round the town past the popular restaurants and cafes and bars, searching for a sight of the pair of them, peeking in pathetically through the windows whenever he could at the diners and inspecting the car parks for a trace of the big, blue jeep. He circled round and round the town like that for ages until in the end he felt sure the doormen were talking into their mobile phones to each other about him and so, out of sheer embarrassment, he branched off and ended up at Rainwater Pond.

It was a starless night and with no moon on high to guide him on his way he got out of the car and crunched across the path towards the house. He would go ahead in, he told himself, and sit dramatically in the half-light and wait for her (or them he should say) to return. He hadn't a clue what he would do or say. Demand an explanation most likely, insist on … something or other. Things might get out of hand of course but …

The door was locked when he tried it. He looked under a stone and found the key. He opened the door and felt around for a light switch and suddenly the whole place was illuminated (alarmingly so): hall, kitchen, bedroom, bathroom, the immediate area surrounding the house; and a whirling alarm went off too that he had no doubt could be heard for miles around. So much for the element of surprise! And to make matters worse, before he had time to rectify the matter, a car pulled up, catching him in the full glare of its blazing headlights.

It was Harry Hall, who let down his automatic window and called out to him.

'Mister Farr,' Harry cried. 'What way are you at all?'

'Not so hot' Michael said, shielding his eyes and plugging his ears and bending to talk to him.

'So I see …' Harry said. '… 11-I-49, in case you're wondering.'

'What? … Oh, right,' Michael said and he stepped into the hallway to punch in the relative numbers and then all was quiet again.

'Yeah,' Harry said. 'That's better … .. All's well with the festival then, I take it?'

'Yeah,' Michael assured him. 'I think so.'

'Good begor,' Harry said. He was wearing an outlandish suit and a bow tie – either on his way to a dress dance or coming home from one. 'So ...' he said, 'what do you make of her?'

'Who's that?' Michael inquired.

Harry laughed.' Who's that, he says! ... . The place is shapin' up nicely, ain't it?' he said then, shrewdly changing the subject and nodding his head towards the complex of unfinished houses.

'Not bad.'

'Not bad! I'll say it's not bad. Do you know how much I stand to make on this project when it's done. Go on, give a guess.'

'I don't know,' Michael said, weary of it all.

'Have a go.'

'Two million?' Michael ventured.

'Ah, here now,' Harry said. 'Have a heart ... .Enough is the answer. Yes, enough.'

He looked at the open door of the cottage and then he peered suspiciously up into Michael's bewildered eyes.

The Furze But Ill Behaves, hah?' he crowed.

'I beg your pardon?' Michael said, clutching the key of the cottage tightly in the palm of his hand.

'*When Uncle Walter Came To Call/ He Hanselled More Than The Hat/The Furze But Ill Behaves/ Until He Is Subdued.* ... Here, let me give you some sound advice before I go. Do whatever you want to do whenever you want to do it and never worry about nothing ... And listen to me, unless they actually catch you with your pants down don't ever admit to nothing either, do you hear me? ... .' He swung the car around so that it was facing the other way. 'What are you doin' out here anyway – at this hour of the night?' he called through the other open window, the engine revving wildly.

'Ah, you know,' Michael answered with a slight shrug of his shoulders.

'Yeah,' Harry said. 'I come out here most nights too around this time. So who am I to talk?'

'Yeah?' Michael said and he waited for some precious gem to fall from Harry's mouth, something about her, anything.

'Yeah,' Harry confessed. 'I like to keep an eye on things, you know,' he said and with a cute, impudent wink he drove back down the same dusty road that had brought him there in the first place.

> Saturated Fields
>> Ramshackle Ditches
>>> Dew Seeping Like Sap
>>>> From The Bowels Of The Earth
>>>>> The Furze But Ill Behaves
>>>>>> Until He Is Subdued.

Michael gazed at the key in his hand and pondered. The sound of beating wings echoed from the darkness. The heron doing his rounds? No, it was a crane, and it flapped right by him, nearly close enough to touch.

He hadn't the heart to go in and wait for them after all of that, and so he switched off the lights, locked the door and put the key back under the stone. And then he went home.

In the morning he was roused from his sleep by the noise of the telephone ringing.

'It's for you,' young Sara called up to him from the kitchen.

He sat up in bed and picked up the receiver. It was Kitty's voice on the other end. She had to catch a bus at eight thirty she said and she needed a lift into town.

'Well what do you expect me to do about it?' Michael barked, angrily.

'Come and get me,' Kitty countered and the innuendo in her voice actually offended him.

'What do you think I am, eh?' he said, 'your hired help or something?'

'Look, can you come and collect me or not?' she pleaded.

'No, I can't,' Michael told her. 'Why don't you get Nicholas Holden to do it?'

'Nicholas?'

'Yeah, Nicholas. He's there with you, isn't he?'

'No.'

'No? Oh, what did he do, slip off early or something?'

'What?'

'Back to his little wife and family in Co Tyrone or wherever it is he lives.'

'What are you on about?' she asked.

'Ah, give me some credit will you,' he said, disgusted.

'What? … .Look, forget it.' she said. 'I'll ring a taxi or something.'

'Yeah, you do that, 'Michael shrieked. 'You hire a taxi.'

She hung up. Michael put the receiver back into its cradle as Eleanor came into the room. He was sitting on the side of the bed in his vest and underpants and his hair on end. She was searching in a drawer for her earrings. She worked in The Angel Boutique three days a week and this was one of those days – selling high priced clothes to women who had more money than sense.

'Who was that?' she wondered as she rooted.

'Nobody important,' Michael informed her.

'Alright,' she said. 'I've to go. What time is your first class at?'

'Not til this afternoon,' he said.

'It's well for you,' she joked, kissed him and left.

Michael rose up, slipped on his dressing gown and went downstairs to make a cup of coffee. The kids were on their way out the door as he loitered in the hall to watch them go. And then when the front door slammed and he was all alone in the house he began to think about it all again, and as he swallowed his coffee and waited for his toast to pop he concluded that this tangled tale he was all caught up in lately was not yet over and done with, not by a long shot. No, there was still more to come, he was sure of it: a twist, a turn, a climax, something he had not bargained for; and soon – before he knew it in fact and without even questioning his motives – he was on his way to Rainwater Pond again.

It was about nine thirty when he got there. The workers were nowhere to be seen, although the cement mixer was turning. Kitty Shaw was, of course, well gone by then. The key was in its usual place under the stone. He went in, punched 11-1-49 and moved around the house, ending up in the bedroom – her bedroom. He stood near the window and looked out at the ocean. He lit up a cigarette. The window was open a fraction and the curtain gently billowed. The bed was unmade and there were a few towels and things lying in an artistic heap on the floor; two empty wine glasses stood on the bedside locker along with an abandoned copy of *Table Manners*; a coffee mug had left its fingerprints on the bare floorboards; some item of clothing hung on the radiator. He was conscious of all these things even though he had his back turned to them. The calendar on the back of the door displayed the wrong month: someone had jumped the gun.

So this is how the story ends, he was thinking as the crane and the heron made themselves known to him again: all alone in a silent house and without any real explanation in sight. He felt like a two bit actor in an avant garde film who had been given no decent lines to say, an immaterial character who could just as easily be rubbed out in the editing room long before the picture went on general release. Laughable really when you think of it, the thought that he thought that he might have a substantial role to play in a story like this. Oh dear, oh dear … He pictured Kitty Shaw laughing at him as she boarded the bus, waving to the young carpenter who had carried her to town; and Nicholas Holden grinning in his motor car; and Jim Belton sighing; and Jenny Sewell saying something; even Harry Hall put in an appearance. Standing room only. Oh dear, oh dear is right.

Michael had a lump in his throat now and a terrible empty knot in his belly; tears welled up in his eyes too and the blood rushed to his face and the room began to reel so that he had to hold on to the window ledge to steady the ship. And then, fearing for his own self-esteem, he bowed his head, grinned and grimaced and geared himself up for the raging storm that he just knew was heading his way. He tried to stop it coming, he really did. He closed his eyes and clenched his fists and let out a long string of curses and repeated the magic words *fool* and *foolishness* over and over and over again in the hope that the genie would stay in the bottle. But of course it did no good. The storm came anyway and blew it all away, all his good work. And when it was over the place was well and truly ransacked and Michael was standing there with a poker in his hand, gazing at his own divided image in the broken hall mirror, one half of him already counting the cost of the damage and dreading its ramifications, the other half, the smug one holding the poker, framed like a torn picture before him.

Young Bobby Harris was there too, peering in over the top of the half door and whistling softly through his teeth. With wayward eyes, Michael turned to regard his handiwork. The bedroom, the bathroom, the kitchen, the tiny hall, the excuse of a scullery, all wrecked: furniture upended, vases and ornaments and dishes scattered and broken, shelves hanging down, table and chairs overturned, bed clothes ripped and torn, the sideboard with its cargo of crockery pulled from the wall, wooden pew dashed, windows smashed, paintings and pictures punctured, bric-a-brac everywhere. Food from the fridge too, hauled out and walked into the ground and shards of glass in smithereens all over the place.

'What's the matter Mister Farr?' Bobby Harris calmly and wisely wondered when the time was right. 'Woman trouble?'

Michael parked his car in the square right opposite The Angel Boutique. He could see Eleanor moving around over there, stocking the glass shelves with all the pretty things she was paid to peddle. The cops would be coming to get him any minute now: sirens going off, handcuffs produced, bundled into the back of the squad car or the black maria like a common criminal and the old familiar blanket over the head. And rightly so. Or maybe it would all be done in an old school tie fashion. No fuss. No scene of any sort. Just a few quiet words from a soft-spoken, pipe smoking detective with a ruddy complexion and a mother living in a nursing home in County Carlow or somewhere; and then a long leisurely stroll along a corridor to fill in the appropriate forms. There would be a court case, naturally enough, and a scandal when it all came out, his name in the local newspaper and that. Disgraced. *Shamed Teacher In Love Triangle.* God! … And even if it didn't all come out, all the sordid details, Eleanor would still put two and two together and kick him out of the house. Out on the street – at his age. Imagine. A flat somewhere. Over The Banjo Bar. On the other hand she might surprise him of course and show some understanding. He had read somewhere that lifers invariably throw a diabolical tantrum somewhere in the middle of their term, break up their cell and bang their heads off the wall and threaten everyone within earshot and that kind of thing. The wardens expect it seemingly, wait for it; and hold no grudges afterwards either. They just console the culprit, make him a nice cup of tea and calm him down while a couple of janitors clean up the mess; and when everything is in order again they lead the poor penitent soul back to his cell so he can finish off the rest of his sentence in relative peace and quiet, no real harm done.

Harry Hall would want his damages, needless to say. And Jim Belton would worry about the reputation of the festival. Probably ask Michael to leave the committee. Or to *stand down* as he'd eloquently put it. The lads on the building site would have a good laugh about it too. Michael was stuck between caring and not giving a toss.

'Aren't you supposed to hire a private detective for this kind of thing?'

It was Eleanor, tapping on the window. He looked up at her sorrowfully.

'Tea break, 'she told him in a muffled, far off voice, looking towards The Coffee Pot Café. 'Come on, I'll let you buy me a doughnut.'

His mobile phone was ringing. Here we go.

'Listen, Michael,' Jim Belton began on the other end. 'Harry Hall's been on to me. Young Robbie Harris just called him.'

Robbie Harris. Not Bobby. Robbie!

'Oh yeah?' Michael said casually. He had no intention of making it easy for any of them. He deserved and expected the third degree.

'Yeah,' Jim Belton continued. 'It's about the little house.'

'What about it?' Michael sort of snapped.

'Well … it seems it's in bits.'

'In bits?'

'Yeah … Ransacked! – apparently! … . Can you hear me?

'Huh?'

'Are you still there?

'Yeah.'

'Where are you anyway?'

'Downtown.'

'Oh, right … Yeah … It seems young Robbie Harris caught a couple of young lads in the cottage this morning, breaking the place up. He chased them off down the railways tracks he said. Unfortunately they gave him the slip. It's a fairly thorough job too by all accounts and it'll take a fair bit of work to clear it up. The thing is we're supposed to have whats-his-name – this Scottish writer – move in there today sometime. Jenny Sewell is going to go out to the house and try to clean up the mess. Will you see if you can stall your man for a while? Pick him up off the mid-day train and take him for lunch or something. Jenny 'll give you a bell when it's all sorted … '

Michael was listening to Jim Belton saying all of this while he watched Eleanor chatting to a lackadaisical window cleaner who was standing beside his ladder outside The Cape Of Good Hope. God only knows what she was saying to him over there. Michael had to admit that he couldn't make head nor tail of her most of the time. She could jump from Billy to Jack in the wink of an eye. One harebrained scheme after another: badminton, bridge, darts, amateur dramatics (back stage department), a new film society, whatever. And travelling – Italy and France and the annual pilgrimage to Medjugorje, (which she organised). And that time in Tunisia (or was it Turkey?) as she dragged him through the labyrinthine medina, stopping at every nook and cranny and cave and cavern that constituted this underground bazaar, to haggle about something or other: a glittering, golden lamp, a pure leather handbag, a silk scarf, a broach or a bracelet, which she'd hold up to her in wonder, a Byzantine candelabra or some other exotic thing; and then off again tirelessly through the maze of market stalls. And later, fed up of it all, he retreated for a quiet smoke and he sat on a rugged plinth and watched her from afar as she bartered with some Arab trader over this Moorish shaped birdcage that she had set her heart on. And when they eventually did the deal the Arab asked her for a kiss and she gave it to him and never even consciously registered the Arab's lusty intent. She just raised herself up on her tippy toes and kissed him. She came back to the bus proudly clutching the birdcage, which was now, incidentally, in her flower filled garden with passion flowers growing in it and twining up through it and trailing profusely all around it. 'How are we supposed to get that thing home?' Michael chided her when he saw it and she pursed her lips and blew him a kiss.

And then she took a great figeary and signed up for French lessons – two nights a week for nearly a year and a half, which Michael had to admit came in fairly handy when that French poet arrived a few years ago without a word of English. Eleanor was assigned to him and he took a great shine to her, went everywhere with her, wrote to her for ages and everything afterwards. So much so that Michael still pretended to be jealous about it from time to time. (Although in his heart of hearts he had to confess that the image of her escorting the Frenchman to his hotel in the rain that night still rankled.) And whenever Michael scolded her about it she would only beam and retort, 'Tu a jaloux toi.'

Yes, she was hard to fathom sometimes all right, no doubt about it. She was a total mystery sometimes.

' … .Anyway Michael, see what you can do,' Jim Belton was saying. 'Harry Hall is going mad, mind you, but as I said to him "Harry, you were the one who told us to leave the key under the stone, that it'd be all right" … '

Michael could not remember what came next, and when the call was over he just sat there for a moment or two and reflected on it all. He eventually got out of the car and crossed the busy street.

'She wants me to go to Medjugorje with her,' the window cleaner called out to Michael when he saw him coming. 'I mean what kind of a proposition is that?'

'You could do worse,' Michael told him from across the way.

'I could do better too,' the window cleaner declared. 'Las Vegas or somewhere. There's a good thing now goin' by,' he said as Father Corish drove through the square, a couple of hurling sticks in the back.

Eleanor waved affectionately at the vanishing priest.

'I mean why not Lourdes or somewhere?' the window cleaner continued as he climbed his ladder at long last. 'You know … somewhere we can all pronounce, like.'

Eleanor shook her head, feigning confusion, and then with her arms akimbo she called out to Michael as he drew near. 'Are you buying me this doughnut or not?' she said.

'Yeah,' Michael cried, putting his hands in the air as if it was a stick up. 'I'm buying, I'm buying,' he said.

He was hoping no one could see the sentimental tears brimming in his eyes.

'Well, come on then, 'Eleanor commanded, linking her arm lovingly into his. 'Buy it and be done with it,' she said. 'And shut up about it.'

SUSSEX GARDENS

I wake up in the morning with crusty, tired eyes and lo and behold there is a new sound added to the mix: the sound of a drill or a saw or something, its humming music conjuring up images of dust and sparks and a bloke in cement-caked boots – *Oi. Gertcha.* The sounds from the street are still there too of course – distant voices below and the noise of the traffic, sirens and alarms and car horns and what-not. Awake half the night, if truth be told. I mean you'd think that sooner or later they'd all go home to their beds, but they never did. Went on all night, a constant … flow. Eventually I drifted off of course but … it was all hours by then.

This room feels fairly cold this morning. I probably should have fiddled with that radiator last night. I'm in a shabby hotel room in Sussex Gardens by the way, just around the corner from Paddington Station, a B and B called *The Miami*; it's a pokey room with a tiny toilet and shower and a miniature basin so that I'm hard set to turn around in the place. I feel like Gulliver to be honest with you, bumping into things and knocking things over and having to stand on the bed to pull my pants up. And God only knows where my shoes are! I got in last night off the boat train. 'Aw, Mister Shannon,' the girl said when I landed. 'We've been expecting you,' like it was The Ritz or somewhere.

'Hotel Lilliput.' I said to Angie when she answered the phone. I actually wanted to touch base with the little one, but she was out at the Girl Guides.

'God, she'll be raging now she missed you,' Angie said in that martyred tone. 'You'd better send us a postcard or something,' she said, and although I promised her I would I knew I wouldn't. Well, I mean what am I going to say? *Wish you were here.*

I could have sent the little one into my mother's house for the few days I was away but she reared up when she heard I was going and Angie was there at the time and what could the poor woman do only volunteer to move in and look after her for me; and what could I do only accept?

'Well?' Angie said into the phone when the pleasantries were out of the way.

'No,' I replied,' not yet. I'm not goin' until the morning,' I told her.

'What's the point in that,' she said. 'I mean what are you waiting for, like?'

'I don't know, 'I said. 'She doesn't work nights as far as I know.'

'Who told you that?' she wondered.

'Your man,' I replied (which was a fib; all he said was that he'd heard that she worked there on and off: The Dog And Bone on The Goldhawk Road.) 'I think she's a cleaner,' I added.

'A cleaner?' Angie said, her voice practically shrieking with disbelief.

'Yeah,' I said. 'Or maybe she does the lunch or something … Anyway I'm going to go there first thing in the morning – or mid-day or whenever.'

I wish I could tell you that Angie was the salt of the earth, but she's not. Well, I mean who is? Nobody! We all want what we want. She wants what she wants and I want what I want and that's all there is to it. There's seldom any salt.

I rise up, shower and shave and before long I'm down in the basement having my breakfast, surrounded by Yanks and Germans and Australian tourists. They put me at a table in the corner, facing the wall: not that the window seat would have been any better, but at least I could have watched the legion of feet shuffling by in the rain. The waitresses are all foreigners, students I'd say. They begrudgingly go about their work, clattering around indifferently, clearing the tables and resetting them again. Not like the London of old. People were kinder then. And the service was far superior too. Everything was … well … better.

We were here on our honeymoon actually, Helen and me – twenty odd years ago … She was young and full of life then, full of mystery. I was young too I suppose although I felt ancient. Twelve years her senior, which she never let me forget. 'You'll be – let me see – sixty when I'm only what … forty-eight. God!' We went to the theatres and museums and art galleries and the cinemas. And we ate out all the time – in restaurants and bars. And she knew nothing about anything and I was acting like I knew it all … My arm around her in the taxi … Flagging the taxi in the first place! … *TAXI!* … And hopping on and off the Tube all the time, reading the map with her looking up at me with that worried, frowny face. I know now, incidentally, that that look didn't mean what I thought it meant at all, it meant something else.

I was in another dimension then, waking up in the middle of the night to find her there beside me, kissing her bare back, knowing in my heart and soul – well sensing it really, deep down, -that I was living on borrowed time with her. That night in the tavern, a few gins and tonics inside her, she rounded on me for no apparent reason – the second last day of the honeymoon it was and out of the blue too. She let rip, called me all sorts of things, brought it up for the first time, my lack of experience. And then she stormed off back to the hotel without me. In the morning she behaved as if nothing had happened, which in time would become more or less the norm I'm sorry to say.

I walk through Paddington Station, beneath its cathedral dome. Taxis zoom on by, up the ramp and away, their honking horns joining the already noisy orchestra of banging doors and whistles and announcements-..*calling at Slough, Maidenhead, Reading, Bristol Parkway, Newport, Cardiff Central, Bridgend, Port Talbot, Neath and Swansea. Change at Swansea for Fishguard Harbour ...* Two lovers at the barrier are holding hands and kissing. Reminds me of all those black and white British films I used to see when I was a young lad: '*Goodbye Darling ... goodbye!*'

I'm heading for the Metropolitan Line, up the steep steps at the far end and down the other side to the Underground. My train is waiting for me when I get there. The driver is looking out his window, his hat tilted sideways and grinning. He sort of winks at me as I climb aboard. I have a feeling he's in on it somehow. Of course I'm on the look out for Ramey Savage. He'll have some soft tack somewhere, you can bank on that – collecting tickets or sitting in a tacky office all day long with his feet up. I mean where did Helen meet that latchiko in the first place, that's what I'd like to know? The snooker hall? The betting shop? The Banjo Bar? He's in that photograph, of course, the one at home on the mantelpiece behind the thing-megig ... He's lurking in the background with his tie

221

undone and his sleeves rolled up: The Loch Garman Band reunion. I'm at a table with my arm around her, the cock of the walk. Helen is like a gin soaked ice queen beside me, staring at the camera. '*Get me out of here,*' she's silently saying. Yes, she started in on me that night too, on the way home. 'A real man knows what he wants,' she snarled. 'A real man takes what he needs.' People passing by noticed and took note – to my eternal shame. I've studied that picture over and over again, looking for some sign, searching for some clue. Did she dance with him that night, I wonder? Or maybe he talked to her at some stage, while I was at the bar maybe? Don't ask me why it matters but … .I only wish I knew, that's all. Details, details, details.

At Ladbrook Grove a busker gets on the train, an African musician in full regalia. He has a strange stringed instrument strapped around him, which he plucks and strums as he sings in some foreign dialect. *Ching ching ching ching cha ching cha ching. Ching ching ching ching cha ching chu* … .He's down the other end of the carriage, alongside a man who looks like a bulldog, singing directly into his idiotic face. I try to decipher the meaning behind all this tongue clicking. *Your Face Is Like A Well Slapped Baby (Click)/ Your Face Is Like A Well Slapped Bum (Cluck)/Your Head Is Like A Turnip (Click) / Your Eyes Are Like Two Tulips (Cluck)/ Oh Froggy Man Where Did You Come From* … The froggy man drops a few coins into the singer's extended hat and then the busker heads my way, singing a similar refrain. God only knows what he's saying about me: *your wife ran away with a loola* or something. *Ching ching ching ching cha ching ching ching ching.*

Of course you know I probably should never have bought that cottage out at Newton's Cross in the first place anyway. 'Cause Helen really hated that place, like you know. She was constantly giving out about it and complaining that she felt sort of cut off from everything out there. She probably thought that I was trying to … I don't know … tame her or something. But she refused to learn to drive, so what could I do? The little one loves it all, mind you, going up the lane to the pond and down onto the stony strand to watch the train trundle by and to feed the swans and that. Helen always maintained that that neck of the woods gave her the heebie-jeebies and I can understand that. I mean you either like that sort of thing or you don't, and she didn't. In the latter stages though, just before she ran away, she took to going up around there on her own for some reason. I'm plagued with the image of her standing on the edge of the pond and gazing into the dark water and thinking her dark, murderous thoughts about me. I sometimes wonder now if maybe she had arranged to meet him up there, the pair of them fooling around in the long grass behind my back. Angie says I shouldn't be dwelling on those kind of things, but I do.

'How long do you intend to wait for her exactly,' Angie asked me one time, her hands on her hips. 'I mean can we put a date on it, like?'

'Yeah, if you want,' I said. 'How does the 12th of Never sound?' I said, which, let's face it, was not exactly what she wanted to hear.

Ching ching ching ching cha ching ching ching … That tune haunts me as I ramble up The Goldhawk Road towards The Dog And Bone.

'Who ever said she's yours in the first place,' Helen said to me once when I brought up the subject of the little one's well being. 'I mean I'm certain sure she's mine,' she laughed, 'but can you be a hundred per cent sure she's yours?' Well, if you put it that way! *Ching ching ching ching cha ching chu* …

223

I slip into a greasy spoon café opposite The Dog And Bone and order a pot of tea and a jam doughnut. I sit near the window where I can see the door of the bar. The lady who served me comes out from behind the counter to refill the sauce bottles. A lorry driver folds his paper and slides it into the inside pocket of his donkey jacket. The sugar is in a sort of a shaker, like a saltcellar. A passing postman drops a letter into The Dog And Bone as I try to picture Angie and the little one, hand in hand, crossing the railway line. Take care, I'm thinking. Go easy … .*Ching ching ching ching cha ching cha ching* …

Ramey Savage will have grown tired of her by now I expect, bailed out with her rings and her jewellery and the last of her savings, left her alone in a dingy room with three weeks rent overdue. She'll need looking after from here on out, I'd say. She'll need … caring for. *Ching ching ching ching cha ching ching ching. Ching ching ching ching cha ching chu.*

VERDANT

'We're going for a walk, Mam,' Joan called in through the half open doorway.

'A walk?' her mother cried from the kitchen.

'Yeah,' Joan replied. 'In the woods.' and her mother made a soft musical sound that was not exactly what you'd call derogatory, but it wasn't all that complimentary either.

Brian Ludlow heard and saw all of this from the hallway where he was waiting, one hand on the latch of the front door; and then with an almost imperceptible, irritable sigh he turned his attention towards his own earnest reflection in the hall mirror: an imposing enough figure in his horn rimmed glasses, peaked cap, trench coat and leather gloves. He could see Joan's father etched there too, sitting on the couch in the living room, fiddling with the remote control, flicking from channel to channel, a crooked, sly grin on his face.

'So he's in on the joke as well,' Brian Ludlow was thinking as Joan waltzed her way down the hall towards him, a red headscarf in her hand, which she wrapped around her throat a couple of times. 'He's in on it too,' he said to himself as he opened the door.

'This way or this?' Joan wondered as soon as they stepped outside.

'This,' Brian said, pointing towards the verdant countryside, ignoring the harsh tone in her voice.

'Oh,' she said then, clearly disappointed.

Brian took control of the situation and started walking
so that she had no other option but to follow him. Joan
lived on the outskirts of Wexford town. Turn right outside
her front door and you were heading towards the town
centre, go the other way and it was sheer countryside. Had
they gone into town they could have walked along the
narrow main street and looked in the shop windows or they
might have nipped down a side street onto the quay and
maybe bought fish and chips or something on the way back
and that would have been something at least; now it was
just going to be a walk and home and nothing in between
and she really needed something in between.

Brian knew well enough what she was thinking as she
hurried to catch up with him. They had had arguments
over this before. In fact lately all they seemed to do was
bicker. They were engaged now, Brian would remind her.
The date was set, the hotel was booked and so was the
band, and all of that cost money, a lot of money, and since
her mother and father were not willing to foot the bill for
the wedding reception then they would have to pay for it
all themselves and the money was not going to drop into
their laps or anything, it was not going to just fall from the
sky. They would have to work for it and save it up. They
would have to make sacrifices. And in the meantime real
life was going to have to lie in abeyance for a while and that
was all there was to it. And she said that she knew all of
that, but that there was no need to take it to the extreme. 'I
mean there's saving and there's saving,' she said, sarcastically; and he reminded her yet again that this was all her
idea in the first place, to get married in a church with a
reception and a band and a list of guests that was getting

longer and longer by the new time – a brace of aunts and uncles and distant cousins he'd never even heard tell of up till now. He was not a religious man, as she well knew. A registry office would have done him. A short ceremony with a handful of people and away to London or someplace for a few days would have been all right with him. But no, she wanted the whole works, the whole shebang, and then nothing would do her only a honeymoon in Rome and Capri for a fortnight. And all that cost a pretty penny and it was money they hadn't got. It was all getting out of hand, he told her. It was all … too much. After all he only worked in a factory. And she worked in a shop. And she said that she knew all of that. She knew well enough where she worked. She didn't need him to tell her that.

And that was what all of this was about, all this pantomime stuff back at the house: her mother's soft musical sound from the kitchen and her father smirking in the living room and Joan's sarcastic *walk in the woods,* speech. It was all a joke, at his expense. The only problem was it wasn't particularly funny. Not from his point of view anyway. Let them make fun of someone else, he was thinking as he strode like a sergeant-major, let them find some other patsy to laugh at.

He had deliberately dressed like this tonight just to provoke her, the hat and coat and gloves. The other night – one night last week – when he turned up wearing this outfit for the very first time she had laughed at him and told him that he looked like a member of the Gestapo. And later she confessed to him that her father said he looked like a spy. 'There's an *agent provocateur* in the hall,' her father had joked, (out of the corner of his mouth if her re-enactment was anything to go by), and after she had told him this she laughed her silly laugh again, snorting through her pudgy nose like a stuck pig. And he had retaliated and told her that her father was no one to talk, sitting there on the couch night after night with his top teeth out and his hair all on end and pretending to be sick just so he could claim benefit and didn't have to go to work. Of course Joan took exception to this and stood up for her father and assured Brian, in an official tone of voice, that her father had worked all his life and that he was entitled to claim benefit if he wanted to and that he was sick, genuinely sick, and was under doctor's orders, that he was not supposed to leave the house or exert himself in any way under any circumstances. And then she had sulked all the way home and when they got back to the house she went in without even asking him to join her for a late night cup of coffee, which had become a sort of a ritual between them lately.

Brian knew now that tonight would be no different. It would end in a rancorous row the same as before and he began to wonder again if it was all worth it. He tried to recall the last good time they spent together and he could not bring any to mind. He could not recall a moment when they had been happy together, although he knew well enough that there must have been times when they'd been fairly happy together, but he could not bring any to mind right now.

At least by walking out into the country they wouldn't have to stroll silently side-by-side along the narrow main street, gazing wistfully into the shop windows at an array of items they couldn't afford to buy. And more to the point they wouldn't have to walk along the quay either. The last few times they had done that they had passed Jimmy Salinger who was clearly working on one of the fishing boats this weather. He would call out to Joan and wink at her and smirk and grin in Brian's direction as if he had the jump on him or something (which in a way Brian had to admit he had). Jimmy used to go out with Joan before Brian came along. They were supposed to be getting engaged at one point until Jimmy met someone else and bailed out and left poor Joan in the lurch. So Brian was well aware that the rumour was going around that Joan had only picked him on the rebound. He was second fiddle. At least that's what one of the jeers in the factory had said to him in the canteen one morning. 'You're only second fiddle there, boy,' he said and the whole place erupted.

Brian didn't really mind all of that except that Joan insisted on bringing Jimmy Salinger's name up every chance she got. It was, 'Jimmy said this and then Jimmy did that ... 'she'd say, smiling at the very mention of his name and showing great delight in relating to him all the mad things that Jimmy Salinger was supposed to have got up to. Anyone would think the way she went on about him all the time that he was some sort of an unsung hero in the town or something when everyone with any sense knew that he was no such thing. He was a corner boy (for want of a better word) who couldn't hold down a job to save his life, always roving from one job to another and from one girl to the next. Snooker halls and betting shops and back street bars were about the size of it with him. And to listen to him talking about all his so called adventures as he bent over the pool table in The Banjo Bar anyone would think that he was a real must to avoid or something. All exaggerated of course. All, well half of it anyway, made up.

And Brian had heard that Jimmy Salinger once bragged about some of the things he'd done with Joan one time in his brother's flat, when his brother and his wife were away for a weekend, of a sexual nature. This was tossed in Brian's face in the canteen in work another day by a puny grease monkey who was only too glad of an opportunity to rub Brian's nose in the dirt in front of everyone. Brian waylaid the culprit out in the toilet later on when no one was around and he gave him a vicious knee in the groin and a box in the jaw that sent him into a cubicle and down beside the toilet bowl, and Brian warned him if he ever mentioned that to anyone ever again he'd put his head into the toilet and flush it on him. And the same wee gentleman was more than a bit surprised, as he lay there, dazed and confused. He was surprised that Brian could flare up like that, surprised too at the strength of him in all likelihood. 'Let the word go forth,' Brian was thinking as he stepped out onto the factory floor again, and he hitched up his pants with his thumbs manfully and took off his glasses and wiped away the condensation with his handkerchief.

But of course Joan wouldn't have a word said against Jimmy Salinger. She said he was a very nice fellow at heart. A heart of gold she said he had. 'And generous to a fault,' she insisted.

'It's very easy to be generous when you've nothing to give away in the first place,' Brian reminded her.

No, he didn't want to walk along the quay tonight and witness Jimmy Salinger standing on the deck of the old trawler, his arms wrapped around the main mast and his hair falling down into his swampy eyes. In actual fact what he really wanted to do was to take Jimmy Salinger up a laneway sometime and give him a good hiding. He would take off his glasses and lay them down on a nearby windowsill, slip off his trench coat and throw his hat aside, roll up his sleeves and beckon Jimmy Salinger to come ahead. He would leave his gloves on though so as not to skin his hands or hurt his knuckles when he'd hit him. And then they'd go to it. Jimmy Salinger would be fairly handy of course, he knew that, everyone knew that, but that wouldn't bother him. Brian would be more than glad to take the kicks and the head butts and the punches initially (sometimes u᷍ in his bedroom at night he'd stand in front of the mirror and rehearse all of this, punching himself in the face just so he would be acclimatised to the stinging pain he might feel when this day did eventually arrive). He'd shake off the blows and push forward and continue to punch-straight and strong and rigid. Straight lefts and rights. Boom boom boom ... There would be no hooks or counter punches. No bending or feinting. No ducking and diving of any sort. No decorations. That's what his uncle Nicky always told him when he was teaching him to box his corner. No need for any decorations. Just brute force and ignorance will be suffice. Straight punches – one, two, three, one, two, three – driving forward all the time, pushing through Jimmy Salinger's guard, driving him back, breaking his resolve so that in the end he would back Jimmy Salinger into a corner up against the wall as one punch followed another until finally his opponent would just lose heart altogether and long for the fight to end. But of course the fight would not end. Long after Jimmy Salinger had conceded Brian would continue to punch and punch and punch, straight and strong and rigid, the back of Jimmy Salinger's head banging against the wall with every blow he'd receive. blood seeping from his mouth and nose and eyebrows, dripping down onto his clean, white shirt. And then, as Jimmy Salinger eventually slid down the wall, Brian would keep on punching and thumping and pucking, head and face and body and ribs. Boom boom boom boom ... He would not kick him or head butt him or anything like that. No, he would just hit him with his clenched fists over and over again until Jimmy Salinger was no longer standing there in front of him. And the next day when Joan wondered about his own cuts and bruises he would just tell her to go and ask Jimmy Salinger about it and she wouldn't know what to say then, and that would be the end of Jimmy Salinger and all the things he ever said and done, that would be the end of all of that.

'Where are we going exactly?' Joan asked as Brian led her through an open gateway and across a green field, skirting the border so as not trample on whatever it was that was supposed to be sown there. And Brian told her he wanted to show her something. 'What?' she asked, but he did not reply.

She had often seen the young men walking through this field from her bedroom window, skirting this very same border, with their hunting dogs and shotguns and Wellington boots. And they would be talking all the time and she'd wonder what they could possibly have to talk about all the time. She felt sorry for them sometimes – for their innocence. And then at other times she sort of envied them and she never knew why she envied them, but she did.

The sea was in front of her now, over this ditch and down this bank and across the railway line and there it lay, dark and dangerous, its foul breath everywhere. She was surprised how close her house was to the sea. She had always been under the impression that she lived far from the sea, mainly because the front of her house faced the other way, out towards the road. But she was not far from the sea at all, just up the road and across this field and there it was. All the time she thought she lived far from the sea and she didn't at all.

A strange shaped tree seemed to bar the way, its crooked, twisted limbs curling up into a pair of arms that waved with the wind, urging her to, '*go back, go back.*' She could almost hears its augural voice crying, '*go back,*' but she could not bring herself to heed the warning and as she climbed through the barbed wire fence she caught her dress in a spike which tugged and dragged and held her firm and when she tried to release it she tore her stocking and got a nasty nick on her wrist so that a tiny gush of blood flowed out to stain her cuffs. She instinctively sucked at the wound to ease the pain, frustrated tears welling up in her eyes.

Brian was moving on ahead, oblivious to her distress, and although she wanted to cry out to him she did not give in to it. She wanted to call his name and tell him to wait for her, but the words wouldn't come. She couldn't bring herself to call his name. In fact at this precise moment in time she could never imagine calling his name ever again. She had a good mind to turn around and amble home without him, without even telling him where she was going, but in a way she had gone too far for all of that now and so she followed him, over the ditch and down the bank of clover and up along the rusty tinted tracks, looking over her shoulder at the tree, which was still soundlessly wailing and wildly beckoning her back.

Brian glanced at her as she hurried towards him. Where had she gone to at all, he wondered – the girl he used to know? She had flaming hair then and sparkling white teeth and her body was contoured. This was when she was going out with Jimmy Salinger. Brian would often see the pair of them scooting about the town, arm in arm. Nipping into The Banjo Bar. Or heading home from a disco. One night he followed the two of them home and on the way Jimmy Salinger took Joan up an alleyway and Brian waited across the street to see how long she would stay up there with him and he waited a long time and would have waited a lot longer only someone he knew came along and asked him what he was doing there and Brian had to make up some lame excuse and go with him; and so he never found out how long she stayed up there with Jimmy Salinger and he had to admit, foolish as it may seem, that the thought of it still rankled even in this day.

Her hair was mousy coloured now, and it was frizzled, especially when it rained. And her teeth were sort of bucked, protruding out from under her upper lip like a rabbit. She looked like a rabbit when she ate, nibbling like a rabbit or a weasel or something of that sort. She wasn't contoured anymore now either. She was fat. Well, bordering on it anyway. He had no desire to hold her or to kiss her or anything even remotely romantic like that any more and he began to think that it was all a mistake, one big mistake. But what could he do? The hotel was booked and the band was hired and the honeymoon was almost paid for. They would lose all their deposits if they pulled out now. They would lose the lot.

His mother had never had any time for Joan of course, right from the word go. He could tell by his mother's face the first time he introduced them to each other.

'Well?' he wondered after Joan was gone.

'I don't know,' his mother replied, dubiously, staring into space as if she were searching for the right words to describe how she felt about her and finding none. And a few days later when Brian pressed her again on the matter she answered,' Well, she's not exactly what I expected, Brian, let's put it that way.'

His mother would sometimes wince when she'd see Joan arriving, wince at the brightness of her clothes or the shrillness of her voice or the cut of her hairstyle. She'd shake her head to indicate that it was all beyond her comprehension, this strange pairing; and whenever Joan tried to speak to her, Brian's mother would only half listen, dismissing nearly everything she'd say as if it was total rubbish or immaterial, and then with some snide remark she'd take herself off to another room. And when it was time to leave Joan would call in to her, 'Goodbye Mrs Ludlow, see you during the week sometime, eh?' she'd say, and Brian's mother would peer out with a quizzical look on her face as if she had completely forgotten that Joan was ever there in the first place and was wondering what difference could it possibly make one way or another to either of them whether she saw her during the week or not. She'd regard Brian with a pitiful expression when Joan was gone and she'd shake her head again and waft the air and open up a window to banish the smell of Joan's perfume from the room.

'She means well, Mother,' Brian would say.

'I'm sure she does, dear,' his mother would reply, 'but …'

She would look at Brian sorrowfully when he came in late at night now, weary from all the bickering; and when he'd go up to the attic to operate his model railway or to listen to his classical records she would tiptoe up with a cup of tea for him and a few biscuits on a plate and leave them down on the shelf beside him and withdraw without a word.

∽

When Joan eventually caught up with him again Brian was standing on the edge of Rainwater Pond. He had his back turned to her and his coat was open, the belt dangling, and his two hands were buried deep inside his pants pockets. His cap was tilted back on his head and he was gazing distractedly into the depths of the grey, dirty water. She deliberately remained a few feet away from him. (In more ways than one there was distance between them now.)

As soon as he sensed her near Brian stepped, uncharacteristically, onto the old broken down quarry wall and walked out to the middle of the pond, the water lapping up around the ends of his trousers, which put her in mind of the time Jimmy Salinger had led her here and he had done the very same thing – kicked off his shoes and socks and rolled up his pants and stepped onto the wall. The tide was high that day and the sea rushed in under the elevated viaduct to flood the pond, submerging the old wall so that from afar Jimmy looked like he was magically walking on the water. And he presented this spectacular feat to her through a pair of gleaming eyes and a set of snow-white teeth and a clear, beautiful complexion and sporting a big brazen smile. And when he beckoned for her to come out and join him she just shook her head and took a backward step and he laughed and pretended to stumble so that she gasped and put her hands to her mouth until he had righted himself again.

And here was Brian now, standing in the very same place where Jimmy had once stood, shattering the illusion somehow. And if Jimmy was the sun that day then Brian was the moon right now, and his very appearance bore testimony to it: dry patches of skin around his nose and flecks of dandruff on his collar; he was partial to sties and pimples and mouth ulcers too and boils that bulged up from beneath his shirt, all outward signs of course of some inner, nocturnal … something or other. And whereas Jimmy was forever laughing and joking about everything under the sun (annoyingly so sometimes) Brian was hard set at the best of times to even crack a smile. And there were other things too, other differences. For instance, Jimmy forgot everything you told him the minute you said it while Brian remembered every minute detail, stored it up and filed it away for a time when it might be drummed up again to punish you for some minor misdemeanour or to remind you of something you once said or done.

And now it was beginning to dawn on Joan why Brian had brought her here today. He knew that she had come here a couple of times with Jimmy Salinger in the past, (he knew that because she had told him so), and he wanted her to know that he had not forgotten the fact. Or perhaps he wanted to teach her something – a lesson of some sort. What was it? Something. He wanted her to know that he was not afraid of this place. He was not afraid to come here, that he would pit himself against any of them any day of the week – Jimmy Salinger or any of them. Swimming, diving, fighting, whatever. Was that it? Or maybe he just wanted her to see this place for what it really was, a dirty patch of ground where the corner boys and the so-called hard cases congregated, and a pond that was filled with rusty things and dead dogs and buckled prams and bicycles and supermarket trolleys and debris of every description. He wanted her to admit that it was a dirty place with no redeeming features whatsoever. None. Jimmy Salinger used to be the kingpin around here once upon a time, walking on the water and all that jazz, but what did that mean? Nothing. This place was nothing and Jimmy Salinger was nothing. He wanted her to admit it, to herself at least if not out loud. 'All right,' she wanted to scream. 'Jimmy Salinger is nothing. This place is nothing. Satisfied?'

Brian, as if intuiting what she was thinking, slowly turned to look at her. She called out to him and asked him if he was all right and she felt outside herself all of a sudden and her voice was not her own. He did not reply of course. Instead he turned sideways to study his own bloated, distorted image in the water: belted trench coat, peaked cap like a squire, gloves on, glasses glinting; and that was when the niggling voice told him that something was going to have to give around here. He always knew it of course and somewhere in her heart she knew it too. Someone would have to take command of this ship or they'd all go down. Rules would have to be written and abided by. Certain things would have to be forbidden. Other things would have to be obeyed. For a start she would not be allowed to mention Jimmy Salinger ever again. It was forbidden. He would not permit it. And he would not be laughed at again either. Not by her and not by her mother and father and not by anyone. She was going to have to get that through her head. To have and to hold was one thing, to honour and obey was another. To honour and obey was the main thing to remember from here on out. But would she listen to him though, that was the thing? Probably not. She could be fairly headstrong when she set her mind to it. She would resist it. She had done it before – resisted him. That time, the one time, when she came to the factory, to bring him his sandwiches (wrapped in tinfoil of all things), and she had stood in the doorway of the canteen watching him as he sat alone at the far end of the room while Jimmy Salinger, who worked there for a fortnight, held sway over a bunch of mesmerised galoots at a nearby table; and he knew what she was thinking, that Jimmy Salinger was everything and he was nothing. And she still thought that now. She still believed that now and nothing he would ever do or say would convince her otherwise, and all the time it was the other way around: Jimmy Salinger was nothing and he was everything. And true, Jimmy Salinger was surrounded that day, yeah, but what did that mean? Nothing. That meant nothing, nothing at all. Galoots.

Anyway, she came to the table where he was sitting that day and presented the sandwiches to him and he couldn't help but notice that there was a certain amount of pity in her eyes. (Laughable as it may sound but that was the truth.) She pitied him. And as she left the room she looked over her shoulder at him and there it was again – pity. She felt sorry for him. This little Wexford girl with the pudgy nose and bucked teeth and big, broad backside going out the door and she felt sorry for him. It made him want to laugh really. And he wanted to cry out to her that he was the one who felt the pity. Pity and shame!.Yes, shame! He was ashamed of her, ashamed of her bucked teeth and her dowdy clothes and her mousy coloured hair. And later that evening he went to her house and told her that she was never to come to the factory again, no matter what. Never. Those sandwiches should have been in his lunchbox, he informed her, not wrapped up in tinfoil like he was some messenger boy, and she had stood up to him, told him where to get off and said some things about his mother and even brought his uncle Nicky into it. And she said all of this in a loud voice so that her mother and father could hear it clearly from the other room. And every time he thought about all that it made him squirm. And even now as he stood here on this old broken down wall he felt himself quake with anger, his feet burrowing into the granite beneath him so that a brief avalanche of stones and dirt fell down into the water below to create a hundred and one tiny ripples that came and went like radio waves.

'Jimmy Salinger is nothing,' he muttered with venom. 'Nothing.' And then he had to take out his handkerchief from his trench coat pocket and wipe a splatter of spittle from the front of his shirt.

When Brian turned to walk towards her his face was red with rage and it was plain to see that there was murder in his heart. It was written on his face. She could see it in his eyes. She wanted to turn and flee but some animal instinct told her it would be better to stay put. He would only pursue her and catch her and drag her into the long grass. She glanced back at the tree, its two arms shielding its spectral eyes now from the impending tragedy. She longed to cry out to someone, but she didn't know what name to call. Her father? Jimmy Salinger? Who? No one would hear her. No one would come. Her main thought was that she was not really prepared to die. And she wondered now how he might kill her? Strangle her in all probability. With his hands, his soft hands. Or he might use his belt. Or her red scarf. Or beat her to death with a stone. Batter her until she fell to the ground and then hammer her face beyond recognition. Or a fence post, maybe. Pull it out of the ground and stab her with the sharp part, through the heart. And then beat her into a pulp with it until the fence post snapped in two. He'd drag her battered body to the water's edge then and frantically fill up her pockets with rocks and stones and fistfuls of dirt and lower her into the pond. And through a pair of sunken eyes he'd watch her sink. Or else he'd leave her covered up among the nettles and weeds and the soothing dock leaves. He'd go home then, shuffling Cain-like down the dusty laneway, and when his mother asked him about the blood on his shirt he'd make up some excuse, that he had a nose bleed or something, and his mother would tell him to go upstairs and change it and he would, and after that he'd retire to the attic to play with his model railway and to listen to his classical records as if nothing had happened. And in the morning the police would arrive to arrest him. They'd take him out to Rainwater Pond and upon his arrival her dead body would suddenly begin to bleed again.

She was thinking all of this as he stepped off the wall and onto dry land and she told herself that she must remain calm and try to placate him somehow. She smiled falsely and reached out to pluck a tread of nothing-at-all from his coat sleeve and she flicked it away fondly; and as he moved closer to her she swatted an invisible insect from in front of his face. But she could tell by his earnest expression that he was not placated and she instinctively retreated in fear when he reached out to touch her. And he grabbed hold of her arm and drew her near to him and he held her fast and firm and he knew that he was hurting her and he didn't care and his cold eyes told her everything. She would not laugh at him again. If she laughed at him again she would be sorry. If she laughed at him or questioned him about anything ever again she would be very, very sorry. And it was forbidden to ever mention Jimmy Salinger again either. Ever! It was not allowed. He would not permit it. Out of the goodness of his heart he would leave things stand as they are, although his better judgement told him otherwise. But no, he would allow it. They would go through the motions now, wedding and reception and honeymoon and all that nonsense, but she needed to understand that this would be the last time he would ever yield to her – the very last time. She needed to understand all of that and he needed to know that she understood it. He told her all of this with his merciless eyes and with his vice-like grip, and she assured him with her frightened eyes that she did understand it and that she would comply. 'Good!' he seemed to say then, and he left it at that.

'Come on,' he eventually mumbled, letting go her arm, which she unconsciously caressed. 'Let's get you home,' he said in a soft voice.

He marched off ahead of her and she raced after him. They went back the roadway, down the dusty lane past the cluster of houses and onto the main road, and she linked her arm into his as if they were already married. When they got to the house she invited him in for a late night cup of coffee, but he refused. He gave her a light kiss on the cheek and set off homeward. She wanted to call out to him as he walked away, but she didn't know what to say to him and so she didn't in the end, she just let him go. She watched him for a long time, watched him as he went, watched as he faded in the distance, watched as he finally disappeared and when he was gone she watched the cold empty horizon where his body had been.

When Brian arrived home that night he paused in the hallway to wipe his feet on the mat. He took off his coat and hat and gloves and hung them carefully in the closet in the hall before calling into his mother in the kitchen that he was going up to the attic. There was a lovely smell coming from the kitchen – rhubarb tart and homemade brown bread. The dog was asleep in his favourite place on the landing. Brian had to step over it to get to where he was going. The grandfather clock at the top of the stairs chimed ten-fifteen as he passed and his mother called up the stairs to him to switch off the chimes, which he would have automatically done anyway.

Up in the attic he set his train and tracks in motion and he stood and watched as it wended its miniature way through Swindon and Reading and Maidenhead and Slough, and finally arrived at Paddington Station, right on time. His mother brought him up a cup of tea and a few biscuits on a plate and when she was gone he drank the tea and ate some of the biscuits and he thought about Joan again. He pictured her climbing into her nightclothes, brushing her teeth and turning out the light. He imagined her tucked up in bed with the light from the moon shining in through the tiny windowpane, falling silvery across the tasselled rug on the floor at the foot of her bed. And then she'd close her eyes and fall asleep and dream of their future life together, and it sort of amused him to think that she'd probably never even know how close she was that night; she'd probably never know how close she came.

SOME SILENT PLACE

It was just a casual remark really, a joke when all was said and done, but for some reason it cut right to the quick this time, touched the very nub of his so called insecurity. After a ferocious workout -twelve broken hurling sticks, one dislocated finger and a calf muscle pulled, and poor Tommy Hawkins carried off the field in a sitting position – the entire squad were being fed and watered in Anne's Country Kitchen: homemade vegetable soup, followed by prime beef steak and baby potatoes and lightly glazed carrots on the side with traditional jelly and ice cream to follow; a riotous feast which gave rise to a medley of conversations and the jangled din of delph and cutlery as twenty six or seven ravenous hurlers yapped about sprained ankles and torn ligaments and damaged cruciates and buxom Jersey girls; the odd glance now and then too of course towards the elevated area where Maurice Dunne the sartorial manager and the other blazered selectors and mentors were seated.

Big Red Devereux ruled the roost at the players' main table, looking for double helpings of everything and offering to polish off anyone else's unwanted dinner, Jaz Corcoran minding his own plate zealously and Tommy Hawkins nursing what turned out to be a cracked tibia; and all the while Anne was weaving her sloe-eyed, gentle sorcery as she glided from table to table: a hand on a shoulder, a reassuring smile, a tie straightened, a button fastened, a tender word, a nod here and there, a coquettish wink, a knowing gesture to some down-in the-dumps player, her soft soothing voice humming some vaguely recognisable tune as she worked the room.

Donie Green, her husband (and official coach to the Wexford squad), occupied the arched opening to the kitchen like a maitre'd, keeping tabs on things. Donie's hair was flecked with grey now and his girth had grown, but he still possessed the slow heartbeat and the grace and noble poise of an aging hurling hero.

'Easy, Red,' Donie joked as he cruised. 'We want our lads to be able to get around you on the day.'

'I'd rather go around him than through him at this stage, Donie,' Jaz Corcoran grinned from a nearby seat, and big Red beat his chest and yodelled like Tarzan.

This tradition of nourishment had started last season and had produced reasonable results too in Donie's estimation and, in spite of the silent cries of nepotism that surely echoed throughout the small town, Donie – with the blessing of the County Board – had decided to continue the practise for at least another term. Anne's cosy French style bistro (well, in design anyway if nothing else – open wooden beams across the ceiling and wine-filled alcoves everywhere and an intricate spiral staircase leading to the decorated loft above) would do well out of it, naturally enough, but at least he'd be sure that the troops were well looked after in the process; and, let's face it, when all was said and done these quaint surroundings certainly put those shabby old clubhouses in the shade.

Father Corish pushed his empty soup bowl aside and tucked into his main meal. The ruddy complexioned priest

– affectionately (and sometimes not so affectionately) known as Corish by all and sundry – was the permanent chaplain to the team. He was also a resident hurl carrier, or as he put it himself, 'he opened and shut a few gates now and then.' The chair beside him was vacant, which caused him to regard it from time to time and sigh miserably and shake his head despondently. Young Kevin Troy, who had a baby face that belied his inner mettle, was on the far side of the empty place, too young and much too hungry to care; and anyway Anne was standing over him now, her hand lightly resting on his shoulder. He looked up at her lovingly as she plucked a speck of something or other from his lapel. Yes, it was true: Jersey girls haunted his fantasies, but, like the rest of the players, it was Anne who invaded his dreams.

'Donie told me I was to try and fatten you up a bit,' Anne softly declared.

'Me?' big Red wondered from across the way.

'No, Red,' she replied. 'Not you, I'm afraid … As a matter of fact he said you're to forgo your jelly and ice cream, actually.'

Red frowned, crestfallen. 'Ah, Anne,' he implored. 'Have a heart.'

'Give his dessert to the child there, Anne,' Jaz Corcoran cried, and young Kevin, fairly used to it all by now, waved them all away.

At seventeen years of age Kevin was indeed the newfound fledgling, in fact this was his first year on the county panel. Spotted in a local club game last season when his team the Faythe Harriers met Oulart-The Ballagh in the second round of the Club Championship. The Harriers were beaten badly that day, but if The Scribe in the local rag was anything to go by, then: *Young Kevin Troy was the one to watch*. It was that beautiful move that did the trick:

stealing the sliotar right from under Jaz Corcoran's nose like that as the thirty two year old veteran, and captain of the opposing side, tried to solo on by with the ball glued to his stick. Kevin just reached in with his hurl and scooped it away from him – *picked his pocket,* as the paper put it – and then without even touching the ball the young player doubled on it and sent it on its merry way to land in the square where his stanch comrade Bertie Bolger waltzed in and rattled the back of the net. Merely damage limitation by that time unfortunately, but nevertheless: *Kevin Troy was on his way.*

Kevin would do some beautiful things on the hurling field in the subsequent years, yet those in the know swear that nothing would ever surpass or even compare to that beautiful move that he made that day. At the time we're talking about now though Kevin still had a lot to learn and even more to prove, and before the season was out he would deliver on both counts.

A phantom icy draught wafted in from somewhere, unsettling the edges of the tablecloths and making the serviettes lightly flitter, and Kevin sensed a definite sea change in the room as Donie shuffled uneasily beneath the arch and the deafening din modulated to a more muted sort of sound. And there were a few other telltale signs too: Father Corish stopped eating, glanced over his shoulder and visibly sighed; Red Devereux put his knife and fork down on the table as if his appetite was on the wane; Jaz Corcoran stopped talking mid-sentence and his easygoing eyes darkened; and the denizens of the top table overhead seemed suddenly all of a dither. Kevin had to turn nearly full circle in his chair to see what all the fuss about.

And there he was, leaning in the doorway, his back to an azure patch of star-stitched night sky, his slouching stance unmistakable. He was eating a big greasy hamburger and carrying a parcel of fish and chips under his oxster, and there was a wreath of dissipating smoke hanging in the vicinity of his shoulder blade, although there was no sign of a spent cigarette anywhere. His kit bag was at his feet, its straps looped around his hurling stick, his very own quiver and bow. He wore a mischievous grin that emanated from a rugged, handsome visage that would be more at home in an old fashioned daguerrtype or profiled on the back of some rusty Roman coin. His nose had been broken, fixed and fractured again and he had a fairly pronounced scar over his right eye that no one was ever allowed to mention. His skin was clear and sallow and his eyes were brown and beautiful. He was not particularly tall – five nine or thereabouts – and his body was squat and compact, a mass of thewed muscle and bone, as anyone who had ever the misfortune to collide against him would readily testify: *a virtual cul-de-sac* was The Scribe's curt description of him. And even now at the tender age of twenty nine you could tell that someday soon – in the not too distant future in fact – he would go to seed: he'd gain a gut and his face would soon become jowled and haggard and more than a little lived in.

If Maurice Dunne was conscious of him in the doorway below then he never let on, although some of the other mentors were not so accommodating. One or two of them actually shook their heads and scowled and Frances Farrell, the County Secretary, had to be restrained from going down after him and saying something to him.

The new arrival showed scant regard for any of them as he strode leisurely across the room, serenading them all with a snatch of his favourite ballad. '*Were I At The Mosshouse/Where The Birds Do Increase,*' he wryly warbled.

Father Corish shifted in his seat uncomfortably and drummed out a agitated tattoo on the tabletop with his fingertips as Mick Hyland slid in beside him to shove back the milk jug and the ornate sugar bowl and the other matching utensils; and then he opened up the parcel on the table in front of him, called out for some vinegar (which, needless to say, went unheeded) and began applying salt in abundance and licking his fingers with relish as he ate.

'Where are you goin' with that shit?' Father Corish snapped at him angrily out of the side of his mouth.

'This?' Mick Hyland replied, 'is just what the doctor ordered, mate.'

'All the good grub here and you go out and ... I don't know ... '

'What?'

'I'm goin' outside for a smoke.' Father Corish griped as he rose. 'Kevin, don't let him near my dessert,' he flung over his shoulder as he fled.

'Next Sunday will be the fourteenth Sunday after Pentecost,' came Mick's fond farewell. 'They'll never catch him.'

Kevin laughed and the hollow sound of his laughter had a lonely old ring to it as Mick Hyland winked at him sideways and proceeded to wolf down his fish and chips, offering them about brazenly, in vain, to this one and that.

Normally Anne would have wagged a remonstrating finger at the culprit of such a prank, or poked him playfully in the ribs or the like, but not this time. No, Mick Hyland was a strange fish, a mystery or, as one well known radio commentator summed him up after a rather tight-lipped interview, *'a tongue-tied enigma!* And so instead Anne just sort of expelled a forlorn, disappointed sound from her pursed lips and her eyes grew melancholy as she moved towards the kitchen, laden with dirty dishes.

Kevin hoped that his laughter had not seemed ignorant or impudent and he gazed from face to face to try and gauge the situation. Big Red definitely disapproved. Jaz

Corcoran was not enamoured either. Tommy Hawkins appeared mildly amused while Donie turned his back on it all, frowned and followed Anne into the kitchen. Donie taught hurling skills, corrected bad habits and pointed out minor faults and failings and more or less took charge of the physical side of things: bad manners was someone else's province. Up above, Maurice Dunne didn't even deign to entertain the commotion below and carried on doing what he was doing all along, chewing the cud with Frances Farrell and writing things down officiously in his notebook – dates and times and telephone numbers.

Mick Hyland was, by definition, the knave of the pack – yes, the genuine article! Or 'a rebel without applause,' as Donie had secretly dubbed him. Look into Mick Hyland's heart (if you dare) and you'd find mutiny there. And defiance. Loyalty? No. Everlasting fealty? Absolutely not. The only thing that saved him was his sometimes genius on the playing field. Hurling lore had it that if Mick Hyland took the trouble to go up for a ball then he very seldom came back down without it; and once he had it you couldn't take it from him. You couldn't hook him and it was twice as hard to block him, and if he took off at a lick it would take a good man to catch him over a short distance. He was tough and he was fast and in a strange sort of way he was fair. Once, or so it goes, he even stood up for a member of the opposing side. Red Devereux was giving this wee lad (Jack Cassidy, the Antrim full forward, who was running rings around the big fellow), dog's abuse on the field – pulling him and dragging him back and hunching and mauling and hurting him. Mick, sheathed in sweat, brushed roughly against Red on the way by and muttered something derogatory in his ear and the big full back took offence and there was very nearly fisticuffs between the two team-mates there and then, the pair of them pulled apart by members of the opposing side, which, as you might expect, caused the ref to scratch his head and wonder about it all. It goes without saying that the dressing room at half time had its own tale to tell, but that's another day's work.

Anne came round with tea and coffee for everyone as if nothing was amiss, a pointing pot in each hand.

'Tea?' she sang, her eyes like saucers. 'Coffee? Anyone?'

Frances Farrell, the greedy bastard, ordered both tea and coffee, which he drank almost simultaneously: a sip of tea first and then a sip of coffee, eventually draining each cup to its dregs and devouring the finger-shaped chocolate biscuits that were placed daintily on each side plate. Anne didn't bat an eyelid when he asked her for both, but anyone could see by her expression that she was perplexed.

'Braces and a belt!' was Donie's description of Frances Farrell when she told him about it afterwards.

Behind Anne's back Jaz Corcoran put his hand on his heart and hummed a sentimental love song to emphasise his secret affection for her – *Love Is Like A Violin* – and Red reached out and wrestled him into a playful headlock.

'She's mine,' he growled. 'Do you hear me – all mine.'

'What do you think of her, Mick?' Tommy Hawkins laughed as the others bumped painfully against him, and he steered a glance in Anne's beautiful direction, her red dress swishing.

'Go away from me,' Mick Hyland grumbled, rolling the grease-ridden paper up into a ball and palming it across the table towards him. 'And don't be annoyin' me,' he added.

'What?' Red wanted to know then.

Mick laughed scornfully and shook his head, which gave the impression that he was having second thoughts about what he was about to say. Red waited for a reply, Jaz Corcoran still held comically captive in his grip.

'Look,' Mick told them all, lowering his voice and scanning the immediate horizon. 'As far as I'm concerned they're all the same in the dark,' he said, 'and it don't matter who they are.'

'Who's that?' Red pressed. 'Women?'

Mick pointed a big fat half-eaten chip at him to confirm that now he was getting the gist of it, and Red's eyes glazed over, as Mick Hyland always maintained they were inclined to do whenever the big fellow was forced to think something through. ('Watch him sometime,' Mick urged Kevin once. 'I mean at the best of times the man's a moron.')

'Yeah, right,' Jaz Corcoran said sarcastically, suddenly emerging from the scrum and fixing his hair and his rumpled attire. 'Dream on, pal!' he said.

'What?' Mick Hyland snarled, a half a dozen players surrounding him now. 'Do you think I couldn't – if I set my mind to it?' he bragged and his eyes darted towards the pay-desk where Anne was standing at the till, raised up on her tippy toes, the ankle and delicate instep of one foot exposed to the elements as she totted and stared vacantly into space.

Silence fell. Nobody wanted to even speculate about something like that. Jersey girls, yeah, sure! But Anne? No. Never. Mick waited for someone to take him up on the offer and when it went unchallenged he just threw his hands in the air and lightly scoffed. Mick was good with women, – well, certain women anyway – everyone knew that. In fact there was a rumour going around that he had sired a couple of children by various girls around the town, although most of that went unacknowledged. But Anne would hardly fall for his usual bullshit and banter. Anne would hardly succumb to that. Still, the thought was there, the notion had been placed or how-would-you-put-it ... planted. Tommy Hawkins stirred restlessly in his seat and

Jaz Corcoran had a pained expression on his face. Red, who was going out with Jean Bradley now (one of Mick's former conquests) looked confused, reading something subliminal into it, an ulterior motive or a slight of some kind.

'What did he say again?' Tom Foley, forever on the outskirts of everything, double-checked, and when Tommy Hawkins repeated what had been said Tom Foley frowned and shook his head, barely cloaking his disgust.

Father Corish came back in the middle of it all, rubbing his hands together and looking forward to his jelly and ice cream.

'Don-fucking-Quan where he is!' Red eventually sneered as he rose and the whole place started laughing. The outburst caused some of the others above to look over the banisters inquisitively and call down merrily to them, 'What's goin' on down there?'

Kevin laughed too and Father Corish, fearing he was the butt of some joke or other, silently wondered what they were all laughing at.

Mick Hyland, however, looked like a man possessed, his face dark and dangerous now.

∞

'Did you ever see the likes of that in all your born days,' Father Corish was saying to Kevin as they watched Mick disappear into the cottage. 'Did you see him?' Father Corish continued. 'Hoppin'off a big hamburger. I mean there's neither sense nor meaning to that … The best of grub there and he goes off and … I don't know … He seems to be hell bent on becoming persona non grata if you ask me. You know? … I mean what's the point?'

They were parked outside Mick's oily garage at Newton's Cross – two petrol pumps and a dingy galvanised workshop attached to a dilapidated two-up-two-down council house in the back of beyond: a man's realm with cowboy books and dirty ashtrays and cups and saucers in the sink and hurling paraphernalia and unironed clothes flung about the place any-old-how, his mother and father long dead and gone by then of course. Kevin had been in the house on several occasions: to hurry Mick up more often than not; or to rouse him from his slumber another time, Jean Bradley sound asleep in the crumpled bed beside him; and once to find him -dirty face and grimy hands and scattered wrenches and the tinny sound of a transistor radio – out in the yard underneath the belly of a suspended automobile as Father Corish waited impatiently out front in his idling motor car.

The three of them had formed a sort of Blessed Trinity of late, travelling to practise and home together again; and sticking together for the games too, Mick refusing to go on the team bus with the others. And Maurice Dunne, who could be a real stickler for protocol at the best of times, allowing the agreement stand, for peace sake, as long as Father Corish vowed to get them there on time and in one piece.

'The first time you're late is the last time I'll allow it,' Maurice Dunne warned Father Corish when he heard of the breach.

'Did you hear him?' Father Corish complained as they wended their way homewards that night -the three of them – the phrase, '*allow it*,' sticking in his craw. 'Giving me orders! I wouldn't mind but I'm after forgetting more about hurling than he'll ever know,' Father Corish went on, and Mick Hyland looked at him askance and mumbled something disparaging under his breath, which of course propelled Father Corish into another tirade about how much he knew and didn't know about the game of hurling.

Father Corish would usually collect Kevin first. 'You be at the gate now, waiting,' he'd tell him and normally Kevin would gladly comply – kit bag, helmet and hurl and angelic appearance, his mother agog at the window. And then they'd nip out to Newton's Cross where Mick would invariably put them through the hoops, Father Corish cursing him into a knot so that poor Kevin would be stuck between the noisy duo, arguing and bickering and complaining all the way to Thurles or Clonmel or Portlaoise or Dublin or wherever the hell they were supposed to be heading.

'It's alright for you,' Father Corish would bellow at the top of his voice. 'I'm the one who gets the shaggin' blame if we're late, God forgive me for cursing.'

Sometimes Nancy Byrne would tag along, sitting in the back seat beside Kevin, hugging her handbag, a chequered, tartan blanket across her lap in the winter months. She'd usually wait in a nearby hotel during the game and afterwards Father Corish would slip off to meet her while the team were having their meal. An hour or so later the pair of them would turn up, smelling of sherry and whisky and, as Mick Hyland slyly put it, 'the reek of hoochie coochie.'

'Is Kitty The Hare comin' with us tonight, Corish?' Mick would tease Father Corish sometimes.

'That'll do you now,' Father Corish would bark and Mick might hum a few bars of 'My Good Luck Charm,' just to add fuel to the fire.

Where had it all begun? In the Craobh Rua clubhouse actually – Mick's old stomping ground. Mick Hyland sitting taciturn on the wooden form in the crowded changing room, his head bent and his left hand cupped around the ball (or the sliotar in hurling parlance), his red helmet at his feet and his old faithful hurl – his name emblazoned along the handle – abandoned in the corner against the wall as if he wanted nothing more to do with it. The sliver of blue sky that presented itself in the broken window behind him was a mere mirage: outside was a wintry late November Sunday morning.

The room, heady with wintergreen, was crammed with players, all togged out and moving about, swapping laces and liniment and corn plasters and masking tape and what-have-you, and slipping out for a leak behind the clubhouse and coming back freezing with the cold, their legs all chapped and their faces on fire: Jaz Corcoran, big Red Devereux, nifty Tom Foley, the diminutive Tommy Hawkins, the cream of the crop in other words from all the numerous clubs, all gathered here for the annual try out with the county squad.

Young Kevin Troy, just turned seventeen, was there too, under false pretence in his own estimation. And Bertie Bolger, his old club mate, grinning like a Cheshire cat, loving it all and relishing the chance to get back into the big league again (although before the month was up, this poor, heart-broken, wounded warrior would be weeded out of the herd).

Father Corish appeared in the doorway, ash stains down the front of his black suit and his trousers shining with a worn patina of age. Kevin had heard about him before, the wayward, belligerent priest who smoked and drank too much and was given to whipping off the collar when cornered and milling into a fight if ever he was called upon to do so.

'Right lads,' Father Corish stoutly bawled. 'Let's get to it,' and like it or not they all rose to brave the elements, pushing and shoving and larking about as they childishly jostled their way out the door. Mick Hyland was the last one on his feet, reluctantly reclaiming his helmet from the floor and his hurl from the corner and falling in line, ungainly enough in the light of day.

Donie stood in the middle of the frost-bound field, the entire squad gathered round him, steam coming from their mouths as they blew into their cupped hands and stamped their feet and swung their arms like windmills. A small band of spectators huddled together on the sideline – hardy snipes who shuffled and speculated: a man and his daughters, an old hurler and his son, a couple of curious connoisseurs, their distant voices echoing eerily throughout the barren frozen playing field.

Anne was there too – Kevin's first faraway sighting of her. She was standing alongside her car, which was parked by the clubhouse, her collar turned up and a cosy scarf muffled around her. She gave a tender wave to Donie, and anyone else that was interested, and then she slipped back into the warmth and comfort of her trendy blue Volkswagen Beetle again.

'How many of us is in it anyway,' Donie was wondering as he calculated. 'Twenty three. All right … '

Two teams were picked to play against each other, ten a side with a couple of lads alternating on the bench. Father Corish would referee the match. 'Take it nice and handy now, lads,' he told them as he threw in the sliotar, the sound of birds all around and the chiming of bells tolling faintly. Donie went out to say hello to Anne, crunching across the crispy field, and returning to the sideline with a flask of tea where along with Maurice Dunne, the new manager, and a few selectors he watched the proceedings and jotted down the more salient episodes.

The game was lack-lustre enough with most of the players just going through the motions: the ground was hard and the ball was soggy and the hurlers rusty after the long winter lay off. Mick Hyland hardly broke a sweat; Big Red Devereux wasn't much better; Jaz Corcoran was no great shakes either; while Kevin, on the other hand, went at it hammer and tongs. So much so that before the second half began the others had good-humouredly christened him Mister

Enthusiastic. 'Give it to Mister Enthusiastic,' someone would say and sure enough they would and when they did Kevin would duly notch up another score to his credit.

'There,' someone said from behind as Kevin lofted another point over the bar from thirty yards out. 'Write that down,' and the new recruit turned to receive a congratulatory wink from Tom Foley, last year's county captain.

They only played twenty minutes each way that morning before going back into the clubhouse again. As they dressed, Maurice Dunne, in his Sunday suit, stood in the middle of the room and gave them all a bit of a pep talk: about teamwork and commitment and the long, hard road ahead and so on. Through the window Kevin spied Anne for the second time as she sat in the front of the car, listening to the radio, tapping out a rhythm on the steering wheel, her cheeks flushed and her eyes twinkling against the cold light of day; and her lovely face lit up with laughter as she spied someone else tiptoeing out for another steaming slash behind the clubhouse; and she shook her head and turned aside, her very essence on display.

By the time the pep talk was over Mick Hyland was fully dressed and, although he only lived a stone's throw away, he went home in Father Corish's battered old car without a by your leave to anyone.

⌒

Over the next five or six weeks the squad met two or three nights a week and the odd Saturday afternoon. After Christmas the deadwood was sent packing and in the end thirty hopeful players were left on the panel. Kevin was one of the lucky ones. Berty Bolger – his sad-eyed club comrade – gave him this advice by way of a valediction: if someone hits you, you hit him back; if someone bites you, you bite him back; if someone kicks you give him as good as you got.

'Don't let no one away with nothing,' Berty counselled him as he emptied his locker. 'And remember we're all proud of you,' he said. 'You're the only Faythe Harrier on the county team now so ... do your best.'

Soon they were training four nights a week and every Saturday and Sunday afternoon – hard, tough, physical work that took its toll on the body and left Kevin feeling sore all over – sore hands, sore fingers, sore thumbs, the backs of his legs aching – and drained of energy. Luckily enough Kevin had a fairly soft, if sometimes tedious, job in the shoe department of his father's drapery store down town and so was not exactly overtaxed during the day; nevertheless, most nights now he was in bed by nine thirty and fast asleep by ten o'clock.

When the National League began Kevin got his chance to prove himself in a game against Tipperary. Tom Foley was called ashore and Kevin, who had to sit out the first two losing games on the sideline, got the shout. He came off the bench, his heart pounding, and ran onto the pitch, past Anne who was hidden in the dappled shadows of the dugout. Kevin smelt her scent first and then he was gazing into those dark, exigent eyes as she reached out and took hold of his hand and squeezed it softly and swiftly for luck on his way by.

Kevin had to mark Ginger Phelan who immediately roughed him up, hunching him and hitting him in the ribs with the tip of his stick when the referee wasn't looking. Kevin, amid shouts and protests from the Wexford contingent, was about to retaliate when Mick Hyland came bounding by like an avenging angel to upend Ginger Phelan on his behalf with a reckless elbow. The whistle was blown and the linesman consulted and names were taken and ultimatums were issued, but the word was out that the novice was to be minded.

Right from the word go Kevin and Mick developed their own intricate geometry on the playing field, weaving out beautiful patterns that were timed to perfection, reading each other's minds, anticipating each other's moves, divining each other's thoughts and intentions; elaborate tapestries of movement – forward and backward steps – that seemed to be set to their very own private melody; two persons in the one God if you like. Or to borrow the Scribe's apt phrase: *They had an understanding.*

Before the start of every game now Mick would automatically partner Kevin in the puck around, the pair of them lining out like a couple of gladiators. *Pick Pack Puck,* the sliotar seemed to say – Kevin's skill with the ball and hurl a joy to watch, Mick distinctive in his gleaming red helmet. Like his Alter Ego (or his Guardian Angel) Mick would sit beside Kevin in the dressing room at half time, borrow things from him sometimes, and, even more surprising, loan him stuff too. Kevin couldn't put his finger on what he did to deserve this honour but soon he was sitting in the back of Father Corish's car as the Blessed Trinity wended their way to and fro from one eventful event to the next – outings to handball matches and point-to-point race meetings and boxing tournaments and charity events and any other Mardi Gras or out-of-the-way dog fight that took their fancy..

Somewhere in there amongst all of that there was Kevin's first visit to old Tadgh O'Toole's workshop so that Mick could pick up his favourite hurl which had been chipped (or injured in Mick's terminology) in the previous game in Thurles. Old Tadgh, the master hurl maker, who put so much care and attention and love into his craft that he was sometimes loath to hand over the finished article at the end of the day so that the hurler in question would have to practically prise the stick away from him with a tender pledge that he'd take good care of it from here on out.

'Any joy Tadgh?' Mick was wondering as he entered, Kevin lagging behind in the doorway, easing his way into the room gradually, 'making strange,' as Father Corish laughingly put it.

The old man used his spit-soaked pipe to pinpoint the repaired hurl on his workbench and Kevin stood to witness Mick reunited with his beloved stick again, picking it up and measuring it and weighing it and swinging it and admiring it, bending it and testing it and wielding it and running his hands lovingly along it, and finally kissing it once for luck as he thanked the pipe puffing old Tadgh kindly. And proud old Tadgh crossed off his name in the dog-eared child's copybook where Mick's particulars were scrawled:

> *Michael Hyland, Newton's Cross (Craobh Rua Club) –Light hurl, narrow heel, full bos, 35 – inch handle ... Mend and band ...*
> *Eamon Sweeney, Kilmuckridge (Buffer's Alley Club) – Heavy hurl, thick heel, Cork bos, 36-inch handle ... ..Splice and trim and shorten ...*

Father Corish kept praising the old man for a job well done and pointing out unnecessarily to Kevin all the pictures on the walls of some of the heroes of yesteryear: Billy and Nicky and Bobby Rackard and Tim Flood, Tony Doran, Hopper McGrath, Willy Murphy and Larry O'Gorman, Donie Green and Darragh Ryan and Paul Codd and Liam Dunne; and of course a handful of the latest crop – big Red Devereux and Tom Foley and Mick Hyland and Tommy Hawkins – all hanging beneath their hardy antecedents. Here and there fairly seasoned old hurls were mounted beside a particular photograph along with some vital statistic or other – *All Ireland Champions 1996 … The Railway Cup 1971.* And Kevin couldn't help but harbour the juvenile notion that his face might one day also adorn these hallowed walls. *Kevin Troy – Young Hurler Of The Year!*

Father Corish must have read his mind because soon he was telling old Tadgh that it wouldn't be too long at all until Kevin's picture would be up there too. 'I'm tellin' you Tadgh, he's handy,' Father Corish vouched and the old timer grunted out some inaudible reply.

The rain was belting down on the corrugated roof as Mick reached out and clasped Tadgh's ancient leathery hand. Meanwhile Kevin – with Father Corish's blessing – snooped about, inspecting the shrine-like nooks and crannies and alcoves where all kinds of treasure could be found: a beautiful shined up old Oireachtas medal, a frameless oil painting of a blood stained Nicky Rackard in action, an aging O'Neill sliotar signed by the entire '96 squad, a battered silver music box which churned out a wobbly *'Boolavogue.'*

A pot-bellied wood stove stood in the centre of the cluttered workshop and a sheep dog lay sleeping in a box by the door. There was a calendar of *Irish Shop Fronts* on the wall and tools strewn haphazardly about the place: a spokeshave, a plane, a stumpy hammer, pinchers and pliers and all sorts of saws and a box of metal bands. There was the smell of glue in the air and pared ash and shavings and linseed oil and varnish of some kind and old stained rags and brushes and some other mysterious aroma that Father Corish fearlessly inhaled and identified as, *'the beautiful smell of someone else's dream.'*

Lined along the rugged benches were vices full of snapped off hurling sticks, and rows and rows of newly made hurls leaned against one wall. A batch of sticks were clumped together ready for collection and a child's tiny camán rested on a cobwebbed cooper's mare in the corner. Kevin would take all of this out into the world with him when they eventually departed, all of this coupled with the germ of a promise (nothing definite now) that old Tadgh just might make him a made-to-measure hurl someday.

There were other adventures too besides those mentioned above: there was the night the three of them went to a dance on their way back from a friendly in Clonmel (friendly in name only, mind you: Brendan Stafford was led off with a nasty, splintered gash on his forehead and there were off-the-ball incidents galore). They were only five minutes in the dancehall when Father Corish slipped off his collar and, just for devilment, he went over and asked this attractive middle-aged woman up onto the floor, the other two standing at the bar, marvelling as Father Corish – to the tune of *By The Wings Of A Snow White Dove* – waltzed the lady effortlessly around the place.

'You never think he was a priest, would you?' Mick chuckled between greedy, illicit gulps of beer.

'No,' Kevin agreed, risking an ale shandy. 'You wouldn't.'

Only that morning Kevin had happened on Father Corish arrayed in the full regalia as he officiated at a funeral mass. Kevin's mother had dropped him out to the remote country parish where Father Corish was now stationed (or exiled, depending on what way you looked at it), and Kevin patiently waited, with his helmet and hurl and kit bag between his knees, in the shadowy nave of the chapel. This was the first time Kevin had seen Father Corish in all his finery and it was strange to discover him immersed in the mystery of it all, to hear him saying '*The Prayers Of The Faithful*,' or to experience him genuflecting and holding the consecrated Holy Host aloft; and later on, as he accompanied the coffin down the main aisle and out to the windy cemetery at the back of the churchyard, to see him swing the thurible, the incense wafting in sanctifying plumes all around him.

Afterwards Kevin went round to the vestry to find the sacristan assisting Father Corish to disrobe, the florid faced priest puffing on a cigarette, shifting it from one hand to the other as the sacristan struggled to get the embroidered chasuble and the long white alb over his big red head.

'Any sign of the other fella yet?' Father Corish gruffly wondered when he noticed Kevin standing there.

'No,' Kevin replied. 'No sign of him yet ... Hang on ... Maybe this is him now.'

Footsteps sounded across the stony yard outside and soon Mick arrived in the ornate doorway. 'Is he not ready yet?' he groaned. 'Come on Corish will you or we'll never get there in time.'

'Hold your horses there now you,' Father Corish repri-manded him. 'One O'Clock I said and if that's not good enough for you then you should have gone on the bus with the others.'

'Is Nancy not with us today, no?'

'No.'

'Why not? Lovers' tiff?'

Father Corish shot him a sidelong glance to remind him that the sacristan was still within earshot.

'She's sick,' Father Corish told him then.

'Oh, the poor thing,' Mick cried. 'She's not what-do-you-call-it or anything I hope, is she?'

'What?' Father Corish foolishly asked.

'You know? ...' and Mick gave a soft comical whistle to emphasise his meaning.

Father Corish shook his head and turned away. 'You'll lock up for me Padraic, will you?'

'Yeah, right, Father,' the sacristan promised. 'No bother.'

'Right. Come on you two ... Let's get to where we're going. For another hidin' to nothin' ... '

'Do you want me to drive or anything, Corish?' Mick offered.

'Why would I want to do that?' Father Corish fished, suspiciously.

'I don't know,' Mick said. 'But sure you probably have a skinful of wine inside you, have you?'

'Don't be so disrespectful all you life,' Father Corish cribbed as he grabbed his jacket and led the way. 'I mean to say there are some things that are just not funny ... '

'Yeah?' Mick countered. 'Like what for instance?'

Kevin picked up his gear and accepted the keys to Father Corish's car, which the sacristan was handing him, and with a gentle shrug of his shoulders he pursued the others out into the chapel yard.

That night ended with fish and chips and battered sausages washed down with tins of Coca Cola in a lamplit lay-by on the edge of Clonmel, Kevin spread out in the back like a sated sultan.

'Her name is Cora, incidentally,' Father Corish informed them out of the blue.

'Cora, eh ... First names terms already ... What's Nancy goin' to say about all this I wonder?' Mick teased.

'You say nothin',' Father Corish warned him, the hint of a cheeky grin in evidence. 'Anyway I only danced with her the twice' he said as he took another smirking swig of coke.

Three nights later they were presented with the new official outfits – black blazers and grey pleated trousers and white shirts and slender neck ties in the Wexford colours of purple and gold. A real ceremonious occasion – supposed to be. The Blessed Trinity arrived late, thanks to Mick insisting they stop off at The Foggy Dew on the way where Father Corish nearly got into a fight with a couple of mountainy men who were harmlessly needling Mick about something or other. Mick had to bundle the vexed priest, red faced and cursing, out the door and into the car. Kevin doubled back to fetch Father Corish's coat which he'd left behind, hanging on the back of a high stool, only to find the drinkers sharing a gleeful laugh about it all.

'He tramped out onto the field and everything after him,' one of them was saying. 'Pulverized him, he did. And I wouldn't mind but he was one of the linesmen that day … '

'There was murders over that I believe,' someone else confirmed, a rather serious individual. 'Hauled in front of the bishop and everything I heard, and banished to the arse hole of nowhere … '

'He's a bit of a head banger all right,' the hefty froggy-eyed barman agreed, his sleeves rolled up and his hands resting on the counter. 'No doubt about it … Did he forget his coat?'

'Yeah,' Kevin answered, blushing like a beetroot.

'No fear of him,' the barman said. 'It's a pity we didn't see that there lads. We could have rifled his wallet … I'm short of a few Johnnies says you … Ha ha ha … Oh now.'

'That's a right little hurler, that fella is,' one of the drinkers remarked as Kevin made his getaway.

They parked out front of The Menapia Hotel that night in a *'resident's only'* parking place and hastened towards the main entrance. Jean Bradley was standing under the canopy with Mary Carmichael, the pair of them smoking the fingers off themselves.

'Yup,' Mick said to Jean Bradley as he passed and then when the trio were safely inside he turned to whisper to the others, 'Do you know what I'm goin' to tell you about that one, lads?'

'We don't need to know, 'Father Corish insisted as he hunted the two of them towards the Alcove – a small room off the bustling lobby – past the disgruntled Frances Farrell who was posted in the doorway, marshalling the event. Kevin scurried to a nearby seat while Father Corish went slinking meekly up to the front to take his place beside the other mentors. Mick remained down the back of the room with his arms folded as Jaz Corcoran and Brendan Stafford modelled the new suits on the stage above, Anne doing the honours at the microphone.

'The tie, as you can see,' she announced, 'is made of pure silk and is of course in the Wexford colours of purple and gold. We have James Dunphy who designed the outfit present here this evening. Are you there James? ... I'm sure James needs no introduction to anyone. He was a well known hurler himself in his time, one of the mainstays of Duffry Rovers in his heyday ... Well done James.'

James Dunphy, the tailor, stepped shyly forward to take his bow. Donie was there too, fitted out handsomely in the gear, standing to the side of the stage as if he was Anne's personal bodyguard.

'Give us a twirl, Jaz,' big Red Devereux heckled from the second row of seats and Jaz Corcoran obliged, walking and twirling and pouting like a supermodel to an ecstatic round of applause and wolf whistles.

And then Mick Hyland was asked what he thought of the design – Jaz hailing down to him from the edge of the stage, 'What do you think, Mick?' – and Mick, a few drinks aboard, pushed his way through the throng. He stepped up to the microphone and told them all that it reminded him of something you might see a brass band wearing, and he wondered if there was a trombone or something handy so that he could play a verse of, *'I'll Sing A Hymn To Mary,'* which managed to elicit a gale of laughter from the gathering, Father Corish covering his face with the palm of his hand in mortification; and then, as if to make amends, Mick burst into song and successfully encouraged everyone to join in with him, much to Maurice Dunne's annoyance who was overheard to say to Frances Farrell, as cameras flashed all round, that this was precisely what he didn't want to happen.

> *Were I At The Mosshouse*
>> *Where The Birds Do Increase*
>>> *At The Foot Of Mount Leinster*
>>>> *Or Some Silent Place*
>>>>> *By The Streams Of Bunclody*
>>>>>> *Where The Waters Do Meet*
>>>>>>> *And All I Would Ask Is*
>>>>>>>> *One Kiss From You Sweet.*

The League was a disaster. The team came out almost bottom of the bunch. The Scribe gave them down the banks-*lethargic, uninspired and very poor* were some of the comments he made, in spite of the fact that he had prophesied great things to come and had actually waxed lyrical about Mick and Kevin (conferring upon them the titles of *Romulus and Remus* by the way) in the centre of the field earlier on in the campaign, which unfortunately he reported turned out to be ... ***nothing more than a half hearted promise in some elusive dream.***

Kevin came out of it all well enough though, scoring a peach of a goal in that game against Tipperary, his celerity breaking Ginger Phelan's heart in the second half, and an overall score of seven points in the remaining three matches. In short, Kevin was in and poor Tom Foley – apart from the odd pointless cameo – was confined to the bench from then on out.

The Championship began with Wexford getting a direct bye into the The Leinster Semi-Final. Wexford V Offaly in Croke Park – Mecca to those in the know. It was Kevin's first appearance there, his head woozy with excitement and the ground quaking beneath him as the whole world slowly spun round and round and time eerily stalled to near stand-still. Kevin's palms were damp and his mouth felt parched as he tried to take it all in. Oceans of acres. A myriad of faces (45,000 was a rough estimate) and unmerciful, thunderous sounds. A marching band playing, *Kelly the Boy From Killane* and a rousing *Minstrel Boy* as the players walked in single file behind, their hurling stick swinging at their sides. Gathering clouds overhead. An inkling of rain. Wheeling, swooping seagulls, squawking in this city by the sea. *Guinness – the black stuff – enjoy it! Getaway With Getaway. Delanty's Mineral Water – pure as snow, cool as rain.* Foghorns and whistles and unfurled flags, and that strange mesmeric, murmurous hum. A minute's silence for some recently deceased veteran of the game. A Wexford harridan shrieking, '*Up Wexford*,' on the cusp of the 60th second. A far off Offaly supporter bawling back a ribald reply. An elevated train in the distance, going about its business, going somewhere else. On a day like this? *The Boys of Wexford* brought a lump to Kevin's throat and a few tears to his eyes and when he tried to tell Mick about it afterwards Mick assured him – amidst the clamour and bustle – that as long as it didn't bring a lump to his pants there was no real harm done.

Mick and Kevin were the mid-fielders and as they pucked around before the game Kevin could hear his father's voice in his ear (a pernickety businessman who knew next to nothing about hurling) as he advised him that morning before he left the house. 'Just do what you're told to do and you should be all right,' he told him sensibly, Kevin's mother nodding nervously in the background.

Mick plucked a blade of grass and scattered it to the wind, watched it sail away. Kevin held his hand out to his marker – the ungovernable Thomas Flynn of '*In Like Flynn*' fame – who refused to shake it; and not only that but Thomas Flynn took off his own helmet and slung it to the sideline antagonistically in an attempt to intimidate the young player. But Kevin was not intimidated. He was confused, however, and wondered what the next seventy minutes would bring. Mick Hyland was having none of it. He barged in between the pair of them and mumbled in Kevin's direction, 'You take the other lad, I'll dance with this fella for a while.'

'No,' Kevin told him. 'Stick to the script.'

But Mick's mind was made up. 'Come on ref,' he barked. 'Throw it in, in the name of Jaysus, and let's get goin' here … '

The referee silently chastised Mick, pointed at him sternly, and then he checked his watch and prepared to blow his whistle.

'If I was you,' Mick Hyland warned Thomas Flynn before the off, 'I'd slap that helmet back on fairly pronto, cause you'd never know what way this aul' thing is goin' to go here today.'

And with that the ball was in and the game was on and with the first beautiful clash of the ash Thomas Flynn's hurling stick snapped in two and he was calling frantically for a replacement as he readjusted his recently recovered helmet.

Kevin had no other option but to go along with the new plan, marking Timmy Twomey, the wrong man as far as he was concerned. He worried about Maurice Dunne on the sideline and the ticking off he'd get in the dressing room at half time for not sticking to the script, his father's innocent words of wisdom ringing in his ears like a message from Purgatory.

∽

Mick Hyland was cursing and swearing and ranting as he came through the jakes doorway at half time, interrupting Maurice Dunne's speech in the dressing room and everything. 'I mean we're like a crowd of fuckin' … camogie players out there,' he cried.

'They're all over us though, Mick,' Jaz Corcoran lamented.

'All over us!' Mick said. 'These lads are not fit to tie our laces, pal. All over us! I'm surprised at you – all over us!'

'Mick's right there,' Father Corish ventured. 'I mean on a good day these fellas are not in our calibre at all.'

'I came here to win a match not skulk around the field like a crowd of nancy boys,' Mick fumed, prowling like a pent up alpha.

'We've no strategy, that's the problem,' Big Red, the current captain, piped from the shadows.

'Strategy!' Mick roared across the room at him. 'Put the ball in the back of the net or over the bar, that's the strategy from here on out.'

'We're nine points down for Christ sake!' Red reminded him.

'Back of the net or over the bar!' Mick repeated. 'Every time! … And make your minds up – either mark your man or get away from him, one or the other … I mean to say meself and the young lad there are working our balls off, runnin' around like a couple of maniacs. We send it in to you fellas time and time again only to have it sent back out again the very second it gets there. And our backs are drivin' it over our heads. I mean where's the point in that when the forwards are winnin' nothin'. Drive it low – to us.

We'll get it into them. And if they can't score then we'll have to go in and do it for them.'

Red scoffed and faced the wall: it was typical of Mick Hyland to blame everyone else when Flynn and Twomey were running riot in the centre of the field.

'What?' Mick challenged him. 'There's four lousy points up on that board – two scored by the young lad and one by me and only one from a forward. And that was from a free we didn't deserve to get in the first place. I mean … Do me a favour … '

'As I was trying to say – before I was so rudely interrupted,' Maurice Dunne began, stepping forward, the tip of a red handkerchief spilling lazily from the top pocket of his tailored suit.

'Interrupted?' Mick muttered under his breath.

'What's that?' Maurice Dunne wondered.

'Look,' Mick said darkly, moving in close to him and Kevin feared that Mick was about to say all the things he had previously told him in private, that Maurice Dunne was nothing only a dressed up gobtaw who wouldn't manage a whorehouse, never mind the county squad; but the door opened just in time and Anne was miraculously standing on the threshold, half in shadow and half in sunlight; and, as she gazed scornfully upon them all, Kevin had to admit that he had never seen this side of her before – this cold, displeased creature who was silently demanding from them the very thing that was in short supply today: call it 'manliness', call it 'heroism', call it downright 'masculinity', whatever you like.(Come to think of it Anne never had much time for obsequiousness of any sort, for Frances Farrell and the likes.) No, she would not tolerate second best today and Kevin felt a sense of shame welling up inside of him and, like the rest of them, he averted his eyes and sort of shuddered as a gentle, myste-

rious zephyr of a breeze swept in from the concrete stairwell.

'I'm goin' back up now, Donie,' Anne eventually sighed,
reaching in to fill up her paper cup from the gurgling water
cooler; and then she took a sip and with one last
reproachful, chilling glance she silently withdrew.

∽

AGAINST THE ODDS! was the Scribe's blazing headline
the following week:

> *Against the odds in a game of two halves is the only
> way to describe last week's Leinster Semi-Final in
> Croke Park. In the first half Wexford were torn apart
> by the Offaly forwards – the Delaney brothers given
> free rein by all and sundry to go on a scoring spree,
> hitting balls over the bar willy-nilly. Or so it seemed to
> this correspondent anyway. Big Red Devereux and his
> cohorts had no answer as the Brothers Grimm went on
> the rampage, exposing all the hidden weaknesses in the
> Wexford defence, turning them everywhichway and
> picking off goals and points at will. Elsewhere – well
> everywhere really – things had turned pretty torrid too.
> The Wexford forwards were beaten in the air, beaten
> on the ground and finally beaten into the ground. Too
> slow, too fat and 'TODAY!' were the words that sprang
> to mind on this occasion. Meanwhile, mid-field, the
> heretofore inspirational partnership of Hyland and
> Troy appeared to have lost its lustre as the bold Thomas
> Flynn (of In Like Flynn fame) lived up to his well
> earned appellation, dodging past his marker time and
> time again to deliver his gifts to one or other of the
> devastating Delaney Brothers; and stealing in in person
> another time to catch a ball on the rebound only to*

bury it in the back of the Wexford goalmouth. A goal and six points down and with no sign of a second coming Wexford heads and hearts were low when the whistle blew for the end of the first half.

Whatever happened in the dressing room at the break we'll never know. Words of wisdom from the manager Maurice Dunne? Divine inspiration? Who knows? Whatever it was it worked wonders, should be bottled in fact. Wexford came out of the traps like Trojans and Thomas Flynn was the first to be notified. Big Red Devereux, who was now taking custody of the square with the strict instructions that no one was allowed over its threshold, decided to put some manners on In Like Flynn with a fair but ferocious shoulder tackle. The dazed Offaly man was cradled pieta-like in the arms of his burly manager who appeared somewhat concerned about the prostrate player. Flynn rose bravely however only to be toppled once again minutes later by Mick Hyland who was making a blistering run up the Cusack Stand side of the field and was definitely in no mood for detours.

Young Kevin Troy was in fine form too as point after point wended homewards from unbelievable angles – five points all in all in the second half from the stick of this talented young turk (two from frees and three from play). Jas Corcoran and Tommy Hawkins both opened deposit accounts on the scoreboard too and, although the Delaney Brothers were still a major threat with two points apiece, things began to look brighter when Brendan Stafford – thanks to a beautiful delivered ball from Kevin Troy – found the net for Wexford in the 56th minute … .

◡

Kevin must have read that article fifty times if not more. First out loud to his mother at lunchtime and later he listened contentedly (and sore all over) as she read it aloud to his father at teatime. And still later again, the next day, when no one was around he cut it out of the paper and brought it up to his room where he read it over and over, his doubled up double mouthing the words in the wardrobe mirror in the corner. There was a prize-winning photograph of Mick Hyland and the two Delaney brothers in combat, the spinning sliotar suspended in mid-air, mud splashing their faces and gansies, and Aidan Delaney's hurling stick bent like a boomerang as Kevin's blurred outline could be discerned waiting in the wings for the breaking ball.

Kevin lay back on his bed and relived it all again. That shot he sent in to Brendan Stafford that time, its trajectory wringing delighted sighs all around the stadium. And those dying seconds of the game when Wexford had snatched victory from Offaly's grasp, who, two points up, must have been under the impression that no doubt they had weathered the storm and done more than enough to secure the win. But no, Mick Hyland was to float one last hopeful ball in around the house, *a precision pass or a Hail Mary shot*, take your pick. Jaz Corcoran caught it, fumbled it and lost it to Tony Gilfoyle – Offaly's gigantic full back – who was determined to whip it out to the wings, which would surely put the game beyond redemption. Tommy Hawkins though had other ideas. He blocked the shot, scooped it up into his hand with a side slice of his hurl, half turned and with one last beautiful strike he slammed it into the roof of the net. Bang! Poetry! And then came the long final whistle and jubilation from the stands; and Tommy Hawkins went down the field, jumping for joy, blissfully unaware that before the week was out he'd crack his tibia in training and wind up hobbling around on crutches for six months or more, miss the Leinster Final and everything over it. No, neither him nor Kevin, as they hugged and kissed each other in the middle of the pitch that day, were yet acquainted with the wise old adage that behind every glorious triumph lurks the ghost of some future downfall.

❧

It was during the run up to the Leinster Final, as far as Kevin could make out, that Mick decided to make his play for Anne. He began to pay her attention whenever the team dined at The Country Kitchen now, stopping to chat to her casually over a cup of tea or smiling up at her as she'd breeze on by, complimenting her and lavishing unexpected presents on her every chance he got: a Saint Christopher key ring, an antique shaving mug to hang on her wall, a tiny framed Jack Vetriano print for which it was no secret - everybody knew - she had a bit of a penchant. He'd find a reason to be near her as often as he could, coming over to help her draw the heavy curtains as darkness fell, or taking some cumbersome thing out to the yard for her, or carrying his own plate and cutlery all the way into the kitchen, worming his way, as big Red deemed it, into her confidence; and once in a while at the end of the evening he'd hang back and sort of smirk and enjoy the exodus of players filing past as if his new found friendship with Anne gave him licence to linger.

Of course the other players noticed and talked about it and sneered at him behind his back, passing snide remarks and making faces to one another along with a variety of vulgar, lewd gestures; they'd mime and mimic him when he wasn't there and it was generally agreed that he was making a holy show of himself this time round.

'The lure of love,' someone said, coining a phrase.

After a while though Kevin became aware that Anne was not entirely indifferent to Mick's advances. She'd redden whenever he'd call out her name and she'd look for him and wonder aloud about him when he wasn't around and she'd try to winkle out his whereabouts. She'd look his way whenever she'd sidle by, a sideways look that was riddled with a mixture of mystery and doubt; and it seemed to Kevin that she lost some of her usual composure whenever, in the midst of the boyish banter, another girl's name was linked, even remotely, with Mick; in fact once when Jean Bradley's name came up she seemed to find it hard to contain her feelings.

There were other things too: the way she'd camouflage herself whenever he'd sidle up to talk to her; the way she'd raise herself up and whisper in his ear – some delicious secret; the way she'd crinkle her nose and laugh at something he'd say or turn suddenly sad and silent and earnest as he walked away from her again. And once when Mick snuck out to the door of the restaurant (for a sly cigarette Kevin suspected) Anne went to join him in the doorway, shaking make believe crumbs from a tablecloth, folding it carefully and then slipping slyly into the shadows where she thought she couldn't be seen.

Kevin was all mixed up over it, jealous if the truth be told. He knew he had no right to be jealous about it (after all she was probably nearly twice his age and a married woman into the bargain), but the truth of the matter was that he was jealous about it and that was all there was to it. He'd wake up in the middle of the night now thinking about them, picturing their two opaque figures out in the kitchen, brushing against the frosted glass; he'd imagine their blurred shadows intermingling, their reflections merging, one behind the other down in the dungeon where the supplies were stored, until in the end, in his mind's eye, the two of them finally became one.

In the daylight hours he envied the stolen moments they shared, the purloined glances, the silent signs and secret signals he had come to recognise: the raised eyebrows, the far too familiar smiles, the unspoken promises; or the time he spied the two of them coming up from the dungeon, sharing some joke or other, her hand tugging at his sleeve in mock disgust at something he said; or that time, of her own volition, she smuggled in a bag of fruit to him in the changing room in Nowlan Park when she thought no one would notice – in a brown paper bag: a banana, an apple and some grapes.

Kevin sometimes wondered what they had to say to one other. He'd study their lips and their body language in an attempt to crack the code. The only consolation was that each time he passed close to them he found that they were usually talking about real mundane things – the beach, holidays, the antics of Anne's oldest boy, some piece in the newspaper or some soap opera storyline or something – and Kevin would somehow try to forgive her and learn to love her again.

One night though, as Father Corish was collared by Frances Farrell in the porch of The Country Kitchen (a ticking off about expenses), Kevin –at the padre's silent behest – went out to wait in the back seat of the car only to observe Mick coming furtively out of the sweet smelling orchard at the rear of the restaurant – a vegetable patch and a tiny greenhouse and a couple of apple trees at the bottom of a sequestered garden: one of the reasons Anne bought the tumbledown shack in the first place, apparently. Mick glanced guiltily about him as he came towards the car, curiously calling out a good humoured, 'goodnight,' to Father Corish and Frances Farrell in the doorway – the oddness of which did not go unnoticed by Father Corish, it must be stressed. Mick got in and buckled his seat belt and absentmindedly browsed through a few books of poetry that were lying around (*The Furze But Ill Behaves* by Kitty Shaw and *In A Time Of Violence* by Eavan Boland), cast them aside and turned on the radio and fiddled with the dial, flicking from station to station and cursing as if he was looking for something in particular.

'What are you lookin' for?' Kevin asked him as he fiddled.

'I don't know,' he said. 'Not Radio Loola anyway ...'

A few minutes later as Father Corish drove away Kevin thought sure he glimpsed Anne's inky outline emerging from the orchard to dart spectrally across the dimly lit yard.

∽

'Any luck?' Father Corish wondered as Kevin came out of the cottage.

'No,' Kevin replied. 'He's not in there ... I'm after lookin' all over the place for him.'

'Try up the lane, so,' Father Corish instructed him, getting out and searching under the doormat for the key to the wooden caboose where the handle for the petrol pumps was located. 'I'm going to top her up,' he said, 'and then we're out of here – with or without him.'

Kevin crossed the road and walked up the rutted laneway towards the pond, Mick's secret hiding place. Mick would come here with Father Corish in the summer months sometimes to sit in the sun or to swim in the dark water or maybe ramble with his gun and dog through the adjoining fields. In the winter months he'd use it as a training ground, running round and round the shadowy lagoon with a sturdy schoolbag full of rocks and heavy stones strapped to his back, Father Corish urging and goading him on. Kevin couldn't believe it when he first witnessed his rigorous routine. Round and round he'd go with a hurl in his hand, catching the balls that Father

Corish would peg to him every so often and driving them across to the far side of the pond, looking somewhat on the roly-poly side with his bulging track suit over layers and layers of jumpers and jackets and shirts; and then up the steep mound of marly earth that stood like a mountain close by, and down the other side to catch another ball and send it sailing skywards. Round and round and up and down he'd go, nipping across the railway line and down onto the rough strand and all around the cluster of newly built holiday homes to circle the pond again and again; another ball, another shot, another steep climb until finally, exhausted, he'd sink to his knees and literally puke in the dirt, scattered balls all over the shop – floating on the water and buried in the mound and lodged in the branches of the red berried holly bush. Mick would do this in the early hours of the pitch black morning, and again in the darkened evening when his working day was done, pushing himself to the brink, his very own purgatory of pain. And now and then Kevin would join him in the old tumbledown house in the weeds which they'd use as a makeshift handball alley, beating the ball against the gable end windowless wall with their hurls, running each other into the ground until once again Mick would sink to his knees and shower curses on the world and its mother.

Kevin was thinking all of this when he happened on Anne's car parked at the top of the lane. His heart sank when he saw it there. He bent his back and peered through the window – although he didn't know why or what he expected to find – at her leather handbag resting on the passenger seat, a child's baby carrier in the back, an E.S.B. bill on the dashboard and a few dejected cassette tapes abandoned and forsaken on the floor.

He tried the passenger door, it was unlocked. He sat in sideways, his feet still outside, the creaking seat moaning beneath him. He picked up the E.S.B. bill and uncon-sciously read it. He opened up the glove compartment and rummaged inside. He filched some chewing gum and popped it in his mouth. He picked up a cassette tape and returned it to its rightful case. He turned round and delib-erately rattled the child's rattler and then he sat there for a moment or two and silently cursed the role that fate had decreed he must play in all of this. Yes, they'd be waiting for him now, huddled together in the long grass – beyond the ragwort, beyond the weeds and wild flowers and forget-me-nots, beyond the foliage of ferns and blackthorn bushes, kneeling beneath the stumpy limbs of a withered old crab apple tree – fingers locked, faces pressed close together, lips lightly touching and softly disengaging again. They'd prob-ably glance his way on his arrival, in a faintly familiar pose they'd borrow from some old faded fresco. It's possible he'd stand there and watch them awhile, and then he'd slowly turn and calmly walk away again. He wondered if they already knew he was here. He had a good mind to sound the horn just to let them know he was coming.

∾

Mick missed as many training sessions as he attended over the next ten days or so and even when he was there it was plain to see that his heart was not really in it, that his mind was elsewhere. On the nights he didn't show up rumours abounded: someone said that they had seen Anne's car parked outside Mick's garage one night on the way into town and that the car was still there three or four hours later when this same person was going home; some other version had it that the pair of them had been sighted together in a coffee shop in Bunclody of all places and that they were supposed to be holding hands and clinging to one another as they walked down the street together. There was another story circulating that they were clocked either going into a hotel or coming out of one in Dublin on a different day; although, taking times and dates and other factors into consideration, this account didn't really hold much water.

Donie was not himself at all these days. On the nights when Mick was present Donie looked uneasy to say the least, and on the nights Mick was missing he was even worse. He had a distant, mournful look about him, pacing the sidelines and glancing at his wristwatch incessantly. If they went back to the restaurant and found that Anne's car was not in the driveway his face would drain and he'd go to the door and stand there, looking up and down the road until she'd make an appearance. Once Kevin chanced to see him going to her as she drew up outside and what followed was an unwelcome (she usually gave as good as she got by the way) whispered cross-examination of her before she even got out of the car.

When Father Corish tried to talk a bit of sense into Mick the two men had a blazing row about it. Kevin was coming out of a training session in Wexford Park when he stumbled on the tail end of the argument in the deserted car park.

'Leave me and her out of this now,' Father Corish was telling him. 'This is not about me.. This is about … '

'It's alright for you to knock her off is that what you're tellin' me?'

'No. I'm sayin' that this is not about me. And it's not about Nancy either – who by the way is not very well so I'll thank you not to bring her name into it … '

'So that's what you're tellin' me … That's it's alright for you but not for me … '

'Mick, if you want now I can take off this collar and the pair of us can go around the back there and sort out this

thing man to man if that's the only language you understand.'

'I'll take that as a 'yes' then!'

'Come on – round the side. Fuck this. Kevin, hold
this coat ...' and Father Corish actually slipped off his
threadbare coat and flung it in Kevin's direction so that
Kevin didn't know whether to remain circumspect or
encroach.

'Alright, keep your shirt on,' Mick snapped, angrily.

'I will keep my shirt on but will you keep yours, that's
what I'm worried about.'

'Ah, go and say a novena somewhere,' Mick hissed,
walking away, and that's when Anne's car came thundering
into view, trailing a light blaze of dust in its wake, the radio
blaring.

The three men stood spellbound in the middle of the
dreary expanse as she circled round and round, a neurotic,
slightly vacant and almost trance-like look about her as she
swept the car in a wide arch to face the exit gate again. And
gone was the Anne of old, the sweet and lovely, and in her
place sat this surly impersonator -down from the attic
Kevin presumed – who bit her nails nervously and glanced
their way defiantly and impatiently waited until Mick,
with brooding eyes and a heavy heart, trudged his way
towards her.

'Mick,' Father Corish called after him as he went. 'Mick
... Mick ... For Christ's sake, Mick!' he said, and he threw
Kevin a sudden, tormented glance that was tinged with a
hint of confrontation.

Kevin, not knowing what else to do, picked up the
priest's dusty coat, brushed it down and helped him into it.
'There, there,' he felt like saying. 'There now.'

'I don't know,' Father Corish mumbled sadly when
he saw them drive away together. 'I mean I just don't

know anymore,' he said, his ginger head bowed and his hands hooked to his hips like a set of clumsy, outmoded wings.

∽

Mick didn't get to play in the Leinster Final in the end. When the panel was posted the day before the big game Mick's name was not up there, not even as a substitute. Needless to say he went ballistic, stormed into Maurice Dunne's office and demanded an explanation, called them all a crowd of tinkers, upended the table and left. He was duly drummed out of the squad altogether the very next day for 'conduct unbecoming,' and without Father Corish to fight his corner for him, that was more or less it really.

Father Corish was otherwise engaged these days, ferrying poor Nancy Byrne up and down to the hospital in Dublin every other day. The poor thing had lost a ferocious amount of weight recently and she was starting to lose her hair and everything. Kevin caught sight of the pair of them once in the Coffee Pot Cafe as he was going by, her two trembling hands clasped in his as see-through tears cascaded down the side of her face: clearly things had taken a turn for the worse.

Kilkenny won the Leinster Final in the end – and deservedly so. Without Mick and without Tommy Hawkins (and, as far as Kevin was concerned, without Anne) Wexford never had a hope. The team tried to come through the back door but they capitulated to Limerick in the next round and that was that.

End Of The Line, the Scribe declared in his column that week. He touched on Mick's sudden departure and, reading between the lines, he seemed to be clued in to what had gone on behind the scenes. He was tipping Clare to win the All Ireland.

Kevin heard on the grapevine that Anne actually left Donie and the children around that time and moved in with Mick – a spontaneous impulse after a clandestine moonlit tryst one night if the stories can be trusted. One source claimed that she was seen working the petrol pumps and that she was supposed to be doing all the bookwork out there, sending out bills and final demands and the like. Kevin was sorely tempted to borrow his father's car sometime and drive out to Newton's Cross just to see for himself. He'd picture her standing in the doorway of the wooden booth and coming towards the car and smiling as he let down the window, and he'd rehearse what he might say to her when he saw her standing there. 'As long as you're happy,' he'd tell her as she topped him up. 'That's the main thing … .'

But unfortunately, as she was soon to discover, loving Mick Hyland and living with him turned to be two different propositions entirely. Mick would go on the rantan for days on end – drinking in the Foggy Dew or the Banjo Bar, staying out all night usually and falling in on top of her at all hours of the morning. There was talk of fights in bars and late night chip shops and other side street shenanigans; there was a run in with a guard that landed him in court, and customers constantly banging on the door and complaining and what-have-you; there were outbursts of temper too, cups and saucers shattered, pots and pans dented and terrible things said or insinuated in the heat of the moment.

Then one night at some unearthly hour Kevin got a call on his mobile phone as he lay sleeping.

'Hello,' Kevin drowsily mumbled from beneath his pillow.

'Kevin, it's me: Corish. This piece of shit is after breakin' down on me again and I'm stranded here. You couldn't come and pick me up by any chance?'

'What … Yeah … Where are you?'

'I'm on my way to Newton's Cross. I'm outside the big warehouse place – right opposite thingmegigs … DeBarry's Lodge … I don't believe this, the friggin' power is going in this thing too – on top of everything else … '

'What?'

'I say this thing's nearly bet.'

'I'll be out there in a minute.'

'What's that?'

'I say I'll be out there in a … He's gone.'

Kevin rose up, got dressed and sneaked downstairs where he picked up his father's car keys from the hook beside the door and slipped silently out into the night. As he was backing out of the cul-de-sac he could see his mother's concerned face appearing in the lighted upstairs window.

Father Corish was sitting in his car when Kevin arrived at DeBarry's Lodge.

'The queer fella's place,' Father Corish told him as he climbed in beside him. 'His nibs is actin' up again it seems. She wants to go home she said.'

'Home?' Kevin echoed.

'Yeah, I know, that's what I said too.'

Ten minutes later Kevin was pulling up in front of the garage at Newton's Cross and Father Corish got out and hurried inside. He returned shortly with Anne in tow, one arm around her waist as if she had just suffered some terrible bereavement. He opened the back door and helped her in. He slammed the back door and opened the front one and placed her overnight bag on the passenger seat, and then he went round to the other side and got in the back with her where he held her hand and whispered words of consolation to her all the way into town.

'What's he's goin' to say though when he sees me?' Anne wept.

'You let me worry about that,' Father Corish told her. 'That's not your problem now … I'll take care of all of that

… He's a bigger man than that … I mean to say we're not talkin' about … Don't cry now … '

Anne whimpered something through her tears, Kevin couldn't make out what it was.

'No one thinks that at all,' Father Corish assured her in a hushed tone of voice. 'I mean, Jesus Christ tonight Anne, you know us all longer than that … I mean. You made a mistake. Everyone makes mistakes. No one's above it. Nobody's what-do-you-call-it … perfect or anything.'

At this point there was another low tearful utterance from Anne, something about holding her head up in the town and other things of that nature.

'What?' Father Corish wondered, bending his ear like a confessor to hear what she had to say.

Kevin's eyes were fastened on them in the driving mirror as she clung to the prodigal priest in the back, murmuring and muttering her secret worries. Her face was all blotched and her hair damply pasted to her clammy head and she had the exhausted, demented look of a sleepwalker about her. Kevin, God forgive him, was plagued with the awful image of her statue crashing from a lofty pedestal; he could almost hear the plaster crack and the sturdy plinth on which she once stood crumble beneath her.

'I mean to say it's not fair on him,' she was saying.

'No, I don't suppose it is, Anne, 'Father Corish agreed, 'but …'

Kevin was driving up the avenue now, past the sheds and outhouses. It was a fairly impressive house with ivy growing on the front facade and an elaborate glass conservatory built on to the side. He pulled up onto the gravel and Father Corish got out and walked across the lawn. He rang the bell and waited. Lights came on in various parts of the building – a bedroom, the landing, the stairwell and hallway. Finally the door was opened and Donie was standing there on the illuminated threshold in his dressing gown. Father Corish began to explain the situation to him, pointing towards the car and obviously appealing to the other man's better nature. From where Kevin was sitting they looked like a couple of knockabout artists, soundlessly mimicking their way through a badly written skit as Father Corish gestured and signalled and pleaded while Donie, hands in pockets, hummed and hawed and grimaced his way to the end of the silent sketch. Anne took it all in too. She sighed and softly moaned in the back and she reached out and placed her helpless paw on Kevin's shoulder.

'Oh, Kevin,' she swooned, her voice fraught with lonely desperation.

Kevin reached back and took hold of her hand and squeezed it gently to comfort her, and he blurted out something that seemed to imply that he understood. But of course he didn't understand. How could he? And not only that but he felt nothing either – well, nothing save a form of numbness that is. He knew he should be feeling something or other round about now but the thing was he didn't really know what it was he was supposed to be feeling and, try as he might, nothing came. 'Is this what people do?' he couldn't help thinking as Father Corish made his way back to the car. 'Let on to understand when they don't and pretend to feel when they can't.'

Father Corish opened up the back door and coaxed Anne to join him.

'What did he say?' she nervously wondered as she climbed out, strangely devoid – from Kevin's prospective anyway – of any sense of pride or self worth now.

'Come on,' Father Corish urged.

'What?'

'You're all right,' he stressed as he retrieved the overnight bag from the front; and then he walked her towards the house, stopping at an appropriate point to pass on her belongings. He waited there awhile and watched as she toddled uncertainly to the front door. To his credit, Donie met her halfway, took the luggage from her and guided her inside, closing the door behind them on the world.

Father Corish retraced his footsteps to the car. He got in and looked directly at Kevin. 'And that's that,' he said matter-of-factly, by way of an explanation.

※

Kevin was knocking around with Tommy Hawkins and Brendan Stafford nowadays and, with no training to worry about anymore, they'd go out clubbing and dancing at the weekends, drinking and carousing and sampling the Jersey girls. One night they spied Mick stumbling into BLITZERS at half one in the morning, a two day growth on him. They watched him dance his way across the dance floor towards the bar, all false flair and wounded bravado. The three of them hid behind a pillar until he was out of sight and then they slipped out a side door and up the street to a different club, Kevin –niggled with a pang of remorse – glancing backwards as he scarpered.

It was on one of these wild nights that Kevin, more than a little tipsy, ended up in the arms of Mary Carmichael in the back seat of someone's car, his pants down around his ankles. 'It's about time,' Mary Carmichael chided him when he kissed her for the first time. She'd been giving him the come-on for ages, she later confessed. It would be just a one off though as far as Kevin was concerned.

'You're not my type,' he informed her afterwards when she wondered if she was going to see him again, and before he knew it he was dodging punches and staving off slaps that rained down on him not only from Mary Carmichael but Jean Bradley too who somehow had mysteriously got wind of the rebuke.

'Not your type!' Jean Bradley was screaming.

'Who do you think you are, eh?' Mary Carmichael kept repeating. 'Who do you think you are?'

'Who is your type don't mind me asking.' Jean Bradley harped on. 'Huh? … Anne Green I suppose … '

'Yes, who do you think you are … .'

'Anne – Butter Wouldn't Melt In Her Bloody Mouth – Green!'

It would make a great story in the clubhouse at a later date. 'Only for big Red arrived they would have torn him asunder,' Tommy Hawkins would loudly proclaim.

Six weeks later in a local club game Kevin got a smack of a sliotar in the lower region and sank to his knees, clutching the family jewels. He rose and played on for a bit but soon the pain became too much to endure and he stumbled to the sideline in agony where he threw up all over his boots.

'It serves him right,' Mary Carmichael was heard to say to Jean Bradley when it happened.

He went home and got into bed with an ice pack between his legs and guaranteed everyone that he would be all right, in spite of the fact that his testicles were black and blue and sore to touch and swollen almost beyond recognition. In the middle of the night the pain intensified and he was forced to struggle out of bed and slip across the landing and wake up his father. He was brought to the hospital, examined and x-rayed and eventually, fearing he might have done some serious damage – a few burst blood vessels or something – he was kept in for further treatment and a few days of observation.

Mick and Father Corish came up to visit him when they heard of his predicament. Kevin, sporting the bones of a downy moustache, was tucked up in bed in a silk pyjamas and a copy of Liam Dunne's, '*I Crossed The Line*,' at hand. He heard them before he saw them, their voices echoing down the hall.

'He's in here,' Father Corish cried when he spied Kevin sitting up in the bed, Mick dallying in the corridor to chat to the night nurse at her station.

'We can't leave you for a minute but you go and get yourself in this mess … I don't know,' Father Corish was trumpeting as he stepped into the ward.

'I know,' Kevin agreed, putting the book aside. 'What did you bring me?'

'Grapes and a large bottle of Seven Up,' Father Corish told him, peeping into the bag.

'Very original.'

'And the blessings of God to go with them … Oh, and a packet of crisps too – cheese and onion. There by default I must confess.'

'What's the other fella at out there?'

'He's talkin' to Sheila Corcoran … How are you feeling?'

'Rough enough … Did you hear what Mary Carmichael said. It serves me right, she said.'

'I heard that all right … Very nice. What are you reading? … I'm mentioned in that I think, am I? Briefly?..No? … Maybe not!'

'How's Nancy?'

'Not too bad at all, thank God … Much better … Rallying … .' Father Corish joyfully announced, although his eyes told a different story.

Kevin had heard his mother and Mrs Kennedy talking about it over the garden fence one day. Poor Nancy had been through the mill they both agreed – losing all that weight, and the wig, and then there was the other thing … They said the Rosary every week for her down in the Ladies Social Club now – the five sorrowful mysteries. When Father Corish's name came up the two women went into a secret form of expression, a sort of Wexford Esperanto if you like, silently mouthing certain words like '*relationship*' and '*hotel room*' and leaving other unspeakable terms out altogether. They clammed up completely when they noticed that Kevin was close at hand.

'Tell her I was asking for her,' Kevin chirped from the bed.

'I surely will, Kevin,' Father Corish pledged. 'I surely will, boy.'

'How's it goin' kid?' Mick Hyland wondered as he came through the door. 'I'm after havin' a word with the nurse there for you,' he said. 'I told her to tell the doctor he's to take away the pain and leave the swellin' … Hey, Corish, stop atin' all the chap's grapes on him.'

'At least I brought him something anyway, more than you did, 'Father Corish berated him. 'I was just sayin' there that I think I'm mentioned in that book – briefly.'

Mick cast him a dubious, skewways glance.

'Well if I'm not, I should be!' Father Corish insisted, indignantly.

And then, as might be expected, the talk turned to hurling, Father Corish planked on the edge of the bed while Mick stood beside the radiator, close to the window. Mick was back playing with Craobh Rua again, thanks mainly to Father Corish who had raised him from the doldrums and forced him back running around the pond once more with the heavy schoolbag on his back. The doldrums, incidentally, reached their zenith – or should that be nadir – one day when Mick got drunk in the Banjo Bar and went out to Anne's house in the evening to bang on the door and curse the nanny crooked when she refused to open the door to him. The children were petrified inside as Mick stepped back to put a big rock through the glass conservatory before he drunkenly lurched across the lawn again.

He stopped off at The Foggy Dew then on his way home where he enticed Jean Bradley back to his own place, only to be awakened a few hours later by big Red Devereaux who had heard and was on the warpath. When the police arrived to question Mick about the conservatory incident they found the two inter-county hurlers beating each other senseless at the side of the house as Jean Bradley – mobile phone in hand – looked on from the kitchen window. Reinforcements had to be called as the two players slipped and slid and wrestled and punched their way out the back to stagger like a couple of stumble-bums over the rusty bonnets and discarded debris that lay like dead carcasses all around. Finally the pair of them were cuffed and bundled into the back of two separate squad cars and carted back into town for the night. Father Corish had to go up to the barracks and bail them out at the break of day. He made them shake hands on the steps outside and then, as big Red – to the accompaniment of birdsong – went home to his mother's house, Father Corish brought Mick, bruised and battered, out to the presbytery for a few days where he nursed him back to health again.

The irony of it all was that Craobh Rua were doing really well in the Club Championship now (demolishing St Anne's in the first round and beating Oulart-The Ballagh by a point in their second match, and hammering The Faythe Harriers in the third round – albeit without the laid-up Kevin Troy on board); and, if The Scribe was to be believed, Croabh Rua were well capable of beating Rathnure in the final.

If Craobh Rua were to win it outright, Father Corish conjectured, Mick would undoubtedly be called back onto the county squad next season; and not only that but if all of that actually came to pass – being the skipper of the winning club – the captaincy of the panel would automat-ically fall to him.

'Wouldn't that be some turn up for the books?' Father Corish gleefully concluded.

'*And All I Would Ask Is/ One Kiss From You Sweet,*' Mick sweetly twittered.

'Did you hear about Mary Carmichael,' Kevin piped when the husky spurt of laughter had died down. 'I was just tellin' Corish about it there. It serves me right, she said.'

'I know,' Mick sympathised. 'I heard.'

'Very nice,' Father Corish said again.

'You stay away from that one,' Mick advised Kevin, pulling up a chair. 'She put the hex on you.'

The following week, when Kevin was well and truly on the mend, his father and mother took him out for a meal. To The Country Kitchen of all places! They were led up the spiral stairs to the loft. 'We're up with the Gods now, Ma,' his father whispered and his mother chuckled with delight.

Kevin could see Anne moving about below, primly setting a table and fussing about something or other the way she was inclined to do, playing her allotted part, true to form. A peal of laughter from an adjacent table caused her to turn and smile and pass a light-hearted comment. She answered some request then, frowned theatrically and moved diligently and earnestly towards the pay-desk. She wore her hair pushed back behind her ears and her apron flapped as she walked. She addressed someone waiting at the till and her soft voice carried the gist of the conversation all the way up to the loft. Water for someone then. Tea for someone else. A candled cake for the Birthday Girl, the whole place plunged into sudden near darkness. *For She's A Jolly Good Fellow* ...

Kevin couldn't help but embrace the notion that all that had happened in the recent past had been some sort of a mysterious ritual that had been enacted sorely for his benefit; and now, job done, the performers had packed up their props and costumes and all gone back home to their day jobs again. He tried to decipher what it was he was supposed to have learnt from all of this. Humility?

Patience? Independence? Some lesson for life? What? ...
But no, it was true that on the face of it life seemed to be
as it always had been, the comings and goings and the tiny
standing stills; underneath though there could no denying,
in Kevin's eyes anyway, that everything and everybody had
been imperceptibly and irretrievably and, for want of a
better word, spiritually altered somehow.

When Anne came up to take their order she was all over
Kevin when she saw him there, and when Donie passed
through the restaurant below she called down to him from
on high. 'Donie,' she said. 'Look who's here,' and Donie
grinned up at him, saluted him and then he slipped noncha-
lantly down to the dungeon as if nothing was ever awry.

FRIENDS OF PILLAR PRESS

Sue Bowden. Andy Bowden. All That Glisters, Thomastown. Margaret Carey. Shem Caulfield. Maura Dieren. Gina O'Donnell. Eva Lynch. Murphy's Bar, Thomastown. Eoin McEvitt. Conor MacGabhann. Helen MacGabhann. Sean O'Neill. Brid O'Neill. Damien Wedge. Colm O'Boyle. Eileen O'Neill. Sean Mahon. Antoinette O'Neill. Aine O'Neill. Frank Neenan. James Hanley. Orla Dukes. Maeve O'Neill. Shane O'Toole. Debra Bowden. Tony Spooner. Elizabeth Cunningham. Richard McLoughlin. Kathryn Potterton. Cormac Buggy. Fiona Shannon.

To become a friend of Pillar Press please contact us at

Ladywell
Thomastown
Co. Kilkenny

Tel: 056-7724901   E-mail: info@pillarpress.ie